D0533144

The Victorian Mystery Series by Robin Paige

(written by Susan Wittig Albert with
her husband, Bill Albert, writing as Robin Paige)

THE *Victorian Mystery* SERIES
1

Death at BISHOP's KEEP

ROBIN PAIGE

SOUTH
DOWNS
CRIME &
MYSTERY

First published in the UK in 2016
by South Downs CRIME & MYSTERY,
an imprint of
The Crime & Mystery Club Ltd,
PO Box 394, Harpenden,
Herts, AL5 1XJ, UK

www.crimeandmystery.club

ISBN
978-0-85730-013-3 (print)
978-0-85730-014-0 (epub)

Typeset in 11pt Palatino
by Geethik Technologies Pvt Ltd., India
Printed and bound by Clays Ltd, St Ives plc

Our deep appreciation goes to Ruby Hild and her late husband, Ron, without whose introduction to East Anglia and to things British this book would never have been written.

We are also grateful to our long-time friend Reginald Wright Barker for allowing us to use his collection of photography books.

I intend to illuminate the Ledger with a blood & thunder tale as they are easy to "compoze" & are better paid than moral & elaborate works of Shakespeare so don't be shocked if I send you a paper containing a picture of Indians, pirates, wolves, bears & distressed damsels in a grand tableau over a title like this "The Maniac Bride" or "The Bath of Blood A Thrilling Tale of Passion."

—LOUISA MAY ALCOTT,
to her friend Alf Whitman

1

"I am in just the mood for a ghostly tale, a scene of mystery, a startling revelation, and where shall I look for an obliging magician to gratify me?"

"Here!"

—LOUISA MAY ALCOTT
The Fate of the Forests

KATE ARDLEIGH GLANCED warily over her shoulder. The late-summer night was black as the pit and stormy, lighted by the intermittent blue-white glare of lightning flashes. The wind skittered like a mad thing through Manhattan's nearly empty streets, twisting Kate's sensible skirt about her ankles and flapping the chestnut vendor's sign. It was precisely the sort of wild night on which Felix Farmore had kidnapped Pearl St. John, in Kate's second story, "Missing Pearl, Or The Lost Heiress." And it was in just such a shadowy street that Felix had apprehended Pearl and borne her off to her fate.

But the figure that Kate saw behind the passing two-horse omnibus was nothing like the fictitious Farmore. It was quite real, and familiar, too, for she had seen it yesterday as well. She quickened her pace, lifting her skirt to avoid a pile of horse droppings and ducking behind a brewery wagon piled with wooden kegs. He (for Kate was quite certain that it was a man, stout and bowler-hatted) had followed her yesterday. And this evening, he had followed her ever since she had left the Fifth Avenue offices of the Frank Leslie Publishing House, where she had finally procured payment for "Missing Pearl." She fisted her gloved hands in the pockets of her trim-fitting jacket and drew her brows together, her apprehension mixed with more than a little annoyance.

In point of fact, Kate would not have been abroad on the streets on a Tuesday evening, a good hour after the closing of the shops, if Mr. Bothwell Coxford, a haughty, self-important assistant editor of *Frank Leslie's Popular Monthly*, had not kept her waiting for the greater part of the afternoon. It was only as the electric lamps were being lighted that a clerk had brought her a bank draft for $225, an amount that would permit her to pay Mrs. Murchison the rent and see her comfortably situated until she had finished her next serial story, which she had tentatively titled "Amber's Amulet, Or The Conspiracy of Death." The money was worth walking a total of forty blocks to fetch, even if the wild night threatened rain.

Kate gave another furtive glance over her shoulder and quickened her step. The shadow had gained ground and was closing fast. Most women would have been frightened to death in such a circumstance, but Kate, independent and self-sufficient, was not given to fright. She stepped decisively around the corner and into the pale halo that encircled the street lamp in front of the Ninth Street Police Station.

The station's stone staircase descended solidly to the pavement and a reassuring light glowed behind the frosted glass door. It was here that her uncle, Sean O'Malley, served as detective sergeant. Uncle Sean was probably at home, presiding over pot roast and potatoes with Aunt Maureen and the two youngest O'Malleys. But inside the station Kate could hear the thunderous voice of Inspector Duggan, the night sergeant, bawling into the recently installed telephone in a voice loud enough to be heard in Brooklyn. If she were to confront the shadowy figure, she had best do it here, where a loud scream would summon reinforcements.

Kate slipped into the shadow of the stairs and waited, holding her breath, until Bowler-Hat turned the corner. He hesitated, stroking his handlebar mustache as he searched the empty street. Then she stepped out and accosted him with greater boldness than she felt, speaking in a firm, unfaltering voice.

"Please be good enough, sir," she said, lifting her chin, "to tell me why you are following me."

Bowler-Hat's mustache twitched and his beefy face registered surprise, alarm, and chagrin, in that order. He hunched his shoulders and shifted his feet uncomfortably, his garments exuding the smoky seasoning of cigars and garlic. Then he collected himself, straightened his shoulders, and cleared his throat.

"You mistake me, madam," he said with great dignity. "I am not following—"

"Stuff and nonsense," Kate snapped. She stamped her foot. "Do you take me for a fool? You, sir, have been trailing a half block behind me ever since I left Fifth Avenue. What is more, you were following me yesterday—and rather clumsily, I must say. Now, do you wish to tell me why you are being such an annoyance, or do you prefer to yield that information to"—she pointed at the brightly lighted door—"Inspector Duggan?"

At that moment, Inspector Duggan was heard to shout into the phone, "Well, then, and a good night to you, too, sir," and to bellow for Corporal Peters, "on the double, dammit!"

His jaw tightening, Bowler-Hat's glance darted from Kate to the lighted door and back again. He hesitated, clearly perceiving that he was in a tight place.

"As you wish," he said sourly. Reaching into the pocket of his tweed coat, he produced a leather card case and handed her a card. "If you will appear at this address on Friday morning at ten, you will be told what you wish to know."

Kate turned the thin gray card to the light. On it was printed, in bold letters, the name Rodney P. Kellerman, and beneath that, Pinkerton's Detective Agency, New York Office, with an address on Second Avenue.

Kate's eyes widened. A private detective! What amazing good fortune! But she did not allow her delight to creep into her voice.

"Pinkerton's?" she asked with cold formality. "And what, pray tell, does Pinkerton's require of me?"

But Rodney P. Kellerman did not appear inclined to answer. He touched his fingers to the brim of his bowler. "Friday at ten, madam," he said, and marched stiffly around the corner.

It began to rain.

2

"In the late nineteenth century the most popular form of narrative was the penny dreadful (or shilling shocker, as it was called in England). Some of the tales were written, pseudonymously, by resourceful women who insisted on making a living for themselves."

—Susan Blake
With Her Own Pen

CLUTCHING RODNEY P. KELLERMAN's card in a cold fist, Kate Ardleigh returned to her bleak third-floor room in Mrs. Murchison's boarding house on Mayberry Street. It was a lodging she had taken only four months before, after the sudden death of her employer, Mrs. Winifred P. Schreiber, whose secretary-companion she had been since leaving Mrs. Dawson's employ in 1889, five years before. Kate could have (and probably should have, she told herself) sought immediate reemployment. Mrs. Schreiber's lawyer would have been glad to give her the highest recommendation, as would Mrs. Dawson, whose three children—dreadful brats!—she had tutored. As she was now a skilled typist (an art she had learned at Mrs. Schreiber's request), she might have sought clerical employment, as well as work as a governess or a companion.

Or she could have returned to her childhood home with her Aunt and Uncle O'Malley, where she would have been greatly welcome. Kate's British father, Thomas Ardleigh, had died before her birth and her Irish mother, Aileen, had similarly succumbed when she was five. The O'Malleys, warmly capacious in their Irish affections, had been mother and father to her, and their six children had been her brothers and sisters. She was deeply attached to them. But while she visited often, returning to live with them would have seemed an admission that she was not capable of making her own way in the world.

Or finally (in Kate's view, it really was a last resort) she could have married. While she was not a conventionally pretty woman, a few men—those not afraid of a strong woman—had been attracted by the intensity of her personality and the depth of her self-composure. She had rejected the attentions of several men, of whom she might have been decently fond if she had made the effort. But she had not. "Decently fond" was not fond enough. Spinsterhood, whatever fear it might strike in the hearts of ordinary women, held no terrors for Kate. She had something else to do, and she intended to do it as long as she could afford private lodgings, lamp oil, paper, and ink—and perhaps, on some glorious day, a typewriter. She intended to be a writer.

Her efforts, under the pseudonym of Beryl Bardwell, had already met with a modest success. "The Rosicrucian's Ruby" and "Missing Pearl" had caught the fancy of Frank Leslie, whose *Popular Monthly* was hawked by every train boy on every railway in the country. Although he had required her upon revision to spice up her tales with a few more sensational passages than she thought altogether tasteful, the stories had been quickly accepted, and almost as quickly paid for—almost, for she had had to fetch the second payment herself, and wait for it, to boot.

But what was nearly as gratifying as the money was the fact that readers were inundating the publisher with a flood tide of requests for more Beryl Bardwell stories, a tide that lifted Kate's spirits as well as raising the *Monthly*'s revenues. Kate felt on the way to supporting herself by her pen, as long as she could manage to scribble for five or six hours daily without interruption. This was why she had not sought immediate reemployment upon the death of Mrs. Winifred P. Schreiber. If she continued to be successful, she might soon be able to afford the $3.50 per month that was required for the rental of a Remington Standard at The Typewriter Exchange at 10 Barclay Street.

But Beryl Bardwell's literary triumphs were not without their complications. The chief difficulty, Kate reflected as she propped Mr. Kellerman's card against the oil lamp and unbuttoned her wet jacket, was the public's unquenchable thirst for ever more lurid sensation.

Kate's original design had been to write tidy domestic dramas to which she could append her own name, like those of Louisa May Alcott. She had even offered three or four of that sort to publishers, but to no avail. One had sniffed, "Morals, my dear Miss Ardleigh, do not sell. The public wants *sensation*. Exotic murder and its detection make an excellent story. Try your hand at something like that, and we should be glad to look at it."

Hence, as only the most thrilling story seemed to satisfy the public taste, Kate determined that hers would be shocking, hair-raising, breathtaking adventures, each one set in an exotic setting and peopled with satisfyingly sinister villains. If her success were to be measured by her readers' responses, she had indeed achieved her goal. But the effort, she acknowledged ruefully as she faced her third such thriller, was beginning to wear. She was getting rather tired of writing sensational shockers.

If, however, Beryl Bardwell's effort was the price of Kate Ardleigh's freedom and independence in a world where such commodities were not commonly available to women, Kate was more than willing to pay the price. She read as many penny dreadfuls as she could, and she had taken to studying the mysteries of Wilkie Collins and Conan Doyle, although she did not agree with Mr. Holmes's disparaging assessment of women, and Dr. Watson seemed unfortunately sycophantic. But Sherlock was no more. Conan Doyle had recently sent his detective off a cliff, no doubt because he was weary of concocting plots that were sufficiently labyrinthian to trap the reader while providing a way out for the detective. Kate was left with such thrilling American detectives as Cap Collier, whose violent adventures had been popular for over a decade in Mr. George Munro's action-packed dime novels.

In truth, Kate was not happy with these models. Her natural inclination was more to the violence of the heart betrayed than to violent action. But Mr. Coxford reported that Mr. Leslie wished for yet more suspenseful action in her stories, and for more dramatic detail. To that end, she was in the habit of mining every fragment of her rather limited experience for plot, setting, and character. That was why she had felt so much delight to discover that she was the object of attention of Rodney P. Kellerman, of Pinkerton's.

So while the storm wore itself out against her window, Kate sat by the oil lamp, dipped her pen, and began to record in a rapid copperplate hand every detail of the evening, down to the odor of cigars and garlic that had enveloped Mr. Kellerman's stout and tweedy self like a savory shroud.

16

3

"What astonishing news you have brought me! A long-lost relative, a sea-voyage, a manor abroad! It is so extraordinary a narrative that I can hardly credit it!"

"Ah, yes. But the tale is not such a simple one, my dear. There is yet a great deal more to be learned."

—ANONYMOUS
A Mother s Plot, 1887

RODNEY P. KELLERMAN GLANCED at his gold-plated pocket watch and pulled a sheaf of papers from a drawer of the desk that Pinkerton's provided him. Five minutes later there was a knock at the office door and a boy in a yellow-and-green plaid waistcoat opened it wide enough to admit his shoulders and a head of unruly hair.

"Young lady t' see you, sir," he said.

"Show her in, please," Mr. Kellerman said, resolving that this interview should be conducted with far greater dignity on his part than the last.

The young woman who entered and took the chair on the other side of the desk was, according to the information he had gathered, an orphan raised by her mother's family, at present unemployed, and a spinster. What's more, she was likely to remain so, in Mr. Kellerman's opinion, because she was already nearing the end of her twenty-fifth year.

And also because she was not the sort who gave herself graces. He glanced at her face as she settled herself and took off her gray knitted gloves. It was a strong face with a too-resolute mouth, heavy brows, and a decisive chin. The eyes were of an intense hazel-green that seemed to see a great deal, the nose was amply dappled with gingery freckles, and the cheeks bore no trace of the paint that some young women, even of the better class, affected. The thick auburn hair, richly highlighted with russet, had escaped from the combs meant to subjugate it, and disheveled locks straggled untidily over her white collar. The costume, a sturdy brown wool suit with plain brown buttons, lacked feminine decoration, except for a bit of cream lace at the wrists and throat.

An unprepossessing person, Mr. Kellerman concluded, and altogether unfeminine, although if he had been truthful, he might have conceded that his judgment was somewhat colored by his chagrin at having allowed her to catch him out so handily on Tuesday night last. That he had been discovered at his work by this observant young woman still greatly nettled him, although, to his credit, he had followed her unseen and done his detecting undetected for the better part of the preceding week. He had watched her, for instance, when she went to seek employment with the publisher, Frank Leslie, whose offices she had visited on Tuesday, and he thought to use that bit of knowledge to his advantage.

"You said you would tell me why you were following me," Miss Ardleigh began with asperity. Her voice, as he had noted in their earlier meeting, was deep and rich, a husky contralto. "I am curious to learn who made it worth your while to go to such effort."

18

As she folded her hands in her lap, Mr. Kellerman observed that the forefinger of the right hand was ink-stained. One would have thought, he remarked critically to himself, that she would have scrubbed away this telltale badge of her previous secretarial engagement. It reinforced his belief that such a person was likely to remain an old maid. A woman who cared about improving her marriage prospects would surely eradicate this tattletale mark of her spinsterhood.

Mr. Kellerman withdrew his attention from Miss Ardleigh's unfortunate hands. "I shall inform you," he replied. He spread out the sheaf of papers and arranged them precisely. "I am in receipt of a letter from your aunt, Miss Sabrina Ardleigh, of—"

"My aunt?" Miss Ardleigh's hazel eyes, which now appeared to be flecked with a deeper green, fastened on his. "Mr. Kellerman," she said firmly, "I *have* no such relation."

"My dear Miss Ardleigh," Mr. Kellerman said with exaggerated patience, "we will never get to the bottom of this if you persist in interrupting me." He moved the top paper a quarter of an inch. "May I resume, please?"

The young woman's mouth tightened. She nodded imperceptibly.

"Miss Sabrina Ardleigh, of Bishop's Keep, Essex, England," he continued, "contacted me several weeks ago through her British solicitors, the firm of Edgecombe, Harcourt, and Harcourt. Miss Ardleigh identified herself as an aunt of yourself, the sister of one Thomas Ardleigh, whom public record shows to have been your father. She wished me to discover whether at the present time you might be a suitable secretary and companion to her. Having made the necessary inquiries, I have conveyed to Mr. Winston Edgecombe, the firm's senior partner and her personal representative, my judgment that, upon a trial basis, you would indeed be suitable for such employment."

"Employment!" Miss Ardleigh exclaimed in a tone of restrained surprise. "In England?"

Mr. Kellerman ignored the interruption. "Mrs. Schreiber, your most recent employer, left ample testimony to your intelligence and integrity and to your competence as an amanuensis. She was apparently much impressed by the fact that you acquired German in order to assist her with her letters and to read to her, and by your skill in manipulating a typewriter. That, at least, is her attorney's recollection. Upon my inquiry, your previous employer, Mrs. Isabella Dawson, certified to me that you were able and industrious in your care of her children"—he cleared his throat—"although not, in Mrs. Dawson's words, 'a natural-born lover of babes.' "

He paused. Miss Ardleigh's head was bowed, her eyes fixed on her laced fingers. "Do you have any question to this point?"

Miss Ardleigh looked up. "Mrs. Schreiber's attorney and Mrs. Dawson—these are the sum of your inquiries?"

Feeling somewhat surprised by the question, Mr. Kellerman countered with a prudent one of his own. "Are there positions I have overlooked—other than your efforts to find secretarial employment with the publishing firm of Frank Leslie?"

The answer, which was tempered with a smile, came with sufficient readiness to satisfy whatever suspicions he might have begun to entertain. "No, sir," Miss Ardleigh said, "there are no other positions. I have been employed for regular wages by no persons other than the two in your report."

He nodded. "Very well, then, I shall proceed. Having received and conveyed these satisfactory reports of your abilities, and the fact that you are presently unengaged and at leisure, I received yesterday a response from Miss Ardleigh, relayed by cable through Mr. Edgecombe. It directs me to make the following offer." He picked up a yellow Western

Union cable and read. " 'In return for a generous annual salary, board, and room at Bishop's Keep, Dedham, as well as the cost of transportation from America to said location, Miss Sabrina Ardleigh proposes to engage Miss Kathryn Ardleigh as her secretary and personal companion for a trial period of twelve months. If the arrangement is satisfactory to both parties, it may be continued indefinitely; if at any time it becomes unsatisfactory to either party, Miss Kathryn Ardleigh will receive wages earned to date and return fare to America.' " He put down the paper. "You are asked to respond by cable as soon as possible."

Miss Ardleigh unclasped her fingers and clasped them again, although without nervousness. Calm as a custard, she was, Mr. Kellerman thought, and her air of thoughtful self-possession disconcerted him. Most of the women of his acquaintance would have been flung into an absolute tizzy by the revelation of a hitherto unknown aunt who proposed employment, not to mention the opportunity of an exotic sea voyage and a visit to the romantic-sounding Bishop's Keep. But Miss Ardleigh, it seemed, was concerned with practical, not romantic or exotic, matters.

"This aunt of mine, of what age is she?" she asked. "What is her health? Is she a traveler or does she prefer to stay at home? What duties are expected of me?"

Mr. Kellerman spoke regretfully. "I am afraid I cannot answer your questions, Miss Ardleigh, for I have not met the lady. Neither she nor Mr. Edgecombe offered further details of the post. I infer," he added, "based on the expense which she incurred to confirm your suitability, that your aunt is quite well off." He coughed delicately.

Miss Ardleigh persisted. "Bishop's Keep. What kind of place is it? What about Dedham? And what does Miss Ardleigh consider a 'generous salary'?"

"Dedham, I understand, is a small village some sixty miles to the north and east of London, ten miles from the town of Colchester. Its chief claim to fame, I recall, is that it lies near the home of John Constable, the famous painter. As to Bishop's Keep, I cannot speak, nor to the amount of the salary, nor to Miss Ardleigh's definition of 'generous.'"

Miss Ardleigh lifted her chin. "I am to know nothing of my employer nor of the position," she said tartly, "and yet I am asked to commit myself to a full year's employment in a foreign land, across the ocean from my own." She paused. "It would appear that I am being asked to buy a pig in a poke."

"So it would appear, madam," Mr. Kellerman said, "although I might note that such a position offers more in the way of . . . say, adventure, than a place at a publishing house. If, indeed, adventure is to your liking," he added hastily. He paused. "Perhaps you wish some time to reflect or to consult those elders who might guide you. Your uncle O'Malley, for instance, or your priest. It is, after all, a matter of some significance."

"It is indeed," Miss Ardleigh said. She looked down at her hands and then up again, her steady eyes clear and direct—quite her best feature, Mr. Kellerman decided, excepting perhaps that deep voice, that reminded him somehow of brown velvet. "However, since there is little information of real substance upon which to reflect, and since no more will be forthcoming, reflection is likely to prove unprofitable. While I respect my uncle O'Malley, his opinion can only be less well informed than my own." Her smile was dry. "And as to a priest, Mr. Kellerman, any Pinkerton's man worth his salt would have ascertained that I am not a practicing Catholic. I am, in fact, a freethinker."

Mr. Kellerman winced. Miss Ardleigh had reinforced his perception that hers was a too-willful nature. But she was regrettably correct. He had not thought to report her failure to attend church services, and he should have; it might have made a difference to her prospective employer.

However, it was too late now. He had tendered the offer and the young woman was pulling on her gloves.

She picked up her reticule and stood up. "Mr. Kellerman," she said, "please reply to Miss Ardleigh's cable with the simple word, 'Yes.'"

Mr. Kellerman stood up as well, surprised by the precipitous response but glad for the end of the interview. Miss Ardleigh was a young woman much too definite in her inclinations, decidedly unfeminine in her appearance, and entirely too forthright. What would be the outcome of this unusual enterprise? How would her new employer respond to this rather too-assertive person?

These questions Mr. Kellerman quickly dismissed as beyond his responsibility. After all, it was Miss Sabrina Ardleigh who was buying a pig in a poke.

4

"With the recent appearance of emulsion papers and the further development of the single-lens reflex camera, photography has become portable, making it an outstandingly useful tool. A single photograph is superior to a half-dozen sketches, for the camera reveals what the eye beholds. With the camera, we may safely say it is no longer possible to harbour illusions."

"Photography as a Tool in Natural Science"
British Journal of Photography 1894

THE STUDENT WAS pale and panting. "Pardon me, sir," he blurted, "there appears to be a dead body in my dig." Sir Archibald Fairfax put down his magnifying glass. He had overseen the Colchester excavation for several months now, and finds—small, to be sure, but quite promising— were occurring daily. Just yesterday, for instance, the team at the Lion Street site had uncovered a patch of excellent Roman mosaic floor, in first-rate condition. As he had written to his colleague Howell, he expected momentarily to make a more stimulating discovery. He had not, however, expected to turn up a skeleton.

"Good show, old chap!" Sir Archibald exclaimed, rising. "There are artifacts?"

The discovery of skeletal remains in the Colchester excavations were surprisingly infrequent, given that the town, the first Roman colony in Britain, was destroyed by Queen Boadicea in a.d. 60 and again by the Danes in the ninth century, and was the site of the Roundheads' famous siege of the Royalists in 1648. Sir Archibald would be pleased to surrender any bones to those of his colleagues who were versed in physical anthropology. Of far greater interest to him were the artifacts found with the skeleton.

"Well, actually—" The student wrung his hands. "That is to say—"

"Come, come, man," Sir Archibald commanded, "get hold of yourself. A good archaeologist must manage his work with dignity, never permitting himself to be swayed by the emotions of discovery." He gave the student a more kindly look. "In what stratum are you working, my boy? Of what period is this skeleton of yours?"

The young man swallowed, his prominent Adam's apple bobbing above his collar. "But you see, sir, it's not a skeleton, at least not yet. The body appears to be recently deceased. And to make a bad lot worse, somebody tumbled dirt in on it. Mucked up my dig a good bit, sir." His voice became anguished. "And I was getting down to the Danes."

Sir Archibald forgot about skeletons and artifacts. He snatched up the pith helmet he affected on site, even in England, where it was hardly required to shade his head from the sun. In fact, even now the sun was well hidden behind a bank of clouds and the late-summer morning was dull and cheerless.

"Right," he said testily. "We'll just go and see, shall we? Can't have people tumbling dirt and mucking up the digs."

The student's excavation was located in the southeast corner of the larger dig. When Sir Archibald reached the site, he found that several people had preceded him and were clustered disturbingly close to the excavation, no doubt tumbling even more dirt. The first, he noted with approval, was a tall, strikingly lean man with a closely trimmed brown beard, a shapeless brown felt hat, and a camera on a wooden tripod. Charles Sheridan and his ubiquitous camera had provided an invaluable service at the dig. Sir Charles was also an amateur paleontologist who understood how to behave on an archaeological site. The second man on the scene, to whom Fairfax took immediate objection, was a uniformed police sergeant, buttons gleaming. The unspeakable third was a seedy young police constable in a uniform shiny in the seat, his scuffed boots run over at the heels.

"I'm sorry, sir," the student panted, reading Sir Archibald's censorious scowl. "The constable happened to be walking by when I made the discovery. He heard my, er, exclamation of amazement. He summoned a superior."

"See here now," Sir Archibald said crossly to the two policemen, "we can't have this. Unauthorized persons at the site. Next thing you know, there'll be tourists." Tourists! As irresponsible as water buffalo. As undisciplined as sacred cows. He glanced at the gentleman with the camera. "Not meaning you, old chap," he added. "Carry on as you will."

Charles Sheridan gave Sir Archibald a restrained smile, took a photographic plate holder out of the large bellows camera, put it carefully into a shoulder bag, and inserted another one.

The sergeant, unperturbed by Sir Archibald's outburst, stepped back from the brink. "I wonder, sir, if you 'ud mind askin' yer chaps t' remove th' dirt, or if you 'ud prefer my man t' do it."

Sir Archibald was incredulous. "*Your* man, sir? In *my* excavation? Absurd! He has no qualifications. Just imagine what would happen should a valuable artifact reside beneath that lot of dirt! Can't have amateurs mucking about with ancient skeletons and irreplaceable antiquities. Simply not done."

"P'raps, sir," said the student, tugging at his sleeve, "you had better have a look first."

Sir Archibald peered into the pit, an area about the size of a double grave, and very nearly as deep. At least, so it had been. Now, one of the sides had caved in, partially covering the floor of the excavation with an untidy heap of dirt and small stones. Out of the debris Sir Archibald saw protruding a human hand and perceived in an instant that this find would produce no artifacts suitable for the collection of the British Museum or for documentation in the *British Journal of Archaeology*. This relic belonged in the morgue.

"Well, sir?" the sergeant asked. "What'll it be?"

Sir Archibald turned to the student. "Right, then, lad," he said, not ungraciously. "Why don't you just pop down and clean out the pit? Down you go, now."

With that, he turned on his heel and marched back to his tent.

5

"You see, but you do not observe."
—SHERLOCK HOLMES,
ARTHUR CONAN DOYLE
Scandal in Bohemia

CHARLES SHERIDAN REMAINED at the lip of the impromptu grave for the next hour, soberly capturing with his camera the progress of the excavation. As the last of the covering dirt was shifted by the student archaeologist, down to shirtsleeves now and sweating in the bright sun that had burned off the cloud, Charles moved his tripod to get a different perspective on the work. While the sergeant and the constable hoisted the stiffened corpse out of the pit, he composed another exposure under the black cloth which covered the back of the camera, and made several others, from different angles, with the body lying face up to the sun. A knot of curious onlookers was kept well to the street by a second police constable, summoned to control the crowd.

Studying the inverted image on the ground glass screen at the back of the camera, Charles saw that the body was that of a slim, swarthy gentleman of foreign appearance. He had high cheekbones, an aquiline nose, and thin lips under a waxed mustache, and was dressed for evening in a black frock coat, double-breasted waistcoat, single-wing collar, and striped trousers. Upon one well-cared-for hand was a curious gold ring in the shape of a scarab, such as Charles had seen among recently discovered Egyptian artifacts in the British Museum. That the corpse was not the ordinary inebriated casualty of several hours' pleasant imbibing at the nearby Red Lion was attested by the fact that a substantial amount of dirt had been deposited on top of him by the landslide. It was more unquestionably indicated by a half-inch cut in the man's dirt-soiled waistcoat in the vicinity of the heart. The cut was surrounded by a rich rosette of crusted blood. The floor of the excavation, onto which he had fallen facedown, was blood-soaked.

The sergeant knelt and jabbed a finger at the cut. He spoke without looking at the police constable standing at attention behind him. "Knife, wudn't yer say, Trabb?"

Trabb penciled nervous jottings in a small notebook. "I'd say so, Sergeant Bat'le."

"Inserted once firmly an' withdrawn?"

"So't appears, sir." Trabb turned his head squeamishly aside. "D'yer recognize 'im?"

" 'Fraid not." The sergeant gingerly inserted his hand into the dead man's pockets, one after the other. "Not a Colchester man, I'd warrant. Don't appear t' have a thing in his pockets. Rob'ry, wouldn't yer say?"

"Indeed, sir," Trabb concurred, writing industriously.

Charles spoke in a quiet voice. "Do you think, Sergeant Battle, that a thief would have overlooked the gold ring? It's worth a few guineas, at least."

The sergeant gave Charles a look in which suspicion and deference contended, then turned back to the corpse. "P'raps yer right, sir," he said with an exaggerated courtesy that seemed to suggest its opposite. "More like, th' thief were in a tearin' hurry t' be done wi' th' deed, or cudn't get the Weedin' ring off."

Charles bent over, slipped the ring off the corpse's ring finger, and handed it without a word to the sergeant.

"Right, sir," Sergeant Battle murmured. He pocketed the ring. Trabb's scribble paused momentarily, then continued.

Charles stood back and surveyed the area. He had for the past week spent the daylight hours documenting the progress of Sir Archibald's dig, so he had a good sense of the lay of the land. The northern border of the excavation was bounded by other digs, making the ground in that direction difficult to navigate, especially in the dark of a moonless night, such as the last. On the southern side of the excavation, however, six yards away, was a dirt cart track that led to the street. According to the student archaeologist, the site was unattended after dark.

Shouldering his camera, Charles slowly paced from the pit to the cart track, head down, studying the sandy surface. There had been a drizzle early in the previous evening. Footprints around the excavation—those left after the rain—had already been destroyed by the tramping to and fro of the police. But as he neared the cart track, a line of footprints emerged out of the muddle. He pulled out an ivory folding rule, laid it beside the prints, and took a photograph, then another. Then he walked a few paces to the cart track and, once again using his rule for scale, took several photographs of what seemed to be the wheel prints of a cab or carriage and the hoof prints of a single horse.

As he changed plates, he noticed on the ground a lozenge of old ivory, about the size of his thumb and curiously carved with minutely detailed leaves and flowers, pressed into the loose dirt by a careless foot. He carefully repositioned his camera and photographed the piece of ivory at the closest range the lens would allow, from three different angles. Then he signaled to the sergeant.

"I think this bit might be of interest to you, Sergeant Battle." Charles pointed at the piece of ivory. "It looks as if it were dropped here recently, does it not?"

The sergeant knelt, squinting, then picked up the ivory and slipped it into his pocket. "P'raps," he remarked carelessly. He glanced at the camera and tripod. "Quite a imposin' instrument, that, sir. I see yer've been busy wi' it."

Charles's camera had been made in Paris in 1890. It had a mahogany front panel which folded down when the camera opened to form the baseboard that supported the square leather bellows and the Eurygraphe Extra-Rapid No. 3 lens. The camera was older and somewhat more cumbersome than others he owned, but was ideal for making detailed exposures where focus was critical and haste in composition no object. It was in his opinion a very fine camera.

"I plan to develop the plates this evening," he said. "If you would find photographic prints of this unfortunate business of use in your investigation, I should be pleased to let you have them."

Charles could see that Sergeant Battle was wary of his offer, and perhaps understandably so. It had been almost seventy years since Daguerre had created his first tantalizingly impermanent images on silver plates coated with a light-sensitive layer of silver iodide, and five years since George Eastman had wound a ribbon of cellulose nitrate on a spool inside a wooden box that he called a "Kodak." The camera was no longer an inventor's novelty used by a handful of eccentrics.

The use of photography in the solving of crime, however, was still relatively unproven in 1894. No doubt Sergeant Battle had heard that Scotland Yard routinely photographed criminals, chiefly as an aid to identification, and perhaps he had even heard a rumor that Alphonse Bertillon, in Paris, was experimenting with detailed photographic records of the crime scene. But the techniques of investigation in the borough police forces were at a decade or more behind those of the Metropolitan

Police, which lagged by yet another decade those of the French *Sûreté*. Sergeant Battle might well not be able to imagine to what use the photographs of this morning's gruesome discovery could be put. After all, there was the corpse, absolutely and indisputably dead, the means of death unquestionably visible in the bloody shirt front. There was PC Trabb, earnestly and meticulously recording each minute detail of the crime scene in his notebook. And shortly, a qualified medical practitioner would examine the body to ascertain whether any instrument or agency other than a knife might have contributed to the victim's untimely demise, and in due course would present his report to the coroner and his jury. What possible service could photographs render in this time-honored process?

But Charles observed that the sergeant was a cautious man, not prepared to reject out of hand a gentleman's offer of assistance, whatever he might do with the photographs once they were in his possession. "T' be sure, sir," he said with a show of earnestness. "If you'd be so kind as t' bring th' pichures t' th' station, I'll see as they gets put t' good use."

"Then I shall," Charles agreed. He pointed at the cart tracks and footprints. "Perhaps your man might want to have a go at these."

"A-corse, sir," said the sergeant, as he stepped on one of the prints.

Observing that there was nothing left to be learned from the scene and little additional help he might offer, Charles took his camera and tripod and walked away.

6

"It is a truth universally acknowledged, that a single man in possession of a good fortune must be in want of a wife."

—Jane Austen
Pride and Prejudice

CHARLES CLIMBED INTO the barouche and placed his camera on the seat, his bag of exposed plates, tripod, and other gear on the floor. The man in the opposite seat lowered his newspaper.

"I must say, Sheridan," he said lazily, "I'm not altogether sure what fascinates you about those old Roman ruins. Not much of value being dug up these days, I'll wager."

Charles sat down with a slight laugh. "Perhaps not. But the remains that were dug up this morning *were* rather of interest. As it happens, there was a bit of foul play."

"You don't say." Bradford Marsden folded the newspaper and raised his voice slightly. "Drive on, Foster."

The coachman lifted the reins and the carriage lurched into its place in the stream of traffic on the cobbled street, behind a brewer's dilapidated dray and a farm wagon filled with baskets of fresh lettuces and cauliflowers.

"A foreign gentleman was unceremoniously dispatched and shoved into an excavation," Charles said. "The local constabulary were on the scene, going about a semblance of investigation." He leaned back in the seat, pulled down his hat brim, and began to reflect on the morning's events. To be truthful, they had stimulated him in a way that he rarely felt stimulated, except perhaps by the discovery of a new species of flora or the sight of an unnamed fossil. One of the hazards of having sufficient money to be at one's leisure was the hazard of continually finding oneself bored by the banality of one's existence and hence forced to seek new forms of intellectual stimulation. Murder was most stimulating.

To engage his mind, Charles had throughout most of his thirty-three years employed himself with various scientific studies. At nine he had accompanied his paleontologist grandfather in the pursuit of fossil shells and corals at Walton-on-the-Naze. At twelve he produced a field guide to local species of edible fungi, hand-illustrated and annotated. At fifteen, he devised a detective camera small enough to be concealed beneath the waistcoat, with the intent to take pictures on the sly. At Eton and Oxford, Charles did not exercise the discipline of narrow specialization in any science, but rather indulged himself in a broad study of all. His natural powers of observation were remarkably keen, exceeded only by his insatiable curiosity, his indefatigable memory, and his unflagging powers of inquiry. But he *did* require something of interest to excite those powers.

"Murder, eh?" Bradford folded the newspaper and tossed it aside. "If that's what it is, no doubt the papers will trumpet it. They're awash in blood. That extraordinary murder discovered in Great Marylebone Street, for instance—the woman who carried off the body of a murdered man in a trunk. One read of nothing else for weeks. I say, Sheridan," he added casually. "I've been meaning to ask your advice about an investment."

Charles glanced at him. "I'm hardly up on commerce. Too busy with other matters, I'm afraid."

"But inventions are rather in your line," Bradford replied as the carriage passed a green park where white-aproned nannies pushed black wickerwork perambulators in the afternoon. He took a cigarette out of a monogrammed gold case. "What do you think about these new motorcars?"

Charles raised his eyebrows. "Motorcars? The mechanical problems are really quite intriguing—particularly those having to do with power transmission and steering. For instance, the rims of the inside and outside wheels do not travel the same distance in a turn. The outside actually travels farther than the inside—"

"What I mean to say," Bradford interrupted, "is what do you think about motorcars as an investment?" He lighted his cigarette.

Charles was thoughtful. "The mechanical problems are not insurmountable. In my view, the primary impediments are social and economic. For example, when cars can travel faster than twelve miles an hour—"

"They can now," Bradford said crossly, "but the law won't allow it."

"The laws will be changed to meet the times," Charles replied, settling into his explanation. "But faster speeds require superior roads, which will mean an increase in taxes. Building an adequate fuel-distribution system will take time, and eventually there will have to be an entirely new maintenance industry. All this could require twenty or thirty years. If the investors are looking for a quick return on their money, they will be disappointed."

Bradford sighed heavily and consulted an engraved gold pocket watch. "We are just in time to meet Eleanor and Aunt Penelope at the railway station. I hope you don't object."

Charles pulled his hat brim down farther. "Object? Why should I object? Your sister is a delightful young woman."

"If constant chatter about weddings does not grate on your ears," Bradford replied, pocketing his watch. He was a handsome man with a certain negligent rakishness. But there were lines of worry about his eyes and he wore an uncharacteristically serious look. Charles wondered if perhaps he had lost more at the Steeplechase than he had admitted to doing. Or whether his worry was connected with motorcars. But Charles would no more inquire about his friend's investments than ask after his mistresses.

"Chatter about weddings annoys you, does it?" Charles replied in a tone of friendly banter. "Just wait, Marsden. When your mother has finished arranging your sister's wedding, she will turn her attention to yours. It must be high time to assure the continuation of the Marsden baronetcy."

Bradford Marsden shuddered and closed his eyes briefly. Then, recollecting himself, he turned to Charles. "You needn't be so smug, my dear chap. It has not escaped my attention that my mother would like to make a certain arrangement where *you* are concerned." The corners of his mouth quirked as he glanced at Charles's dusty hat. "Despite that ridiculous hat of yours."

Charles sobered. He had accepted Bradford Marsden's invitation to spend a month at Marsden Manor for the purpose of documenting the Colchester dig, as well as pursuing various interests, among them a few rare local flora and some fascinating Cenozoic coelenterates. He had no intention of being ambushed by a maternal attempt at matrimonial arranging .

"I presume," Charles said somberly, "that you are referring to Patsy."

If Charles was rarely frustrated in his determined search for knowledge, he was frequently frustrated when it came to the fairer sex. This had certainly been the case since his arrival the previous week at Marsden Manor. He had sensed from the outset that Lady Henrietta Marsden had her own aims for his visit, and that those aims involved her younger daughter. To make things worse, the daughter's intentions in the matter were clearly those of the mother. The two were in cahoots.

Bradford raised his eyebrows. "Would that be such a disaster, old man?"

Charles's response was carefully diplomatic. "Your sister is liberally endowed with Marsden beauty and grace, as well as Marsden wit. But she is, after all, barely eighteen and not yet out. I am deeply honored and complimented by Lady Henrietta's consideration, but I think she would do well to look to someone nearer Patsy's age. I am too old for her."

He did not add, although he might have, that Patsy Marsden was a flibbertigibbet whose conversation flitted like a butterfly between balls and bonnets. She was the last woman in the world that he would have considered.

"Damn it all, man," Marsden grumbled, "don't talk as if you were poised on the verge of the grave. You're only thirty-three, even if you are a musty old scientist. And you come from excellent family. The Marsdens would be honored—*I* would be honored—to entrust Patsy's future to you."

Charles smiled. "You forget," he said, happily falling back upon his strongest argument, "that I am a younger son."

Younger sons, as Bradford Marsden very well knew, were generally left without inheritance, while the family jewels, the family estate, and the family title, if there was one, were bestowed in their entirety upon the eldest son. In Charles's situation, the fact that his brother Robert had inherited the bulk of their father's money was fortuitously offset by a sizable legacy from his maternal grandmother— in other words, he was possessed of a substantial fortune. But Charles had several times successfully deployed his status as younger son as a shield against the menace of matrimony. He expected it to work in this instance as well.

But Bradford only laughed. "Come now, Sheridan, you can't hide behind that ruse with me. We've been friends too long. I know, as does Mother, that you've enough to support Patsy quite comfortably." Bradford did not add that the Marsdens (whose fortunes had slipped into a lengthy decline precipitated by Grandfather Marsden's regrettable losses at the gaming table and exacerbated by Bradford's father's equally regrettable love of expensive but ill-fated horseflesh) would be greatly relieved if their younger daughter were to marry into Charles Sheridan's respectable family and quite ample fortune. His pale blue eyes twinkled. "And who knows? Perhaps a few months spent traipsing in out-of-the-way corners of the world, carrying those cameras of yours, might sober her sufficiently to allow her to think beyond the next new gown and slippers." In the distance, the train whistle could be heard, and the chugging of the engine, and Bradford leaned forward to tap the coachman's shoulder. "The whip, Foster."

"Patsy is quite delicious just as she is," Charles lied, as the carriage moved forward smartly. "I would not change her for the world. No, Marsden, you and your mother will have to indulge me. Patsy will make some fortunate man a loving, if not dutiful, wife, but I have not yet found the right woman. Perhaps—"

He paused. On the graveled footpath beside the street, two rosy-cheeked young women with elaborately piled hair and ruffled silk parasols smiled flirtatiously at the occupants of the carriage. For Bradford's benefit, he spoke heavily, a man weighted by disappointed hopes.

"—Perhaps I never shall."

"Nonsense." Marsden said, tipping his bowler at the two young women. "And don't be so quick to reject Patsy. She's young yet. With a husband's firm hand guiding her development, she could become a charming wife."

Charles pursed his lips. A wife, charming or otherwise, was not in his scheme of things.

7

"You have read in the newspaper our murder I hope—you cannot think how much more interesting a murder becomes from being committed at one's door."

—JANE CARLYLE
to her cousin Jeannie Welch

AS THE TRAIN from London pulled into the Colchester station, Kate eagerly rose from her seat in the first-class carriage she had shared with Eleanor Marsden and Garnet, Miss Marsden's personal maid.

"We're here," she cried excitedly, leaning from the open window to glimpse what she could of the platform. "At last!"

Then she remembered herself and pulled back from the window, flushing. Miss Marsden was rising in a leisurely way, directing Garnet to gather her cloak, her exquisite dyed kid gloves, her parasol, her reticule, and the half-dozen bags and bandboxes she had brought with her from London, stuffed with (as Kate had been hearing for the last several hours) wedding finery. To the sophisticated Miss Marsden, Kate thought, her pleasure in the sights and sounds of her arrival must seem terribly inexperienced and gauche, rather like a schoolgirl on an adventure.

Kate tossed her head. But she *was* inexperienced and this *was* an adventure for her. She could scarcely wait to see the massive walls of Bishop's Keep rising like a mossy ruin out of the surrounding grove of ancient oaks, the sunset gilding its great stone turrets. If the truthful expression of pleasure in either her journey or her arrival was amusing to her elegant traveling companion, so be it. So she repeated with enthusiasm as she reached for her carpetbag, "How lovely to be here at last."

Eleanor Marsden inspected the fluff of silvery blond bangs and the tilt of her plum-colored straw hat in the small mirror that Garnet held up for her. "You must be appallingly tired, my dear Miss Ardleigh. It is such a long, tedious journey all the way from New York."

It had been a long journey, Kate thought. But hardly tedious. To her surprise and pleasure, the steamship passage Mr. Kellerman had arranged at her aunt's direction, as well as the railway tickets from Liverpool to London and from London to Colchester, had been first-class accommodations, an acknowledgment, no doubt, that she was an Ardleigh, albeit a distant one. Had she been a mere secretary-companion, she would have been sent third class.

But although Kate's unfashionable clothing and flyaway hair set her apart from the extravagantly gowned and coiffed transatlantic voyagers, she did not feel the least uncomfortable. On the contrary, the excitement of the journey had charged her. Her imagination examined each sight, each exchange, each person, as possible subject matter for the sensational stories that Beryl Bardwell had promised to post (Kate's secretarial schedule permitting) to Mr. Coxford. After all, Kate reminded herself, she had not accepted her new position because she needed the money (she was confident of supporting herself with her pen) but because she deeply desired *adventure.* If she were going to write sensational stories, she needed to live a sensational life. It was impossible to describe from the heart what she had not experienced! It had been the rarest and most wonderful chance that Aunt Sabrina had risen like a specter out of the mists to offer her this Excalibur of widened horizons. She would not squander the least moment of her journey. She would take note of it all.

So she was especially gratified when Mrs. Snodgrass's priceless diamond necklace was discovered to be missing and the gossip at the table implicated the ship's steward, a man of (it was rumored) Egyptian origin, a swarthy fellow with slender, tapering fingers and an evil look. For the following two days, Kate alternately posted herself in the stuffy hallway outside Mrs. Snodgrass's stateroom and loitered on deck near the office of the steward, pretending great interest in the starboard vista. But to her frustration, she was not afforded the opportunity to enter either room unobserved (whether she *would* have was quite another question) and had to content herself with polite inquiries as to Mrs. Snodgrass's health and a casually phrased remark to the steward about camels, which met with a blank stare. She was downcast when Mrs. Snodgrass's maid turned up the missing jewels in the laundry. Thus it was that the embryonic "Deadly Diamonds" (which was to have followed "Amber's Amulet," on which she was just getting a start) was rudely aborted.

But everything else about her journey had been perfect, down to the perfect coincidence of discovering that her fellow traveler in the first-class carriage from London to Colchester was Miss Eleanor Marsden, of Marsden Manor, daughter of a baronet—and her aunt's neighbor. Marsden Manor, it turned out, was only three miles from Bishop's Keep. Life was indeed stranger than fiction!

Kate was very glad to have met Miss Marsden, whom she liked immediately. Clearheaded though she was about many things, Kate was given to forming quick opinions on the basis of short acquaintance. It was a character trait that Aunt Maureen had often cautioned her to curb, although Kate stubbornly felt it a strength to be cultivated. A writer, she thought, should be a quick study of personality, able to see through the social facade straight to the heart. In the case of Miss Marsden, the heart did not seem far to seek. She wore it like a talisman on her sleeve and loved to talk about what was in it.

"There they are," Miss Marsden called over her shoulder to Kate as she tripped across the platform, plum kid boots peeping from under the deep flounce of her elegant plum-colored traveling suit. "Yoo-hoo," she cried, waving. "Bradford, Charles! Here we are!"

Kate watched with interest as a strikingly handsome, fair-haired young man ambled toward them. He was dressed in stylish gray flannels, flawlessly tailored, and wore a smart gray bowler. He was accompanied by a man whose clothes were markedly less formal.

"If it isn't our favorite spendthrift," the fair-haired man said jauntily. "Did you leave anything in the Regency Street shops, Ellie?"

Miss Marsden tapped him smartly on the arm. "Not a solitary ribbon or plume, dear brother. And since poor Garnet could not carry the half of my extravagances, I ordered most of my purchases sent down by post. Wait until you see the lavish waistcoat I have brought for you, in the same shade of peacock as the one I purchased for Mr. Fairley."

Mr. Ernest Fairley, Kate knew from Miss Marsden's voluminous railway confidences, was Miss Marsden's Intended. His grandfather, the genius of Fairley's Finest Fancy Candies, had founded the family fortune on chocolate. If Miss Marsden's report were to be trusted, the marriage, which would take place at Christmas, was considered the match of the year. Kate had been aghast to learn that Mr. Fairley, a widower, was nearly twenty-five years older than his bride-to-be. Still, Miss Marsden, who from the moment of their meeting had scarcely stopped talking about Mr. Fairley's courtship, their impending vows, and the splendid Fairley family home in Kensington, did not seem unduly troubled at the thought of surrendering her carefree soul to a man who was her senior by a quarter of a century.

Kate, for her part, could not imagine such a thing. Or rather, she could imagine it all too clearly, and the image made her shudder. How could any thinking woman yield up her independence to the whim and will of some man who would become her guardian both in the eyes of the law and society? How could she bear to be treated as if she were a wayward child who required adult protection from the dangers of the world and from her own naive and ungovernable willfulness? Not for her, such a fate!

The stylish man was peering toward the train hissing on the track, while the conductor shouted and slammed the coach doors, porters jangled baggage trucks, and passengers scurried to board. "Where is Aunt Penelope?"

"She developed a frightful cold," Miss Marsden said carelessly, "really quite severe, poor old thing. The doctor advised her to take to her bed. Rather than wait, I came on without her."

The young man frowned. "Papa will not be at all pleased, Ellie. You know his feelings on the subject of women traveling unescorted."

Miss Marsden gave him a dazzling smile, "But I was not *alone*, Bradford. My dear friend Miss Ardleigh was kind enough to accompany me, and of course I had Garnet. I am sure Papa could not object." She drew Kate forward. "Miss Kathryn Ardleigh, may I present my dear brother, the Honorable Bradford Marsden, and his friend, Sir Charles Sheridan, who is staying the month with us. Gentlemen, Miss Ardleigh is the niece of Miss Sabrina

Ardleigh and Mrs. Bernice Jaggers. She has come to live with her aunts at Bishop's Keep."

Kate's amusement at Miss Marsden's adroitness in giving their accidental meeting the appearance of a planned jaunt was nearly lost in her astonishment. There were *two* aunts? But she could not question Miss Marsden without revealing her ignorance about the situation into which she was walking, as Uncle O'Malley would have said, as blind as a bat. In spite of her intuitive liking for her companion, her own railway confidences had been discreetly reserved. She was anxious to know whether Bishop's Keep was indeed as romantic as she imagined, but she had not asked. Nor had she disclosed either her secretarial employment or the existence of Beryl Bardwell. And she had asked nothing about her aunt, leaving it to Miss Marsden to think what she wished.

"Charmed, I am sure, Miss Ardleigh," Bradford Marsden drawled, bending in a polished greeting over her hand. "How nice that you have come." He cocked a wry eyebrow. "And how felicitous for Eleanor. Now she will have a friend directly at hand. No doubt you will be required to properly admire her nuptial finery and envy her choice of husbands. Most of her friends, regrettably, fail to serve these necessary purposes, for they live in London. You will certainly be useful."

"I am glad to share Miss Marsden's joys," Kate said quietly, retrieving her hand.

Miss Marsden made a playful face. "Come now, Bradford, *do* behave." She turned to the other gentleman, who stood slightly behind her brother. "Sir Charles Sheridan, my dear Kathryn, is a masterful photographer, famous for some picture or other that he took of the Queen at her Jubilee, and thereby earned his knighthood. You will have to persuade him to take your portrait, as he did the Queen's, and Mrs. Langtry's. But don't let him talk to you of fossils," she added with a playful gaiety.

"Once given leave to begin, the man scarcely knows how to make a stop, and must be reined in with the firmest possible hand."

Kate nodded at Sir Charles with interest, half expecting him to wear some visible token of his grandness. But as a knight, he was a stunning disappointment, especially in comparison to the impeccably groomed, grinning Bradford Marsden. Sir Charles's brown canvas jacket needed brushing. It was covered with lumpy pockets, stuffed, from what she could see, with odds and ends of scientific paraphernalia—magnifying lens, an ivory rule, a pair of calipers. His tweedy Norfolk breeches were tucked into scarred, heavy-soled leather boots, and a soft felt hat, a broad-brimmed, brown thing with a shapeless crown, was pushed back on his curly brown hair, cut overlong, so that he looked like a buccaneer. From the look of him, Kate deduced that his knighthood was not a distinction he valued highly.

"Kathryn—" Miss Marsden took her arm. "May I call you Kathryn, my dear? And you really must call me Eleanor. I require it. It is so tedious to be formal." Without waiting for a response, she went on. "Dear Kathryn has arrived a day sooner than expected, so I have offered to take her to Bishop's Keep."

Mr. Marsden pursed his lips. "But my dear sister, I fear that five is too many, given your monstrous load of parcels."

Kate disengaged her arm. "I can wait here," she said hastily. "I can send word to Bishop's Keep to let them know I have arrived, and someone will be sent to fetch me, I shall not mind staying, truly."

She would not, either. Beryl Bardwell would spend the time writing down everything she had seen on the clanking, steam-belching journey from London to Colchester and as much of Eleanor's chitchat as she could remember, as well as full descriptions of the elegant Bradford Marsden and Sir Charles Sheridan, he of the

45

lumpy pockets. And she would give her thoughts to what adventures and great mysteries lay ahead at Bishop's Keep, which she imagined as an enormous stone pile of arches and towers, shrouded by a mysterious haze and haunted by ghosts of dead Ardleighs. Now that she was almost there, she had to admit to some anxiety. The sense of being alone in a strange place, so distant from the life she had known, the feeling of utter dependence on the goodwill of her unknown aunt—her *two* unknown aunts!—made her feel apprehensive. Apprehension was not an emotion Kate was used to. She didn't particularly like it.

"Actually, I prefer to stay behind," Sir Charles said. "I shall return to the scene of the murder and see if anything new has been found out—although," he added, as much to himself as to them, "judging from Sergeant Battle's muddled methods, I rather doubt it."

Kate swiveled to look at Sir Charles. Eleanor squealed and clapped her hands.

"Murder!" she cried. "How delightfully shocking! Charles, you naughty man, what dreadful scrape have you gotten yourself into now? You must tell us all about it as we ride. There is nothing I love quite as much as a good murder, especially when one of our party is *involved* in it." She possessed herself of Kate's arm once again. "And it is absolute balderdash to think of anyone's staying behind," she added firmly. "We will hire a man with a cart to take Garnet and the boxes, whilst we enjoy a leisurely drive through the countryside. You should know, dear Kathryn, that the painter John Constable, who has memorialized our Dedham Vale in his landscapes, was Sir Charles's estimable great-uncle. Come now, everyone."

Kate smiled. Clearly, problems were readily solved if one had the money to hire the solution. But even though she continued to smile as Eleanor led them toward the carriage, she was at the same time surveying Sir Charles with greater interest, wondering exactly what sort of murder he meant.

The carriage, with Kate's boxes roped at the rear, proceeded through the Essex countryside, resplendent in late-summer glories. Blackbirds sang in the hawthorn hedges, apples ripened in the orchards, and golden stubblefields were studded with standing sheaves of grain. But the sun was a flat silver disk, mist-shrouded, in a pearl-gray sky. As they rode, the air thickened into a damp, cool fog. Bradford Marsden seemed preoccupied, while Eleanor wheedled out of Sir Charles a full account of the dead body in the dig and Beryl Bardwell made careful mental note of every grisly detail that might enrich "Amber's Amulet."

So far, her story was little more than character sketches of an Egyptian gentleman (greatly resembling the ship's steward in appearance and demeanor) and a mysterious medium named Mrs. Amber Bartlett, who wore an amulet and conducted séances in darkened rooms. It did not presently involve a murder, if only because Kate had not yet thought it all out, but the story would undoubtedly be the better for one. She made a note to herself to look for the newspaper accounts of the Colchester tragedy, and at Sir Charles's mention of the photographs he had taken that morning, she asked to see them.

"But my dear Kathryn," Eleanor protested in a shocked voice, "they are photographs of a dead man. And not merely dead, but shockingly *murdered*! One presumes that there was a great deal of blood." She shuddered with an eager delicacy. "The mere thought of it makes one quite faint." Then she smiled and patted Kate's hand. "But I forget. You are an American and American women are reputed to be amazingly venturesome. *You* would not be daunted by a bit of blood, perhaps not even by the Chamber of Horrors at Madame Tussaud's." She turned to Bradford. "Perhaps Miss Ardleigh would consent to your escorting us to Madame Tussaud's, dear brother. I understand that Cecil Hambrough's dreadful murderer has been newly installed, holding the very gun from which the fatal shot was fired."

Having already heard of Madame Tussaud's famous waxworks and feeling that the jaunt would yield excellent story material, Kate instantly agreed to Eleanor's proposal. "It is not that I am particularly adventuresome," she added. "It is simply that I am fascinated by all facets of life—even death." She smiled at Sir Charles. "Hence my interest in your photographs."

Bradford Marsden roused himself from his preoccupation. "Sheridan, old chap," he said, "you are in luck. Someone actually wants to see those wretched snapshots of yours." He turned morosely to Kate. "Take my advice and don't encourage the fellow, Miss Ardleigh. He will not only insist on showing you his photographs, but his fingerprints as well."

"Fingerprints?" Kate asked, finding that her opinion of Sir Charles was in need of revision. "You know about fingerprints?"

Sir Charles held out his hand, palm up. "Indeed," he said. "The skin of each finger exhibits a unique set of ridges. Each time the finger touches a surface, it deposits a print, rather like a stamp."

"That much I know," Kate said.

Sir Charles frowned. "You know?"

"I read *Pudd'nhead Wilson*," Kate explained. "Mark Twain's novel, published last year in *Century Magazine*. The murderer is convicted when the detective shows an enlarged drawing of a fingerprint to the jury."

"Astonishing," Sir Charles murmured.

"Absurd," Mr. Marsden said. "Shows how far novels are from the real world. Convicting a man on the flimsy print of a finger!"

"Nevertheless," Kate said bravely, "at some time when you would care to explain more about fingerprints, Sir Charles, I would be interested in listening." And she sat back, fearing that she had called too much attention to herself already, when attention was the last thing she wished. In order for Beryl Bardwell to conduct her clandestine observations, she must remain discreet and undiscovered behind the mask of Kathryn Ardleigh, docile, decorous secretary-companion. But how interesting to encounter a man (however arrogant he might be) who could teach her something more than she already knew about fingerprints—*and* to encounter a murder. Not just fictional murder, either, but murder most *real*!

So, as Eleanor Marsden pointed out landmarks of interest along the way, Beryl Bardwell was devising a catalog of things she needed to discover. Who was the murdered man? From whence had he come? And, above all, who had done the deed and why? It was up to her to find answers, or, rather, to create them. When it came to thrillers, Beryl Bardwell was constrained neither by truth nor by fact.

8

"The splendour falls on castle walls"
—ALFRED, LORD TENNYSON
The Princess

To Charles Sheridan's surprise, he found the drive to Bishop's Keep rather interesting. Marsden was sitting like a stick, busy with his thoughts. Eleanor was no less feather-witted than usual. But Miss Ardleigh—

Ah, yes, Miss Ardleigh. Charles occasionally amused himself by drawing conclusions about people's characters and personal histories from appearance and odd bits of conversation. It was not difficult to conclude, from the plain cut and plainer fabric of her costume, that Miss Ardleigh was a poor relation. The woman was not particularly young, and not particularly beautiful. She lacked either the interest, the skill, or the funds—perhaps chiefly interest, since most women managed to pretty themselves no matter what their funds—to devote much attention to her appearance. The undisciplined mass of auburn hair, for instance, bespoke both a lack of concern for elegance and an unruly will, while the second finger of the right hand bore inky tribute to her acquaintance with the pen. That, and her age, indicated a type: the American spinster abroad, greedily consuming every delight of the excursive experience, and writing volumes about it in the form of letters home.

But there seemed to be more to Miss Ardleigh than that, Charles acknowledged. The unruly hair was quite lovely and the forthright hazel eyes under straight dark brows unusually striking. She would photograph well. And more, she had intrigued him with her odd remark about Mark Twain's use of fingerprints. It had betrayed an unusual interest. What sort of woman read detective stories?

Three-quarters of an hour after leaving the station, the carriage with its four passengers turned off the road and onto a curving lane lined with mist-cloaked beeches. Miss Ardleigh seemed to be holding an excited expectation in stern check. "I suppose Bishop's Keep is very medieval," she said in an offhand way, glancing across the fog-wreathed landscape.

"Medieval?" Eleanor asked in surprise. "Why, no. Why did you—Oh, of course. The *Keep*."

Charles suppressed a smile. Americans harbored endless misconceptions about England. All the fault of Byron and Wordsworth and those other soulful purveyors of the Romantic view. Caught up in a New World whirlwind of invention and innovation, Americans loved to take a holiday from progress to revel in the picturesque, the macabre, the mist. That's what came of having virtually no history of their own, and no castles. And very little fog, either.

"You have been reading thrillers," Bradford remarked. "Towers and turrets and dead bodies in great chests, and bats in all the belfries."

Charles was distracted from his reflections on the American temperament. "Ah, bats," he said energetically. "D'you know, there is a bat in this locality that is quite a rare little fellow, a—"

Eleanor's laugh was a melodious tinkle. "I am sure Kathryn will have more exciting things to do than spy out bats for you, Charles."

"Are you saying that Bishop's Keep is not really a castle?" Miss Ardleigh asked, clearly disappointed but trying not to seem so.

"There once was a castle," Bradford said carelessly, "the country seat of some great churchman or another. But Cromwell pulled it down during the Civil War, and there is little left save the odd flint rubble wall. The present residence is less than seventy years old. Not as romantic as a castle, but a damned sight less drafty, I warrant." A little of his flirtatious good humor seemed to be coming back, and he grinned. "If it's romance you're after, Miss Ardleigh, you must visit Marsden Manor. No ruin, but we have our own resident ghost."

At the word "ghost," Charles noticed, Miss Ardleigh leaned slightly forward, her face eager. She was no doubt impressed by Bradford's attention, as were most women. The brief sigh that escaped his lips as he turned away was largely unconscious.

Sir Charles could not know, of course, that Kate was far less impressed by Mr. Marsden's person and manner than by his last remark. "Is there truly a ghost?" she asked, trying to keep the hopeful note out of her voice.

"Truly," Bradford said solemnly.

Eleanor patted her hand. "Do come and be introduced to him, Kathryn. Bradford will give you the life story of the wretched creature, and I shall show off my wedding dress."

Kate smiled. "I certainly shall," she said. "I don't imagine your ghost goes to weddings," she said, hoping to prompt Mr. Marsden to say more.

The corners of Bradford's mouth twitched and his pale blue eyes were amused. "No, but he's quite civil, all the same. If you will do us the honor of staying over the night, we can put you in the chamber which he frequents. In search of his missing head."

"His head!" Kate exclaimed. "You mean, he was *murdered?*"

"*Bradford!*" Eleanor protested.

"Ah," Bradford said knowingly, and to Kate's disappointment, lapsed into silence. Eleanor launched into a lengthy description of the gown she planned to wear to the next ball, while Kate feigned interest. Eleanor's chatter seemed to plunge her brother further into gloom. Sir Charles sat quiet, thinking, perhaps, of his bats.

Kate was half listening to Eleanor and watching the mist-draped groves on either side of the road when the carriage turned a sharp bend, a meadow opened, and Bishop's Keep loomed through the silver fog. She suppressed a little "Oh!" and leaned forward eagerly.

But what Kate saw before her was not the splendor of castle walls that Beryl Bardwell had conjured up in her novelistic imagination. It was instead a large and rather dull-looking Georgian residence built of gray brick and decorated only by monotonous rows of tall windows capped with white-painted pediments. A pair of stone lions, more like sour toads than royal beasts, flanked the slate steps that led down to the drive. Kate's disappointment stuck in her throat like a bitter pill. Bishop's Keep, despite its romantic name, was only an ordinary house. No doubt the life she would lead there would be equally ordinary, conventionally routine, and boring.

Sir Charles glanced at her, the corners of his mouth amused. "Does Bishop's Keep meet your expectation?" he asked mildly.

Kate's lips thinned. The man had seen through her. How intolerable!

"In every detail," she lied tartly. She gathered her skirts, accepted Bradford Marsden's hand, and alighted from the carriage.

The farewells took but a moment and, after a round of promises to exchange calls, Kate found her bags sitting beside one of the lions and herself standing on the lowest step, waving. The coachman's whip cracked, the Marsden carriage disappeared into the mist, and Kate turned reluctantly to face her fate. She stood looking for a moment, then stuck out her tongue at one of the lions and marched up the stairs and down the walk to the massive oak door. She lifted her hand to the brass knocker.

Bishop's Keep might not be a castle, but like it or not, she was here.

9

"The majority of servants would be judged criminal if their backgrounds and their actions were fully known. Many were previously discharged for lying or theft and have obtained their present places with forged credentials, while not a few supplement their honest wages by acting as paid informants for housebreakers. The careful mistress must beware of those who pretend to serve."

—THE PRACTICAL HOUSEHOLD, 1884

"I CONTINUE TO believe, Sabrina," Bernice Jaggers said, feeling quite cross, "that you are making a most dreadful mistake. This young woman's reputation is not personally known to you, and it is the utmost folly to trust the word of some Pinkerton person on the other side of the Atlantic. We must be vigilant. Persons hired into our household must be of the most trustworthy sort."

Sabrina Ardleigh put down her pen and turned from the small rosewood desk in the withdrawing room. "I am not hiring a servant, Bernice. I am employing Brother Thomas's daughter."

"I hardly see the difference." Bernice sat down on a carved mahogany chair and twitched the skirt of her black bombazine, which she wore in mourning for her husband, Captain Reginald Jaggers, of whom in the last years of their marriage she had not been fond. He had fallen with General Gordon at Khartoum nearly a decade before, but like the Queen, Bernice lived daily with her husband's memory. She drew her brows together severely. "She is an American. Worse yet, *Irish*." Her mouth puckered on the word. "You have managed for years without knowing that Thomas had a daughter, and you have managed without a secretary as well. Why must you have one now? And why is Thomas's daughter the only one who will do?"

Sabrina rose from her chair and crossed the Turkish carpet to the window that gave a view of the sloping lawn. She spoke without turning. "We have discussed the matter fully, Bernice. You are always insisting on the virtues of Christian charity. It is scarcely Christian of you to reject an opportunity to assist a woman of our own blood—"

"Christian!" Bernice shrilled. "You talk of Christianity, when you persist in consorting with those wretched spiritualists and taking part in shamefully immodest pagan rites at that horrid Temple of Morris—"

"Temple of Horus," Sabrina corrected her mildly. "Horns was the son of Isis, the most revered of Egyptian goddesses. And the rites to which you refer—"

The mention of Egyptian deities added fuel to Bernice's fire, for she was a strict Nonconformist who attended chapel three times a week and demanded that the servants do likewise. "Morris, Horus, it's all one," she snapped. "I simply do not understand Vicar Talbot, encouraging you to involve yourself in this Order of the Golden Fawn—"

"Golden *Dawn*." Sabrina turned. "Really, Bernice, you could at least learn to listen, even if you object to—"

Bernice snorted. "Ever since then, you have been entirely lost to good sense. Séances, magic, fortunetelling cards. You might as well leave Bishop's Keep and set up as a palm reader in Colchester."

"And leave the Ardleigh fortune to you, my dear sister?" Sabrina asked lightly, smiling a little.

Bernice closed her eyes. "I am content," she said piously. "You have been overgenerous to your poor sister, whom God in His infinite wisdom saw fit to leave with little."

But Sabrina had slipped, so to speak, a dagger into the dark heart of her sister's discontent. In her youth, Bernice had been a carefree, willful young woman. After a tempestuous courtship, she had eloped with a military man of little family and no prospects. In stern consequence, her father had disinherited her. Meanwhile, Thomas, her brother and the Ardleigh heir, had quarreled with his father, renounced his fortune, and fled to America. Through attrition, then, the sizable Ardleigh estate, gained through shrewd dealings in the woolen industry, had fallen into Sabrina's hands. It was only due to her assent—not freely given but coerced with a certain compelling piece of information—that Bernice had lived at Bishop's Keep for the past four years. For the profligate Captain Jaggers, true to his father-in-law's dire predictions, had upon his demise left his wife only a meager pension, scarcely enough to permit the purchase of a decent annual bonnet. For Bernice's part, she bore her widow's fate with perpetual resentment and never resigned herself to her dependency upon her sister. It was the grossest injustice that Sabrina alone had inherited what should have been shared between them!

A moment's silence followed Bernice's outburst, and then the tentative clearing of a throat. Bernice opened her eyes to glare at Amelia, the parlor maid, a brown-haired, generously endowed wench whom Bernice suspected of having an eye for the coachman.

How long had Amelia been standing there? How much had she overheard? Servants simply could not be trusted.

They battened on family discord like vultures on carrion. One was at their mercy, just as poor Lord Russell had been at the mercy of his valet, who had been inspired to murder by reading a dreadful shilling shocker. Or the tragic Mrs. Thomas, who had been hacked to pieces and parboiled by her savagely cunning maid-of-all-work, an Irishwoman. Yes, *Irish!* and named Kate! Bernice shuddered.

The parlor maid took a step forward, hands folded over her starched white apron. Bernice noticed that her frilled white cap was crooked.

"What is it, Amelia?" Sabrina asked.

Amelia sketched a curtsy. "A lady t' see ye, mum."

"Where is her card?" Bernice asked testily. "Have I not instructed you how a guest is to be admitted? You are to receive the card on a silver tray. If from a footman, present it unaltered. If from the lady herself, turn up the right corner." She pursed her mouth. "And straighten your cap."

There was an unmistakable flash of defiance in Amelia's brown eyes before she obediently raised her hands to the back of her head. "Th' lady don't have no card, mum."

Bernice chose to ignore the look. "No card? What lady would come calling without a card?"

"It is Miss Kathryn Ardleigh, mum. Wot was expected tomorrow. I showed her to th' mornin' room."

"Miss Ardleigh!" Sabrina exclaimed. "Kathryn!"

"What did I tell you, sister?" Bernice said, with meager satisfaction. "The Irishwoman has scarcely set foot in the door, and already she makes herself a bother."

"Nonsense," Sabrina replied, lifting her chin. "Amelia, we will have tea for three, please. Tell Mudd to prepare the best silver service."

With a disdainful harrumph, Bernice followed her sister out of the room. Had she noticed Amelia's glance, shadowed by some darkly unfathomable emotion, she might have been less inclined to fret about her niece and more inclined to distrust the parlor maid.

10

"From all blindness of heart; from pride, vain-glory, and hypocrisy, from envy, hatred, and malice, and from all uncharitableness, Good Lord, deliver us."
—THE PRAYER BOOK, 1662

THE EXTERIOR OF the house might be dull and rather ugly, Kate thought, but the morning room was quite lovely, done in silver-green bamboo wallpaper, with pale green velvet drapes at the windows and a carpet of deeper green. On one table was a blue bowl filled with lemons, on another a collection of framed photographs, one of which Kate recognized with a start as her father as a boy of sixteen or so, stiff and solemn in a frock coat and an absurdly elegant top hat. Somehow the sight of the photograph made her connection to Bishop's Keep seem very real, and she realized with a start that until that moment the place had seemed imaginary, make-believe, like the setting in one of Beryl Bardwell's stories.

She stared at the photograph for a moment, feeling a wave of loss and grief for the father she had never had a chance to love. What had he been like as a boy? As a young man? How different might her life have been if he had lived to bring his wife and daughter home to England?

Home—the word had an odd ring to it, and she lifted her head to look around. Her father had grown up here, had run and played and laughed and cried in these rooms, on the lawns, in the woods. This place had been her father's home. Was it now to be hers?

"My dear niece Kathryn!" a huskily melodic voice exclaimed behind her. Kate turned. "How good it is to see you—and a full day early!"

The handsome older woman who seized both Kate's hands had warm gray eyes under heavy brows. A gracious smile lighted a face marked by intelligence and individuality, with fine lines of age etched about the eyes and mouth. She was dressed in a loose, lace-trimmed mauve gown with fluid sleeves. The color highlighted the silvery streaks in the soft wings of hair on her forehead, the loose coils on top of her head. She wore no jewelry except for an intriguing golden pendant in the shape of an Egyptian scarab.

"Hello, Miss Ardleigh," Kate said, liking her at once. "I hope it is no bother that I have come early. The ship docked sooner than expected."

With a last squeeze, the woman dropped Kate's hands. "Of course it is no bother. And please, call me Aunt Sabrina." She turned to the woman standing behind her. "This is my sister and also your aunt, Mrs. Bernice Jaggers."

Bernice Jaggers stood stolidly fastened to the floor, a lady of late middle age, her plump white hands clasped over her full black skirt, a sour, pinched look on her round face. She acknowledged Kate's greeting with a brief inclination of the head and the chilly instruction to address her as "Aunt Jaggers."

Smiling, Aunt Sabrina led Kate to a green damask settee. "Bernice and I are delighted that you have come."

Hardly, Kate thought, seeing the twist of Aunt Jaggers's narrow, thinly compressed lips. From the look of it, the woman bitterly resented either Kate or her sister's inviting their niece to Bishop's Keep—or life in general. Apprehensively wondering which it was and how her attitude would color their relations, Kate sat down.

Aunt Sabrina seated herself in one of the damask armchairs and leaned back in a comfortably casual pose, one that would not have been possible, Kate knew, if the sitter were stiffly corseted. "Now, my dear, tell us about your journey. I hope you found enough of interest to distract you from its tribulations."

After a brief sketch of her railway travel and sea voyage (omitting the fertile intrigue that had enlarged the notebooks of Beryl Bardwell), Kate concluded by relating her encounter of Miss Marsden and her trip from Colchester with the Marsdens and Sir Charles Sheridan.

"So you have made the acquaintance of some of our neighborhood aristocracy," Aunt Sabrina remarked, smiling. "Well, you will meet the rest of the family this evening. Only this morning, we received an invitation from Lady Henrietta to dinner tonight. I am certain she will wish you to join us."

Aunt Jaggers moved to a straight chair and sat on its edge, arranging her voluminous black skirts. She cast a steely-eyed gaze at Kate, then turned her attention to Aunt Sabrina.

"Please recall, sister," she said stiffly, "that Miss Ardleigh has not come to Bishop's Keep to participate in society. She is here to serve as your secretary and assist you with your . . ." She gave a loud sniff, as if she were rejecting a piece of spoiled fish. "Writings."

"Be that as it may," Aunt Sabrina said firmly. "If she is not too tired, I am sure she will be welcome at tonight's dinner."

"Thank you," Kate said sincerely. "I enjoyed meeting Miss Marsden and her brother. I should like to come." She glanced from Aunt Jaggers to Aunt Sabrina. Sisters they might be, but they did not look it. Aunt Sabrina, who bore some resemblance to the faded photograph of Kate's father, was at this moment toying with an escaping tendril of feathery hair. Her graceful posture, her tilted head and loose hair, her mobile and generous expression—to Kate these were the attributes of a woman who enjoyed an enviable ease of movement and freedom of mind. Aunt Jaggers, on the other hand, was straitly corseted and as tart as the lemons piled in the Delft bowl. In the look she darted at Aunt Sabrina was enough malice to make Kate shift uneasily in her chair.

Kate cleared her throat. Other thoughts pressed into her mind, and she had to speak them, the sooner and the more frankly, the better. "I am very grateful to you for asking me to come to Bishop's Keep," she said to Aunt Sabrina. "Your invitation was a great surprise, as was the fact—if you will pardon me—of your existence. I had not known that any members of my father's family survived him."

Aunt Sabrina's eyes went to Kate's father's photograph, then back to Kate. Her face was somber, as if the thought of him were a long sadness. "When my brother went to America, he expressed the wish to permanently dissociate himself from the family. Your grandfather, George Ardleigh, was quite willing to concur in his son's decision. He imposed his concurrence upon the rest of the family, including your grandmother Madeline, who was deeply grieved by Thomas's absence. No doubt both father and son had good reasons for wishing a permanent separation. But they took those reasons to their graves. When I made belated inquiries last year about your mother and discovered that she had borne a daughter, I felt it was not fair to impute to you your father's perhaps impulsive estrangement from his family." She fell silent for a moment, and when she spoke again, Kate felt the melancholy weight of her sadness. "I am sorry for your loss of both your parents, Kathryn. And I have come to view our estrangement as a great loss. I hope to remedy it."

Aunt Jaggers straightened her shoulders, her mouth pinched and parsimonious. "I must speak frankly, Niece Kathryn," she said. "My sister's sentiments are in no way to be attributed to me. It was my sad duty to counsel her against inviting into this house a young Irishwoman whose character is not directly known to us, who has been brought up in America." Her tone sharpened. "It has frequently fallen to me to counsel my sister against various ill-conceived schemes, to no avail. It was no different this time. My counsel was ignored." Her dark eyes glittered like bits of chipped glass. "But I insist upon making my position clear."

Aunt Jaggers's ill will was so extraordinarily plain that it momentarily robbed Kate of speech. But Aunt Sabrina spoke for her, in an odd tone that was at once a rebuke and a conciliation.

"You have indeed made yourself clear, sister. But I trust that your opinions are not entirely fixed, and that you will allow our brother's daughter to demonstrate her own character and abilities." The words were reasonable enough, but beneath them there was an undertone of anger held back, as if Aunt Sabrina wished to say more, but was reluctant, perhaps even fearful. What lay between the two sisters? Whatever it was, it made one angry, the other apprehensive, and each nettled with the other.

Kate felt it was time to ask the other questions that pressed on her mind. "I would like to know about my duties," she said to Aunt Sabrina, "and why it was I whom you chose to be your secretary. You no doubt could have hired someone nearby and saved yourself the considerable expense of my travel, not to speak of the uncertainty of hiring someone sight unseen."

With a quick glance at her sister, Aunt Sabrina began to speak carefully, as if she were picking her way along a thorny path through a subject that had been the cause of considerable disharmony between them. But beneath the restrained words, Kate heard a note of unrestrained excitement and guessed that Aunt Sabrina was talking about something in which she had a passionate interest.

"I have recently been appointed historian of a particular . . . society. My responsibilities involve the writing of a history of the society and the keeping of a detailed and confidential record of . . . certain activities peculiar to the association."

Kate could have wished for greater specificity, especially where the curious "confidential record" and the tantalizing "certain activities" were concerned. But she contented herself for the moment with Aunt Sabrina's answer.

Aunt Jaggers, however, was not content. "You should tell this young woman that it is your intention to drag her into that spiritualist taradiddle of yours," she said snappishly. "That Order of whatever-it-is."

"The Order of the Golden Dawn," Aunt Sabrina said distinctly. Her fingers went, unconsciously, Kate thought, to the scarab pendant at her throat.

"Yes." Aunt Jaggers sniffed. "I am sure that when Niece Ardleigh is informed of your real purpose for hiring her, no doubt she will refuse to be associated with your deviltry. Egyptian magic—blasphemy!"

Kate shifted, her interest suddenly heightened by these unexplained hints. In what sort of spiritualist taradiddle was Aunt Sabrina engaged? How had she become interested in Egyptian magic?

Aunt Sabrina ignored the intrusion and continued calmly. "This work, which I will explain in detail at a later time, is not especially onerous, nor will it encompass all your hours. But it does require intelligence, attention to detail, and a clear facility in writing, as well as a mature, judicious discretion." She smiled gravely. "These are virtues, Kathryn, in which I am told you excel."

Kate felt that she could meet Aunt Sabrina's qualifications without difficulty. But she had been given only part of an answer.

"Thank you for your confidence," she said. "But surely you might have discovered these virtues in any number of young women close at hand."

"Perhaps." Aunt Sabrina returned her direct look. "But you can operate a typewriter, and you read and write German. This combination would have proved most difficult to find, even in Colchester. Furthermore, I have begun to feel that it is important to become acquainted with *you*, Kathryn. While the work you will do is certainly important to me, it is your person in which I have the greater interest."

"I see," Kate said, more softly. Aunt Sabrina's eyes had saddened and her gaze had gone to her brother's photograph. For a moment there was silence, as Kate reflected on the fact that the sins of the fathers could often be visited upon the daughters as well. Perhaps Aunt Sabrina hoped to make up to her niece and herself what George and Thomas Ardleigh had denied them both. Watching the older woman, something in her warmed and she was glad she had come—not for the sake of Beryl Bardwell's grand adventure, but because, in some way Kate did not quite understand, she felt that Aunt Sabrina had called her home.

Aunt Jaggers broke the silence. " *Your* emphasis, Sabrina, may be upon the . . ." She coughed. "Familial relationship. As I am responsible for the household, mine must rest upon practical matters. The matter of employment, for instance." She turned to Kate. "You will talk with me soon about what is expected of you during your stay here, however short or long it may be. For the moment, I will simply say that we keep the Sabbath strictly, and that I expect daily attendance at prayers and weekly at chapel.

At *chapel*," she repeated meaningfully. "And, not least, novel reading is *not* permitted of the servants."

Aunt Sabrina spoke quietly, but though her rebuke was muted, her anger was plain in her short reply. "I hardly think your below stairs regimen should affect Kathryn's reading habits, Bernice. And her religious practices are a concern proper only to God and herself." She turned to Kate. "You and I can continue our discussion of your duties in the morning."

Kate nodded, glancing from one to the other. She could read in their faces the concealed truth of the relationship: that Aunt Jaggers hated her sister and that Aunt Sabrina both disliked and feared Aunt Jaggers. It was an obviously complex and painful situation in which the two women found themselves entangled, Kate thought, and then stopped herself, with an unexpected flash of consternation.

Whatever the source of Aunt Jaggers's malice, *she* was now entangled in it too, and blindly, for she did not understand it. She would have to be on her guard not to offend—something to which she was not temperamentally inclined! And she would have to take special care to safeguard the secret of Beryl Bardwell's existence. Kate could imagine the fracas should Aunt Jaggers learn that not only did she read novels, she *wrote* penny dreadfuls—and the most luridly sensational kind!

Aunt Sabrina glanced up as a butler in a dark morning coat and formal trousers sailed into the room at the helm of a large, heavily laden tea cart, a gleaming silver urn like a figurehead at its prow. He was followed by the brown-haired, brown-eyed maid who had shown Kate in.

"Ah, our tea has arrived," Aunt Sabrina said with some relief, as the cart was rolled into place at the end of the sideboard.

Mudd—rather younger than Kate would have expected of a butler, and more dandified, with carefully trimmed side-whiskers and a modish tie—filled a bone china cup and brought it to Kate. When tea had been served, Mudd and Amelia retired to a corner of the room, where they stood invisibly at attention, blank as pie, fixed as furniture.

They were not, however, invisible to Kate, and behind the curtain of their bland impassivity, she sensed a silent scrutiny, a furtive watching, tinged with—what? Kate was sure that some deep passion lay behind the hooded eyes of the brown-haired Amelia, when she handed the tea tray round again. And while Mudd's face was immobile, the working of his mouth betrayed an intense emotion; what it was Kate could not tell. She sat back, intrigued.

Such currents and crosscurrents of powerful feeling flowing between sister and sister! Such secret passions hidden behind the inscrutable faces of the servants! Beryl Bardwell would not have to leave this house for raw material—indeed, for the rawest, the deepest, the strongest of human emotions.

Then suddenly, Kate felt cold. The muted violence, the envy, hatred, and malice that she sensed in this room was not the stuff of novels. It was quite *real*. And because it was real, it had the power to wound, to maim, even to kill.

Kate shivered.

11

"Manners make the man, but manors make the nobleman."

—PUNCH, JAN, 27, 1894

SOMEWHAT TO HIS surprise, Charles was enjoying his visit to the Marsdens' country manor. His intellect was entertained by Bradford's dry wit; his curiosity was piqued by the dig at nearby Colchester, and especially by the morning's discovery; and his throat was soothed by the clean air of the country, a welcome change from the irritating London fog, which was tar-flavored and thick as treacle. As well, he loved the Essex countryside, for as a lad he had spent summers with his mother's family at East Bergholt, only three miles away across the River Stour. It was there he had taken to photography, capturing on photographic plate the same landscapes that his famous great-uncle, John Constable, had earlier captured on canvas.

But evenings at Marsden Manor, Charles felt, were less to be enjoyed than endured. On this particular night, he itched to get to the temporary photographic laboratory he had installed in the scullery, which he had equipped with a Carbutt's Dry Plate Kerosene Lantern that allowed him to develop photographs in the absence of gas or electric light. But he was prevented from satisfying his wish by the requirement to dress for dinner, to which, Lady Henrietta had informed him, guests were invited.

Dressing was not Charles's favorite activity, and he did not particularly enjoy social dinners with persons he did not know. For Charles, the social ritual of dining was rather a burden, requiring that he exert himself to be pleasant when he would have much preferred a cold bird and a glass of wine with Bradford, followed by a game of chess and an article in his latest scientific journal.

But tonight's dinner promised to be of some little interest, for the guests included Barfield Talbot, the village vicar, and the Marsdens' nearest neighbors, Miss Sabrina Ardleigh, Mrs. Bernice Jaggers, and their newly arrived niece, Kathryn Ardleigh. So it was that Charles found himself, sherry in hand, seated on a chair in the drawing room, across from a sofa on which sat Miss Ardleigh, whose simple blue dress severely (but pleasantly, Charles thought) contrasted with the elaborate gowns of Eleanor and her younger sister, Patsy.

"Imagine my surprise and pleasure," Eleanor told Charles excitedly, "when I learned that dear Kathryn and her aunts would be at dinner tonight."

"And mine," the vicar put in. He was a stooped, wiry man in his late sixties, with a lion's mane of silver hair and a droopy white mustache. His smile at Miss Ardleigh lighted pale blue eyes. "Your aunt has told me how glad she is that you were able to come to England. She has for some time felt the need to be closer to her only niece."

Miss Ardleigh met the vicar's smile with an inquiring look. Charles thought she was about to ask a question, but after a brief hesitation, she only said, "I am glad to be here."

The vicar turned to Charles. "And I am delighted to meet you, Sir Charles. I understand that you are assisting Fairfax with the Colchester dig. I must confess to being something of an antiquarian myself. The Colchester site has long held a great fascination for me."

Eleanor's eyes were sparkling. "Then you may be interested to hear, Vicar, of Sir Charles's *latest* find." Her voice took on a tone of muted excitement. "He discovered a dead man in the dig this morning!"

There was a horrified gasp from Miss Ardleigh's two aunts, seated across the room with Lady Henrietta. "Eleanor!" Lady Henrietta exclaimed.

"But it's true, Mother," Eleanor protested. "He'd been murdered!"

"How perfectly appalling!" Patsy Marsden cried in a coquettish fright, clapping her hands.

"Indeed it is appalling," Lady Henrietta said sternly. "Not at all a fit subject. Shall we speak of something else?"

"Murdered, was he, Charles?" Lord Marsden asked from his chair beside the columned and pedimented mantelpiece. The baron was a balding gentleman of immaculate white waistcoat and imposing stomach, testimony to a long-standing devotion to saddle of Dartmoor mutton and excellent port.

"You're in for it now, Charles," Bradford said, helping himself to the sherry decanter on the sideboard. "You'll have to tell the whole thing."

Charles looked at Lady Henrietta.

"Oh, very well," she said. But Charles could hear, beneath the grudging reluctance of her tone, an unacknowledged curiosity, so he gave an abridged and slightly sanitized account of the discovery of the dead man and the activities of the police. His attention, however, was focused less on the story than on Miss Ardleigh, whose interest in the narrative was intense, but nothing like the self-dramatized horror exhibited by Eleanor and Patsy.

"A foreign gentleman, you say?" the vicar asked, knitting bushy white brows.

"Continental," Charles replied, "from the cut of the clothes. He was wearing a scarab ring that suggested travel in Egypt, or at the least, Egyptian interests."

"A scarab?" Miss Ardleigh asked quickly. Her glance went to her aunts. The elder aunt, who sat on the sofa with an easy grace that was very different from the frowning abruptness of her sister, colored slightly and turned her head.

"What is a scarab?" Patsy asked.

"A dung beetle," Bradford said. His mother made a noise in her throat.

"An Egyptian magical amulet," the vicar said quickly.

"The beetle is associated with the transit of the sun," Charles explained, "and hence the resurrection."

The fussy aunt sniffed. "Egyptian magic," she said in a tone that suggested hellfire and perdition. "No wonder he was murdered."

The vicar shifted uncomfortably and cleared his throat. "My dear Mrs. Jaggers," he began, but was interrupted by Lord Marsden.

"Robbery, to be sure," the baron said gruffly. "Country's gone to the dogs. Nobody's safe since we've ceased giving riffraff the boat. Damned anarchists can plant their bombs anywhere, blast it all. That Frenchie who blew himself up at Greenwich, for instance. If the bloody bomb hadn't gone off in his hands, it would've taken out the Royal Observat'ry." He scowled at his elder daughter. "That's why women must *not* go about unescorted, Eleanor. Never know when you might be blown up."

"Yes, Papa," Eleanor said, meekness itself. She cast her glance sideways at Charles. "Sir Charles has photographs of the dead man," she added with a certain coyness.

Lady Henrietta pulled herself up. "I simply do not understand," she remarked acidly, "the current attraction of crime, particularly murder, among younger people."

She gave Eleanor and Patsy a severe look down the length of her rather horsey nose. "No lady concerns herself with such vulgar matters." She turned the same severity upon Charles, but indulgently relaxed, as if to say that his transgression, for transgression it was, was understood and forgiven. Men were expected to interest themselves in vulgar matters, while women were expected not to notice.

Charles bowed. "Your pardon, Lady Henrietta. I do agree. Murder is hardly a drawing room matter."

Lord Marsden cleared his throat. "Bought another mare from Peel today," he announced to no one in particular.

"Aim to breed her to Farleydale."

A look that might have been of misgiving crossed Bradford's face. "From Peel?" he asked. In a low voice, he added, "With respect, sir, I thought we had agreed not to—"

The baron's thick neck reddened fiercely. "A beauty, my boy. Excellent bloodline. High spirits. Grand bargain."

Bradford subsided, although Charles thought his friend looked uneasy, and he wondered again what was troubling him. From horses, the baron's passion, the subject turned to hunting, and from hunting to balls, and from balls, inevitably, to weddings—specifically, to the wedding of Eleanor to Mr. Ernest Fairley, which would take place in three months' time. Precisely at nine, dinner was announced, and the company removed to the large dining hall.

Kate was pleased when she found herself seated next to Sir Charles at dinner, for she meant to ask him a question. They sat upon heavy gilt chairs with rose damask seats, under a cut glass chandelier filled with lighted candles. The light radiated over the long rosewood table, casting shadowy glimmers over the frowning likenesses of Marsden ancestors hung along the paneled wall. The candlelight also illuminated the fine china, delicate crystal, and ornate silver that gave the table an air of almost unimaginable magnificence.

Or so it seemed to Kate, who had never before sat down to such an elegant table, in such elegant company, a knight of the realm on one side of her, and a lord and lady at opposite ends of the table. But she did not feel overwhelmed by the elegance; instead, she was entertained, and intrigued. It was as if she were a spectator at a play in which the characters (some of them anyway) thought they were real, while she knew differently. Perhaps it was because she was an American, she thought, seeing the British gentry through alien eyes.

The dinner, regrettably, did not live up to the distinction of the table. The menu proceeded from a thin oyster soup to a gluey fricassee of chicken, and thence to a saddle of mutton with caper sauce and vegetables and after that a Tewkesbury ham, climaxing in a quivery blancmange that Kate thought notable only for its near total lack of taste. Throughout most of the dinner, the conversation consisted only of polite exchanges of appreciation for the food (feigned, on Kate's part), exchanges of local gossip, and various bits of fashion news from London, primarily pertaining to bridal finery. But when the blancmange was served, Kate turned to Sir Charles and asked the question she had had on her mind for most of the evening, ever since he had mentioned the dead man's scarab ring.

"If it was robbery," she said without preamble, "why did the thief not take the gold scarab ring?"

Sir Charles put down his spoon. His brown eyes fastened on hers. "*Gold* ring?" he asked. "I do not believe I said—"

"To be sure," Kate said, irritated at herself for jumping to an unwarranted conclusion. Just because Aunt Sabrina's scarab was gold didn't mean—"I have assumed too much. The scarab was made of a gemstone, then?"

"No," he admitted, "it was gold. And I do agree—robbery hardly seems consistent with the facts of this case." He paused. "Why do you ask?"

Kate allowed her glass to be refilled with champagne for the third time. "I am merely curious," she said lightly. "One does not encounter a murder very often—outside of fiction, that is. Particularly a murder that is documented with photographs."

"And do you often encounter murder in fiction as well?" Sir Charles asked. "Documented or otherwise?"

His words sounded like a challenge, and Kate knew what he was thinking. Women did not read stories with murders in them. Ordinarily, Kate might have answered his question with an evasion, but the champagne emboldened her. She answered his challenge with one of her own. "It is a pity, don't you think, that women and men lead such different lives?"

Sir Charles took a sip of his champagne, put down the glass, and parried with another question. "You do not agree that our differences make life interesting?"

"Hardly!" Kate exclaimed. "At least, not from a woman's point of view. Women are hedged about with rules of what is right and proper. No one evidences surprise when men read—or write—a book with a violent crime in it. But a woman cannot." She frowned and pushed her champagne glass back. She was saying too much.

But Sir Charles seemed to have taken her remark seriously. "I fear," he said, "that you are right. Women's lives are far more circumscribed than men's, although that seems to be changing as women venture into the world." He turned his stemmed glass in his fingers. "But do you see it as useful to them to develop an interest in crime? How have you profited from its study, Miss Ardleigh?"

Kate perceived that her impulsiveness had nearly landed her in a trap. A pace or two more, and Beryl Bardwell might find herself in peril of discovery. She flushed, wondering how to extricate herself. "Well, I—"

She was saved by her hostess, who rose at the end of the table to signal that it was time for the ladies to withdraw.

"Perhaps crime is of general interest to you," Sir Charles persisted. "Or perhaps it is *this* crime that fascinates you."

"Charles," Eleanor said, "if you wish your port and cigar, you must allow Kathryn to leave with the ladies. We cannot abandon her here."

Kate rose with great relief.

12

"The chief part of the organization of every living creature is due to inheritance; and consequently, though each being assuredly is well fitted for its place in nature, many structures have now no very close and direct relations to present habits of life."

—CHARLES DARRIN
The Origin of Species

WHEN THE LADIES had gone, Bradford motioned to the butler to bring the port and offered a cigar to the vicar. He did not offer one to Charles, who was getting out his pipe, nor to his father, who had fallen asleep over the blancmange and was now sprawled in his chair, bald head fallen forward, mouth open, snoring in his sleep like a Yorkshire pig. Bradford looked at him, anger thick at the back of his throat. How much had he paid Peel for the damned mare? Too much, no doubt.

But then, any amount would have been too much, according to the family solicitors and accountants, who were becoming positively tiresome about the condition of the Marsden accounts. Damn it, Bradford thought ferociously, why couldn't his father *listen* to them? The anger settled into a heaviness that lay on his chest like a pleurisy.

But he could understand—a little. After all, his father had come of age when the old Queen was young, when landed fortunes seemed solid as Essex earth and eternal as the sun, which never set upon the far-flung Empire. But Victoria was past her fifty-fifth year on the throne, the Empire was in a half-dozen tight patches, and the agricultural economy had been blighted by the repeal of the Corn Laws almost fifty years ago, allowing cheap foreign grain to flood the home market. There was no money any longer in horses, especially when one's judgments about bloodlines were as—Yes, let it be said! As feeble and faulty as his father's.

From the music room came the sound of the piano. Patsy, playing a Schumann song, passably well. Eleanor's soprano, untrained but acceptable, and a contralto—Miss Ardleigh's, he assumed. Bradford sipped his port, thinking unexpectedly of the American—part Irish, from the look of her. Not pretty, certainly, but rather handsome, when one actually looked at her. And one did look at her, for her calm self-assurance, her composure, was such a contrast to the stylish, self-conscious flourishes of the women around her, including his sisters.

Miss Ardleigh. Kathryn. Bradford frowned. Nothing could come of it except a little harmless flirtation, of course, for although she was the niece of a neighbor and primly enough dressed, she was Irish, and American. But of course, such a combination offered certain advantages. One might guess from looking at that wonderfully unruly mop of hair what a willful creature she must—

He set down his glass of port hard. No. No, this would not do. What he required was not a mistress to bed but an heiress to wed, and the sooner the better. He was beginning to feel desperate enough to acknowledge that the woman's other qualifications—appearance, demeanor, temperament—did not matter, as long as she was sufficiently rich. If the solicitors were right, he might soon have to resort to such a stratagem.

Bradford stared at the candles gleaming in their silver candelabra down the center of the long table. It was unkind to blame his father's faulty judgment for their situation. He had simply continued to live in the old manner, which was no longer suited to the times. And in any case, Bradford himself was not blameless, far from it. He had taken matters into his own hands in a way that, as he thought about it now, quite appalled him. He had poured a substantial amount of money—truth be told, much more than he could afford—into a venture he knew little about, on the word of a man of uncertain reputation. He had bargained with the devil, and if he had to pay the price, the fault was only his own.

Bradford picked up his glass again. However reckless his action, at least he had not closed his eyes to the need to ensure the reliable survival of the Marsden landed fortunes into an unreliable future. He had been looking out for the family. For his sisters, whose dowries had to be provided; for his mother, to whom the opinion of society was the inspiration of a frivolous life; for his father, and his damned bloody horses.

The candle in front of him guttered and went out. Even the assurance that he had done it for family seemed flabby, and Bradford felt suddenly chilled to the bone. If only Landers didn't require so much money to stay in the game. If only he'd been somewhere else when the man came along, dangling his damned patents like diamonds. He wished him dead. He wished him in hell!

"As to the corpse, Sir Charles," the vicar was saying. "What will you do with the photographs?"

Startled, Bradford brought his attention back to his guests. Charles and the vicar were talking about the wretched murder. Had they no other topic of conversation?

"I shall develop the prints and take them to the police," Charles replied, stoking his pipe. "The sergeant did not seem keen on them, however," he added. "I rather fancy he agreed to receive them only because he feared to offend."

"P'rhaps," the vicar said, thoughtful. "Juries do prefer rhetoric to scientific proof. Witness the Lamson trial in '82."

"Ah, yes," Charles said, accepting a light for his pipe from the butler. "A friend of mine, Dr. Thomas Stevenson, gave evidence. His testimony was based on his investigation of plant alkaloids—very fine research, too, very solid."

"Well and good," the vicar reminded him, "but Lamson was convicted upon his confession, not by the expert testimony of a scientist. Juries are confused by science."

Bradford stirred uneasily. All this talk about trials and juries made him apprehensive. He changed the subject. "Speaking of investigations, Vicar, how are yours progressing?" He turned to Charles with a wry humor. "The vicar has a compelling curiosity about the afterworld. He is bent upon proving the physical existence of the soul."

The vicar inclined his head. "Some persons—they shall be nameless, of course—take pleasure in deriding my investigations." He waved a benign hand in Bradford's direction. "But my treatises on the nature of Spirit have been quite well received by the London Spiritualist Alliance." He lowered his voice. "This is a subject that is spoken of, you understand, only among friends."

"Of course," Charles said gravely. "I myself have an academic interest in such dealings. My camera and I have been invited to several séances to photograph ectoplasmic manifestations."

Bradford grinned and pulled on his cigar. "And what did you observe? Did your camera capture the soul, or did you find the ectoplasm to be merely flimflam?"

Charles was about to reply when the vicar interrupted spiritedly. "It does not matter what was observed! What matters is the commitment to unbiased observation, carried out in the service of Truth." His voice grew louder and his white mustache, impassioned, quivered violently. "What is important is the application of scientific method of the study of the Soul." He leaned forward, blue eyes fierce, leathery face intent. "If this inquiry is your aim, Sir Charles, you are in luck. There is within our very neighborhood, in nearby Colchester, an association of persons dedicated to this pursuit. It is called the Order of the Golden Dawn, and I am a member."

"In Colchester?" Charles asked with surprise.

"Indeed," the vicar said tartly. "Why should inquiry into spiritual matters be confined to the metropolitan centers?"

"Why indeed?" Bradford asked. He gestured to the butler. "Hawkins, wake his lordship." He stood and pushed back his chair. "Shall we join the ladies, gentlemen? Better their nonsense, I think, than our own."

13

"By the 1890s, the Spiritualist movement had spread to England, where mediums set up shop in every city and even royalty attended séances. Spiritualist journals abounded, and kabbalism, Rosicrucianism, Theosophy, and Freemasonry flourished. Out of this rich occult mix was crystalized, by a kind of social alchemy, the Order of the Golden Dawn. It became the most famous of all occult societies."

—LENORE PENMORE
Spiritualism in England, 1870–1920

ON HER FIRST morning at Bishop's Keep, Kate stepped out of the breakfast room into the hall. "Pardon me," she said tentatively to the parlor maid, "can you show me the way to the library? I am to meet Miss Ardleigh there."

Amelia dropped her eyes, but not before Kate had caught the fearfully sullen glance. It was the same look she'd seen on the face of the young chambermaid, a girl of fourteen or so, who had opened her draperies this morning and brought her tea. Mudd, of course, had been too well trained to display any overt emotion as he directed her to the breakfast sideboard. But she could see it in the tense line of his jaw, the half-furtive look of the eye. The orderly, placid surface of life at Bishop's Keep concealed a black undertow. The tension made Kate shiver.

"This way, 'f ye please, miss," Amelia said without inflection, and started off down the dark hallway.

As she followed Amelia's modestly beribboned cap, it suddenly occurred to Kate that if Beryl Bardwell planned to include a servant as a character in "Amber's Amulet," she needed to know a great deal more than she already knew about the servants' lives. Perhaps she should set aside her apprehension and make an effort to befriend Amelia.

"It is such a very large house, there must be a great amount of work to do," Kate said, catching up to the maid, who seemed to have wings on her feet. "Is there a large staff?"

"Sev'ral, miss," Amelia said, quickening her already fast pace.

Kate lengthened her stride. "Have you been here long?" she inquired.

"Only since winter, miss."

"Well, I suppose with a large staff, people are bound to come and go." Kate smiled and made a friendly gesture. "I am sure you have already discovered a great deal about life at Bishop's Keep, while I am a newcomer. I have quite a few questions."

Amelia's reaction was not quite what Kate had expected. She stopped short, blanching. Her chin began to tremble. "Don't be askin' me, I beg ye, miss, please," she pleaded shrilly. " 'Tis not my place t' say wot happened to Jenny."

Kate stared at her, startled. Who was Jenny? What had happened to her? What fear had the power to turn Amelia pale?

"I don't mean to frighten you, Amelia." Kate reached out to touch the girl's white-cuffed sleeve. "I would only like to—"

"That'll do, Amelia," Mudd said severely, materializing out of the darkness. The parlor maid dropped a stricken curtsy and fled down the hall as if dragons flew at her heels. Mudd turned to Kate, his smooth face tightening.

"You were seekin' the library, I believe?" He pointed stiffly. "It's that door. And if yer don't mind, miss, please direct any questions about the workin's of the ouse to me or to Cook." His restrained Cockney was strongly flavored by menace.

Kate dropped her eyes. "Thank you," she said. "I will." Wondering what nest of secrets she had stepped into, she went to the door. She was conscious that Mudd stood watching until she opened it and went inside.

The library was long and narrow, with oak-paneled walls, shelves of leather-bound books, a desk untidily littered with papers, and a fireplace with a fire burning against the morning chill. The bright morning sun fell through a stained glass window done in the style of Edward Burne-Jones, and a Morris chair stood near the fire. On one wall Kate recognized a copy of Millais's pre-Raphaelite painting of Ophelia, and copies of Oscar Wilde's *The Picture of Dorian Gray* and his play *Salomé* lay on an ebony table, in the edition that also contained Aubrey Beardsley's erotic drawings. Kate was a little startled when she saw it. Her aunt's tastes were interestingly modern.

Aunt Sabrina was seated at the desk. "You rested well, I trust?" she inquired. She was wearing an unbelted peacock blue morning gown, and her gray hair, streaked with silver, was knotted loosely at the back of her neck. Kate noticed that she was not wearing the gold scarab pendant. "Your room is satisfactory?"

"Yes, thank you," Kate said. She seated herself in the leather chair beside the desk. "But my curiosity has caught fire," she added with a smile. "Your remarks yesterday about my work only fueled it, I fear."

Aunt Sabrina aligned a stack of papers. "I must be . . . circumspect when your aunt Jaggers is present. She does not fully appreciate my interests, which she views as eccentric and not altogether respectable, perhaps even . . . dangerous."

"I see," Kate murmured. "And those views are—?"

Aunt Sabrina picked up a gold letter opener in the curious shape of a heron, turning it in her fingers. "I have had for many years an interest in spiritualism and the occult. Some time ago, Vicar Talbot, whom you met last night, solicited me to membership in the Order of the Golden Dawn. The vicar is an antiquarian and an occultist of unblemished reputation." She hesitated slightly. "The Order is an esoteric society organized for the study and practice of ritual magic."

Kate—or rather, Beryl Bardwell—could not help herself. "How interesting!" she burst out.

Aunt Sabrina smiled slightly, then continued. "The authority for the Order of the Golden Dawn is ancient, having been handed down from Christian Rosenkreuz, the fifteenth-century father of Rosicrucianism. Our chief is Dr. William Westcott, who obtained this authority through an accidentally discovered cipher manuscript. Dr. Westcott founded the first temple several years ago in London, and authorized others, such as Mr. MacGregor Mathers's temple in Paris. Florence Farnsworth has just established the Temple of Horns in Colchester."

"That is the temple of which you are a member?" Kate asked.

Aunt Sabrina nodded. "Recently, I was asked to serve as the Order's Cancellarius, or secretary-historian." She gestured at the stacks of papers on the desk and the large box that stood in the corner. "I have been entrusted with many valuable papers, letters, relics, documents, and so on—all of which must be sorted through, cataloged, and described before a history of the Order can be begun. As well, there is the continuing work of correspondence, membership lists, and so on—a very great deal of writing to be done." She paused and looked directly at Kate. "That is why I need you, Kathryn. To make the work easier, I have ordered an American typewriter for you, a Remington, I believe it is called."

"Oh," Kate breathed. Beryl Bardwell had longed so much for a typewriter—and to think it would be hers!

"We have not yet spoken of remuneration," Aunt Sabrina said. "I propose a salary of fifteen hundred pounds a year. I hope this is acceptable."

Kate did a rapid calculation in her head. It was more than acceptable. "Thank you," she said.

Aunt Sabrina nodded. "But the question your aunt Jaggers raises is a pertinent one," she continued. "While I am assured of the propriety, even the significance of this work, it may seem to you like so much"—the corners of her mouth twitched— "'taradiddle and deviltry,' as my sister calls it."

Kate thought of "Amber's Amulet," whose chief characters were the mysterious medium, Mrs. Bartlett, and her lover, the Egyptian gentleman. "The occult is of very great interest to me," she said, speaking with greater truthfulness than Aunt Sabrina could appreciate. "I should be pleased to consider myself your employee, even"—she paused, and looked Aunt Sabrina straight in the eye, so there could be no mistake—"your apprentice."

Aunt Sabrina gave her an equally direct look. "That is your wish?"

"It is indeed," Kate said firmly. The more she could learn of magical ritual, the more realistic Beryl Bardwell's story would be. "The typewriter. Will it be available for my personal use—during my free time, of course? I have some

85

work of my own to pursue. Nothing very important," she added hastily. "It is just something that—"

"By all means, leave ample time for your own work," Aunt Sabrina said. "But there is something else I must ask," she added, her voice darkening. "The unfortunate gentleman whose body was found in the excavation at Colchester—" She paused and shifted uncomfortably.

Kate looked at her, remembering the odd coincidence of the golden scarab. "Yes?"

"I wish to know more about him," she said, "but I cannot myself make inquiries. Would you mind going to ... could you ... ?"

"You would like to find out the identity of the dead man?" Kate asked.

Aunt Sabrina looked relieved at Kate's matter-of-fact response. "I would," she said. "I regret that I cannot give you my reasons just now, and I also regret that I must ask you to undertake such an unseemly inquiry. But I—"

Impulsively, Kate leaned forward. "Dear Aunt," she said, "I have no objections at all to looking into this matter for you." Kate's face was serene and her voice calm, but deep within her, Beryl Bardwell was jumping up and down, clapping her hands. A murder to investigate! An opportunity to learn the methods of criminal detection first-hand!

Aunt Sabrina looked pleased. "Well, then," she said, "I propose that Pocket drive you to Colchester immediately after luncheon. The purpose of your trip, of course," she added, "must be private, between us."

"Of course," Kate murmured.

Aunt Sabrina straightened. "In the meanwhile," she said, "I believe that your aunt Jaggers wishes you to speak with her."

"Yes," Kate said with a noticeable lack of enthusiasm, and stood.

Aunt Sabrina put her hand on Kate's arm. "Kathryn, one more word, please."

Kate sat back down, regretting that she had not concealed her feelings. She and Aunt Jaggers had not gotten off to a good beginning. But Aunt Jaggers was as she was, and there was nothing to be done about her unpleasantness. It was not fair to Aunt Sabrina to so openly reveal her feelings that discomfort was created between *them*.

Aunt Sabrina's mouth tensed, then relaxed, as if she were forcing herself to speak calmly. "Your aunt—I speak in confidence, of course—is a deeply unhappy woman. She married very young, against your grandfather's wishes. He was a man with a great concern for the appearance of things, and denied her any share in his estate. She was widowed some years ago, and left with nothing, a situation that she quite naturally resents. At . . . ah, my suggestion, she returned here, to our family home. At her wish, she manages this household." Aunt Sabrina shifted uncomfortably, as if she were speaking of something that gave her pain. "My sister relieves me of domestic responsibilities I do not relish. In gratitude for her willingness to undertake these chores, I have given her a free rein below stairs." She hesitated. "Too free a rein, perhaps. I daresay I bear some guilt in that unpleasant business last spring."

Kate said nothing, but the situation was coming clear. With Aunt Sabrina deeply engaged with her own interests and disinclined to involve herself in below stairs matters, Aunt Jaggers was free to do as she liked. But what was the business about last spring?

Aunt Sabrina turned the letter opener in her fingers, continuing with evident discomfort. "I trust, Kathryn, that your aunt will not seek to impose a strict discipline on you, as she does on the servants. If this occurs, please discuss the matter with me."

"Thank you, Aunt Sabrina," Kate said, quite sincerely. She sensed again, as she had yesterday, the complexity of the relationship between the sisters. If Aunt Jaggers was so profoundly disliked, perhaps even feared, why was she permitted to stay at Bishop's Keep?

"Do remember, Kathryn," her aunt said, and the words were clearly a warning. "Come to me, first."

"I shall," Kate murmured. But as she rose to leave the room, she told herself sternly that she would not trouble Aunt Sabrina to intervene. Whatever difficulties Aunt Jaggers posed, she would deal with them herself.

14

"Remember, that whatever your situation be, housemaid, or through-servant, or nursemaid, your mistress will expect you to obey her orders. The first and chief of your duties is, to do what you are desired to do."

—TEACHER, SERVANTS' TRAINING-HOUSE,
Townsend Street, London, 1887

AUNT JAGGERS'S SUITE of rooms lay in the west wing of the house. When Kate answered the summons to enter, she stepped into a dim and crowded twilight. Aunt Jaggers obviously adhered to the principle that a room was not quite furnished unless it was *full*. This one held no fewer than nine chairs, a Chesterfield settee and a chaise, four occasional tables, a red lacquered Japanese cabinet and a mahogany cupboard, a large burnished gong, and a tall green vase filled with dyed pampas plumes and peacock feathers. The fireplace mantel was elaborately draped in wine-colored velvet, and not another vase or bowl could have found a place on the mirrored mantelshelf. In the corner, a red-and-green parrot clacked and complained in a tall bamboo cage half-hidden behind ferny fronds.

"Mind that dog." Aunt Jaggers spoke sharply from her chair beside a fire that made the room unbearably hot. She was knitting what appeared to be a black wool muffler.

Kate lifted her skirt and looked down. At her feet stood a small terrier, plump as a piglet. It bared yellow teeth and growled.

"Nice doggie," Kate said nervously. She had never gotten on with dogs.

The parrot gave a malicious squawk. "Step to it, men!"

"The dog bites," snapped Aunt Jaggers. Her knitting needles clicked ferociously. "Don't provoke him."

"I'll try not," Kate said, moving to the red velvet settee. The terrier flopped on the hearth, chin on paws, and regarded Kate with red-eyed suspicion. She sat, feeling very much like Alice with the Red Queen, wondering when Aunt Jaggers would cry out, "Off with her head!"

Aunt Jaggers did not look up from her knitting. On the wall behind her hung a large multisectioned picture of the Plagues of Egypt. "I have asked you here to ensure that you understand the rules of the household. If you are staying, that is," she added waspishly. "Perhaps you have reconsidered your rash decision to accept employment from my sister."

Kate pressed her lips together. "I have not."

"More's the pity," Aunt Jaggers remarked, her eyes still fixed on her knitting. "You will find, when you involve yourself with that unspeakable Temple of Doris—"

"Horus, I believe it is called," Kate said diplomatically.

Aunt Jaggers's shoulders went rigid with disapproval. "Its name is of no importance. As I have said to my sister very often, what matters is that its work is of the devil—séances, incense, astrology, cards, magic." Her voice became shrill. "Should you become an apprentice to these sorcerers, Niece Kathryn, you will endanger your immortal soul. As does my sister."

"Thank you, Aunt," Kate murmured. "I appreciate your concern. I shall strive to guard my soul."

"Don't be sarcastic, miss! It is unbecoming. You will not get on in the world that way."

"No, Aunt," Kate said humbly.

"To your post," snapped the parrot. "Attention!" These military orders were followed by a silence, broken only by the furious clicking of needles and the terrier's asthmatic wheezing.

After a moment, Aunt Jaggers dropped her knitting into her lap. "My sister has expressed her belief that your Ardleigh kinship raises you above the level to which your occupation consigns you. I do not concur, but my opinions clearly have no weight. You should nevertheless be aware of the conditions of service in this household. God has given the young and malleable hearts of the servants into my trust," she added with passionate intensity, "and it falls to me to see that they perform the duties for which He has fitted them."

"Damnation," the parrot remarked amiably. "Rule Britannia."

Aunt Jaggers got up and threw a velvet drape over the parrot's cage. The bird subsided with a surly cluck. Sitting down, she said, "We observe the Sabbath strictly. No hot meals, no hot water, fires only in winter. Prayers each morning of the week at six-thirty in the back parlor. No jam, butter, tea, sugar, and most especially beer are permitted to the servants. In these practices, I am supported by *The Young Servant's Own Book*, which warns against excessive eating and drinking." She reached for a well-worn book on the table beside her, opened it to a marked page, and began to read. " 'Eating too much is bad for the health, and drinking too much leads to misery. It is not wise for servants to accustom themselves to drink strong tea with a great deal of sugar; for, should they have to buy for themselves, they will find it very expensive to do so.' " She shut the book and turned to Kate, her eyes feverish with passionate intensity. "You see, by guarding those in our employ against their own wicked desires, we do them a service for which they will be grateful in later years." She dipped her hand into a box of candy on the table beside her and put a chocolate into her mouth.

"I see," Kate said thoughtfully. Was Aunt Jaggers's severe guardianship the reason for Amelia's fear and Mudd's warning? Somehow, she thought not. Her own earlier employer had been almost as strict, without any noticeable effect on the servants. No, if the servants' fear and bitterness were directed at Aunt Jaggers, it flowed from some other source, darker and deeper than mere resentment.

The terrier had fallen noisily asleep, and Aunt Jaggers's voice became hoarsely sententious against the background of its snore. "It is our duty to reprove and correct those in our employ and to guard them from their own natural inclinations to become apprentices of misrule. That, of course," she added, but not as an afterthought, "is why the reading of novels is prohibited."

In other circumstances, Kate might have laughed. Now, seeing Aunt Jaggers's face, her upper lip beaded with sweat, she knew this was nothing to laugh about. "You do not deem novels fit reading," she ventured cautiously.

"A sign of moral depravity," Aunt Jaggers replied firmly. "Witness this teaching from *The Christian Miscellany and Family Visitor*." She took a booklet from the table, adjusted her glasses, and again read aloud. " 'Novel reading tends to inflame the passions, pollute the imagination, and corrupt the heart. It frequently becomes an inveterate habit, strong and fatal as that of a drunkard. In this state of intoxication, great waywardness of conduct is always sure to follow. Even when the habit is renounced, and genuine reformation takes place, the individual always suffers the cravings of former excitement.' "

"A horrible fate," Kate murmured, thinking of Beryl Bardwell's embryonic story in the writing desk in her room upstairs, through which she fully intended to intoxicate the imaginations and inflame the passions of her readers. She would have to be more careful to conceal the evidence of her moral depravity.

Aunt Jaggers lowered the booklet and fixed glittering eyes upon Kate. "I trust that you will agree to do as I desire out of courtesy, if not out of strict requirement."

"I thank you," Kate said, "for communicating your concerns to me." She took a deep breath. A lie would finish this unpleasant business in an instant. Was it honesty or sheer stubbornness that made her so contrary? "But I cannot agree to keep a rule made by another," she said, "when I would not make the same rule for myself."

Aunt Jaggers took off her glasses and stared at Kate. "Impertinence!"

Kate bowed her head. "I do not intend it so, Aunt. But I do plead guilty to candor."

Aunt Jaggers's thin lips pursed into a knot. "You will reap the wages of your transgression!"

Kate stood. "I daresay, Aunt," she said, and walked to the door. As she closed it behind her, she heard the parrot squawk again. "God save the Queen."

And as she turned to go down the gloomy hall, she glimpsed the flying ties of Amelia's lacy white apron fluttering like startled doves around the corner.

15

"When constabulary duty's to be done,
A policeman's lot is not a happy one."
—GILBERT AND SULLIVAN
The Pirates of Penzance

INSPECTOR HOWARD WAINWRIGHT sat at a small table in his dingy office in the even dingier basement of Town Hall, frowning down at the hastily scribbled autopsy report Sergeant Battle had laid before him. His frown deepened to a scowl, and he wished fervently that the borough police could afford one of those new typewriters. It would make Dr. Forsythe's crabbed hand legible.

But his superiors were not likely to authorize the purchase of a typewriter, the inspector knew. And even if they did, his sausage-fingered sergeant would have to learn to operate it. One eventuality was as improbable as the other, and either was as unlikely as the installation of a telephone, which the inspector also fervently desired.

Inspector Wainwright was a practical man and knew the limitations of his position. But he was also ambitious and wished for the tools that would not only help him do his work but assist him to rise in his profession. His experience with the Essex constabulary, however, had made him pessimistic about the future. His pessimism pervaded his view of his work, indeed, of his life, and deepened his naturally melancholy state of mind.

The inspector was still squinting at Dr. Forsythe's indecipherable scribble when a figure darkened the doorway. He looked up impatiently. "Yes, Sergeant?"

Sergeant Battle came in and closed the door behind him. "'Tis th' gennulman from th' dig, sir," he said, *sotto voce*. "Th' one wot I tol' yer 'bout. He's got th' pichures."

"Has he?" Inspector Wainwright put down the report. He looked at Sergeant Battle's fat, oily fingers. Not only improbable and unlikely, but impossible. "Well, show him in."

The gentleman who came into the room was carrying a large leather portfolio. Inspector Wainwright stood.

"I fear I neglected to introduce myself to your subordinates yesterday," the gentleman said, taking off his dusty felt hat. "My name is Charles Sheridan." The sergeant retired discreetly and shut the door.

The inspector was at a disadvantage, and he knew it. He had been absent from the murder scene yesterday because he had been summoned to look for some missing plate at Hammond Hall—plate that had turned up in the kitchen slops while he was questioning Lady Hammond's cook. If he had been at the dig instead of pursuing his futile errand, he would have forbidden the gentleman to take photographs. It was not that he had anything against cameras; quite the contrary. He was firm in his opinion, however, that the documentation of crime should be done by the police—and the borough force, which possessed neither typewriter nor telephone, possessed no camera.

"I was about to have a cup of tea," the inspector said. "Would you take some?"

"Thank you, yes," Mr. Sheridan replied, unstrapping his portfolio.

The inspector went to the corner, where a kettle was boiling on a gas burner, and took down two crockery cups, neither very clean. By the time he returned with the tea, Mr. Sheridan had laid out a dozen photos on the table.

The inspector set down the cups and leaned over the photographs. "Ah," he said to himself after a moment, and then "Oh," and finally, "Yes, I see." When he finished his examination, he took up his cup and sat down, feeling even more gloomy than before. He had viewed the corpse in question, laid out on the mortuary table while Dr. Forsythe stood at the ready. He had viewed the excavation this morning and had seen what there was to see, which wasn't very much. But Mr. Sheridan's photographs of the body *in* the excavation gave him a far more complete understanding of the situation than either his belated inspection or the report of Sergeant Battle and PC Trabb. The fact quite depressed him.

Mr. Sheridan sipped his tea. "You've had experience with photography in criminal investigation, Inspector?"

Inspector Wainwright examined the questioner over the rim of his cup. A man of obvious breeding and intelligence, the sort of man whose social position the inspector could not help but envy. "Can't say as I have," he said sourly. "A local photographer shoots everybody who is arrested. Criminals don't fancy the business, of course. They contort their faces and bodies so that even their mothers wouldn't recognize 'em."

"And what do you do with the photographs, once obtained?"

Inspector Wainwright laughed shortly. "What else?" He gestured toward a cabinet. "We keep 'em. Of course, it's no mean trick to find one that's wanted again. Not many men give a truthful account of their names." He looked at the photograph of the dead man, stretched out on his back, his aquiline features clearly visible, as was his clothing, the ring on his finger, the knife wound in his chest. "But this, now," he said thoughtfully, almost to himself. "This is dif'rent. If I had a camera, and more coppers, a picture like this could be taken round to innkeepers, the stationmaster, cabbies. P'rhaps somebody could identify the bloke." He put down the photo. "If I had a camera," he repeated morosely. "And more coppers."

"You don't know who he was, then?"

Inspector Wainwright shook his head. "PC Trabb's out inquirin', but there's nothin' yet. Got the autopsy report, though," he added, "for what it's worth." He scowled at the nearly illegible document.

"Anything unexpected?"

"Only that the tip of the knife was recovered. Broke off against a rib." The inspector picked up the envelope that had come with Dr. Forsythe's report and spilled the contents onto the table. Among the items was a triangular bit of metal about a quarter inch on a side.

"Ah," Mr. Sheridan said, picking it up. "Sharpened on two edges. A dagger. A weapon designed for killing." He looked at the other items that had spilled out of the envelope with the knife tip: a railway ticket, a cut off clothing label, and the gold scarab ring. "The ticket was found in the victim's pocket?"

The inspector nodded.

"Return ticket, London to Dover," Mr. Sheridan mused. "He came from the Continent—from France, if we trust the evidence of the Parisian label—on a brief errand, planning to return shortly. But something waylaid him. Or rather, some*one*." He picked up the ring and examined it. "You have noticed the inscription inside this ring, no doubt."

"Inscription?" The inspector frowned. "I noticed somethin' that looked like child's scribblin'."

"Permit me to copy it," Mr. Sheridan said. From a pocket he took out a jeweler's loupe and inserted it into his eye, holding it firmly between his brow and his cheek. From another pocket he took out a pencil and pad, and commenced to sketch a series of stick figures—hands, birds, snakes, and other, unidentifiable objects.

The inspector took in Mr. Sheridan's industry without a word. The man was adept, no doubt about it. The last fellow he had seen working in such a nimble-fingered way had turned out to be a forger. Warily, he asked, "And what do you propose to do with this copy?"

"The inscription may tell us something about the ring's owner," Mr. Sheridan said, taking the lens out of his eye.

"But it can't be read," the inspector objected. "It's gibberish."

"It can't be read by us, certainly," Mr. Sheridan agreed, pocketing the pad. "I believe it is Middle Egyptian. It appears to me that there are two names here, perhaps a prayer." He pointed to the last figure, which appeared to be a cross with a loop. "This is an ankh, which represents eternal life. That's as much as I can make out, more's the pity. However, there's a chap in the Egyptology section of the British Museum who reads hieroglyphics as if he were reading *The Times*. With your permission, I propose to send this copy to him."

Feeling pinned, the inspector said, "I s'pose you may as well give it a go." He sat back, his gloomy curiosity fully aroused. Most men of Mr. Sheridan's class scarcely spoke to police, even when they were required to do so by official business, deeming it beneath their dignity to associate with someone at the level of sweeps and rat catchers. He frowned, curiosity darkening to suspicion. Why would a gentleman go to the trouble of photographing a dead body, bringing the photos to the police station, and engaging in a discussion of the evidence—especially a gentleman with the fingers of a forger? He straightened up.

"I don't b'lieve you've said, sir, where you're stayin'. In case I might have a need to talk further with you about this case."

Mr. Sheridan was shuffling photographs. "I am a guest at Marsden Manor, Dedham," he said absently. "If I am needed, you may send for me there." He laid two pictures in front of them. "Did you notice these, Inspector? The one on the left is a photograph of a pair of footprints."

The inspector frowned. Upon his arrival at the excavation at daybreak this morning, he had discovered to his chagrin (but not to his surprise) that Sergeant Battle had once again neglected to secure the scene of a crime. All footprints had been obliterated. The sergeant had reported that there were some, and Trabb had provided a clumsy drawing, which lay now in his drawer. But neither drawing nor report provided any useful detail. The inspector had thought that the footprints were gone forever—but he had been wrong. They were preserved here, in this photograph.

"And this on the right," Mr. Sheridan continued, tapping it with his thumb, "is an enlargement of that on the left. Observe the enhanced detail. Much more can be seen in the photograph than the naked eye might observe at the actual scene of the crime."

"Can it, now?" the inspector said darkly. Contrivances like the camera—and the typewriter and the telephone—were helpful and labour-saving. But he knew where to draw the line. A device that revealed *more* than the eye was not, in his opinion, to be fully trusted. Such an art could fabricate as easily as it could inform.

"It most certainly can." Mr. Sheridan took a pencil-sized silver case out of his pocket, flicked a button, and out popped a pointer. "Observe this footprint," he said, tracing its outline on the left-hand photograph with the pointer. "It is clearly that of a man's shoe. Here"—pointing—"are a second and a third, all directed toward the excavation—and rather unsteadily at that. Notice the unequal distances between the prints, and the uneven distribution of weight, first upon one foot, then the other."

He shifted his pointer to the enlargement. "This print, this small round indentation—is it not the print of the walking stick upon which the man is leaning heavily?" He reached into another pocket and took out a hand-held magnifying glass, which he handed to the inspector.

Still nursing his chagrin over the ineptness that had denied him the first-hand view of the footprints to which he was entitled, the inspector took the lens and scrutinized the enlarged indentation. "But no walking stick was found," he growled.

"No," Mr. Sheridan said, "it was not."

The inspector narrowed his eyes. He could not object to the gentleman's conclusions, although they struck him as being of the hocus-pocus variety, rather like that preposterous "consulting detective" whose exploits were all the rage. He might, however, question the gentleman's motives for interesting himself so deeply in this case. He might, in fact, suspect the gentleman himself. "And what, sir, is *your* business in the Colchester area?" he asked, putting down the lens.

Mr. Sheridan reshuffled the photographs. "As I said, I am visiting the Marsdens. As well, Sir Archibald has invited me to make a photographic record of the progress of the excavation here in Colchester." Another photo. The pointer again. "See here, Inspector. These are wheel prints in the cart track near the excavation."

The inspector folded his arms, no longer to be seduced. "What of 'em? Looks like the victim came by cab, don't it? He must have done, anyway. Bit out of the way to walk, for an unsteady man who's got to use a walking stick."

"But notice the ivory rule," Mr. Sheridan said, gesturing energetically, "which indicates the gauge. The distance between the wheels is only five feet. The axle width of a hansom cab is six feet." Two more photographs, side to side. "Moreover, observe this mark in the print—that of a partial break in the iron rim of the right wheel. Here it is in this photograph, and here"—pointing again—"in this one, at an interval of approximately twelve and one half feet."

Inspector Wainwright pushed his lips in and out. "Meanin'?"

"Meaning that this vehicle was not a cab, sir. Its wheelbase is much too small. Further, the diameter of the wheel is only about four feet, while that of most hansoms is roughly five." At the clouded look on the inspector's face he added, "You recall pi, of course. The diameter of a circle equals its circumference divided by three and fourteen sixteen ten thousandths."

"Of course," the inspector said, humoring him. "Pie."

Mr. Sheridan nodded. "But that is less important than the fact that this vehicle's wheels have iron rims, while hansom cabs have rubber tires. It is clear, sir, that this is a rather small carriage, lightweight, of the about-town variety, with a break in the iron rim of the right wheel. Further, if you will be so good as to notice the hoof prints— here, and again here—you will observe that the vehicle was drawn by a horse lame in the left hind leg."

The inspector managed to suppress a smile, the first of the day. "And what kind of harness would you say this horse was wearin'?"

Mr. Sheridan appeared not to notice the inspector's amusement. He stacked the photographs, placing those of the corpse on top. "I have prepared these copies for you and have retained the plates," he said crisply. "If you require additional prints, you have only to ask. Should your inquiries uncover the victim's identity, please be so kind as to inform me of the particulars." He took out a gold pocket watch and looked at it. "In the meantime, I shall attempt to discover the meaning of the inscription in the ring. I also plan to return to the excavation. While I fear that the area has already been tramped, the cart track may have remained undisturbed, at least sufficiently to allow

me to acquire certain additional data that may be useful."
He took up his empty portfolio and his hat. "Good day to
you, Inspector."

The gentleman had scarcely cleared the stoop when the
inspector bellowed out, "Battle!"

The sergeant appeared at the door. "Sir?"

"That gent who was just here," the inspector said
urgently. "Put somebody on his back, smartish."

"But I don't have nobody to put on 'im," the sergeant
protested.

"Got *yourself*, haven't you?" The inspector spoke icily,
feeling that Battle should put forth some extra effort to
atone for his sins of the day before. "Fetch your bicycle,
man, and hop to it!"

"Yessir," the sergeant said, and disappeared.

The inspector went back to his table, balled Dr. Forsythe's
unreadable autopsy report, and pitched it against the wall.

16

"The archaeologist must be something of a detective, in the sense that he must extract from the site enough evidence to allow him to conclude what happened there, when it happened, and to whom. If the archaeologist is also an historian (and the best are), he weaves this information into a larger narrative which allows him to conclude why it happened."

—WILLIAM ALBERT
An Introduction to Historical Archaeology

AN HOUR LATER, Charles was seated in Sir Archibald Fairfax's field tent at the excavation, declining an offer of tea. "Thank you," he said, "but I just had a cup with Inspector Wainwright."

"The police!" Sir Archibald exclaimed, concerned. "My dear boy, is everything quite all right?"

"Oh, quite," Charles said. "I dropped off my photographs of yesterday's find."

"With the police?" Sir Archibald asked, puzzled. "But I fail to see—" His face cleared. "Oh, to be sure. The dead man in the dig. I'd forgotten. We made a discovery yesterday afternoon—another mosaic. Drove the miserable wretch straight out of my mind."

"It's the miserable wretch I've come about, actually," Charles said. "I've been to the excavation after more photographs, but the place is a muddle. Yesterday's police work was altogether negligent. No attention paid to roping off the site or maintaining proper custody of evidence."

"What did y'expect?" Sir Archibald asked pettishly. "Bad mannered as bison, police. Brainless. Tramping about, never minding where they put their boots. Almost as bad as women," he added, "whisking along in their deuced skirts. Shifty as a squadron of street sweepers."

"It's hardly the fault of the police, I suppose," Charles reflected. "Not much training, little education, no money for equipment or adequate staff. Not held in high regard by society."

"And not a thought in their heads for the preservation of history," Sir Archibald went on, as if Charles hadn't spoken. "Police *or* women."

"I suppose you can hardly expect them to have a proper scientific attitude," Charles said, half to himself. "Their outlook is dictated by tradition. Scarcely disposed to the progressive point of view."

"Puts me in mind of the way our business was done twenty years ago—*still* done, on most sites." Sir Archibald stood up and started to stride back and forth. "No attention to the proper documentation of artifacts, to stratigraphic records, to analysis. Does no good to dig, if carelessness results in the loss of proper *in situ* information. Like that great oaf Schliemann, you recall, the idiot who destroyed Troy while he was digging it up. Bloody treasure hunter, yanking artifacts out of the ground like turnips. Once something's dug up, it can't be put back." He raised his hand in an imperial gesture. "Our paramount responsibility is to extract every ounce of information that the ground can reveal. Without that, what's in the museum is of no more worth than bits salvaged out of the dustbin."

"Just so," Charles said hastily, remembering that Sir Archibald's animosity toward Heinrich Schliemann could lead to an hour's impassioned discourse. And while Sir Archibald's remarks opened several intriguing parallels between archaeology and criminal detection, he needed to get on with the business.

"I have a question for you, Sir Archibald," he said, "regarding vehicular access to the dig. Specifically, the cart track behind the spot where the body was found. What vehicles might be expected to use that track?"

"None, sir," Sir Archibald said firmly. "Horses are as destructive as police—worse, when one considers the size of the beast. Once when I was working at Mycenae, a horse went berserk and crashed into a field tent, smashing a grand lot of urns, not to mention two fine young archaeologists. No, no, horses won't do at all. Debris is removed to the spoil heaps by barrow."

"I see," Charles said. "So any hoof prints—"

"Don't *tell* me that you have found hoof prints!"

"I'm afraid so. Along the cart track."

Sir Archibald shook his head. "Patrols," he muttered. "There will have to be patrols, day and night. And a cordon, and—"

Charles stood up. "I leave it to you, Sir Archibald," he said. "I am confident that you will take every measure in your power to protect the site from intrusion."

"Oh, I shall, sir," Sir Archibald said, with great fervor. "You can depend upon it." He sat down heavily. "Police," he muttered. "Horses." He dropped his head into his hands. "Next thing you know, it'll be women."

"Excuse me, sir." Charles did not turn, but he recognized the voice from the doorway behind him. It belonged to the student archaeologist who had started the whole thing.

Sir Archibald looked up. "What is it?" he asked testily. "Well, well, speak up. Not another dead man, I hope?"

"No," the student said. "Actually, it's a woman."

Sir Archibald leaped to his feet, his face filled with horror. "A dead woman?" he cried.

"Oh, no, sir," the student said hastily. "She's very much alive."

Charles glanced over his shoulder. The first thing he saw was a pair of ankle-high black boots and a dark serge divided skirt, almost like full-cut trousers, so short as to show an inch of black stocking. Startled, his gaze traveled upward—past slim dark jacket, white shirt, manly tie—and came to rest on the woman's face, topped by a mound of undisciplined auburn hair.

It was Kathryn Ardleigh.

17

"O let us love our occupations,
Bless the squire and his relations,
Live upon our daily rations,
And always know our proper stations."
—CHARLES DICKENS,
The Chimes, 2nd Quarter

"AN' BLESS THIS food to our use an' us in Thy service," Mudd said. "Amen."

" 'men," chorused the servants obediently, from benches arranged along both sides of the staff dining table.

From her place at the foot of the table, opposite Mudd, Cook saw Pocket slip a boiled egg under his jersey. "Pocket," she remarked, "if yer'll be so good as t' put that egg on yer plate, Mr. Mudd'll ladle th' soup."

Reddening, Pocket—at seventeen, he served as groom, doubled as footman and coachman, and did a great deal of the garden work beside—placed the egg on his plate. "Thought I'd 'ave a bit o' snack a'ter," he muttered. "Didn't mean nothin', Mrs. Pratt."

"That's all right, Pocket," Amelia comforted him. "Th' times *is* long t' tea. I gets hungry m'self, and I don't have yer heavy work."

Cook looked down the table. The household staff was gathered for the midday meal in the servants' hall, a damp room lacking the comforts of fire and carpet, with a patch of mildew the very shape of Ireland on the wall beside the door. Cook blackly credited the room's cheerlessness to Jaggers, who, when she ordered the carpet removed and the fireplace blocked up, had had the gall to *read* the explanation to Cook out of one of her household manuals. *From Kitchen to Garret*, Cook remembered with some bitterness, by a Mrs. Panton. "Carpets should not be installed in the servants' hall nor fires laid" (Mrs. Panton wrote and Jaggers concurred), because such luxuries might induce the servants to loiter instead of getting on with their tasks. Mrs. Panton also permitted the installation of a discarded sofa or armchair, but grudgingly. "If the servants are young, heedless, or have not lived any time in the establishment, these little additions to their comfort are not necessary." It was Jaggers's opinion that one side chair was sufficient and a sofa superfluous.

That, Cook thought resentfully, was only *one* of the wretched Jaggers's opinions, on a par with her strict economies with the servants' food. The joint that Cook roasted for the dining room, for instance, was expected to reappear on the servants' table for at least five midday meals, variously incarnated until it concluded in a hash that was mostly cabbage and potato. As to tea and cakes, as there'd been in cheerful abundance until the coming of Jaggers four years ago—Well, such treats now were had only on high holy days, such as Christmas and Boxing Day, and even then, the quantity was stinting.

And where, Cook asked herself with a tightening of the jaw, were *her* perquisites—the drippings she'd sold to the candlemaker, the cony wool that had gone for seven shillings a pound to the hatter and the muff maker, the old tea leaves—all the valuable salvage that she had been permitted by the old Mrs. Ardleigh and by Miss Sabrina Ardleigh after? Why, they'd been sacrificed with the fire and the carpet, of course, on the altar of Jaggers's ha'penny economies.

In her mind, Cook could not pay Miss Ardleigh's sister the compliment of calling her *Mrs.* She was Jaggers, like any other servant, for that's what she was—a servant gotten above herself. And a younger sister gotten above an elder, too, which was most mysterious. Cook couldn't for the life of her fathom how Miss Ardleigh had allowed it to happen, or what mysterious hold the younger sister had over the elder.

Waiting for her bowl of steaming oxtail soup to be relayed hand to hand down the table, Cook frowned. In her experience, penny soul never amounted to tuppence, and Jaggers would sooner or later get what was coming to her, if she had to see to it herself. Then Miss Ardleigh would resume her proper authority above stairs, and below stairs would be left to Cook (which was her natural right, seeing as Mudd was young and a come-lately with a great lot to learn). And when that happened, Cook intended to have not only a carpet and a sofa, but a fire as well—not for herself, either, but for the young ones, seeing that their lives were so bleak and work-filled.

Cook received her soup, scowling. And so it should be, shouldn't it? She was senior in this house, wasn't she? She thought back to the day, twenty-one years ago next month, when the shy and awkward young Sarah Perkins, as she had been called before her marriage to the unfortunate Mr. Pratt, was hired as scullery maid by the late Mrs. Ardleigh. Sarah had grown in skill, had prospered in her perquisites and tradesmen's commissions, and had kept her place through the various comings and goings of maids, butlers, drunken cooks, and careless housekeepers—comings and goings that, since Jaggers, had picked up speed like a runaway cart on a steep downhill grade. Harriet and Nettie were only the latest in a long line of kitchen maids and tweenies, while Mudd at twenty-six was the third butler in four years. Impressed by himself, Mudd was; he had been hired from a London agency, and in his previous place had been only a footman. And Amelia at barely eighteen was the fourth parlor maid coming directly after poor Jenny.

Jenny. Cook could still not think of her without a black hatred boiling in her heart toward Jaggers. Not that the girl hadn't been foolish, but most girls were, now and again, and were forgiven and welcomed back into the fold. No, Jaggers's sin was by far the worst, and she'd be damned to bloody hell for it. Cook tore a piece of bread into her soup, her scowl darkening. If Miss Ardleigh had done what was proper when she was told about the situation, instead of shirking it onto her sister, what had happened would never have happened. Cook was sure of it.

Amelia turned to Nettie, worried. "Ain't yer found it yet?"

"I've looked ever'where, truly I 'ave," said Nettie. Her thin face was frightened. "I can't think where it's got to. 'Twas there afore this mornin' an' now 'tis gone. When she finds it missin', I'll be blamed, sure."

Cook pushed away the thought of Jenny and gave Nettie a reproachful look. "I've told yer a dozen times, child, yer must have extra diligence 'n her rooms. Clean th' grate an' black it, make up th' fire, empty th' slops, dust th' shelves, sweep th' carpet wi' damp tea leaves t' keep down th' dust, an' scrub yer hands afore yer change th' linen."

"But I do!" Nettie wailed. She was a few months shy of fourteen, lonely and heartsick, Cook knew, in her first place. "I'm ever so careful when I dusts, an' she always looks at my fingernails t' be sure they're clean afore I makes up th' bed. But there's so many lit'le pieces o' everythin', so many bits o' china an' glass an'—"

"P'rhaps she won't miss it," put in Pocket hopefully, fishing in his soup with a spoon for a bit of meat. He was a great tease. Only now, he was as concerned as the others.

"Oh, she'll miss it, all right," Mudd said with a grim look. "Eyes like a bloody 'awk, that one 'as. Greedy as a 'awk, too," he added. "Always first to the tea cakes."

Cook nodded. She and Mudd did not agree on everything, but on this subject, they were in total harmony.

"Anyway," Harriet said, patting Nettie's hand, " 'tis only a pincushion." Harriet was two years younger than Nettie, but her commonsensical cheerfulness often made her seem older.

"But th' *queen's* pincushion!" Nettie cried, stricken. "Wi' th' *queen's* pichur ringed round in *pearls*. Worth a year's wage, at least!"

"Come now, Nettie," Cook admonished, "hold yer tongue. We'll 'ave no more loose talk." She looked down the table at Mudd. "How's th' young miss settlin' in?"

"That one?" The butler arched an expressive eyebrow. "She's not so young, Mrs. P., truth be told. But nosy. Asks too many questions." He gave the parlor maid a stern glance. "Amelia nearly gave us away th' other momin'."

Cook glared at Amelia. "Ain't yer bin told not t' talk?" she demanded roughly.

"I din't talk," Amelia replied, lifting her chin with a pert defiance. "Not really. She took me by surprise. She's sly, that one. Talks back, too. I heard her tellin' Mrs. Jaggers that she wouldn't mind th' rules."

"Garn!" Harriet exclaimed enviously. "Wish *I* could do that!"

Cook frowned at Harriet until she squirmed and dropped her bread. "An' just how did yer *happen* to hear her talk back, I wonder?" she inquired of Amelia, her voice rich with sarcasm.

111

The girl's fair face flushed. "I was dustin' th' table in th' hall outside Mrs. Jaggers's sittin' room. Th' young miss an' Mrs. Jaggers was talkin' loud, they was, over th' clatter o' that barmy-brained parrot." She scraped bacon drippings on her bread. "T'were my parrot, th' wretched bird'ud be in th' stewpot aready."

Amelia had to clean the parrot's cage because Jaggers did not trust Nettie with the task. The bird had belonged to Jaggers's dead husband, and the silly woman had been daft enough to keep it. Cook snorted under her breath. Any husband of *hers* who had died possessed of a parrot would find it dead in the dustbin before the last clod fell onto his coffin.

"She reads, too, the young miss does," Nettie said, putting her fright over the pincushion behind her. "Shillin' shockers. She's got one called *The Mummy's Curse* layin' on her table, like, in plain sight."

"*Garn!*" Harriet's brown eyes were saucer like. "Wish I could read it." She looked at Cook. "No, I don't," she amended quickly. "I'd be too a-scared. Mrs. Jaggers 'ud beat me. Anyways, I can't read that good."

"She beats yer," Cook said fiercely, "yer tell me. She's not t' lay a hand on th' staff—Miss Ardleigh give orders." That much Miss Ardleigh had done, although it was after the fact. Little enough, too, but Cook meant to see that Jaggers obeyed.

"There's more." Nettie dropped her voice. "The young miss reads th' newspaper. There's a copy o' th' Colchester *Exchange* on her dressin' table, wi' a circle drawn round a story 'bout a *murder.* Some for'n gent wi' a knife in his heart, heaved int' a hole."

Nettie could read, and did so, much to Cook's chagrin. In this regard, Cook subscribed to the same moral principle as did Jaggers: that women, and particularly girls, should not fill their minds with what appeared in the newspaper.

At this intelligence, Harriet was speechless, and even Pocket looked impressed. "Better not let Mrs. Jaggers catch her readin' 'bout murders," he remarked.

"Nor you, Nettie," Mudd put in sternly, mindful of his place of authority over the servants. "Rule's a rule. No newspaper readin'. Mrs. Jaggers'll flog you, sure as soot."

"She'll flog me first," Cook muttered.

"She can't flog th' young miss," Nettie reflected. "That'un belongs t' Miss Ardleigh."

"Anyway, she's fam'ly," Amelia said, resentful. "She's not like us. She don't have t' do as told."

"She wears wot she pleases, too," Pocket said knowingly. He cast a glance at Cook to see if she had spied him putting three boiled eggs on his plate. "The both o' us was sent t' Colchester this morning, an' she went in trousers!"

"Trousers!" Amelia and Harriet gasped in one voice, and Cook almost choked.

"Gawd's truth," Pocket said solemnly, holding up one hand while the other deposited a boiled egg under his jersey. "*Short* trousers, wot showed her ankle."

"She better take care, is all I got t' say," Mudd put in. "Jaggers may not flog 'er, but she's got 'er ways. She's a mean'un, Jaggers is."

"Yes," Amelia said. Viciously, she stabbed the knife into the bread. "That's wot Jenny used t' say. Mrs. Jaggers is a mean'un."

Mudd's cup crashed into its saucer.

Cook cleared her throat, mercifully ignoring the second egg that Pocket was spiriting under his jersey. "We don't talk 'bout Jenny," she said. "An' yer young ones, yer guard yer tongues. Ye don't know 'oo might be listenin'."

A nervous silence fell upon the table.

18

"With the Divine permission I will apply myself to the Great Work, which is to purify and exalt my Spiritual nature, that I may at length attain to be more than human, and thus gradually raise and unite myself to my Higher and Divine Genius."

—CANDIDATE'S OATH,
The Order of the Golden Dawn

ON THE MORNING following her excursion to the Colchester excavation, Kate went with Aunt Sabrina to the library, taking with her a pad and paper and her fountain pen. On the newly installed desk in an alcove by the window sat a gleaming black-and-gold Remington Standard typewriter, arrived the day before. Kate couldn't keep her eyes off it, imagining how speedily Beryl Bardwell would now be able to produce chapters of her story, for which she had a new title—"The Conspiracy of the Golden Scarab"—which reflected some important modifications she had decided to make in the plot.

Aunt Sabrina sat down at her desk. "Did you discover anything at Colchester?" she asked. Her tone was half-anticipatory, half-apprehensive, Kate thought.

"I discovered that Sir Archibald Fairfax doesn't permit women on the site of his archaeological excavations," Kate said. "I was summarily hauled into his field tent and instructed to leave the premises—in front of Sir Charles Sheridan, who was there, he told me, to discuss the murder."

Aunt Sabrina frowned. "The murder? Sir Charles remains interested in the murder?"

"Yes," Kate said. "He had earlier been to talk with Inspector Wainwright, of the Colchester police."

Aunt Sabrina's face was intent. "Has the identity of the dead man yet been determined?"

Kate shook her head. "Unfortunately, no. After we left Mr. Fairfax, Sir Charles told me of the few clues he and the police have obtained."

After being taken to the field tent yesterday, Kate had listened at length and with as much forbearance as she could summon to Sir Archibald's opinion of women, who were in some incomprehensible way, it seemed, as potentially devastating to historical inquiry as horses, water buffalo, and policemen. When the archaeologist had at last stopped shaking his turkey-red wattles at her, she had taken her leave. Sir Charles, who seemed startled by her sudden appearance at the door of the field tent and wryly amused by her walking costume, accompanied her to the spot where Pocket was waiting with the dog cart. On the way he told her what he had learned from his meeting with Inspector Wainwright.

"The police have recovered a knife tip that appears to be from the murder weapon," Kate told her aunt, "as well as a railway return ticket from London to Dover. In addition, Sir Charles has discovered that the victim appears to have driven to the excavation in a light carriage, iron-wheeled, drawn by a horse lame in the left hind foot. The victim walked unsteadily, probably assisted by a walking stick. And the scarab ring," she added with a close look at her aunt, "is inscribed."

"Inscribed?" Aunt Sabrina asked quickly.

"Sir Charles copied the inscription, which appears to consist of hieroglyphics, and has asked an Egyptologist to decipher it."

"I see," Aunt Sabrina said. Her expression was unreadable. "But the police have no suspect?"

"No," Kate said. "And according to Sir Charles, they may not discover any. He does not have a high opinion of their abilities."

Aunt Sabrina straightened her shoulders. "In the circumstances," she said briskly, "I believe we can conclude our inquiry into the matter, Kathryn."

Kate frowned. "But I haven't seen Sir Charles's photographs of the murder victim," she objected. "They may offer some clue—"

"They may indeed." Aunt Sabrina's mouth was firm. "But I must insist, Kathryn. I do not wish you to press the matter. Most particularly, I do not wish you to call attention to my interest in this affair. If Sir Charles happens to show you the photographs, that is one thing. But you must not press him for them." She leaned forward, her look intent. "Do you understand?"

"Yes, Aunt," Kate said reluctantly, feeling a sharp disappointment. Her murder investigation, closed before it had scarcely been opened! But it wasn't just disappointment she felt. She was deeply curious. Why would Aunt Sabrina ask her to look into the murder and then force her withdrawal before anything definite was learned? What was Aunt Sabrina's interest in this matter?

"In any event," Aunt Sabrina said, shifting some papers on her desk, "we have other important things to command our attention. I would like to give you an introduction to the Order of the Golden Dawn, so that you will understand the work you will be asked to do." Her face tightened imperceptibly. "But I must have your promise, Kathryn, that you will not reveal what I tell you.

The business of our Order is quite secret, and the history is meant for initiates only."

"Of course, Aunt Sabrina," Kate said, pushing the murder investigation out of her mind and settling herself to take notes. She would reveal nothing she learned about the Golden Dawn. But that did not mean that Beryl Bardwell could not borrow an idea or two.

"The Golden Dawn," Aunt Sabrina said, "is a secret fraternity dedicated to exploring mysteries of the spirit through magical and occult practices."

"I believe you said that it was recently established," Kate said.

"Recently, yes, but on age-old authority. Seven years ago, Dr. William Westcott found, by accident, an ancient manuscript written in cipher."

"How interesting," Kate said. She sat forward in her chair. An ancient cipher document would be a marvelous plot device in her story.

Aunt Sabrina rose and went to the fireplace. "After some effort, Dr. Westcott discovered the key to the cipher and transcribed the document, which revealed the outlines of an ancient occult order. Dr. Westcott was in a position to understand its significance, because he is a Freemason and a student of Western occultism, as well as a medical doctor of good reputation and coroner for North-East London." With tongs, she took a lump of coal from a japanned black coal box and added it to the grate. The fire blazed into a shower of sparks. "Dr. Westcott then asked MacGregor Mathers to expand the outlines and create a series of rituals."

"This Mr. Mathers," Kate said. "He is the one you mentioned yesterday? The man who established the temple in Paris?"

"Yes," Aunt Sabrina said. "The Ahathoor Temple. Mathers is a—" She returned to her chair and sat down, her brows pulled together. "I don't mean to be uncharitable," she said reluctantly, "but I must confess to disliking the man. He is arrogant and conceited, quite pretentious about his magical knowledge. And always in need of funds. He sponged on Dr. Westcott for some years, and now Annie Horniman virtually supports him and his wife, Moina, in Paris." She made an exasperated gesture. "But to give the devil his due, the man is an excellent ritualist. He expanded the materials in the cipher documents to create the initiation rites for the Order."

Kate was thoughtful. There were so many frauds about— the Order of the Golden Dawn would need unimpeachable credentials. "The authority you mentioned," she asked. "Where did it come from?"

"From a certain Fräulein Anna Sprengel, a chief of a German Rosicrucian order called *Die Goldene Dämmerung*. Dr. Westcott found her name and address in the cipher document and wrote to her. She wrote back, authorizing him to establish a London temple. He called it the Isis-Urania Temple, and invited Mathers to join him as co-chief. Fräulein Sprengel and Dr. Westcott exchanged several letters, until he received the news that she was dead."

"There are other temples beside those in London and Colchester?"

"Five, altogether," Aunt Sabrina said. "And several hundred members. But we do not have a reliable membership roster. That will be your first task, Kathryn. You will write to each of the temples and ask them to send a correct list of their members. When you are finished, I will ask you to sort and organize the rather disordered mass of papers that Dr. Westcott had accumulated, which now reside in the boxes under your worktable. When that is done, I would like you to copy the cipher manuscript for one of our members, Willie Yeats, an Irish poet, who wishes to make a study of it. You will enjoy meeting him, I think. He has a deep interest in the tarot, which is used quite frequently in our rituals."

"The tarot?"

"The tarot cards are esoteric cards derived from an ancient Egyptian magical system. Those we use have been drawn by Moina Mathers from her husband's design. Each card represents a particular psychic state, a sort of station along an allegorical journey toward higher spiritual knowledge. As such, the deck serves as a kind of Bible for the Order."

"Ah," Kate said thoughtfully. Beryl Bardwell was becoming quite interested. "I would like to see the cards, when it's convenient."

Aunt Sabrina shook her head. "I'm afraid you can't see the cards, Kathryn. The privilege is open only to members."

"I see," Kate said. Then, being a person who acted upon the impulse of the moment, she added decidedly, "Well, then, I must become a member." It was not so much that she wanted to join a magical society—Kate was naturally skeptical, and although she respected her aunt's occult interests, she was doubtful about mystical orders in general. But the story Beryl Bardwell was writing featured the beautiful medium Mrs. Bartlett, who might be expected to understand and use such things as tarot cards. If becoming a member of an occult society would give Beryl Bardwell ready access to a magician or two who might serve as models, Kate was more than ready.

Aunt Sabrina gave her a searching look. "Are you quite sure you want to join? You're not just seeking to please me?"

"I'm seeking to please myself," Kate assured her. "Is it difficult to become a member?"

Aunt Sabrina smiled. "Not at all. In fact, your joining would make our work much more enjoyable, and I would feel more at ease in sharing the material. But I suggest that you attend a gathering or two before you make up your mind. The next one is on Saturday afternoon. Several members from London will be there, as well as a few visitors. It is said that Oscar Wilde will come—he is an admirer of Mrs. Farnsworth, and his wife, Constance, formerly belonged to the London temple. He is to bring a man of his acquaintance, Doyle, I believe. The writer of those detective mysteries that have become so popular."

Kate's heart leaped up. Oscar Wilde was chiefly a literary curiosity—at least, that's how American papers portrayed him. But Conan Doyle! Perhaps she could speak to him and find out why he had allowed Professor Moriarty to fling Sherlock Holmes into the abyss, thereby bringing the series to an untimely end. If the successful Holmes had been Beryl Bardwell's character, she would not have killed him!

19

"Is there, in human-form, that bears a heart— A wretch! a villain! lost to love and truth! That can, with studied, sly, ensnaring art, Betray sweet Jenny's unsuspecting youth?"

—ROBERT BURNS
The Cotter's Saturday Night

KATE WAS AT the typewriter that afternoon when her work was interrupted by Amelia.

"Yer wanted in the drawin' room, miss," she said.

Kate looked up, frowning. She had just finished her aunt's work for the day and settled down to Beryl Bardwell's latest chapter. She did not wish to leave it, for she was trying to extricate her heroine from a particularly perilous situation. "Thank you, Amelia," she said, "but I would rather—"

"There's callers, miss," Amelia said flatly, and withdrew.

Kate, resigned, tidied her russet hair into a semblance of neatness and smoothed the dark gray serge skirt she wore to work in. Her gray cotton shirtwaist was badly rumpled and one white cuff was ink-stained. Well, that was just too bad, she thought defiantly, collecting her papers and hiding them in the desk. Whoever had interrupted her writing time would simply have to take her as she was, dressed for work rather than attired for afternoon callers.

Kate wasn't entirely surprised when she saw that one of the visitors was Eleanor Marsden, attractive and vivacious in china-blue silk. She was, however, a little nonplussed when Sir Charles Sheridan stood and bowed.

"Miss Ardleigh," he said.

Kate felt herself reddening under his inquisitive glance. "Sir Charles," she murmured, immediately conscious of her soiled cuffs and workaday costume. She sat down, remembering his dry amusement at her walking suit the day before and wondering if he thought that she was in the habit of wearing unladylike dress. She hoped he would not mention encountering her in Sir Archibald's field tent, for across the room, Aunt Jaggers was scowling over her cup of tea. It would not be easy to explain why she had gone to the excavation without implicating Aunt Sabrina.

Eleanor's eyes widened slightly when she took in Kate's appearance, but she leaned forward. "My dear Kathryn!" she exclaimed. "How good it is to see you again!" *Her* cuffs were elegant with lace, and a blue straw hat, jauntily beribboned, perched on the back of her head. Dainty blue boots peeped out from beneath her skirt.

Kate smiled. "I'm glad you came," she said with genuine warmth. "I had hoped to see you again before very long." She looked curiously at Sir Charles. Some devil stirred in her and she said, lightly, "Did you come to inquire after the bats, Sir Charles? I understand the ruins are quite full of them." Aunt Sabrina had told her about the remains of the old keep across the little lake at the foot of the lawn. She planned to go there as soon as she could.

At the mention of bats, Aunt Jaggers made a sputtering noise. Sir Charles looked regretful. "I'm afraid that Miss

Marsden would not permit such an excursion today," he said. "But I certainly hope to make a later investigation. The bat in question is quite a wonderful—"

"Sir Charles!" Eleanor admonished, tapping his wrist. She turned to Kate. "Really, Kathryn, you mustn't encourage him."

Aunt Sabrina sat back in her chair, chuckling. "And how is your mother, Miss Marsden?"

"Quite well," Eleanor said, "although simply maddened with wedding plans. There is *so* much to do." She smiled. "She asked me to inquire whether you plan to invite the G.F.S. to hold their annual tea at Bishop's Keep this year."

Aunt Sabrina nodded. "Tell Lady Marsden that I have already informed the vicar that I would be glad for the Society to come. But he has not yet fixed upon a day."

Aunt Jaggers narrowed her eyes. She seemed about to say something, but Kate spoke first. "The G.F.S.?" she asked. "Is that some sort of organization?"

Eleanor giggled. "The group is often referred to as the God-Forsaken Spinsters," she said. Amelia's back, turned to Kate, seemed to stiffen.

Kate glanced from Eleanor to Amelia and frowned. "How old must one be to belong to this group?" she asked innocently. Sir Charles cleared his throat, and she caught his glance. His lips were twitching and his brown eyes were wryly amused.

But Eleanor was not amused. "Oh, not *you*, my dear Kathryn!" she exclaimed, brows arched in horror. "You could never—"

"Perhaps I'm *too* old," Kate persisted. Sir Charles began to cough into his napkin.

Aunt Sabrina laughed. "The Girls' Friendly Society," she told Kate, "is an association of young women in service. Its annual tea is arranged by the vicar and sponsored by several of the ladies of the parish. Many of our girls are away from home for the first time, you see, and—"

"And at loose ends," Aunt Jaggers put in. "They should do better to stay in their places and work, rather than gallivanting about, footloose, in gowns and gloves."

Teasing forgotten, Kate spoke up in protest. "But surely the servants are permitted to do as they like with their half days, Aunt."

"I hardly imagine, Niece," Aunt Jaggers remarked icily, "that you are sufficiently acquainted with the servant class to have formed a valid opinion."

Kate bit her tongue. Aunt Sabrina moved in her chair but said nothing. The uncomfortable silence was broken by Mudd's murmured direction to Amelia to replenish the tray of tea cakes.

Across from Kate, Sir Charles sipped his tea. His glance met hers over the rim of the cup, and she was startled to find it appreciative. He put down his cup and inquired, "Are you enjoying the autumn countryside, Miss Ardleigh? I can recommend the mill and the locks at Flatford, on the Stour. It is not a long walk from here, and quite picturesque."

"I'm afraid I have been much too busy with my work to gallivant about the countryside," Kate said. She glanced at Aunt Jaggers. The devil spoke. "With or without gloves."

Aunt Jaggers snorted. Aunt Sabrina looked distressed. "How inconsiderate of me, Kathryn," she said. "Really, you *must* take some time off, if only to see the ruins. You are working much too hard."

Eleanor's cup rattled. "Working?" she asked, staring at Kate. "Why, Kathryn, whatever are you *doing*?"

"I have come to Bishop's Keep to serve as my aunt's secretary," Kate said. She displayed her inky cuff ruefully. "As you see, it can be quite a messy business."

Eleanor's cornflower-blue eyes widened. "Your aunt's . . . *secretary*? But I thought you were . . . I mean, I had hoped we could be . . ."

Kate lifted her chin. Eleanor's voice trailed off before she finished her sentence, but her meaning was clear. She had thought that Kate was a member of the leisure class, just as she was, and that therefore they could be friends. Kate felt a sharp disappointment. But she should not blame Eleanor, who could hardly help being brought up to despise honest work, and to think of it as something done only by her inferiors. *She* was the one who was at fault. She should never have allowed Eleanor to think that she was something other than what she was.

"I'm sorry if I deceived you, Eleanor," she said quietly. "I did not come to Bishop's Keep to be a lady of leisure." She hesitated, hoping that there might still be a chance for a friendship. "But if you were about to suggest that we go for a walk or a short drive some afternoon, I am sure that Aunt Sabrina would be glad to let me take an hour."

"Certainly," Aunt Sabrina said warmly. "I am only sorry I did not think to suggest it myself. I—"

"Excuse me, mum." The door had opened to admit Amelia, hesitant, and without the tea cakes. "There's someone t'see yer, mum, but I misdoubt that—"

"Stop blathering and show them in," Aunt Jaggers snapped.

Amelia frowned uncertainly. "But he's a constable, mum."

Aunt Jaggers's face grew dark. "Then send him to the kitchen."

Aunt Sabrina intervened. "Did he say what his errand was, Amelia?"

Amelia's head bobbed. "He said 'twas news, mum. Important news."

"Then show him in, please," Aunt Sabrina said.

In a moment Amelia reappeared. With her was a portly man, balding, with a pockmarked face. His navy serge uniform was grimy, his boots sheened with dust. He held a tall hat under one arm and a newspaper-wrapped parcel under the other. He looked uncertainly from one person to the other, as if unsure whom to address.

Aunt Sabrina relieved him of his uncertainty. "Good day, sir," she said. "I believe you have news, Constable—"

"Clay, mum," the man said, stepping forward. "From Chelmsford." Kate recognized the name of a town that the train had passed through, about thirty miles from London. "I'm some sorry t'intrude, mum, but I've brought somethin' t'was left f'r yer. I was on me way t' Dedham, y'see, an' thought it best t' bring it t'yer, rather than send it by post, seein' what it was."

"Something left for me?" Aunt Sabrina frowned. "How odd. I know no one in Chelmsford."

The constable shifted his bulk. "T'be sure, mum," he mumbled. "But happen that th' girl bin an' died yesternight 'n th' workhouse, y'see, an' she left—"

"The girl?" Aunt Sabrina spoke sharply. "What girl?"

The constable frowned. He managed to secure his hat under the same arm that held the parcel, and fished in his pocket, pulling out a soiled scrap of paper. "Name o' Jenny, 'twere," he said, reading from it. "Jenny Blyly."

Suddenly there was a piercing shriek, the cry of a soul in torment. All eyes in the room went to Amelia.

"Not Jenny!" she cried. "Dear God, not Jenny!"

Cook stood in the kitchen, staring down at the opened parcel on the table. "An' how'd she die?" she asked, her voice a brittle thread.

The constable lifted the mug of hot tea Nettie had given him. "In th' workhouse," he said. He looked up. "Th babe died afore her."

Amelia's muffled sobbing could be heard from the corner by the fire. Harriet was huddled beside her knee, trying to comfort her. Pocket stood an uneasy distance away, his face working. Mudd sat at the other end of the table, head bowed.

Cook lifted the ragged dress from the table. That and the green knitted shawl and the worn shoes were all that was in the parcel. "Nothin' else?" she asked the constable.

"I'm her aunt. I'm who has t' tell her pore mother how she ended."

He countered her question with one of his own. "D'you know some un called Tom Potter?"

Amelia's sobbing grew louder. "I do," Cook said shortly. "Why?"

"T'was a note fer him in th' pocket o' th' dress," the constable said. He fished in his trousers. "Here 'tis."

Cook took the crumpled bit of paper from his hand. "I'll see't he gits it," she said.

The constable had been gone several minutes before Cook roused herself to smooth out the note. She went to the lamp and held it up so that the poorly penciled script was illuminated by the golden light. Finally, she turned and spoke into the silence.

"Nettie," she said, "fetch me shawl. I've an errand."

Nettie's mouth made a round O. "But there's the dinner!" she said. "Mrs. Jaggers'll—"

"Jaggers kin go t' bloody hell," Cook said fiercely. "That's where the Lord sends the murderers of pore babes and young girls!"

Mudd lifted his head and spoke. "An' if th' Lord don't dispatch 'er quick," he said through clenched teeth, "I will."

From the doorway, there was a stifled gasp. Cook looked up to see the startled face of the young Miss Ardleigh.

Aunt Sabrina was not eager to talk about what had happened, but Kate managed to wring a little information out of her that evening, after they finished the cold supper that Nettie and Harriet scraped together in the unexplained absence of Cook. Jenny Blyly, barely nineteen, had been Amelia's predecessor. She had disappeared six months before under circumstances that Aunt Sabrina would not divulge but which seemed to involve Aunt Jaggers. In fact, having heard what she had in the kitchen, it was clear to Kate that the servants blamed Aunt Jaggers for Jenny's disappearance and her death.

But even though Aunt Sabrina would not discuss the details of Jenny's story, its sad outline was not hard for Kate to reconstruct. The girl must have become pregnant. Aunt Jaggers, discovering the fact, would have heaped recriminations on her head and discharged her on the spot, with no hope of a character. Penniless, despairing, she had found her way to the Chelmsford workhouse, where her newborn baby had died and she shortly after.

Jenny's tale was the stuff of Beryl Bardwell's novels, and under other circumstances, Kate might have pursued the details with a writer's interested curiosity. But echoing in her mind was Amelia's tortured cry and Cook's impassioned consignment of Aunt Jaggers to hell. And when she saw Mudd the next morning, face impassive, eyes hooded, arranging the creamed eggs and kidney on the breakfast sideboard, Kate remembered his ominous threat with a shiver of cold foreboding. She was too practical for presentiment, but even she could not escape the certainty that something dreadful was going to happen at Bishop's Keep.

20

"The reputation of Scotland Yard was unfortunately
sullied by corruption during the latter eighteen-
hundreds. One day the superintendent met a stranger
who resembled a former Yard official. 'Were you
not on our staff?' he inquired. To which the stranger
replied, 'No, thank God, I have never sunk that low.' "

—GEORGE DAINSBURY
Police in Great Britain

ON THE DAY following his call with Eleanor at Bishop's
Keep, Charles was once again taking photographs at
the dig. It was interesting, and he enjoyed chatting with
Fairfax, who was a curmudgeonly old fogey but for all
that, a dedicated archaeologist. After Kathryn Ardleigh's
unauthorized incursion, he had instituted an entire set
of new regulations that constrained horses, police, and
women from straying onto the site of the dig.

Kathryn Ardleigh. Charles could not think of her
without smiling, remembering the sight of her in the
doorway of Sir Archibald's field tent, neatly garbed in
what the dress reformers called "rational attire," a divided

skirt actually suited to freedom of movement. And the next day, appearing in front of callers in a rumpled shirtwaist and inky cuffs. Of course, as a man, Charles did not know much about women's costumes. But he knew what he liked: dress with a practical bent. He admitted to thinking that the bustle (before it went out of fashion a few years before) was the most absurd appendage a woman might strap onto her derriere, and the corset almost as ridiculous. He had the suspicion that Kathryn Ardleigh would be loath to wear either, especially if she spent much of her time, as it seemed she did, at secretarial labors. It appeared that she was a woman who resisted the dictates of fashion and made up her own mind about the way she dressed. He wondered if this unconventionality reflected her general outlook on life, and he hoped she had not been too deeply offended by Fairfax's misogynistic tirade.

In addition to photographing the dig, Charles also called from time to time at the police station in the center of town. There, he began to perceive that Inspector Wainwright, while an intelligent and dedicated policeman, was handicapped by a lack of trained assistants. Battle, Trabb, and two other inexperienced PCs were the whole of the force in his ward, and their efforts were chiefly dedicated to patrolling the streets, dealing with rowdy soldiers from the nearby army barracks, and directing carriage traffic. As a result, any investigation was necessarily limited to accumulating basic facts from cursory examination or direct interview. Given this situation, Charles thought, any criminal who found himself in the Colchester jail probably got there through his own criminal stupidity or through sheer bad luck. His suspicion was confirmed by the paucity of evidence offered at the coroner's inquest, which returned a verdict of unlawful killing by person or persons unknown.

So it was that after several unsatisfying discussions with the pessimistic Inspector Wainwright, Charles concluded that, if it were left to the Colchester constabulary, the unfortunate victim's identity would never be known. And without that, the murderer's identity would remain undiscovered. True, PC Trabb had been sent round with the photos of the dead man to the stationmaster, the cabbies, and all the inns, but his circuit was to no avail. No one would admit to recognizing the dead man. And while the Colchester *Exchange* regaled its readers with the lurid details of the killing and pleaded for information from the public, no informants came forward. Sensing that Wainwright had arrived at a dead end, Charles tentatively advanced the suggestion that perhaps this was a case for the Criminal Investigation Department of the Metropolitan Police—Scotland Yard.

Inspector Wainwright bridled. "The Defective Department?" he snorted. Charles recognized the reference to an infamous *Punch* cartoon of a few years before that had expressed the commonly held view that the CID was at bottom corrupt, as well as incompetent. "Had the Yard in on a killin' three years ago," Wainwright added gloomily. "Didn't come up with a bloody thing. Waste of time. Won't do it unless I'm ordered to."

Charles was sympathetic to the inspector's dilemma, but that did not take them any farther toward solving the crime. Concluding that the floundering Wainwright was not going to ask for a helping hand, he determined on his own private course of action. So the next morning, instead of driving as usual directly to the dig, he took copies of his photographs and began to retrace the steps of PC Trabb, going first to the railway station, where he hoped to meet someone who remembered the dead gentleman.

"Nope, never seen 'im," was the stationmaster's reply to the question Charles asked when he presented the full-face image of the deceased through the painted metal of the grille window. "When'd yer say 'e come?"

131

When Charles mentioned the date, the stationmaster cocked his head. "Well, I never seen 'im," was his reply. He leaned his elbows on the wooden counter and adjusted his green eyeshade. "But that's 'cause I wudn't at work that partic'lar day, which I'd've cert'nly said t' the PC if he'd had th' wit t' ask. Goods wagon rolled over me foot an' laid me up proper. 'Twas Jarrett wot was here in me place." He turned and raised his voice over the hiss and clatter of the departing train. "Fetch Jarrett."

When Jarrett was fetched, he proved to be a tall, thin man with a bulbous nose, bright red, and a bumpy chin. He stared at the photo for a moment. "Yep, I seen 'im," he allowed helpfully. " 'Cept 'is eyes was hopen at th' time."

The stationmaster gave Jarrett a scornful glance. " 'Course his eyes was open, Jarrett. This here's a pitchur of a *corpse*."

"Can you recall anything special about the man?" Charles asked. "How do you come to remember him?"

Jarrett stretched his lips over teeth as yellow as antique ivory. " 'E cudn't speak th' Queen's English. Frenchy fella, 'e was, all slick talk an' smiley unner that waxed mustache. Wanted a 'orse to 'ire."

Charles frowned. "A cab?"

Jarrett wagged his head from side to side. "A 'orse to 'ire," he repeated emphatically. "An' a carriage, a-corse. Said 'ee'd drive 'isself. Said as 'ow 'e didn't trust cabbies. 'E's right, too, 'if I *am* th' one wot says. 'Alf th' cabbies cheat, partic'larly if th' fare's a for'ner. Drive 'em ten miles at ten pence a mile, jus' t' get t' th' pub around th' corner. Bucks is th' worst, a-corse," he added confidentially. "Them wot lost their license an' only drive at night, when they c'n rob th' fares wot 're drunk or asleep." He laid a grubby finger beside his nose, so flagrant it seemed to glow with its own light. "Know fer a fac', I do. Me brother-in-law's a cabbie. Many's th' story 'e tells 'bout bucks an' baddies, chargin' 'xorb'ant fares an' givin' short change. An' racin', an' haccidents, an' sick 'orses, and—"

"Which jobmaster'd yer send th' bloke to?" The stationmaster intervened, bringing Jarrett's recital to a full stop. "Edge or Prodger?"

"Prodger," Jarrett replied. He looked at Charles. "On North 'ill. Tell 'im Jarrett sent yer," he added. " 'E'll treat yer right. 'E's me wife's second cousin."

"I see," Charles said thoughtfully. "Perhaps I should visit Prodger."

"Indeed, Sir Charles." The female voice, deep and rich, came from behind him. "I think that would be a fine idea."

Charles turned, removing his hat. "Good afternoon, Miss Ardleigh," he said. "How coincidental that we should meet again." She was not wearing her rational dress today, he noticed, merely a dark suit and sensible boots.

"Yes," she said. "Miss Marsden has gone to London for a day or two. She invited me to ride to the station with her, and I agreed. Her train has just departed. I came in to—" Her glance went quickly to the stationmaster, and back again. "To obtain a new timetable," she said.

"I see," Charles said, surmising from her look that it was a conversation with the stationmaster she had come for, rather than a timetable. He could not believe that her presence here was merely coincidental. She had shown an unusual interest in the murder, had appeared at the dig— without adequate explanation of her presence—and now at the station. Was she following the same trail he was following? His question was answered in the next breath.

"I wonder if I might accompany you on your visit to Mr. Jarrett's wife's second cousin," she said in a serious tone. "I must confess to wishing to meet the man."

Charles took her elbow and drew her outside. "And I must confess," he said in a low voice, "to some curiosity. To my recollection, Miss Ardleigh, we have had four encounters, and in each of them you have evidenced a great fascination for murder. Why is this?"

She turned to face him, her hazel-green eyes clear, her expression straightforward. "I was afraid you would ask me that question," she said, "and I wish that I could answer you. Will you accept that I cannot, Sir Charles, and be satisfied?"

He looked at her for a moment. She was not the kind of woman he could easily persuade to tell him what she did not wish him to know. Perhaps it would be good to have her where he could watch her. By so doing, he might be able to deduce for himself her reason for pursuing this case with such an uncommon interest.

"Very well, then," he said, resigned. He turned toward the street. "You may come along. I have a chaise. It is full of photographic gear, but there is room for a passenger."

"Thank you," she said. She stopped at the carriage stand to ask Eleanor's coachman to wait until she returned, and then climbed into the chaise beside Sir Charles without waiting for his hand in assistance.

21

"Yankee Doodle came to town
Riding on a pony:
Stuck a feather in his cap
And called it Macaroni."

KATE HAD TOLD the truth—part of it, at any rate. She had come to the station with Eleanor. Miss Marsden had stopped in briefly the day before, having apparently decided that her friendship with Kate was not to be sacrificed on the altar of Kate's secretarial labors. She had invited Kate to spend the weekend with her in London. Kate had demurred. She proposed accompanying Eleanor to the train instead, which would take only the morning, and not several days.

But Kate did not intend to leave the station the instant Eleanor's train departed, for the same thought had occurred to her that had obviously occurred to Sir Charles: that the murdered man could hardly have arrived in Colchester without attracting some notice, and that the railway station would be the logical place to inquire. Even though Aunt Sabrina had requested her to leave off her investigation, Kate had not *promised* that she would do so. In any event, Beryl Bardwell's curiosity was far stronger than Kate's sense of propriety. So it was that she found herself seated next to Sir Charles, driving up the steep incline of North Hill in pursuit of a dead man.

Prodger proved to be the largest jobmaster in Colchester. The shop, a drafty wooden building at the rear of a cobbled yard filled with horses and carriages, sheltered a number of vehicles—growlers, Victorias, barouches, phaetons, carts, chaises, broughams. Kate saw that it also housed a substantial stable, a carriage- and harness-repair shop, and, at the rear, a smithy with a smoking forge from which a rhythmic clanging could be heard, punctuated by shouts and a loud hissing. Prodger himself was stout and affable, and his ruddy, full-featured countenance conveyed the satisfied good humor of a man for whom life is going according to plan. He had barely to glance at the photograph Sir Charles held out to recognize it.

"T' be sure," he said, stroking his grizzled chin whiskers. "The gentleman hired a chaise and a gray geldin'. Was quite partic'lar as t' horse and harness. Wanted somethin' smart." His chin whiskers took on a knowing look. "T' impress a lady, I surmised," he added, inclining his head in Kate's direction.

"Did he say anything about the gelding's lameness when he returned it?" Sir Charles inquired.

Prodger pushed out his lips and pulled them in again, giving thought to his reply. "Well, now," he came out with finally, "I can't say as the gentleman was the one who returned it. The rig was left here the next mornin', accordin' to prearrangements. As to lame, Jip'll know."

Jip was the stableboy, a fresh, bright-eyed lad of fifteen, full of the importance of his work. "Ay, Mr. Prodger, sir, th' 'orse *was* 'alf-lame, 'e was." He wiped his hands on his blue denim apron. "But 'e's right agin now, never worry. T'was only a splinter in 'is left 'ind 'oof, an' easily took care of."

Kate watched as Sir Charles turned around, to look at a row of light two-wheeled chaises arranged along one side of the main building. The second carriage leaned tipsily to the right, one red-painted wheel missing. He studied it for a moment as if he were measuring it with his glance. "Where," he asked, "is the wheel that belongs to that chaise?"

Prodger jerked his head in the direction of the smith. "Trotter's got it," he said. "He's ironin' it."

"Ironing it?" Kate asked, wondering how one ironed a metal wheel rim.

"Ironing it!" Sir Charles exclaimed. "For God's sake, man, that wheel's *evidence!*"

Kate stared at him, uncomprehending. "Evidence?" she asked. But Sir Charles paid no attention to her. He hastened after Prodger to the smithy, with Kate trailing along behind. Trotter was standing over a wooden wheel, about to cut the iron tire with a chisel. Behind him, a group of workmen were creating a terrible din, clanging and shouting.

"Stop!" Charles shouted, holding up his hand.

The smith looked up, hammer poised over the chisel. His face was charcoal, his eyes white marbles. "Sez 'oo?" he retorted, and struck the chisel a ringing blow.

Behind the smith, Kate saw that two journeymen and two apprentices were working on another, larger wheel, which rested flat on a circular stone platform. A red-hot iron rim was being fitted to the wooden wheel and driven into place with blows of the journeymen's sledges. The apprentices doused the smoking rim with water from sprinkling cans. Steam replaced smoke with a great hissing and a stench of charred wood, while the iron tire contracted violently and the wheel snapped and creaked. Kate watched with fascination. So *this* was how one ironed a wheel.

Sir Charles turned to Mr. Prodger. "I need to examine the wheel," he said loudly, over the noise. "The last man to hire the carriage from which it came was murdered."

"Murthered?" the smith exclaimed, and dropped his chisel.

Kate stared at Sir Charles. How could he be so sure?

Prodger raised his hand to quiet the workers. Into the sudden silence, he said, "Murdered? D'you mean that the gent I read about in the *Exchange* was Monsoor Armand?"

"That was the name of the man who hired this carriage?" Sir Charles asked.

"That was the name he give me for the ledger," Prodger replied cautiously.

Armand, Kate thought—a French name. A Frenchman with a scarab ring.

"I would like to photograph this wheel," Sir Charles said. "It is evidence in a murder case. I am assisting Inspector Wainwright," he added, by way of explanation.

"Wainwright needs assistin'." Prodger's chin whiskers quivered disdainfully. Then, with an air of resignation, he addressed the smith. "Well, Trotter, I don't suppose it'll harm that wheel to let the gentleman make a photograph of it."

By way of answer, the smith leaned the wheel against a tree and turned his back on it, going to oversee the progress of the men with the sledges and sprinkling cans. While Kate waited beside the wheel, Sir Charles went to the chaise, got his camera and tripod, and set them up. As she watched curiously, he unfolded his ivory rule, propped it against the wheel, and photographed the wheel and the rule, following that with several close-up views of the break in the iron rim. Then he marked the spot where the break touched the ground, carefully rolled the wheel one revolution until the break touched again, and measured the distance with his rule.

"Twelve feet seven inches," he muttered to himself. He turned to Prodger. "I would like to photograph and examine the chaise from which this wheel came."

Prodger led him back to the row of carriages. "What I want to know," he said, as Sir Charles set up his camera, "is how you knew which wheel you was after."

"The break in the rim," Sir Charles said, taking a photo. "It left a mark at the scene of the crime, which revealed itself in the photographs I took. As good as a fingerprint for identification."

"Fingerprint?" Prodger asked, mystified. "What's that?"

Kate spoke quickly, forestalling Sir Charles's inevitable lecture. "The distinctive mark left by a person's fingertips," she said. "A fingerprint can be used to distinguish one person from another."

Prodger grunted. "Seems to me a man's face ought to be bettern' his fingers, for that purpose."

Sir Charles straightened up. "Did Monsieur Armand offer any identification?" he asked, changing the plate in the camera. "An address, perhaps?"

"He offered th' hire in advance, an' a generous tip," Prodger replied with dignity. "In this business, that were sufficient identif'cation."

"Did he mention his purpose for traveling to Colchester?" Kate asked. She ignored Sir Charles's irritated frown. He wasn't the only one who could question an informant. "Or the name of someone he planned to meet while he was here?"

The jobmaster pulled his mouth first to one side, then the other. "He asked after a street—Queen Street, I believe. But I disremember th' number."

Kate felt a stab of excitement. Queen Street! Perhaps they were getting somewhere!

Sir Charles stepped out from behind the tripod. "Would you object to my examining the interior of the chaise?" he asked.

"Examine all you like," Prodger said with a shrug. "But our carriages is clean swept after ev'ry hire." He dragged over a wooden block and placed it under the axle of the missing-wheeled chaise, balancing the vehicle. "If it'll help t' have a look, climb up."

Kate looked on while Sir Charles examined the carriage carefully. Prodger was right. The floor had been swept, the leather seat polished, the side panels wiped clean. But on the smooth handle of the whip, Sir Charles pointed out a clear fingerprint, which he photographed. "Well, that appears to be it," he said, stepping out of the chaise.

"You've missed the feather," Kate said.

Sir Charles frowned. "Feather?"

Kate picked it out of the corner of the seat and held it out. The feather was of an iridescent blue hue, such as she had never before seen. It was broken.

"Aha!" Sir Charles exclaimed. With a triumphant smile, he grasped it and held it up to the light. After studying it for a moment, he folded it into a piece of paper and put the paper carefully into his pocket.

Kate frowned. "You're welcome," she said pointedly, feeling in her heart the unfairness of playing Watson to this self-absorbed Holmes.

Sir Charles turned to look at her for a long moment, his smile fading. "Forgive me," he said, very seriously. "Thank you, Miss Ardleigh, for spying the feather. You have sharp eyes."

Kate smiled.

"What c'n you tell from a brok'n feather?" Mr. Prodger asked.

"That depends upon whether it is possible to locate the remainder of it," Sir Charles replied.

"Indeed," Kate said, "and upon who has possession of it."

Mr. Prodger gave his whiskers a rueful shake. "I've heard of lookin' for a needle in a haystack, but lookin' for one partic'lar feather in a town the size of Colchester—" He barked a laugh. "All I c'n say, sir, is if you find it, you're a sight sharper'n Wainwright. He couldn't find a feather if the bloody thing was stuck in his cap. Or ticklin' his arse." He looked at Kate. "Beggin' yer pardon, ma'am."

22

"Until the end of the nineteenth century, British jurisprudence was ruled by oral and documentary evidence. New investigative technologies, such as fingerprints, ballistics, and toxicology were often regarded as irrelevant and even frivolous by those whose task it was to summon the criminal before the bar. What counted was the criminal's confession to obtain."

—ALISTAIR CARRS,
Criminal Detection in the Nineteenth Century

ON SATURDAY MORNING, Charles applied himself to solving a murder. The jobmaster Prodger had given the victim a name—Monsieur Armand. Whether it was the man's real name remained to be seen. Charles offered the information to Inspector Wainwright, whom he found once again seated at the small table in the chilly basement office, surrounded by stacks of papers.

"Armand?" Wainwright asked irritably, when Charles had finished the narrative of his investigations. The pallid light fell upon the table through the dingy window, illuminating a wire basket containing official memoranda, an inkstand and fragment of much-used blotter, and a Prince Albert red-and-gilt ashtray filled with a quantity of cigarette butts. The inspector scraped back his straight wooden chair, rose, and went to warm his hands over the kettle, which was heating on the gas burner.

"Armand," Charles repeated. He took the other chair, which was missing two of its wooden turnings.

Wainwright rubbed his thick hands together. His brown wool coat was worn at the elbows and in want of brushing, and his collar had already seen several days' service. "Don't know that a name takes us anywhere," he said, his voice heavy with an irreversible gloom. He took the tea canister from the shelf and shook out the last spoonful of loose tea into a cracked white china teapot. He poured hot water from the kettle into the pot, took down a tin of My Lady's Tea Biscuits, and returned once more to his chair. "We already knew he was French, from the coat label. 'Armand' probably isn't the real name."

"Perhaps," Charles said. "But I have found something else that may help us." He took out a piece of paper and unfolded it carefully.

The inspector opened the biscuit tin. "What's that?"

"A fragment of feather," Charles said, turning it over with a pencil. "Certainly a nonindigenous species. *Pavo christatus*, I believe. From the breast of a male bird. This specimen does not bear the familiar 'eye' of the splendid tail plumage, of course, but the iridescent blue color reveals its—"

Wainwright pulled out several crumbly biscuits and put them on the table. "Where'd you find it?" He gestured at the biscuits. "Tea will be ready shortly. Have a biscuit."

"No, thank you," Charles said. "It was found in the chaise hired by the victim." By Miss Ardleigh, he thought to himself, but did not say. The interested, interesting Miss

Ardleigh, who absolutely refused to relate the reason for her interest.

The inspector made a growling noise deep in his throat.

"Observe that the feather is broken," Charles said, pointing. "With the aid of a microscope, it would be possible to match it to—"

"Haven't got a microscope." Wainwright picked up a biscuit and bit it. It crumbled in his hand. With a muttered curse, he dropped the crumbs on the floor. He got up, fetched the teapot and two cups, and brought them to the table. "Anything else?"

Charles retrieved the feather, folded it into its paper, and put it back in his coat pocket. From his portfolio, he took an enlarged photograph. "This," he said, laying it on the table. "Tell me, Inspector, has Monsieur Armand yet been buried?"

"Yesterday." The inspector squinted suspiciously at the photograph. "What is it?"

"It is the enlargement of a fingerprint on the whip handle of the chaise hired by the victim." Charles picked up a pencil and pointed to a ridged whorl. "Observe this unique configuration."

"And just what d'you expect to prove with that?" As Wainwright picked up the teapot and began to pour, his voice was laden with something like scorn.

"It is regrettable that the corpse has been buried. If it were to be exhumed and the man's fingerprints compared to—"

Wainwright set down the teapot so smartly that hot tea splashed onto the photograph. "Exhumed!" he exclaimed.

Charles retrieved the photo hastily. "Have you read Mark Twain's *Pudd'nhead Wilson*?"

The inspector stared at him.

Charles tried a different tack. "It is unfortunate that fingerprints are not generally in use. But with the proper equipment and training, an astute police officer like yourself could make quite a name—"

"Not got proper equipment," Wainwright growled, picking up his cup, "and not likely to get it." He blew on it, bitterly. "Have to buy even my own tea and biscuits. The superintendent won't give me a farthin' for fingerprints or photos or feathers, when he won't give me a telephone or a typewriter. Or a microscope. Of course," he added with ill-concealed resentment, "a learned gentleman like yourself wouldn't understand that."

Charles frowned. He felt, he thought, the same frustration that Dr. John Snow must have felt forty years before, when he tried to explain his theory of the transmission of typhoid to the Ministry of Public Health. Such stubborn unwillingness to accept anything new!

"But my dear fellow," he said urgently, "if this fingerprint does not belong to the victim, it must belong to the *killer.* Don't you see? We have here the opportunity to establish—"

"A confession," Wainwright said into his teacup.

"Beg pardon?" Charles asked.

"A confession." The inspector set his cup down. "That's what we need to solve this murder. That's what a jury would understand."

"I see," Charles said. He cleared his throat. "I wonder, though," he said mildly, "just how a confession is to be obtained from a killer who has so far eluded detection?"

"Your tea's gettin' cold," the inspector said. "Drink up."

23

"Glendower: I can call spirits from the vasty deep.
Hotspur: Why so can I, or so can any man; But will
they come when you do call for them?"
—WILLIAM SHAKESPEARE
Henry IV, Part I, III, i

ON SATURDAY AFTERNOON, Kate, as a proposed neophyte,
was to be introduced to the Order of the Golden Dawn.
She and Aunt Sabrina drove to Colchester, where the Temple
of Horus was to meet at Number Seven Keenan Street.

As they rode through the warm autumn sunshine,
past fields hazy with the smoke of burning stubble, Kate
considered whether she should tell Aunt Sabrina that she
and Sir Charles had the day before discovered the name
of the dead Frenchman. But Aunt Sabrina seemed to be
in quite a gay mood, talking animatedly about this and
that. Perhaps she was relieved that the matter of the dead
man was behind them. In any event, Kate hated to bring it
up again, and to disclose her mischief. Aunt Sabrina had
terminated the investigation. If she knew that her niece
had violated her expressed wish by going detecting with
Sir Charles, she would be deeply disappointed.

Furthermore, Kate told herself, there was nothing concrete to report. That the dead man had given the name of Armand to Mr. Prodger meant very little. It could have been a false name. No, the only *real* evidence they had turned up was the fingerprint and the blue feather. And the name of a street—Queen Street—which, on the one hand, might have been the murdered man's destination and, on the other, might have nothing to do with his death. Kate would not know unless she could go there herself and inquire, and she could not for the life of her think how she might accomplish that.

But although the jaunt seemed to have yielded little useful information, Kate could not regret the fact that she had gone. For one thing, Beryl Bardwell had enjoyed the opportunity to exercise her wits. For another, Kate had enjoyed the hour she spent with Sir Charles, observing his methods of patient and painstaking analysis. She had not thought that so much was to be learned from a single wheel.

As Sir Charles drove her back to the Marsden carriage, waiting at the railway station, Kate had renewed her request to see the photographs of the dead man, somewhat diffidently, since her aunt had instructed her not to pursue the matter. To that request, she added that she would like to see the photographs of the wheel print that he had taken at the site. In reply to his surprised, "Why?" she had replied evasively, "I hope it is not too much trouble." She could not tell him that Beryl Bardwell was toying with the idea of using a broken wheel as a clue to the solution of a murder.

Number Seven Keenan Street was a three-story brick house, with a modest frontage on the street. The parlor and the dining room directly behind it were quite crowded, Kate saw, and she thought as she was introduced to her hostess that the gathering looked more like an afternoon *soiree* than a meeting of magicians. Beryl Bardwell, who viewed the afternoon as a time for research, was making mental notes.

"Miss Ardleigh, my dear." Mrs. Farnsworth extended her hand with a warm smile. "It is kind of your aunt to bring you. She says you are making wonderful progress in your research."

"Research?" Kate asked. She was momentarily startled, before she realized that Mrs. Farnsworth was referring to her secretarial work, not Beryl Bardwell's covert inquiry, of which Mrs. Farnsworth herself was the current object. "Oh, yes. The membership lists."

"Indeed," Mrs. Farnsworth replied. "The Order is growing so fast that it is well-nigh impossible to keep account of its membership." She smiled easily at Aunt Sabrina. "When you leave, my dear Sabrina, be sure to take with you the packet of letters and other documents I have assembled for you."

Mrs. Farnsworth was oddly fascinating, Kate thought. Her figure was petite, sprite like, almost a child's figure, but it was her face, under a wealth of brown hair, that captured and held the viewer's attention. Her luminous eyes were brown, with large, dark irises; her lips were full and sensual; her mercurial mouth seemed capable of almost any expression, and with every change of expression her face seemed completely remade. Unlike her guests, most of whom were conventionally garbed, her costume was dramatic: an emerald green robe with a low-cut gauze-sleeved green bodice, decorated with blue-green feathers with exotic markings. She wore a gold pendant at her throat which, Kate saw in an instant of startled recognition, was similar to her aunt's.

Mrs. Farnsworth's theatrical dress was no doubt explained by the fact that she was a retired actress. Quite recently retired, it seemed, from the collection of colorful playbills Kate had remarked in the hallway. Two of George Bernard Shaw's were prominently featured, *Widowers' Houses* and *Arms and the Man*, and Shakespeare's *As You Like It*, which had apparently enjoyed a long run at the St.

James. Mrs. Farnsworth had recently changed her name, it seemed: on the playbills, she appeared as Florence Faber. Kate couldn't help but think she must have made a fetching Rosalind.

Like the lady, Mrs. Farnsworth's parlor was dramatically decorated. The plum-colored walls were hung with Oriental-style draperies and ivory fans; sculptures of Egyptian deities stood on painted columns in the corners; and hieroglyphic paintings—copied in the British Museum, Aunt Sabrina confided in a whisper, by Mrs. Farnsworth herself—occupied prominent places in the dimly lighted room. The Oriental carpets that overspread the floor were of rich blues and purples, although they were worn, as were the furnishings. It was the room of someone who had a more exotic taste than ready money.

But the room was quite small, and its decor was hardly visible in the crush of people. Aunt Sabrina made her way through the crowd, murmuring greetings here and there, Kate a step behind. They paused on the outskirts of a group gathered in front of the fireplace. Dominating the group was Oscar Wilde, a tall man, several inches over six feet and portly. His dark brown hair fell nearly to his shoulders and his lips were full and finely chiseled in a face that spoke of dissipation. He was elegantly dressed in a lavender tailed coat, flowered waistcoat, and white silk cravat, loosely tied. Listening, Kate thought that his sentences, although they were clearly extemporaneous, seemed as perfectly composed as if he had constructed them in writing and delivered them from memory.

The conversation was not about some mystical topic, but on the subject of America. "Of course," Mr. Wilde said, drawling out the words with wry humor, "if one had enough money to go to America, one would not go." With languid grace, he tapped his cigarette into the fireplace behind him.

"I fear you are right, Wilde," said the tweedy, heavyset gentleman beside him. He adjusted his polka-dot tie with one massive, beringed hand. "I will be launching an American tour in a few days, but I must say I am still smarting over what happened with my *Study in Scarlet*. Virtually purloined by Lippincott."

Kate looked at the man, surprised. He must be Conan Doyle! How odd. In her imagination, the author had resembled his character—lean and gaunt, with piercing eyes and a hawk like beak of a nose. But Mr. Doyle was clearly fond of his table. He was stout and hearty, with the thick hands and the wide, flat nose of a boxer. He had the appearance of a man who had never read a book in his life and had not noticed the absence.

"Ah, yes," Wilde said lazily, leaning one elbow against the green marble mantel and pulling at his jowl with his fingers. "Until quite recently, American publishers took what they liked without the annoyance of parting with their money." He rolled his eyes dramatically. "Americans. Always in hot pursuit of the next moment, as if they were catching a train. It is a state of affairs not favorable to poetry."

"Perhaps," Kate said quietly, "Americans do not require poetry to accompany their affairs."

All eyes shifted to her. The corner of Doyle's mouth quirked. Another man—intense and dark-haired, with fine-cut intellectual features under heavy brows—smothered a laugh and ended by breaking into a violent cough that shook his double pince-nez from his nose.

Wilde cocked one eyebrow, scantily amused. "Quite good, *quite*, quite good, my dear lady," he drawled. He paused, letting the silence lengthen while Kate felt her cheeks redden. "An American, I presume." He turned to the dark-haired young man. "One can always distinguish American women by their exquisitely incoherent speech, Willie. Like exploding crackers. One is reminded of

149

Sheridan, in *The Rivals*. They are as 'headstrong as an allegory on the banks of the Nile.' "

The young man with the pince-nez spoke up. "I hardly think the lady's remark was incoherent, Oscar. In fact, I rather imagine she bested you." His voice held more than a hint of the Irish. His soft gray tie was inexpertly and crookedly tied, and he wore a small cluster of feathers in his lapel. Kate's eyes widened slightly when she saw them—blue feathers, bright blue, iridescent blue—and she realized that they were very like the feather she had found in the carriage. The young man smiled at Kate. "Well done, Miss . . ."

"Gentlemen," Aunt Sabrina said, "may I present my niece, Miss Kathryn Ardleigh. Mr. Wilde, Mr. Doyle, and Mr. Yeats. As you have guessed, gentlemen, Miss Ardleigh is an American by birth—"

"But Irish by nature, I perceive, as well as by name and appearance," Wilde interrupted elegantly. He took Kate's hand and bowed over it with an extravagant flourish. "My friend Willie Yeats is quite right, Miss Ardleigh. You have bested me. But I confess it willingly, for besting Oscar Wilde is allowed only to that exquisite divinity who boggles him with her beauty."

"Then I fear you are easily boggled, Mr. Wilde," Kate said, retrieving her hand. Her eyes fastened on Willie Yeats's blue feathers. "And therefore easily bested."

Wilde's eyebrows went up. Yeats chuckled dryly, and Kate realized that he must be the man for whom she was copying the cipher transcript. She would somehow have to pursue the matter of Yeats's feathers. But she was momentarily sidetracked by Conan Doyle's remark about *A Study in Scarlet*.

"Is it true about the copyright of your work, Mr. Doyle?" she asked, turning to him. "It was stolen?"

"Yes," Doyle allowed, "it was. Though to be fair, the theft was rather made up by what Lippincott paid me to write *The Sign of Four*." He coughed. "Don't know that the offer would've been quite so handsome if American readers hadn't already gotten onto *Scarlet.*"

"You certainly have many American readers," Kate said, thinking to turn the conversation toward the question she wanted to ask. "They have banded into Let's Keep Holmes Alive clubs to protest the unfortunate demise of your famous detective."

Doyle thrust his hands in his pockets. "Chap's dead," he said. "Let him rest."

"But why?" Kate persisted. "If one of my characters were to win such a fervent following, I do not believe I would dare to—"

Doyle's half smile was patronizing. "My dear young lady, I doubt you can understand the situation, not being an author."

"But I—" Kate checked herself on the brink of betraying Beryl Bardwell. "Perhaps you are right."

"The truth is that I am no longer interested in detective stories," Doyle remarked with a self-important air. "My aim is to write serious books. *Micah Clarke* is one such effort. Have you read it?"

"I must confess that I have not," Kate said.

"An admirable work, my dear Doyle," Wilde put in lazily, "if somewhat wearying. Still, one rather does enjoy robust adventure—when someone else does the adventuring."

"Holmes gets in the way of my other writing, y'see," Doyle said to Kate, ignoring Wilde. "And my psychic research, which is most interesting to me." He looked around. "Which of course is why I am here."

"Ghost-hunting," Yeats said with some scorn.

"My dear man," Doyle replied, raising his chin, "that is not an attribute one applies to the Society for Psychical Research."

Kate regarded him with interest. "But why can you not write both serious literature and detective stories?" she asked. "Surely the two are not exclusive."

Doyle spoke as if he were speaking to a child. "My dear young lady, you clearly do not understand the labors of authorship. The difficulty is that each short story needs as clear-cut and original a plot as a longish book would do." He frowned. "At any rate, Holmes is dead. Even if I wanted to bring the fellow back to life, I could not. He lies at the bottom of a vast precipice."

"But Sherlock Holmes can hardly remain dead," Kate objected pertly. "Your readers will not allow it. And I think it would not be difficult to call him from the vasty deep, sir."

Wilde's full lips curved slightly upward. "Ah, but will he come when you do call for him? *That*, dear Doyle, is the question."

"He will come," Kate said, "if you call in the right way. He should reappear in some interesting disguise, I think, so that the manner of his reappearance distracts attention from the fact of it. He should then explain to Dr. Watson that he sent Professor Moriarty into the dreadful chasm in his stead, perhaps with some sleight of hand, such as baritsu."

"Baritsu?" Doyle asked doubtfully.

"A form of Japanese wrestling," Kate said.

Mr. Yeats smiled. "The lady is ingenious, Doyle."

Doyle pulled his brows together. "You are forgetting the tracks," he said. "In *The Final Problem*, Dr. Watson observed that *two* persons went down the path and none returned."

Kate raised her brows. "I imagine that a man of Mr. Holmes's resourcefulness could scale a cliff or two. I also imagine that he might go into hiding to escape the Professor's confederates, while entrusting to his brother Mycroft the maintenance of his Baker Street lodgings. That would explain his absence from London and his failure to communicate with Dr. Watson."

Wilde's puffy-lidded eyes were amused. "As Holmes would say, my dear Doyle, 'The impression of a woman may be more valuable than the conclusion of an analytic reasoner.' " He pursed his lips. "There you have it, dear sir. The plot, trotted out *in toto*—or is it *en tutu?*" Ignoring Willie Yeats's groan, he added, "What do you say, Doyle, to Miss Ardleigh's spirited resurrection of Sherlock Holmes?"

Doyle shook his head, stubbornly beetle-browed. "Fellow's dead and dead he stays. I shan't have him bullying me for the rest of my days."

Wilde leaned toward Kate and lowered his voice confidentially. "I perceive, Miss Ardleigh, that we have hit upon our friend's sore spot. Like Frankenstein, he has created in Holmes a being with eternal life. Like Frankenstein, he cannot be rid of the monster. Such a fate is truly something to fear."

"Don't see what you're getting at," Doyle said. He looked around, scowling. "When's the séance?"

"Ah, yes," Wilde said. He turned to Mrs. Farnsworth, who had just come up. "I told him there was bound to be table rapping, Florence. When do we begin?"

"I am sorry, gentlemen," Mrs. Farnsworth said, "but there is to be no séance this afternoon."

"No séance!" Doyle protested.

Mrs. Farnsworth smiled. "If I had known that's what you wanted, Mr. Doyle, we could have arranged something." Her smile became playful. "But spirits certainly abound here. They may communicate with you if you make your willingness known. Do be on the lookout."

"Oh, I shall," Doyle said with enormous seriousness. "I shall indeed. No spirit shall get by me!"

Kate was suddenly seized with the urge to laugh.

24

"Errors, like feathers, on the surface flow;
She who would find the truth must dive below."
—AFTER CHARLES DRYDEN,
All for Love

WITH A MURMURED excuse to Aunt Sabrina and the others, Kate left the group and looked around, wondering suddenly why everyone had come. If Beryl Bardwell had expected to witness magical rites or meet unconventional people, she was disappointed, for the men and women crowding the rooms, with the exception of Mrs. Farnsworth and the effete Oscar Wilde, were quite ordinary in their dress and demeanor. The only interesting thing about them, she realized suddenly, was that most of the men wore a cluster of blue feathers in their buttonholes, while the women wore some item of exotic feather jewelry—feathery earrings, a brooch, a pendant.

She looked around her, trying not to stare. What was the significance of all these feathers? Was the feather she had discovered in the seat of the chaise connected to the feathers in this room? Or was it all simply some vast coincidence?

Kate ventured into the dining room, where an elaborate tea was laid out on the sideboard. She put a cucumber sandwich on a china plate, allowed a maid to draw a cup of tea from a large silver urn, and went to stand behind a leafy thicket of potted bamboo, where she could watch and form an opinion without being observed. Over the next few minutes, she counted no fewer than nine men arrive at the table wearing blue feather boutonnieres in their lapels.

She was distracted from her observations by Mrs. Farnsworth, who appeared at the table with a well-fed gentleman with neatly trimmed gray side-whiskers. Above the whiskers, his cheeks were a mottled red, and his gray brows were drawn together in a scowl. The two of them stood together on the other side of the bamboo, talking intently, so deeply engrossed in what they were saying that they paid little attention to their surroundings. Kate, feeling as invisible as one of the servants, moved a step closer.

"Damned charlatan," the gentleman exploded furiously. "How can he behave with such unfraternal ingratitude?" He hunched his shoulders inside his frock coat, and his mouth twisted. "I have been completely misled."

The cords of Mrs. Farnsworth's neck tightened, but when she spoke her voice was soft, her touch on the gentleman's arm delicate. "My dear Wynn, I do understand your dismay. But you must not allow Mathers's churlish behavior to distress you. I am sure that his accusations—"

"Are utterly unfounded!" the man exclaimed. "Reckless, baseless, unsubstantiated! And I shall prove it." His voice rose and his side-whiskers trembled with passion. "I shall *prove* it, in open court, if need be! I have documents attesting to the antiquity of the manuscripts. A letter from Woodford, an affidavit from the German translator—"

Mrs. Farnsworth made a small mouth. "But if you so openly answer the man's effrontery, do you not also open our Order to public challenge? That, I fear," she added with light reproach, "would be a disaster."

Mrs. Farnsworth's reproof was casual and the toss of her head perfectly artless. But Kate heard the artful modulations in her tone, and saw that her glance spoke even more subtly. The woman was a skilled actress. And there was a great deal of passion concealed by her art.

The gentleman pulled himself up. "But it will be a disaster if he makes this challenge public and I do not answer him!"

"Then we must do all in our power to keep the wretched man from making the challenge public," Mrs. Farnsworth said. Her tone was silken, but there was a barely definable edge. "If the confidence of the members is shaken, or the reputation of the Order tarnished in the eyes of others, we could all be ruined. There will be *no* public display." Kate had not the least idea what she meant, but the man appeared to understand and, reluctantly, to agree.

"Ah, very well," he said disgustedly. His face was flushed with anger and his neck bulged over his stiff wing collar. "I will agree to say nothing—at this time." He raised his voice slightly. "But I cannot promise for the future, Florence. I have my honor to consider, and my good name. If that miscreant Mathers continues to make unprincipled charges against me—"

"My dear, *dear* Wynn," Mrs. Farnsworth said with easy affection, "that is all I ask. A few weeks' reprieve, while I shepherd our fledgling group here in Colchester through its delicate formative phase. Our new temple will be consecrated shortly, and *then* you may have it out with Mathers and end his absurd challenge to Fräulein Sprengel's warrant and your authority." She stopped and looked up at the man. Her voice held a brittleness so slight it was almost indiscernible. "I believe you understand me."

The man puffed out his cheeks. "I do, my dear. Yes, of course I do. I certainly do. And I am prepared at any moment to defend—"

"Thank you." Mrs. Farnsworth smiled lightly, but there was a shadow in her eyes. "And where are the papers in question?"

A slight frown crossed the gentleman's florid face. "The papers? They were left with the other historical documents."

Mrs. Farnsworth's remarkably mobile face darkened into a frown. "Is that not . . . dangerous?"

The man made a harrumphing sound. "I hardly think so. Their significance is not apparent to—"

"You are quite right," Mrs. Farnsworth said, half to herself. "Their significance would only be apparent under the most expert examination, and that they will not receive." She reached up to touch his cheek with the tip of one finger. It was the lightest touch and hardly indiscreet, but it revealed a long-standing intimacy. The man impulsively caught her hand and kissed it.

"Thank you, my dear," he said fervently. "You have ever been the genius of my better self."

"Yes," she said. The man moved away into the crowd, leaving Mrs. Farnsworth standing alone, lost in thought. After a moment she seemed to recollect herself and stepped to the other side of the table, where she smilingly engaged in conversation with Vicar Barfield Talbot, whom Kate had been expecting to see. The vicar, too, was wearing a cluster of blue feathers. Kate waited her chance to slip unobserved out from behind the palm, only to bump immediately into Aunt Sabrina.

"Ah, here you are, Kathryn," Aunt Sabrina said. She looked around at the table, heavily laden with silver trays of olives ranked like fish scales, radishes arranged like the rays of the sun, and anchovies interlaced, basket-style, in an elaborate display. There were fine plates piled with meringues, jellies, and crystallized fruits, and the whole was centered with an elegant trifle. "Is this not a fine repast?" She picked up a small plate and began to help herself. "Oh, look—mushrooms, stuffed! I never miss a chance to eat mushrooms in any form."

At that moment, the vicar said an affectionate farewell to Mrs. Farnsworth and came toward them. "Good afternoon, my dear Miss Ardleigh," he said to Aunt Sabrina.

"My dear Vicar," Aunt Sabrina said warmly. She looped her arm through his and drew him closer. "And of course you know our proposed Neophyte, my niece Kathryn."

"Ah, Miss Ardleigh," the old man said. His bow was gallant. "I am glad to learn that you wish to join our Order, my dear. I applauded your aunt's wish to be reunited with you and to use your skills to our advantage, but I admit to feeling much more comfortable that the Order's historical material is in the hands of members. The Golden Dawn is an esoteric society, and its rituals must be guarded from the eyes of the world."

"Of course," Kate murmured, although she hadn't happened upon anything so far that the eyes of the world couldn't see. She wondered whether the Order's much-vaunted secrecy might be a smoke screen that concealed its lack of substance.

"Do you have any questions I might answer, my dear?" the vicar inquired.

"Yes," Kate said promptly. "Please tell me about the blue feathers you and the others are wearing. What is their significance?"

"Ah, yes, the feathers," the vicar said, touching his own feather cluster with a finger. "Our new temple has adopted the peacock as an emblem."

Of course! Kate had never seen a peacock feather, but she had read of the bird.

"For centuries," the vicar was saying, "the bird has represented immortality. The eyes depicted on its splendid tail feathers suggest the supernatural ability to see deeply into the spirit. And, of course, that is what we of the

Golden Dawn are about. Seeing deeply into our hearts, in search of our souls."

"I see," Kate said thoughtfully, wondering to herself whether she should convey this information to Sir Charles or keep it to herself.

Aunt Sabrina put her arm around Kate's shoulders. "You must come and be introduced, Kathryn. Annie Horniman wants to meet you, and Rachel Cracknell. And of course, our dear Dr. Westcott, the founder of our Order, for whom we all have such deep affection and respect." She smiled at the vicar. "If you will excuse us, Barfield."

"By all means," the vicar said, bowing. His eyes held a special warmth as he looked at Aunt Sabrina. "It is always good to see you once again, Sabrina. Soon, perhaps?"

"Indeed," Aunt Sabrina murmured, and took Kate's elbow.

After several other introductions and polite social conversation, Aunt Sabrina steered Kate toward a corner. "Dr. Westcott," she whispered in Kate's ear.

To Kate's surprise, Dr. Westcott proved to be the same man who had spoken so heatedly with Mrs. Farnsworth. But the mottled red had faded from his cheeks, and he smiled graciously when Aunt Sabrina introduced them.

"Welcome to our Order, Miss Ardleigh." His words were resonant, his sentences fully rounded.

"Kathryn is assisting me with our history," Aunt Sabrina put in. "She has an interest in ritual magic."

Dr. Westcott's look became stern. "You understand, I trust, that our magical practices are not parlor amusements. They are handed down from the ancients through a long line of individuals—priests—who communicate the sacred teaching to those who are willing to accept its esoteric discipline." He lifted his hand, as if in blessing, and his voice took on an even richer timbre. "This sacred work enables us to raise ourselves to an understanding of our inner truth, our unerring and divine genius."

159

Kate inclined her head, feeling almost obliged to say "Amen." She couldn't help wondering how Dr. Westcott's unerring and divine genius had allowed him to be misled by the miscreant Mathers.

And what, if anything, the Order's emblem had to do with the broken blue feather she had found in the carriage that had borne a man to his death.

25

> "'And yet you've gay gauntlets and blue feathers
> three!—'
> 'Yes: that's what we wear when we're ruined,' said
> he."
>
> —AFTER THOMAS HARDY,
> *The Ruined Maid*

GIVEN THE INSPECTOR'S chilly reception of his first two pieces of evidence, the feather and the fingerprint, Charles had not thought it helpful to mention the third: the name of the street for which Monsieur Armand had been bound. And since it did not seem likely that Wainwright would release either Sergeant Battle or PC Trabb to make inquiry in Queen Street, he decided to do it himself. On Monday morning he borrowed Bradford's saddle horse and rode to Colchester through a chilly gray drizzle. He left his horse at Taylor's Livery Stable and asked directions of a vendor of hot pies. Having purchased a fragrant, crusty pork pie, he ate it with relish as he walked.

Queen Street proved to be a residential street a stone's throw from the old castle. Chimney pots poured sooty smoke over roofs of gray slate that rose steeply above the narrow three- and four-story houses, closely spaced to conserve land. Charles noted with disapproval that here, as in the new suburbs of London, the roof lines of the ill-proportioned brick houses were interrupted at irregular intervals by gables, turrets, battlements, and dormers, so many and so varied that they confused the eye. The houses fronted directly on the street, so that there was not even the relief of a square of grass fenced by a few sprigs of privet.

Having arrived at his destination, Charles opened his portfolio and took out a photograph of the dead man. He looked once over his shoulder to ascertain that Miss Ardleigh was *not* following after him; then he climbed the first stoop and rang the bell. His summons was answered by a stiff-backed parlor maid with a long face, a trace of dark mustache over her upper lip, and the saddest eyes he had ever seen.

"Good day, miss," Charles said, raising his brown felt hat. "I am making inquiries for the police about—"

"Tradesman's entrance round back," the maid said. She gave his canvas coat a scornful glance and shut the door.

Charles frowned with irritation. His hand was poised to ring again, but he thought better of it. He would return later, and trust that a more receptive person might answer his knock. He went back down the stoop, out to the sidewalk, and up the stairs of the next house. This door was opened by a butler with a brilliant red nose. Taking no chances, Charles swiftly inserted his foot in the opening.

"I represent the police," he said, "in an inquiry of great importance." He held up the photograph. "This man is said to have visited a house on this street. Have you seen him?"

The butler sniffed. "I have not," he said with grave dignity. "Are you the police?"

"No," Charles said, "I merely—"

"Pray remove your foot, sir."

Charles held his ground. "I would like to inquire of other members of your household. Perhaps your mistress—"

The butler's right arm disappeared behind the door and reappeared again with a silver-tipped cane. "Your foot, sir," the butler said, and stabbed Charles's toe smartly.

The third door, which Charles approached with trepidation and a slight limp, was not answered at all. The fourth, however, was opened by a middle-aged man whom Charles took by his dress and manner to be the gentleman of the house. He was apparently on his way out, for he wore a velvet-collared chesterfield and held one end of a leather leash, the other end of which was attached to a fluffy white poodle about the size of a lady's muff, furiously yapping. When he saw Charles, he looked alarmed.

"If it's the money you're after," he said over the dog's din, "I have already—"

"I am not a bill collector," Charles said with dignity.

"Good," the man said. He looked down, obviously flustered. "Be quiet, Precious." The poodle ducked behind the man's ankle and glowered at Charles, continuing to bark. From somewhere within the house, a woman's voice fretfully commanded, "Take that dog out of here, Frank, before my brain explodes."

"Yes, Irene," Frank replied nervously, over his shoulder. "Precious and I are just leaving." He looked out at the gray drizzle. "Is it raining?" he asked Charles.

Charles held up his photo. "Have you seen this man?"

"Can't say that I have," Frank said, giving the photograph barely a look. He reached behind the door and Charles stepped back quickly. But when his hand reappeared again, it held only a gray bowler and an umbrella.

"Are you sure?" Charles persisted. "It is a matter of some importance. The police—"

"Frank!" The female voice was loudly petulant. "Can't you manage to do even one simple thing? Get that dog out of—"

"Yes, my dear," Frank replied, putting his hat on his head. Precious launched a swift sortie at Charles's trouser leg. He retired to the top step. Frank yanked the dog back, stepped out of the door, and closed it behind him. "Never saw the fellow," he muttered, pushing past Charles. "I say, old chap, I really must be off."

Charles stared at him. A jaunty trio of peacock feathers was inserted into the band of trim that encircled Frank's bowler. He couldn't be sure, but it looked as if one were broken. He was seized by a sudden excitement. "Pardon me," he said, gesturing at the hat, "but I wonder if you would permit me to have a look at those feathers."

Frank frowned. "Feathers? I don't know about any—" He apparently recollected them, for he reddened and, still holding the leash, snatched off his hat and pulled out the cockade of feathers. Precious took advantage of Frank's inattentiveness to lunge at Charles's shoe.

"Do the feathers have a special significance?" Charles asked. "Perhaps—"

"I tell you," Frank said loudly, "there are *no* feathers!" He stuffed them into his pocket, jammed his bowler back on his head, and put up his umbrella. He walked smartly away, dragging Precious with him. As he did so, a gentleman wearing a caped Inverness came toward him. The two were apparently acquainted, for as they passed on the sidewalk, Frank tipped his gray bowler and the other inclined his head. As the man in the Inverness drew nearer, Charles saw that in his lapel was fixed a cluster of peacock feathers.

26

"It's worse than wicked, my dear, it's vulgar."
—PUNCH

CHARLES WAS FULLY soaked by the time he retrieved Bradford's horse from Taylor's Livery Stable, but the rain stopped as he rode back to Marsden Manor, his portfolio under his arm. He was able to contemplate the outcome of the morning's inquiry in the pale light of an afternoon sun, as he rode under trees that scattered raindrops with every breeze.

But there was regrettably little to contemplate. His efforts on Queen Street had come to nothing—well, almost. There was still the matter of Frank's feathers to be looked into, and those of the man in the Inverness. Surely some significance lay in those odd lapel decorations. For the moment, he couldn't imagine what it was, and although Charles was resourceful, he had been pulled up short. Hunting a single peacock feather was hard enough. Hunting one peacock feather in a blizzard of peacock feathers was much harder. Still, he was confident. Something would come to him.

Something did, but not quite in the way he might have imagined. To Charles's surprise, the Marsden stable yard was crowded. The indoor and outdoor servants were standing in a circle, talking and gesturing excitedly. As he dismounted and turned his horse over to a groom, he saw that everyone was looking at a motorcar, a Panhard-Levassor with a forward-mounted vertical engine, tiller steering, and a red parasol canopy. An elegant machine.

"Charles!" Eleanor cried breathlessly, running up to him with Patsy behind her, and, to his surprise and quickly stifled pleasure, Miss Ardleigh. "Whatever do you think?"

Charles regarded the motorcar with interest. He had considered buying a similar model the year before, but its engineering problems had deterred him.

"I doubt," he said, "that you bought this in London. The Honorable Thomas Milbank must have favored us with a visit."

"Indeed he has," Eleanor said. "Have you and Mr. Milbank met?"

"Actually, yes," Charles said. "Last autumn, on the occasion of his driving this car through Windsor at the speed of fourteen miles an hour."

"*Fourteen* miles an hour on the road?" Miss Ardleigh was aghast.

"Indeed," Charles said.

"But what about the Red Flag Act?" Eleanor asked. "Did the police not arrest him?"

"No, blast it," drawled a lazy voice. They were joined by a tall, thin young man in a khaki-colored twill dustcoat, leather helmet and goggles and leather gloves. Bradford Marsden accompanied him.

"Hello, Tommy," Charles said cordially.

"Hullo, Charlie," the young man said. They shook hands.

"They did *not* arrest you, Mr. Milbank?" Patsy's tone and glance were openly admiring, and Charles wondered if he might be about to experience a reprieve from the matrimonial sword Lady Marsden and her daughter were holding over his head.

Milbank took off his helmet and goggles. "They were meant to, but I'm afraid the pater's connections discouraged 'em."

"Which is not to say," Charles said to Patsy, "that Mr. Milbank's action was anything but heroic. Quite the contrary. He deliberately flouted the law."

"Mr. Milbank's father," Bradford explained to Miss Ardleigh, "is Lord Howard Milbank. He is influential in Whitehall circles. The police were understandably reluctant to collar his son and haul him off to jail like a common criminal, even though he volunteered."

Miss Ardleigh looked confused. "I'm afraid I don't understand any of this," she said. "What did you do wrong, Mr. Milbank? And why should you have wanted to be arrested?"

Milbank unbuttoned his dustcoat. "It's the Home Office, y' see, ma'am. Rules of the road. Parliament has set a speed limit of four miles an hour in open country and two miles an hour in towns. And a man has to walk twenty yards in front, carrying a red flag."

"It's to ensure the citizens' safety," Patsy explained excitedly to Miss Ardleigh. "Motorcars go so exceedingly fast that—"

"Safety be damned," Milbank said with a snort. "Begging your pardon, ma'am. It's the commercial interests, y' see. The railroads, chiefly. They fear competition."

"So Mr. Milbank has made a cause of it," Bradford told Miss Ardleigh. "He travels about, lecturing on the promise of the combustion engine and breaking the law wherever he can."

"Breaking the law!" Patsy cried, wide-eyed. "How wonderfully *wicked*!"

"Right," Bradford said emphatically. "Shouldn't wonder if he'll be arrested yet."

"Shouldn't wonder," Charles agreed affably, glancing once more at Patsy. He was gratified to see the blush on her cheek as she looked at her new hero. Eleanor's eyes, as well, were fixed on Milbank. Miss Ardleigh, he saw, merely looked thoughtful.

"I suppose the combustion engine will make some people very rich," she observed, stepping back to look at the machine with a critical eye.

Milbank and Bradford Marsden exchanged glances. "To be sure," Milbank said, "provided that the Home Office takes the blinders off before it's too late. The Self-Propelled Traffic Association, of which I am proud to be a member, is trying to persuade 'em."

Bradford looked somber. "What do you think of the chances, old man?"

Milbank shrugged. "Could be worse," he said. "We could be trying to bargain with the Royal Navy."

There was a commotion on the other side of the stable yard, and the lookers-on began to scramble. "I demand to know the meaning of this!" a voice roared. Charles turned. It was Lord Marsden, striding formidably across the yard in his riding clothes.

With a look of trepidation, Bradford stepped forward. "Let me present the Honorable Mr. Thomas Milbank to you, Papa. He has stopped on his way back from Cambridge to show us his—"

"The *dis*-honorable Mr. Milbank," Lord Marsden thundered. He raised his riding crop in a threatening gesture. "Sir, I'll thank you to get your bloody contraption out of my stable yard. It's scared the horses and fouled the air. And there's not been tuppence of work out of anybody since you got here." He glared at the motorcar. "Not only wicked, but vulgar," he muttered.

"But Papa," Eleanor objected hurriedly, "we've asked Mr. Milbank to stay to tea."

"Didn't ask *me*," Lord Marsden snapped, and stalked off.

Bradford looked chagrined. "Fearfully sorry, old chap," he *muttered*. "The guv has no love for motorcars. But I didn't think he would be insulting."

"Not to worry," Mr. Milbank said comfortably. "I'm continually being insulted. The motorcar has a way of stirring men up." He buttoned up his dustcoat. "Should be off, anyway. Dining in Colchester tonight. Friend of mine—actress—has removed there from London. D'you know her? Mrs. Farnsworth. Florence Faber, she was, when she was on the stage."

"Oh, yes," Miss Ardleigh said unexpectedly. "My aunt introduced me to her last Saturday. Quite an interesting lady."

Eleanor stared, her sensibilities obviously shocked. "An . . . actress? And you found such a person . . . interesting?"

Miss Ardleigh smiled. "I did indeed," she answered. "It was at her house that I met Conan Doyle, the author of the Sherlock Holmes mysteries—and Oscar Wilde, as well."

"Dear Kathryn," Eleanor said with a nervous turn of her head. "Murder mysteries and Oscar Wilde. You constantly amaze me." She paused, seeming to reflect. "But then, you *are* an American. I suppose that is the explanation."

"Doyle *and* Wilde, eh?" Milbank remarked with a laugh. "That's Florence Farnsworth, to be sure. She dares to be both wicked and wonderful at once, and everyone flocks to her. What a creature."

What a creature indeed, Charles was thinking. The object of his attention, however, was not Tommy Milbank's Farnsworth, but Miss Ardleigh, absorbed just now in her conversation with Eleanor. The woman at once intrigued and exasperated him. Stumbling onto the dig as if by accident, pretending that she had chanced into the railway station in search of a timetable, intruding upon his investigation of Prodger, finding that fragment of feather—blast it, the woman was ubiquitous! The more he thought about her, the more outrageous her behavior seemed to him. It was a wonder he had been able to get to Queen Street and back today without her turning up.

While the women talked, Bradford pulled Milbank aside. "I wonder, Milbank," he said, lowering his voice, "if I might drive into Colchester with you. I have some questions about motorcars. In particular, about Mr. Harry Landers. He has acquired a number of patent licenses and is planning to float a new company, which he calls the British Motor Car Syndicate. Are you acquainted with him?"

Charles turned his attention from Miss Ardleigh to Bradford. Harry Landers? If his friend was involved with *that* charlatan, no wonder he had been worried of late. Anything Landers turned his hand to be likely to prove a confidence game.

Milbank jerked on his helmet. "To be sure, I know Landers," he said. "Wish I didn't, either," he added.

"I think we had better talk," Bradford said quietly. "I'll get my coat."

A few minutes later, Charles watched Bradford and Tommy Milbank drive off, accompanied by the vulgar belchings of the motor, the exultant shouts of small children, and the excited yapping of the manor dogs. Eleanor picked up the skirt of her green dress. "I suppose we might as well go in to tea," she said with evident regret. "Although how Papa could be so rude—"

"Yes, he *was* rude, wasn't he?" Patsy said, frowning. "I can't think why." She shook her golden curls, clearly nettled. "Mr. Milbank is such a *handsome* gentleman." A veiled glance at Charles suggested that her remark was intended to inspire jealousy.

Charles responded with a quick smile. "Handsome and rich," he said agreeably. "The Milbanks, of course, hold quite a prominent role in society." Patsy lapsed into a thoughtful silence.

As they turned toward the manor house, Miss Ardleigh adroitly allowed the sisters to move ahead and fell in step with Charles. Although he was perfectly disposed to be irritated with this forward behavior, which so nearly resembled her brash intrusions of the past few days, he could not help noticing that the pale gold of her wool costume, reminiscent of champagne, was striking against her mahogany hair. And if he had not been distracted by the odd compound of irritation and admiration that swirled like an alchemist's brew inside him, he might have been prepared for the observation that followed her greeting. Instead, it startled him.

"I wonder," she remarked, "whether the portfolio under your arm contains the photographs of which we have spoken."

Charles clutched his portfolio tighter. If he had looked into his feelings at this moment, he might have remarked that he was holding on to it exactly as a drowning man holds on to a life preserver. But he did not. "As a matter of fact, it does," he said stiffly. "But I do not think it is especially prudent to—"

"You promised to show them to me," Miss Ardleigh reminded him. Her sidewise glance seemed oddly merry, as if she were making fun of him. "You think my interest . . . wicked? Or vulgar?"

"Neither." He frowned. Actually, he found her interest both disconcerting and stimulating, but he could hardly tell her that. He settled for a caution that, even to his ears, sounded remarkably like something Sir Archibald or Lady

Henrietta might say. "They are, after all, the photographs of a dead man."

"To be sure," she said. She turned her head. "Please do not think me callous if I say that the man's condition, while piteous, will not distress me, Sir Charles. And I hardly think that at this point it can distress him."

In spite of himself, Charles almost smiled.

"Of course," she added gravely, "if showing the photo to me would offend *your* sensibilities . . ."

Charles opened his portfolio and pulled out a photograph of the dead man, stretched out on his back, hands resting on his midriff, and another of the wheel tracks.

Miss Ardleigh paused on the path and held the photograph in one gloved hand. A flicker of guarded recognition crossed her face. The corners of her lips tightened imperceptibly. She glanced up.

"Have the police progressed in their inquiries?"

"Frankly, no," Charles confessed. "You know as much as do the police. The only physical clues are those we discovered in Prodger's chaise—a peacock feather and a fingerprint. I doubt that even Doyle's ingenious Holmes could make much of either."

"Indeed," she said in an easy tone, brushing back a lock of rich auburn hair that escaped across her cheek. But she was still studying the photograph, as if memorizing it.

"The local police," he said, watching her closely, "appear to have reached the limit of their resources. Unfortunately, Inspector Wainwright refuses to call in the Yard. I gather that he had some former difficulty with them."

There was a moment of silence. "Have you enjoyed any success in your pursuit of the feather?" she asked.

"None," Charles said, "although I have seen similar feathers in the lapels of two men. I plan to continue my search."

"I see," Miss Ardleigh said, handing back the photograph. "And the ring the dead man is wearing—does it seem to you to be significant?"

The scarab ring? Charles realized that he had not considered the import of the ring's motif in any detailed way, interested as he had been in the problem of deciphering its inscription. "If it does," he said honestly, "I did not think to inquire into it." He turned toward her, hoping to flush out her interest with a direct question. "Do you have a particular reason for your inquiries, Miss Ardleigh?"

She half turned away from him, and there was another silence. When she finally spoke, it was not in answer to his question. "I have a thought, Sir Charles. I suggest that you show the photograph to Mrs. Florence Farnsworth, in Keenan Street, Colchester. She may perhaps be of assistance to you."

"Mrs. Farnsworth," Charles said. "Is that not the lady of whom Mr. Milbank spoke a moment ago?"

"It is," Miss Ardleigh replied, and began to walk in the direction Eleanor and Patsy had taken, leaving Charles standing in the path.

The finality in Miss Ardleigh's words made it clear that she intended to conclude the interview, and a deep frustration added itself to Charles's initial irritation and discomposure. From her reaction to the picture, he judged that she knew something about the dead man. She had even appeared to recognize him, or something about him.

Charles frowned. What did Miss Ardleigh know? And how did she know it?

27

"Who can wonder that the laws of society should at
times be forgotten by those whom the eye of society
habitually overlooks, and whom the heart of society
often appears to discard?"
—DR. JOHN SIMON
City of London Medical Report, 1849

A s KATE RODE home in the chaise through the pearly
twilight, she thought over the events of her afternoon
visit to Marsden Manor. She had enjoyed her tour of the
manor, which she found truly impressive, with its Tudor
half-timbering and its wide vistas of green lawn and
colorful gardens. She had marveled at the vast display of
Eleanor's wedding finery, on exhibit in one of the many
second-floor bedrooms. Although the promised ghost had
failed to materialize, Beryl Bardwell had garnered a fine
stock of material for the next chapter in "The Conspiracy of
the Golden Scarab," in which she now planned to feature
an English country house. And a motorcar, for Tommy
Milbank's machine, with its elegantly sleek finish and
astounding capacity for self-propelled speed, had made
a strong impression on Beryl, who was already imagining

her heroine fitted out in dustcoat and goggles, her hand firm on the tiller. The afternoon had been quite pleasant.

But thought-provoking as well. As the chaise turned onto the lane toward Bishop's Keep, Kate's thoughts turned to another subject—Sir Charles Sheridan. She had been pleased to see him, more pleased than she was willing to admit to herself. Over their last several meetings, she had begun to feel a marked interest in him, not only in his knowledge of investigative procedures and methods of analysis, but in the man himself, lumpy coat, camera, and all. She had even felt—or had it been her imagination?— that he looked at her attentively, as if he were actually listening to what she said.

But she couldn't help wondering whether she had been entirely wise to suggest that he call on Mrs. Farnsworth. Her recommendation had seemed to pique his interest, although she was sure that he thought her both whimsical and overbold, intruding once more into an investigation in which she had no part.

It was, of course, the sight of the scarab ring on her finger of the dead man that had prompted her to speak. That, and the peacock feather. Sir Charles had seemed to think neither important, but Kate could only conclude that, taken together, the two items were of singular and rather troubling significance. There was, although Sir Charles did not know it, a third: Aunt Sabrina's interest in the murder. When Kate put that together with the fact that Aunt Sabrina and Mrs. Farnsworth each possessed a scarab pendant, and that most of the people at Saturday's gathering had worn the emblem of the peacock feather, she could reach only one reasonable conclusion, and its corollary: Monsieur Armand had visited Colchester with the intention of seeing some member of the Order of the Golden Dawn, and Aunt Sabrina suspected as much. Further, Aunt Sabrina did not wish anyone to know of her suspicions. Kate could not suggest to Sir Charles that he speak to her aunt on the subject, but she could suggest that he consult with Mrs. Farnsworth, who must be acquainted with all the members of the temple she had organized.

But still, Kate felt troubled. She certainly had no wish to embarrass either Aunt Sabrina or the Order. And she liked Mrs. Farnsworth, who evidently dared to be as audacious in the way she behaved as in the way she dressed. If Sir Charles did indeed take up her suggestion, she hoped he would be discreet in his inquiry. She wished that she had thought to ask him not to mention her name.

It was approaching nightfall when the cart arrived at the stable yard of Bishop's Keep. Kate alighted and went in through the kitchen entry. She was greeted as usual with the ripe fragrance of pickles, potatoes, apples, and coffee, for the entranceway led through a storeroom crowded with jars, crocks, bins, and barrels. To furnish its tables, Bishop's Keep relied on its own gardens and pastures and on the local vendors of meat, fish, and fowl. Staple items—flour, sugar, salt, tea—were purchased infrequently at Dedham or Colchester.

The brick-floored, stone-walled kitchen was chill and dusky, lighted only by the fire in the large fireplace and a single oil lamp hanging over the worktable. Cook—Mrs. Pratt, Kate called her, thinking it demeaning to name her by her function—stood over the table, kneading bread. She was a thickset woman in a gray dress covered with a starched white apron. She had a dour mouth and piercing black eyes under heavy black brows that met in the center, giving her a suspicious look. But she had warmed to Kate and usually greeted her with the twitch of her lips that passed for a smile.

This evening, however, there was no smile. Mrs. Pratt's brows were knit together in a scowl and her frilled cap was dangerously askew. Her arms were white to the elbows with flour and she was pummeling a mound of stiff dough as if it were her bitterest enemy.

"Good evening," Kate said, pulling off her gloves. She was surprised to see Mrs. Pratt engaged so late in the day with a task that she usually completed much earlier.

"Evenin'," Mrs. Pratt muttered, dealing the innocent dough another hard blow.

Kate sniffed. Amidst the comfortable smells of the kitchen—the lingering odor of the luncheon onion soup, the smoke of the fire, the sharp aroma of lamp oil—she caught the unmistakable perfume of Aunt Sabrina's best port. Mrs. Pratt had been at the tipple.

Kate put her gloves in her pocket. "I trust all is well," she remarked in an idle tone, although it was clear to her that it wasn't.

Mrs. Pratt gave the dough a quarter-turn and a smart smack. "An' how culd anythin' be well in this house," she said, slurring her words, "wi' sweet Jenny dead an' that woman struttin' round proud as Herself in a temper?"

Kate was distressed by the bitterness of Mrs. Pratt's remark, but not surprised. She had known since the Friday before that the servants' resentment of Aunt Jaggers was not an ordinary hostility, derived from the accumulated aggravation of small slights. It was a sustained ferocity that brooded, like a bird of prey on its nest, over a long-held and deeply felt injury. When Kate had overheard Mrs. Pratt's threat, she had understood why. "Jaggers'll be in bloody hell," Cook had said savagely. "That's where the Lord sends the murderers of pore babes and young girls!" Mudd had echoed her feeling with an almost equal violence.

Kate looked at Mrs. Pratt's dark face, troubled. A storm was brewing. Was there anything she could do to help the household weather it? It was not that she gave two beans for Aunt Jaggers's feelings. If the woman had wronged Jenny Blyly, she deserved to suffer for it. But she wanted to shield Aunt Sabrina from the worst of the blow, if she could. And she had come to feel an honest affection for the people who devoted their honest labors to make Bishop's

Keep comfortable. It would be a terrible pity if the storm shipwrecked their small security, such as it was.

"I would be interested in hearing your concern if you care to tell me," Kate said quietly. She sat down on a stool beside the fire. "Perhaps there is something I can do."

"Do?" Mrs. Pratt asked bitterly. "Ain't nothin' can be done."

"But still—" Kate said, and left the sentence hanging, hoping that Mrs. Pratt would tell her about Jenny Blyly. But that wasn't where Mrs. Pratt began.

" 'Tis Nettie," Mrs. Pratt said finally, stripping shreds of dough from her hands. "Nettie an' th' pincushion." She pulled two fingers of lard from a tin bucket and began furiously to grease a brown earthenware bowl as large as a small washtub.

"Pincushion?" Kate asked, surprised.

"Wi' th' image of the queen on't. 'Tis gone missin'." Mrs. Pratt thumped the heavy bowl on the table so hard that the crockery rattled on the sideboard. "Jaggers whipt her fer stealin', she did." There was deep indignation in her voice, and frustration.

"Whipped!" Kate exclaimed. "Over a pincushion!"

"Aye," Mrs. Pratt said darkly. "Whipt, wi' a leather strop. Nettie missed th' pincushion a while ago. We hoped it'ud turn up, like, under th' carpet or at th' back of the drawer, th' way lost things does. But Jaggers wanted it yestiddy, an' it culdn't be found, nowheres. She accused Nettie of thievin' an' give her till this arternoon to put it back." She gathered up the mass of glossy dough with both hands and dropped it into the bowl. "When she cudn't, she whipt her an' took away her half days fer a year."

"Oh," Kate whispered miserably. "Poor, poor Nettie." The girl was little more than a child, thin and pale-faced, with narrow hunched shoulders and lank hair. "Where is she now?"

Mrs. Pratt turned the dough lardside-up with a swift motion. "In th' cellar, cleanin' coal boxes. Jaggers give her a can'le an' set her to't afore tea."

"How unkind!" Kate exclaimed. Being sent to the damp, black cellar with only a candle would of itself be a horrible punishment, let alone sent there to clean the coal boxes.

Mrs. Pratt looked at Kate, her glance narrowed and bitter. "There's no dealin' wi' th' wretch," she said bleakly. "An' no use appealin' to Miss Ardleigh."

"But surely, if my aunt knew—"

Mrs. Pratt's voice was fierce. "An' wot'ud she do? It were th' same when Jaggers drove Jenny away last spring. Miss Ardleigh din't do nothin' then, neither." She shook her head. "No, Jaggers has got a hold on Miss Ardleigh somehow, otherwise she wudn't be tolerated here fer a bloody minute."

"Please, Mrs. Pratt," Kate said painfully, "tell me about Jenny." She didn't want to hear the story, because she had already guessed its outline. But it might help Mrs. Pratt to tell it.

Without speaking, Mrs. Pratt covered the bowl with a damp towel and set it on the hearth. Putting the bread to rise at this late hour meant that she would have to get up for the baking well before dawn. It was a measure of just how far things had slipped out of kilter today.

Kate knit her fingers together. "It's too late to help Jenny," she said painfully, "but I can do nothing for the others unless I know the whole story."

Mrs. Pratt dropped into the chair on the other side of the fire. "Can't do nothin' anyways," she muttered, wiping her hands on her apron. "Nobody kin do nothin'." She took a small flask out of her pocket and pulled on it.

Kate waited. In a few moments, the port loosened the cook's tongue. Mrs. Pratt began to speak, slowly and painfully, as if the tale were being wrenched out of her like an abscessed tooth, the pain of it undeadened, even by drink.

"Jenny were th' parlor maid afore Amelia," she said. She put the flask back in her pocket. "Me sister Rose's oldest girl, Amelia's sister. Pert as a daisy an' prompt in 'er work. But she wudn't put on an int'rest in religion, which soured Jaggers, an' sometimes she had a tart mouth." Her jaw tightened. "When Jaggers found out that she were wi' child—"

Kate pulled in her breath, imagining Aunt Jaggers's fury. And Jenny had been Amelia's sister! No wonder the girl had been so distraught.

"Floggin' was first," Mrs. Pratt said thickly. She put her work-roughened hands on her knees and leaned toward the fire. "Then Jaggers sent her out. No char'cter, no money, 'cept what little we culd scrape t'gether among us. Fair broke her mother's heart, it did."

Kate closed her eyes. It was a familiar enough story— one she had even written herself, complete with shy maid, sly seducer, and flint-hearted mistress. But Jenny's was no made-up story. It was *real*. Kate could feel the girl's hopelessness and despair, and her heart brimmed with an answering compassion. How could girls like Jenny and Nettie endure such terrible treatment? How could they live in a society of such wretched inequalities, where their sad poverty could at every moment be measured against the abundance above stairs, where a parrot merited more casual affection than a parlor maid? But she had not yet heard the worst of it.

Mrs. Pratt clenched her hands. "Hadn't bin fer Jaggers, we'd a' come through it, Jenny an' us, fer th' father were a village lad, an' loved her. He were happy to marry her an' give th' babe his name, straightaway." Her voice sharpened. "But Jaggers shamed her till she b'lieved hersel' worse 'n worthless, an' not gud enuf fer th' one she loved." Her mouth twisted, her words full of poisonous hatred. "*Jaggers* is who killed Jenny, with her hard blows an' her harsh words. All o' us knows it. All o' us hates her fer it. Tom Potter most of all."

"Tom Potter?"

"Jenny's young man. Th' constable who brought th' news o' her passin' also brought a note from her t' him. A love note, like." She smiled grimly. "But yer needn't worry none, miss. Jaggers'll get her reward. It'll all be made right in th' end." A coal broke on the hearth, scattering shimmers of spark. "An' if it ain't, Tom'll make it right, or Mudd will, or me."

Kate stared at her, apprehension rippling through her like a hissing snake. "No," she whispered. "That's not the way."

"Yes," Mrs. Pratt said darkly. "Yes, 'tis."

28

"Find me some material, though it is no bigger than a fly's foot, give me but a clew no thicker than a spider's web, and I'll follow it through the whole labyrinth."
—WILKIE COLLINS
Foul Play

CHARLES SPENT THE next day following the two clues he had—the peacock feather and the dead man's photograph. Buttoned up in a mackintosh and wearing a hat against the drizzling mist, he rode into Colchester, where he stabled his horse and walked to Queen Street. At the fourth house, his portfolio under his arm, he pulled the brass bell. It was answered this time by a pert little maid with red cheeks and a ready smile who gave Charles a demure look under her eyelashes when he asked to see the master. He handed over his card, on which he had written, "A matter of paramount importance."

"I'll tell Mr. Murdstone yer here, sir," the maid said, leaving him standing in the narrow hall. He passed the time by examining a series of gilt-framed etchings of the Charge of the Light Brigade, hung against the rose-patterned wallpaper. Precious was nowhere to be seen but could be heard, yapping briskly but faintly in a distant room, and the rich perfume of cooked onions arose from the back of the house. A moment later the maid returned to take his coat and lead him to the parlor.

Frank Murdstone was roasting his feet on the small fender in the lace-curtained parlor immediately off the hall, comfortable in a soft jacket and loose tie, reading a newspaper by the light of a hissing gas lamp. He was a man with a horsey nose, a high forehead, and tufted eyebrows.

"Oh, it's you," he said, removing his boots from the fender. He put down his newspaper, his ears reddening. He obviously remembered yesterday's encounter with some embarrassment. "What can I do for you, Sir Charles? What's this business of 'paramount importance'?"

"As I said yesterday," Charles said, taking the photograph out of his portfolio, "I am attempting to identify this man."

Murdstone stood up, glanced briefly at the photograph Charles handed him, and shrugged. "Can't help you, I'm afraid."

"Do you mind taking one more look?" Charles prodded, watching Murdstone's face. The fire cast flickering shadows across his cheeks, highlighting the dome of his forehead.

Murdstone took a pair of gold-rimmed glasses out of his pocket, hooked them over his ears, and peered through them at the photograph. His eyes widened slightly. "Dead man, is he?"

"Murdered."

Murdstone shook his head firmly. "Never saw the chap." He handed the photo back and took off his glasses. "If you don't mind my asking, why are you inquiring, and not the police?"

"It is a matter of interest to me," Charles said vaguely. At this point he was not entirely sure why he was pursuing the matter. The police had given it up as a bad job and offered absolutely no encouragement. Perhaps he was led by his feeling that the dead ought to inspire at least some interest among the living; perhaps it was merely his enjoyment of the labyrinthian process of puzzle solving. "One more question, Mr. Murdstone. Yesterday when we met, you were wearing a cockade of peacock feathers in your hat. The gentleman you greeted on the street was also wearing peacock feathers. Is there some special significance to that fact?"

There was a moment's silence. The coals shifted in the grate. Murdstone pulled at his lower lip and turned so that his face could not be seen. "I don't see what a few silly feathers have to do with anything," he said.

Charles persisted. "Is it the insignia of a secret society?"

Murdstone turned around to face Charles. "If you must know," he said pettishly, "it's one of my wife's silly involvements." There was a shadow of something in his face—resentment, or deceit? Was he hiding something? "Wouldn't have gone, myself, but she insisted. And when Irene insists—"

Charles heard a flurry of yaps in the hallway, and a sharp female voice. "Frank, it is time for Precious to have her walk."

Murdstone's resentment—for that's what Charles thought it was—darkened in his face. "Coming, m'dear," he said. He pulled off his jacket and reached for his coat, hanging on the back of a chair. "The chap you saw on the street. He's one of 'em. Freemason. Obsessed by magic. Dotes on abracadabra, passwords, all that rot." He shrugged his arms into his coat.

"This society," Charles pressed, fearing that he was about to lose his informant to the custody of a poodle. "Can you tell me its name?"

Murdstone moved to the mantel mirror to straighten his tie. "Order of the Golden Dawn," he muttered. "Lot of foolishness, 'f you ask me. Mumbo jumbo, cards, astrology, séances. Sheer flummery. But Mrs. Murdstone—"

"Frank!" The door was flung open and an overly stout matron in a gray dress came into the room, leaning on a silver-headed stick. She held a red leather leash in her hand, the poodle dancing at the other end. "Are you going to dither all—" She stopped when she saw Charles.

Murdstone turned around. "Sir Charles Sheridan," he said, with a careless wave of his hand. "Mrs. Murdstone. Sir Charles is inquiring about the affair last week, m'dear. Over at Florence-what's-her-name's—"

"Florence Farnsworth," Mrs. Murdstone said peevishly. She had at least three chins, receding one after the other like foothills into her mountainous bosom. "Why you can't manage a simple name—" The poodle made a quick sally in Charles's direction and was pulled back. She retreated sulkily behind her mistress's full skirts.

"Ah, yes, Farnsworth," Murdstone said, rocking on the balls of his feet. "Farnsworth," he repeated to himself, as if trying to memorize it.

Charles frowned slightly, remembering that Miss Ardleigh had also directed him to Mrs. Farnsworth, and his suspicion of yesterday that there was some connection between her and the dead man. What did she know? How did she come by her information? She had appeared to recognize something about Monsieur Armand's photograph—how was that possible? Had she seen him, spoken to him, perhaps in London, before she came down to Bishop's Keep? If that were true, Miss Ardleigh was almost certainly other than she seemed.

But those questions, however compellingly they were beginning to prod him, had to be postponed for the moment. "I would like to learn more about the Order," Charles said.

Mrs. Murdstone turned to Charles and her manner changed. "Are you interested in becoming a member, Sir Charles?" she inquired ingratiatingly.

Charles bowed slightly. "One does not wish to commit oneself on a matter of such importance without some previous intelligence of the group. What can you tell me of it?"

Mrs. Murdstone's plump face took on a mysterious look and she lowered her voice. "Only that if you are interested in the occult, sir, I daresay you will find it a most fascinating group. I cannot speak further without revealing important secrets, you understand—"

Mr. Murdstone shaped "flummery" with his lips, but did not speak the word.

"Of course," Charles murmured. "I would not for the world ask you to violate a sacred trust."

"The Society's charter was obtained from a very ancient Society in Germany," Mrs. Murdstone continued. "Unlike the sham societies one sees so much of these days, it enjoys an entirely legitimate lineage, with roots going back to the Rosicrucians and even to the magicians of Egypt. Its authority is transmitted through our respected chief, Dr. William Westcott, whom all the world knows as a man to be admired and trusted. Our temple is named the—" But here she clapped her hand over her mouth. "Forgive me, sir, I go too far," she said coyly, through pudgy fingers, heavily ringed. "It is permitted to speak the name of our temple only to initiates."

"To be sure," Charles said. "Mrs. Farnsworth—would the lady live in Keenan Street?"

"Indeed," Mrs. Murdstone said helpfully, "Number Seven. Some two years ago, she left a distinguished career on the London stage to marry Mr. Farnsworth, a gentleman who made his fortune in railroads. Unfortunately, she was left a widow shortly after their wedding, and has now taken on the task of establishing and organizing our temple—a rather difficult task, if I may say, requiring a great investment of her time and personal attention." She paused and gave Charles a benevolent glance. "If you require introduction, you may say that Mrs. Murdstone recommends you to her as a Seeker after Truth."

"I most certainly shall," Charles said, bowing low. "Thank you for your help, Mrs. Murdstone." He inclined his head toward her husband. "And yours, Mr. Murdstone."

"Glad t'oblige, sir, glad t'oblige," Murdstone said heartily, and Charles took his leave. As he retrieved his hat from the maid at the front door, he could hear Precious's yapping bark and Mrs. Murdstone, scolding sharply. The smell of onions followed him out of the house.

The houses in Keenan Street were as undistinguished as those in Queen, built of brick, high, with only a modest frontage. Charles raised an eyebrow. Was it possible that Prodger had misunderstood his customer's accented English? Had Monsieur Armand been in search of *Keenan* Street, not Queen? Again, a compelling question, but not capable of answer, since the seeker was unfortunately dead.

The stoop of Number Seven, like those of its neighbors, descended directly to the sidewalk without the amenity of hedge or grass. To the right of the stoop was the bow window of the parlor hung with lace curtains and filled with a small forest of fern. There was no evidence of Mr. Farnsworth's railroad fortune, for the door was answered by a maid-of-all-work with a mop in her hand and a churlish frown on her narrow face. She hung Charles's wet coat and hat on a wooden coat tree, and showed him into the small parlor.

The room was cheaply furnished, but a few exotic touches gave it something of distinction. A plaster statuette of the Egyptian god Seth stood on a pedestal in the corner; several unframed hieroglyphic tomb paintings were prominently placed; and the floor was spread with Turkish carpets of purple and blue, much worn. The furnishings were of Japanese design, and a painted Japanese screen was angled beside the fireplace. Peacock feathers were artfully arranged on the walls. The only evidences of Mrs. Farnsworth's acting career were the framed playbills that Charles had seen in the entry hallway, where the name Florence Faber was prominently featured.

"Sir Charles Sheridan?"

The woman who came toward him was small and slight, but her features were sharply defined, with a classical balance and a jaw that hinted at a firm will. Charles would not have called her beautiful, but some, no doubt, would have. A gold net bound her softly waved brown hair away from a face that was dominated by large, luminous eyes and a mobile, mercurial mouth. Some time had passed since the loss of her husband and she was no longer in mourning; her pale green dress was loose and flowing with a pre-Raphaelite simplicity, but she did not, Charles thought, have the pre-Raphaelite aura of untouched innocence and wondering naïveté. She wore instead the look of a weary Bohemian.

"Thank you for seeing me, Mrs. Farnsworth," Charles said, bowing over her hand. "I come at the recommendation of Mrs. Murdstone, who suggests that you can provide me an introduction to the Order of the Golden Dawn."

"Ah, yes, Mrs. Murdstone," Mrs. Farnsworth murmured. She waved at a gold velvet settee. "Please, sit down, Sir Charles. Your interest in such matters is—?"

"—is of long standing, ma'am," Charles said deftly. He parted his coattails and sat down. "As a child I early discovered a great fascination for things beyond the realm of ordinary human knowledge."

He paused. That was true, although his interest in the unknown lay largely in the sciences of the natural, rather than the supernatural. But the temperament of persons attracted to the occult had long held a scientific interest for him. What was there about the supernatural that fascinated certain people? What sort of people were they? Mrs. Farnsworth, for instance, seemed a woman of the world and not one to be taken in by charlatans. What was the source of *her* interest? Was it the experience of the occult—some satisfaction she gained in the practice of magical ritual? Or was it the power the practice gave her? Looking at the strong line of her jaw and a certain arrogance in the lift of her chin, he could believe that it was the lure of power that had brought her to the Order. Perhaps the founding of the Colchester temple lent her a certain authority, a certain prestige. Or perhaps the drama of ritual magic had replaced the stage dramas of her acting career.

"You were saying—" Mrs. Farnsworth remarked. Her voice was casual, but her probing glance made Charles feel that he was the object of her critical assessment.

Charles shifted. "Forgive me. I do not want to take up your time with talk about myself. You established the temple here, I believe?"

Mrs. Farnsworth took the light bamboo chair beside the settee. "I did," she said with simple authority. She leaned back, arranging her arm so that one hand hung gracefully from the arm of the chair, and fixed him with a direct gaze. "But you must understand that I can speak of it only in general terms. It is, after all, a *secret* order. One does not expect a Freemason to divulge the sacred rituals of his lodge."

"Quite so," Charles said. He paused. "I wonder, though . . . Is membership in your Order confined to Colchester?"

Mrs. Farnsworth's laugh was throaty, amused. "My dear man, how is it that you do not know already of the Golden Dawn? The Order has temples in London, Edinburgh, Bradford, Paris. It is the foremost organization of its kind in the world."

"Indeed," Charles said with interest. "In Paris?"

"Mr. MacGregor Mathers has established the Ahathoor Temple there, as well as a school of occult sciences." A

189

smile softened Mrs. Farnsworth's lips and she raised her hand in a studiedly playful gesture. "Our little temple in Colchester is but one star in a distinguished galaxy."

"I do indeed see," Charles said, "and I am much impressed. Perhaps—"

He left the sentence hanging, placed his portfolio on his knees, and opened it. He might ordinarily have had some compunction about showing the photograph of a dead man to a woman of delicate sensibilities, although he had cropped this one so that it did not reveal the fatal wound. But Mrs. Farnsworth had been an actress, and actresses were women of the world. Such a thing should not shock. He took it out and handed it to her.

"This is a photograph of a man who, I believe, may have been associated with your Order. I wonder what you can tell me about him. The name I know him by," he added, watching her closely, "is Monsieur Armand. That may not be his real name."

Mrs. Farnsworth took the photograph and studied it for a few moments, her face revealing nothing. When she handed it back, her glance was casual, her tone devoid of any significance or feeling. "I fear I cannot help you," she said. "The gentleman is a stranger to me." She arched expressive brows. "If you are in doubt as to his identity, why not simply ask him?"

"Because," Charles said, "the man is dead."

Mrs. Farnsworth shook her head. "A pity," she murmured. "His death was untimely?"

"He was murdered," Charles said.

She looked startled. "Why on earth do you bring the photograph of a murdered man to me?"

"Because," Charles replied carefully, "I understand that he visited a member of your Order."

Mrs. Farnsworth frowned. "My dear Sir Charles," she said, "our temple is quite large. Surely you cannot imagine that I am acquainted with the private business dealings of individual members?"

Charles felt rebuked. "Well, I—"

She rose from her chair. "Am I to take it, then," she said with evident distaste, "that your interest in the Order is connected with your interest in this dead person?"

Charles rose also. "That is correct, ma'am," he said. "It is of urgent importance that I discover where he spent the last day of his—"

"Then I very much fear that you have wasted your time inquiring here." She gathered her skirt and turned toward the door. "And now if you will excuse me, I have pressing matters to attend to." She swept out of the room, leaving behind her the lingering scent of roses and a host of puzzling questions.

29

"It is no use telling me there are good aunts and bad aunts. At the core, they are all alike. Sooner or later, out pops the cloven hoof."

—P. G. WODEHOUSE
The Code of the Woosters

WHILE CHARLES WAS on his way to Colchester, Kate was on her way to the library. She had almost finished copying out the cipher manuscript and its transcription for Mr. Yeats. It had been tedious labor, for the crabbed glyphs were written in faded sepia ink and were hard to decipher. The paper on which they were written bore a watermark of 1809—or, rather, some of the sheets did. Others bore no mark at all; curiously, they appeared to be much newer, although the script and ink were the same. And there was a further curiosity: the name and address of the German woman to whom Dr. Westcott had written for authorization of the Order of the Golden Dawn were in the same hand that had produced the cipher. Odd, Kate thought, since the woman had died only recently. Kate mentioned these puzzling facts to Aunt Sabrina, but she seemed unable to shed any light on the matter.

Aunt Sabrina, meanwhile, had been copying out her tarot deck. The precious cards had been designed by MacGregor Mathers in consultation (it was said) with his spirit guide, and hand-drawn by his wife, Moina Mathers. This original deck was loaned to each member in turn, so that a personal copy could be made. The member was required to keep the deck closely guarded and pass it on when he or she had finished copying it.

But Kate was thinking neither about the cipher document nor the Golden Dawn tarot. After what Mrs. Pratt had told her last night, she was filled with a firm determination. She would have a frank talk with Aunt Sabrina. It was too late to help Jenny, but something had to be done to restrain Aunt Jaggers, and Aunt Sabrina was the only person who could do it.

But when Kate came into the library, Aunt Sabrina was not alone. Aunt Jaggers, dressed in her customary rusty black, stood in front of the fire, while Aunt Sabrina, wearing a pale blue morning gown, was sitting at her desk, where she had been copying the cards. From their strained faces and tense postures, it was clear that the two were quarreling.

Sensing that she had stepped into a private and perhaps embarrassing exchange, Kate turned to leave. But Aunt Jaggers caught sight of her.

"What do you think you're doing, miss?" she cried violently, stamping her foot. "Eavesdropping, like the other servants?"

"Calm yourself, Bernice," Aunt Sabrina said, rising. "Kathryn was merely—"

"Don't tell me what she was doing," Aunt Jaggers snapped, shoulders squared, face wrenched into angry ugliness. "I've seen how this girl toadies to you and your foolish sorcery. Before she came, there was at least peace in this household." She pulled herself up. "Clearly, your experiment is not working. She must go."

Kate gasped as if a bucket of cold well water had been splashed over her. Go?

"You aren't serious, Bernice," Aunt Sabrina said quietly.

"I am *very* serious," Aunt Jaggers replied with a lofty look. "We did agree, did we not, that if this person"—she glanced coldly at Kate—"did not suit, she would be returned to America."

Aunt Sabrina's voice was low, controlled. "But she *does* suit. She suits very well. Her work is exemplary, her manner cooperative, her—"

"She does not suit *me*," Aunt Jaggers said flatly. "But you needn't worry about the details. I have already written to the steamship agent in London to arrange return passage for her. As soon as possible." Her triumphant look at Kate said, How do you like *that*, miss? as plainly as if she had spoken the words.

"You are challenging me in this way," Aunt Sabrina said, "because you know how I feel about what you did yesterday. After that disgraceful business with Jenny, I told you that your power to discipline the servants did not extend to physical punishment or discharge. What happened with Nettie sickens me, Bernice. I intend to—"

"Be careful what you intend, sister." Aunt Jaggers's voice was flint like, her words barbed. "Remember what I *know*."

Aunt Sabrina seemed to flinch and turn away, and Kate was startled to see something very like fear come into her eyes—fear and hatred. What could Aunt Jaggers possibly know that could make Aunt Sabrina afraid? What secret could be so compromising that it would force her to submit to her sister's tyranny? Kate was stunned. Aunt Jaggers was a *blackmailer!* No wonder Aunt Sabrina hated her.

Aunt Sabrina's face was white, without expression. When she spoke, her voice was so low that Kate had to strain to hear the words. "You may use your ill-gotten knowledge once too often for your own welfare, sister."

"Perhaps I have not used it often enough," Aunt Jaggers retorted, "for my own welfare." She felt she had the upper hand; Kate could see it in the confident lift of her head and the aggressive line of her jaw. "Perhaps I should use it with your dear friend the vicar as well. Perhaps he would be willing to—"

Aunt Sabrina's hand moved so fast that Kate almost didn't see the slap. But she went cold inside as she heard the smart smack of flesh against flesh, and heard Aunt Jaggers's shriek.

"You struck me!" she cried furiously, her hand going to her cheek.

Aunt Sabrina's shoulders slumped suddenly, all the rigidity gone out of her, and a look of self-disgust crossed her face. It was as if having stooped to physical violence, she had lost the high ground of her moral position. "I am . . . sorry," she said, struggling for control. "Forgive me, Bernice. I did not intend—"

But Aunt Jaggers's eye had fallen on the Golden Dawn tarot deck. "Fortunetelling cards," she shrilled. "Oh, Sabrina, how low you have fallen!" Her nostrils flared at the painted figure on the card. "I see the mark of the cloven hoof in your forehead!" She was shouting now, fixing all her inflamed morality, her burning hatred, upon the pieces of cardboard.

Aunt Sabrina took a step forward. "Don't touch those cards, Bernice," she said. "They are not mine. They belong to—"

"The Devil!" Aunt Jaggers shrieked. And with one wild gesture, she swept up the cards and hurled them onto the blazing fire. As Kate stared in paralyzed horror, the thin pasteboard cards flared brightly in the flames, curled into ash, and were gone.

"Bernice!" Aunt Sabrina whispered, horrified. "What have you done?"

Aunt Jaggers seemed to have taken strength from her action. "I have done what I should have done weeks ago. I have taken a stand against evil." She raised her hand in a commanding gesture, her eyes like silver coins. "Mark me, sister. I have burned your cards. And unless you banish the rest of this deviltry, I promise you I will burn it, as well!" She stepped smartly to Kate's alcove and shoved Kate's box of letters onto the floor.

Aunt Sabrina straightened her shoulders. She seemed to be grappling within herself. "If you don't get out, Bernice," she said between clenched teeth, "I will . . . I will—"

Aunt Jaggers lifted her chin. "You will do what, sister?" When Aunt Sabrina did not answer, a thin, triumphant smile crossed her face, and she turned to Kate. "I will let you know when arrangements have been made for your departure," she said.

In the fireplace, the flames flickered brightly.

30

"If we believe a thing to be bad . . . it is our duty to try to prevent it and to damn the consequences."

—LORD MILNER

AUNT SABRINA LEFT the library a few minutes after Aunt Jaggers, saying only that she was going to her room and did not wish to be disturbed. Feeling as if she had been caught in a furious crossfire (as perhaps she had), Kate retrieved two or three cards that had escaped the flames and picked up the correspondence that Aunt Jaggers had flung on the floor. She noted that it contained a recent, already opened letter to Mrs. Farnsworth from Mr. Mathers, from Paris. The letter, marked "Private and Confidential," must have been inadvertently included with the correspondence of the Order, which Mrs. Farnsworth had given to Aunt Sabrina.

Kate put the envelope on Aunt Sabrina's desk and busied herself with the typing of the cipher transcript for Mr. Yeats. Given Aunt Jaggers's threat to deport her, it was difficult to concentrate on her typing. But Kate pushed her worries to the back of her mind as best she could, and simply let her fingers do their mechanical work. If Aunt

Jaggers was determined that she should not stay, there was hardly anything she could do to prevent her.

Kate was not surprised that Aunt Sabrina did not reappear when it was time for luncheon. The argument with her sister had been bad enough, but the loss of the tarot deck must be even more cruel. To members of the Golden Dawn, Mr. Mathers's precious deck of cards was a spiritual document, a map of the journey to self-transcendence and transformation. The cards were literally irreplaceable, their destruction inconceivable. Kate could not imagine how her aunt would explain it.

When Kate went at one o'clock to the kitchen to make herself a roast beef and pickle sandwich, the house was a tomb. Aunt Jaggers had ordered luncheon brought to her room; Aunt Sabrina was still absent. Mrs. Pratt was stonily silent, Harriet crept about like a mouse, and poor Nettie was nowhere to be seen. Perhaps she had been exiled again to the cellar, Kate thought with a feeling of sad helplessness. Amelia and Mudd were somewhere above stairs, going invisibly about their work.

It was another gray, misty day. After she had eaten, Kate pulled on wellies, wrapped herself in a shawl, and went with an umbrella into the garden, where stalks of purple asters vied for pride of place with mounds of yellow chrysanthemums and fragrant lavender. But not even the wistful autumn loveliness of an English garden could keep her mind from Aunt Jaggers's threats, and she turned them over uneasily in her thoughts. What hold did the woman have over Aunt Sabrina? Could she *really* compel Kate's return to America? And what was that odd business about the vicar? What role did he play in the lives of these two women?

After a while Kate came back inside and built up the library fire once again, noticing that Aunt Sabrina had been in the room and had taken Mr. Mathers's private letter to Mrs. Farnsworth from the desk. Ten minutes later, as she was settling down to work, she heard the sound of wheels on gravel. She opened the French doors that led onto the terrace outside the library, and saw that Pocket, a mackintosh cloak thrown over his shoulders against the rain, had brought the carriage round.

Kate turned away from the French doors as Aunt Sabrina came into the library, wearing a coat and fur hat. There was a wild, almost frantic look about her.

"Why, Aunt," Kate said, immediately concerned, "whatever is the matter?"

"I must go out," Aunt Sabrina replied distractedly. She was holding Mr. Mathers's letter in her hand.

"Must you?" Kate asked. "It's chilly outside, and wet. If you wish to return Mr. Mathers's letter to Mrs. Farnsworth, I'm sure I could do it for you just as well."

Aunt Sabrina was trembling. "What I have to do, *I* must do," she said, almost incoherently. "Only I can prevent—" She stopped. "It is a matter of the utmost urgency."

"Then permit me to go with you," Kate said, beginning to be frightened by her aunt's strange behavior. "If you will wait just a moment while I get my—"

"No," Aunt Sabrina said, disregarding Kate's hand on her arm. She pulled on a glove, dropping the other in her haste. "My errands may take some time, Kathryn." She picked up the glove and yanked it on. A button snapped off and bounced across the floor, but she did not notice. "I shall likely not be home until after tea."

Kate stepped back, dismayed. What could be so urgent about Mr. Mathers's letter that it had to be returned on such an inclement day? Why did Aunt Sabrina herself have to do it? And what did she hope to prevent?

Perhaps, though, the letter was not the real purpose of her errand. Perhaps it was Aunt Jaggers's wanton destruction of the Golden Dawn tarot deck that she was in such haste to communicate to Mrs. Farnsworth. Kate moved to the fireplace and stood, watching her aunt. It was only conjecture that Aunt Sebrina was going to Mrs. Farnsworth's. Perhaps she was going to see someone else. Who could it be?

But Aunt Sabrina's white, thin-lipped face made it clear that there would be no answer to this question. Kate reluctantly bade her goodbye and went to the French doors to watch the carriage depart, Pocket giving an encouraging chirrup to the wet horse. When the drive was empty, she returned to her chair and resumed her typing. But while she tried very hard to focus on her task, she could not help worrying about Aunt Sabrina, driving through the rain to some unknown destination, to fulfill some unknown purpose. She could not help worrying about herself, too, and her mind kept returning to the question she had asked herself in the garden. Could Aunt Jaggers actually compel her to leave Bishop's Keep and return to America?

In spite of her troubled thoughts, Kate managed to finish the transcription of the cipher manuscript by teatime. She wasn't quite sure what use Mr. Yeats would make of it. The magical rituals were fragmentary, not very interesting, and actually rather silly. As far as she could see, its real value was not in its hocus-pocus, but in its history: it was, after all, supposed to be very old, written down by some long-ago secret society and passed from one adept to another, carefully safeguarded by its communication in cipher.

Well, Kate thought, putting the transcript aside, whatever the value of the document to Mr. Yeats, it was typed, and neatly, too. At least he would be able to read it clearly. Her next task—and by far the most important she had undertaken so far—was to translate the letters Fräulein Sprengel had written, in German, to Dr. Westcott, giving him the authority he needed to establish the Order of the Golden Dawn. She was looking forward to the work, for she enjoyed translating. While she was not expert in German, she felt she knew it well.

But as Kate began to work, she discovered something that both surprised and puzzled her. Fräulein Sprengel was supposed to be an educated German woman, but her letters contained several very elementary mistakes in grammar, not to mention numerous spelling errors, the sort usually committed by English speakers with an imperfect knowledge of the language. For example, the word *adressiert*—address—was spelled with two d's when it should have had but one; the English word *secretary* appeared in place of the German *Sekretar*, and "Lodge" had been used instead of *Loge*. Kate pressed her lips together and shook her head. If she had not been told differently, she would have guessed that the letters—which were of vital importance to anyone concerned with the Order's legitimacy—had been written by an Englishman who was only superficially acquainted with German! This guess would have been further supported by the fact that Fräulein Sprengel's name and modern address were part of a document which purported to be quite ancient.

But the business of the cipher document seemed academic. Kate had a larger and more immediate problem to worry about—and, anyway, it was getting late and she was tired. She folded the letters and put them back in the box, her mind returning to her own dilemma. What would she do if Aunt Jaggers insisted that she leave and Aunt Sabrina had neither the will nor the strength to withstand her sister?

Kate stood up and went to the French doors to look out at the afternoon. The rain had stopped, the clouds were clearing away, and a pale, translucent light seemed to suffuse the landscape. She rested her cheek against the cool glass and stared out at the rain-wet trees.

What could she do to prevent Aunt Jaggers from sending her back to America? She had been at Bishop's Keep only a few weeks, but already she felt at home here, and the idea of leaving was surprisingly painful. She twisted a lock of hair around her finger, considering what she should do. Unfortunately, there did not seem to be many choices. She suspected that Aunt Sabrina might find it easier to let her go than to confront her sister, whose threat of revelation— revelation of what?—had almost seemed to annihilate her. And without Aunt Sabrina's protection, she would be, like Jenny Blyly, homeless.

But not, Kate thought, helpless. She straightened her shoulders and her lips firmed. Aunt Jaggers might be able to eject her from Bishop's Keep, but she could not force her onto the boat. In the circumstances, Aunt Sabrina would probably be generous in the matter of severance pay. She would have what she had earned so far, and Beryl Bardwell was due a payment from *Frank Leslie's Popular Monthly* when she delivered "The Conspiracy of the Golden Scarab." She might be able to find a cottage to let in Dedham or in Colchester, where she could see Aunt Sabrina from time to time.

Kate stepped back from the window, already beginning to feel better. No, she could not prevent Aunt Jaggers from doing whatever she chose to do. But she was not by nature one who surrendered easily. If she were forced to leave, she was resourceful enough to fend for herself. Unlike Jenny Blyly, she knew she would survive.

31

"A prudent mistress disciplines without resort to the whip, for a servant violently dealt with will respond in kind."
— MRS. AUGUSTA MANNERS
The Arts of Household Management, 1886

A HALF HOUR later, Kate finished her work, set her desk in order, and covered the Remington with its black oilcloth shroud. Aunt Sabrina had said she wouldn't be home for tea, and Kate, who was not yet accustomed to having people wait upon her, hated to put the servants to the bother of doing something she could do perfectly well for herself. She left the library to go down to the kitchen and find something to eat.

But the kitchen was the scene of chaos. Harriet was huddled in a heap on the floor, her apron pulled over her head. Aunt Jaggers, cap, hair, and face streaming water, was shrieking in fury at Mrs. Pratt. And Mrs. Pratt, her cheek and eye reddened as if from a smart blow, was holding the half-empty slops pail at the ready.

"Slut!" Aunt Jaggers cried. "Fat, lazy—"

"Hold yer tongue!" Mrs. Pratt cautioned fiercely, raising the bucket. "Or I'll douse yer again. Th' nerve o'yer, hittin' a pore child with yer fist!"

"You are dismissed, Cook!" Aunt Jaggers shrilled. She raised her hand and stepped forward as if to strike Mrs. Pratt another blow. "Pack your bags and—"

"Stop, both of you!" Kate commanded sharply. "What in heaven's name has happened?"

"She hit Harriet i' the face with her fist," Mrs. Pratt said in a tone of outrage, "an' then she hit me. The woman's out o' her bloody mind!"

"I won't have brazen insolence in my house!" Aunt Jaggers cried. "The girl is impertinent."

" 'Tis not yer house," Mrs. Pratt retorted with great dignity. " 'Tis yer sister's house, and none o' yers."

Aunt Jaggers stamped her foot, her face livid. "Send Pocket for the constable, Niece Ardleigh. I want this woman jailed for assault."

Mrs. Pratt's eyes were narrowed, her glance steely. "As to assault, 'twas Jaggers who struck th' first blow, against pore Harriet. All I did was—"

Aunt Jaggers pointed a trembling finger. "You threw a bucket of slops on me!"

" 'Twere a half bucket," Mrs. Pratt replied calmly. "An' if need be, I'll use th' rest of it, an' th' bucket besides." Her mouth tightened. "An' as fer packin' me bags, it was a Ardleigh wot hired me an' it'll be a Ardleigh wot sacks me."

"I think," Kate said firmly, "that we had all better calm ourselves." She looked at her aunt. "I do not believe this is a matter for the constable, Aunt Jaggers. My uncle O'Malley is a policeman, and I know that they are reluctant to intervene in domestic matters. And there would be the embarrassment of—"

"Who asked you to intervene, miss?" Aunt Jaggers's face was wrathful. "When the constable comes, I will order him to—"

But Kate did not discover what order her aunt intended to give the constable, for Mudd came into the kitchen at that moment, carrying a coal scuttle. Aunt Jaggers, apparently feeling outnumbered, choked off her threat, glared balefully at the three of them, and stamped out. Crooning words of comfort, Mrs. Pratt bent over the sobbing Harriet and lifted her to a chair. With a savage look at Aunt Jaggers's departing back, Mudd thumped the scuttle on the hearth and went outside, slamming the door behind him.

"Do you think we should summon the doctor?" Kate asked worriedly, with a look at Harriet. The girl's cheek was heavily bruised, and her right eye was beginning to swell.

"No," Mrs. Pratt said, smoothing Harriet's hair away from her face. "I'll make a comfrey poultice. Th' doctor culd do no better." She went toward the pantry.

Impulsively, Kate bent over the frightened girl. "It will be all right," she said, touching her cheek gently, but she was at once swept by a feeling of sad helplessness. How could she promise Harriet that Aunt Jaggers's brutality would be restrained, when she herself was vulnerable to the woman's whims? If Aunt Sabrina would not do what should be done, no one could protect the servants.

Biting her lip and wishing she had not offered such an easy comfort when there was none to be had, Kate turned away to prepare her tea. She kept her eyes on what she was doing, but as she heard Mrs. Pratt moving about the kitchen, preparing Harriet's poultice, a gnawing apprehension, a kind of fearful expectation grew in her mind.

"Jaggers is who killed Jenny," Mrs. Pratt had said bitterly. "All o' us knows it. All o' us hates her fer it." Kate could not escape the terrible feeling that a hurricane was about to strike above stairs, and a volcano to erupt below, and that both events would leave behind a scarred and barren landscape that none of them would recognize.

There was a soft knock at the back door. With an unreadable glance at Kate, Mrs. Pratt moved toward it. "Who's there?" she called out quietly.

"Tom Potter," a muffled voice replied.

Kate frowned. Tom Potter?

All o' us hates her fer it. Tom Potter most of all.

Mrs. Pratt faced Kate. "If yer done makin' yer tea, miss," she said pointedly, "Mudd'll take that tray up fer yer."

Kate picked up the tray she had prepared. "Thank you," she said, "but I can do it." She walked toward the door to the stairs. When she reached it, she turned.

Mrs. Pratt had already admitted Tom Potter, speaking to him in quick, hard sentences. He was a slender, boyish-looking young man in a rough brown coat, brown trousers, and brown felt hat. A fierceness shone in his eyes, and when he stepped to the fireplace to bend over Harriet, his voice was soft but vibrating with a scarcely restrained anger.

"Don' cry, child," he said quietly. "We'll make it right, I swear t' yer. She'll not be beatin' yer again."

Mrs. Pratt stepped swiftly forward, interposing herself between Kate and the visitor. It was clear that there would be no introduction. Instead, she said, her voice level, "I'm grateful t' yer, miss, fer what ye did this evenin'."

"I wish I could have done more," Kate said.

"Ye did what ye culd." She squinted at Kate, considering. " 'Tis true yer uncle's a copper?"

"Yes," Kate said.

"Ah," Cook said thoughtfully. She seemed about to say something else, but instead grasped the stairway door and opened it so Kate could go through. "Well, ring if yer wants anythin' else."

"I shall," Kate said. "Thank you."

The apprehension did not leave Kate as she carried her tray upstairs to her room; rather, it was magnified by the recollection of Jenny's lover, vowing to right Harriet's wrong. All considerations of morality and ethics aside, Aunt Jaggers was inviting trouble when she mistreated the servants. It was not unheard of for them to take revenge, for the person who felt entrapped and powerless to turn to crime. There was the Belgian maid who strangled her elderly employer. And the Irish maid-of-all-work who was hanged at Newgate for bludgeoning her employer, hacking her body into pieces, and—

Kate shook herself. She couldn't dismiss the fears that menaced her. They were legitimate, for the wrongs Jenny and Harriet had suffered were real wrongs, just as the Belgian maid and Kate Webster were real murderers, and not merely characters in Beryl Bardwell's sensational thrillers. But she couldn't give way to her apprehension, for if she did, she would have to ask herself what would happen to *her*, caught as she was in the web of her aunt's malice.

Kate carried her tray into her room, lighted the fire, and sat down to eat, grateful for the silence and the opportunity to be alone. When she was finished, she pulled off her shoes and took out the manuscript of "The Conspiracy of the Golden Scarab." If she expected to meet her deadline, she had to work—regardless of what storms might be brewing around her.

She scribbled furiously for several hours, pausing only to refill her teacup and mend the fire. When she finally laid down her pen and gulped the last of the cold tea, her draft of the next chapter—set in an English country manor and featuring characters that greatly resembled Sir Charles Sheridan and Bradford and Eleanor Marsden— was done. It was a trifle short on sensation, she thought critically, but it was satisfyingly full of the realistic details her readers loved. Perhaps she could devise a startling plot twist—a death or some other disaster—involving the medium, whose character was beginning to seem to Kate more and more ambiguous. She still had the notes she had scribbled after her visit to Mrs. Farnsworth's. She might even work Oscar Wilde and Conan Doyle into the plot—suitably disguised, of course.

And the Irish maid who had been hanged at Newgate for bludgeoning her mistress.

32

"But answer came there none."
—Sir Walter Scott
The Bridal of Triermain

IT WAS RAINING in a drizzly, half hearted fashion when Charles got back on his horse after leaving Mrs. Farnsworth's house on Keenan Street. If the lady had any answers, she had not imparted them to him. But perhaps there was another way to get to the bottom of the affair. He rode toward the village of Dedham, three miles to the north of Marsden Manor, along the River Stour.

Charles remembered Dedham quite well from the days of his youth. It was a market town for the hamlet of East Bergholt, where he had spent summers that he still recalled with joy and wonder, visiting his grandparents and wandering the wooded hills and sweet, shallow vales. Dedham lay on the south side of the river, whose lush green banks sloped into deep water, verges fringed with willow and hawthorn and populated by choirs of songbirds. Barges moved slowly westward on the river from the harbor at Manningtree, through locks at Flatford and Dedham and Stratford St. Mary.

Dedham's High Street ran east and west along one side of a small square. On the northeast corner stood The Marlborough Head, a half-timbered building of respectable vintage that had served as a wool market in the fifteenth century, an apothecary in the seventeenth century, and finally, after 1704 and the Battle of Blenheim, as an inn, named for the first Duke of Marlborough. It had from time to time offered the young Charles a place to warm himself and eat a hot pork pie while waiting for his grandfather to complete his business. Across High Street stood the brick Grammar School, a fine Georgian building with a calm facade and stately demeanor. And on the corner opposite stood the pride of the village, the Church of St. Mary the Virgin, its tower foursquare and of commanding height, founded on the wealth of the woolen industry and raised before King Henry's bold interference in the divine order of things. The walls were faced with stone from Caen and local knapped flint had been used to construct the tower. The buttresses were outlined heavily by large quoins of dressed stone, and in the plinth of the tower was an arrangement of quatrefoiled shields, alternating with crowns. It was altogether an impressive church, the cornerstone of village life.

The vicarage was much less picturesquely impressive, designed not to celebrate the spirit but to answer the needs of the body for shelter and comfort. It stood beside the church, a solid, tidy brick residence with a slate roof, a respectable number of chimney pots, and green shutters. A carriage waited in the street, the mackintoshed driver hunched over his reins, clearly unhappy about the wet. As Charles rode up, a woman in a fur hat came out of the front door, her mouth set, her face marked by evident distress. She climbed into the carriage and drove off.

In the front hallway, Charles's damp coat was taken by the solicitous housekeeper and he was shown into a small, dark parlor warmed by a brisk fire. A few moments later, Vicar Talbot appeared, a troubled look on his lined face and his lion's mane of white hair disheveled, as if his pastoral shoulders still bore the burden left behind by his just-departed parishioner. The vicar was followed by the housekeeper with the tea tray, and the next few moments were spent in the business of pouring and passing. By the time Charles was settled in his overstuffed chair by the fire, teacup and muffin plate on the table beside, the vicar's ruffled hair and troubled expression seemed somewhat soothed.

"Well, Sir Charles," he said, relaxing into his chintz chair opposite. "What brings you out on such a dismal day?"

"A question or two," Charles said, "concerning the man whose body was found in the Colchester digs."

The vicar raised an eyebrow. "Ah, yes," he said, filling his pipe with tobacco. "And what has been discovered thus far about the unfortunate gentleman?"

"Very little," Charles admitted. "We have a nationality—French—and a name—Monsieur Armand—although whether either are precisely correct is difficult to say."

"We?" the vicar asked. "That is, you and—"

"The police, of course," Charles said. "Inspector Wainwright refuses to bring the Yard into a matter that clearly requires more resources than he has. I am doing what I can, which I fear is deuced little."

"To be sure," the vicar replied. He sipped his tea. "Nothing else has been discovered?"

"The carriage he hired, in which I found a fingerprint. Unfortunately, the victim has already been buried, so I cannot discover whether it is his fingerprint or belongs to someone else. If a suspect is found, I shall certainly attempt to take his prints and look for a match. And something else," he added casually. "A bit of feather. *Pavo christatus*."

The vicar glanced up sharply, then went back to his pipe. Watching, Charles thought he saw an intensification of the troubled look the old man had worn when he came in the room. "Found the carriage, did you?" he remarked, propping his feet on the chintz-covered stool in front of him. "That took a bit of luck." He smiled. "Or deft detecting."

Charles nodded. "The peacock feather, I have been told, is the insignia of the Order of the Golden Dawn."

The vicar puffed calmly on his pipe. "Quite so," he replied. "But peacock feathers have been the rage for some years now. Everybody has them. Even I." He gestured at a ceramic vase of dried grass fronds and peacock feathers in the corner.

"Of course," Charles said thoughtfully. "Still, it is a clue, and there are bloody few of them in this affair." He paused. "You are a member of the Order, if I understood you correctly the other evening."

"I . . . am." His reply was slow, almost reluctant.

Charles gave the other man an inquiring glance. When they talked previously, the vicar had seemed impressed with the Order, had even recommended it. Had something occurred to change his view? He spoke quietly. "I wonder, sir, if you would oblige me by telling me something of it."

The vicar made a small grimace and shifted in his chair. "What do you want to know?"

"Something of its history, perhaps."

"Well, then," the vicar said, as if resigned. "I first heard of it six years ago, at a meeting of the Metropolitan College of the Society of Rosicrucians. Wynn Westcott spoke of it. He is a coroner of London—then and now, a man of utterly impeccable repute." He shook his head slightly. There was in his face a kind of regretful disappointment, as if he were speaking of someone about whom he had held a mistakenly elevated opinion and could scarcely believe that he had been in error.

He came back to himself and began to speak again. "Dr. Westcott invited me to a meeting of the temple—the Isis-Urania Temple, it was called, newly established in London. I was delighted to be asked to enter as a Neophyte." A

211

tone of wry irony colored his words. "A neophyte, indeed. I fear I had much to learn, although I thought at the time I knew quite a lot."

"Neophyte is a rank of entry?"

"Yes. The members progress through various ranks, as do the Freemasons. With the proper study and the passing of certain tests, I advanced through the grades of the Outer Order—Neophyte, Zelator, Theoricus, Practicus, and Philosophus—and thence to the Second Order, where I now stand at the Sixth Grade, as an Adeptus Major."

"It sounds as if there is much effort involved in this work," Charles remarked.

"I have always been interested in the magical arts, and count the time as study of little consequence." The vicar's mouth set in a firm, fixed line, and bitterness crept into his tone. "I have prided myself on my commitment to scientific inquiry into the occult, not out of superstitious credulousness, but on the firm foundation of objective science. To learn now that I may have been—" He bit off his sentence.

"May have been what, sir?"

The vicar straightened. "I think, Sir Charles, that I have said as much as I am able—more, perhaps, than I should have done. The Golden Dawn is, after all, a secret society, and its practices must remain confidential."

Charles took a different tack. "How long has Mrs. Farnsworth been a member of the Order?"

The vicar's gaze went back to the fire. "Ah, yes. Mrs. Farnsworth." He puffed on his pipe and a wreath of smoke rose over his head. "I first encountered the lady in the Isis-Urania Temple. An actress, then Florence Faber. Have you met?"

"This morning," Charles said. "I called on her."

The vicar nodded. "Her stage career, it appears, came to something of an abrupt conclusion. She apparently refused to honor a contract, which angered the play's producers.

Subsequently, a larger difficulty arose over a substantial sum of money she is said to have ... borrowed." He paused. "I have not inquired into the details, you understand, but I gather that there were accusations on both sides, and that the matter was concluded without litigation only on the condition that her departure from the London stage be a permanent one."

"In other words," Charles said, "she has been blacklisted."

"So it would seem. She married an admirer—a Colchester merchant who was said to have made a substantial fortune in railroad stock. But he died shortly after the honeymoon, leaving her to discover—with some understandable shock, I daresay—that the expected fortune had melted into a sea of debts. She only just managed to keep the house on Keenan Street from going on the auctioneer's block."

"How does she support herself?"

"By the contributions of the wealthier members of the temple. They are glad to give generously toward the establishment of the Order in Colchester. Mrs. Farnsworth has been energetic in seeing to its expansion, and the membership here now exceeds that in Edinburgh, Bradford, and Paris, combined. She is also supported because she is a friend of Westcott's," he added. There was a touch of acid in his tone. "In the view of the members, Westcott is a god."

"She does not plan to return to acting, then."

"On the contrary, she does, although not at the present in London. Some friends of hers and Westcott's—again, wealthy members of the temple—are working toward that end. She will play Rosalind in *As You Like It*, when the Grand Theatre opens early next year."

"You mentioned Paris," Charles said reflectively. "There is a Parisian temple, operated by someone named Mathers, I believe."

The vicar pulled rapidly on his pipe. "Mathers. Indeed. Mathers."

"Is he connected with the Order here in England?"

"He *was,*" the vicar said. The pulling became so agitated that it turned into a spate of coughing. "Fancies himself an occultist," the vicar choked out. "Involved with the Kabbalah, astrology, the tarot. An eccentric with an exaggerated sense of his own importance, in my opinion. And a troublemaker."

"But no immediate connection with the British Order?"

The vicar's knuckles whitened around his pipe stem. The thought of Mathers seemed to waken some deep emotion in him, anger, perhaps even fear. "None, Sir Charles, that I am at liberty to discuss at this time." He pushed himself to the edge of the chair. "I have only partially answered your questions, and I am distressed to thrust you out once more into the wet. But I fear that my Sunday sermon is still in a state of disrepair and requires my active attentions. Do you mind?"

"Of course not," Charles said, setting his cup on the table. "But before you go, perhaps . . ." He opened his portfolio. "Can you tell me if you recognize this man?"

The vicar took the photograph. "This is the murdered man?" he asked. A tic appeared at the corner of his right eye.

"Yes," Charles said.

The vicar handed back the photograph and stood, not meeting Charles's eye. "I am afraid I cannot help you," he said.

Charles rose as well, hearing the evasion in the clergyman's words. There might be answers here, but for the moment Vicar Talbot was keeping them to himself.

33

"What secrets are hidden behind the tapestry of dark?"

— MRS. BLEDSOME
The Aunt's Revenge, 1886

IT WAS NEARLY eight when Kate heard the carriage return. A few minutes later, she heard Aunt Sabrina's slow step on the stair, and the closing of her bedroom door. Thinking that her aunt was surely tired and hungry, Kate put on her shoes and went out into the passage. Outside Aunt Sabrina's door, she tapped gently. When she heard a blurred sound she took to be an assent, she opened the door and went in.

Aunt Sabrina was sitting at her dressing table with her back to the door, her head in her hands. She did not look up or turn around.

"You must be tired, Aunt Sabrina," Kate said gently. She needn't tell her now about the altercation in the kitchen, or Tom Potter; the tale had to be told, but it could wait until she was rested. "Would you like me to fix you a bit of hot supper? I could bring it up on a tray."

Aunt Sabrina raised her head and looked at Kate in the dressing table mirror. Her face was gray and old-looking and her eyes were darkly hollowed, but she managed a small smile. "You needn't bother, dear," she said. "I am not hungry."

Kate stared at her aunt's reflection in shocked silence. What had happened during her meeting with Mrs. Farnsworth—if that was where she had gone—to turn her skin the color of putty?

Aunt Sabrina turned around. "My dear Kathryn," she said, and then stopped. For a moment she hesitated, as if deciding whether she should speak and how much she should say. Then she seemed to come to some painful resolution and began again, her voice faltering a little.

"Kathryn, I know you are concerned for my well-being, and I very much wish that I could share with you what has transpired today. But I cannot." The lines around her mouth were deeply drawn and the crepey skin below her eyes was smudged with weariness.

"I understand," Kate said, genuinely touched by her aunt's obvious dilemma. She turned to go, but Aunt Sabrina gestured, seeming to want to speak. Kate waited.

"There is one thing more," she said at last. "Please do not distress yourself about your aunt Jaggers, Kathryn. Whatever I must do, I shall do, and quickly." Her voice took on a brittle metallic ring and her eyes, steely now, met Kate's directly. "You will *not* be sent away. And if something should happen to me, I have seen to it that your future here at Bishop's Keep is secure."

"Thank you, Aunt," Kate said. But she was frightened by the tone of her aunt's voice. What did Aunt Sabrina fear that she would have to do to restrain Aunt Jaggers?

But it was not a question Kate could ask, and when she sought her aunt's eyes again, they were hooded and remote. Kate sensed that she had come at last to some decision, to a choice that brought with it both a desperate regret and a profound pain, so pervasive and wounding that Kate could only guess at its depth and dimension.

Aunt Sabrina turned around again. "Now please allow me to be alone," she said. "I have a great deal to consider." Her shoulders slumped and her voice dropped, so that Kate almost did not hear her next words. "I fear that my future has been greatly altered—and not just mine, but that of persons for whom I care."

The distance between them was only a few steps. Kate ached to cross it and put her arms around her aunt. But she could not. Whatever was troubling Aunt Sabrina was something she had decided to bear alone. With a murmured "Sleep well" she left. She had the disquieting sense that she was closing the door on a tragedy.

Back in her room, Kate considered whether she should go to bed. But if she did, she would only lie restlessly awake. So she gathered up her papers and went downstairs to the library, where she lighted the oil lamp beside the shrouded Remington. It was after eight o'clock and the old house was silent, the servants in their quarters, Aunt Jaggers in her west wing suite, Aunt Sabrina in her room. It was a good time to type the chapter she had just completed, and to revise and expand it as she went.

Caught up in her work, Kate spent far more time than she had expected. According to the loudly ticking grandfather clock in the corner, it was close to eleven when she finished the last page to her satisfaction. She poked up the dying fire, added coal, and sat beside it in the tall wing chair to read what she had written. Then, seeing that the lamp was about to run out of oil, she turned it out and sat for a few minutes longer in the dark, watching the last flickers of the fire, letting her mind go to the questions that seemed most central to her life at Bishop's Keep.

What was the source of the enmity between Aunt Sabrina and Aunt Jaggers? But, of course, that was an unanswerable question, for it was impossible to know what secrets were buried in the intimacies of sisters. The complex tapestry of the present was woven out of threads of the past, of old loves, old hates, old sins, even old slights. The thing that seemed most trivial, most innocent in intention, was often most deeply felt and long remembered.

But the question still remained, as tantalizing as a book in some foreign tongue. What ancient silence did Aunt Jaggers threaten to break? What secret did she know that Aunt Sabrina feared to have revealed—so greatly feared that she allowed Aunt Jaggers to violate moral principles that she held dear? How did this matter concern the vicar, who seemed like an entirely pleasant and harmless old man? And how did Aunt Sabrina intend—if that was her intention—to break her sister's hold over her? Kate shifted in the wing chair, drawing her stockinged feet up under her. And what had happened during the afternoon and evening to bring Aunt Sabrina home looking like death warmed over?

Kate pondered the question for a long time, while the fire burned down and the room grew colder. They were questions like those she often created in her story-making, but they had a real-life urgency that she never experienced in her writing. And they were unanswerable precisely because she did not have control over what real people did or thought or believed, as she did over the characters in her novels. It was easy enough for her hero to solve the crime that she put before him, complete with clues that invited his deduction. Not so easy for her to understand the intricacies of a plot she had not contrived, or the hearts of people whose secrets were hidden from her, and perhaps even from themselves.

Kate stirred. She was just concluding that there was nothing to be gained from sitting in the dark, mulling over questions that had no answers, when she heard the noise. It was only a tiny click, and she might not have heard it at all if her ears had not been attuned to utter silence. She twisted around in the chair, startled. Behind her, in the dimness, she saw one of the French doors begin to swing open. Someone was entering the library!

Quick as thought, Kate reached for the poker. With a wild yell, she leaped out of the chair, brandishing the poker, and dashed for the door. On the dark terrace outside, she heard the scramble of feet, a clatter, and a muffled oath as the intruder knocked over a flowerpot, and the sound of running footsteps on gravel. A moment later, there was the thud of a horse's hooves galloping down the lane. The intruder had made good his escape.

"Wha's happ'nin'?" came a sleepy voice from the direction of the servants' wing. A casement window flew open and Mudd, in his nightshirt, put out his head. "What's goin' on out there?" he demanded. "What's all th' noise?"

Kate stood in the doorway, shoeless, the poker still in her hand. Now that the danger was over, she could feel herself shaking. "A thief tried to break in, Mr. Mudd," she replied, trying to steady her voice. Mudd's head disappeared.

Kate went back into the library and, with shaking hands, lighted a candle at a dying coal on the hearth. She stepped out onto the terrace again, sheltering its flame with her hand. There was nothing, of course. The intruder had gotten completely away.

Then her eye fell on something lying on the clipped grass, beside the tumbled flowerpot. She picked it up and turned it in her hands.

The intruder might have escaped, but he had left his brown felt hat behind.

34

"Them that asks no questions isn't told a lie."
—RUDYARD KIPLING
A Smugglers's Song

KATE WAS OUTSIDE early the next morning. The rain had stopped well before dawn and the morning was a cheerful one, mild and bright, promising a fine day. With Aunt Sabrina and Mudd, Kate made a tour of the shrubbery, trying to identify the intruder's route of escape. But if he had left footprints or his horse any hoof prints, they had been obscured by the heavy rain that fell shortly after midnight. Mudd sent Pocket to notify the constable about the attempted break-in, and Kate and Aunt Sabrina returned to the library.

"So the only clue to the intruder's identity is the brown felt hat," Kate said, turning it over in her hands.

"Hardly a clue, I should think," Aunt Sabrina said. "It looks as if it came out of a dustbin."

"Perhaps you are right," Kate said slowly. She would have to tell Aunt Sabrina about the man who had visited the kitchen the day before. Jenny Blyly's young man, Tom Potter. He must have been the intruder, and he was clearly up to no good. And there was the matter of the altercation

220

between Aunt Jaggers and Mrs. Pratt. Aunt Sabrina would have to know about that, as well.

But perhaps not at this very moment. Aunt Sabrina did not look well. Her eyes were smudged, her voice strained. Her costume this morning was a navy blue dress fitted far more conservatively than her usual loose gowns, and she wore a gold watch clipped to a brooch on her lapel. Her gray hair was arranged in a tidy knot at the back of her neck. Her appearance was more severe than it had been since Kate's arrival, and her mouth was set, as if she had come to some conclusion that she did not relish.

"Tramping about the shrubbery so early has made me rather hungry," Aunt Sabrina said. "Shall we have some breakfast?" She paused a moment, and then added, as if in afterthought, "We shall not be working this morning, Kathryn."

Kate looked at her aunt in surprise. "No?"

"No." Aunt Sabrina's tone was flat. "I have determined to set the history aside for the moment. When I am ready to resume work, I shall tell you."

"But I have already begun to translate Fräulein Sprengel's letters," Kate objected gently. She frowned, remembering the questions and reservations about the letters that had arisen in her mind the afternoon before. But that seemed so long ago, and of much less consequence than the events that had occurred since. There was really no point in mentioning her concerns, especially if they were not going forward with the history.

Aunt Sabrina's face had darkened. "Ah, yes, the letters. Please collect them for me, and the cipher document and its transcription, and any copies you may have made of either." Aunt Sabrina's voice was firm and authoritative, and her manner invited neither remark nor rebuttal.

"Yes, Aunt," Kate said obediently, and began to gather the documents into a neat stack. She handed it to Aunt Sabrina.

"Is this all?"

"Yes, Aunt."

Aunt Sabrina took them. "Thank you," she said. "Please follow me." Without a word, she went from the room, with Kate a half step behind, wondering at the determined set of the other woman's shoulders. What had happened during Aunt Sabrina's absence yesterday to change her so decidedly? Where had she gone? Whom had she seen? What had she learned?

In her bedroom, Aunt Sabrina took a framed oil from the wall. Where the painting had hung was a small safe, which Aunt Sabrina opened with a key she took from the top drawer of a delicate Queen Anne desk.

"The documents are to remain here until they are asked for by the vicar," Aunt Sabrina said. She put them into the safe, and secured it with the key. She looked directly at Kate. "Were I to answer your questions about the letters, my dear, I would have to lie." She turned away with a firmness that absolutely concluded the matter.

But there was something else Kate needed to say, and she could not delay any longer. She cleared her throat. "Aunt Sabrina," she said, "something happened in the kitchen yesterday evening that I feel you should know about."

Aunt Sabrina replaced the painting on the wall. "Do not tell me," she said gravely, "that my sister has been at the servants again."

"I am afraid so," Kate said.

Aunt Sabrina was resigned. "What happened?"

"Aunt Jaggers struck Harriet. Mrs. Pratt came to her defense and dumped a half bucket of water on Aunt Jaggers." Kate hesitated, and then added, "Aunt Jaggers fired her."

Aunt Sabrina's mouth tightened. "Bernice discharged Cook!" she exclaimed in surprise. "What *can* she have been thinking of!"

Kate smiled a little. "I don't believe she was thinking at all. Perhaps by now she has cooled. At any rate, Mrs. Pratt stood her ground. She is awaiting your decision about her future employment."

"I will speak to Cook," Aunt Sabrina said with taut anger. There were spots of color high on her cheeks, and her nostrils were flared. "And then to Bernice. If I had not already decided to put an end to her threats and petty cruelties, this would be the last straw."

Kate stared, surprised at her aunt's anger. If she were reacting to her sister's treatment of Harriet and Cook, surely her response was exaggerated. But Kate already suspected that there was something else between them, some bitter secret Aunt Jaggers had been holding over Aunt Sabrina like a dagger. It looked as if Aunt Sabrina had decided to take matters into her own hands. What was she going to do? Was she willing to risk the disclosure of the secret information that Aunt Jaggers seemed to hold?

Aunt Sabrina turned. "I find I have lost my appetite for breakfast," she said, "but I wish to speak with the servants. Would you mind, Kathryn, accompanying me below stairs?"

"Of course not," Kate said. "There is something else, though." She hesitated, wondering whether she should tell Aunt Sabrina about Tom Potter. But perhaps it would be well to speak with Mrs. Pratt first. She made up her mind. "There is something else, though," she repeated. "It's a small thing, but I'm afraid it must be dealt with this morning. During my visit to Marsden Manor on the day before yesterday, I invited the Marsdens—Eleanor, Patsy, and Bradford—and Sir Charles to luncheon here today. I meant to speak to you about it yesterday, but an occasion did not present itself. Today does not seem the best time for a social call. When Pocket returns from the village, may I send him with a note, postponing the luncheon?"

"No." Aunt Sabrina's voice was firm. "I am glad that you have invited your friends. Come. We will do our business with the servants, and then speak to Cook about the luncheon. She is a competent cook, but a plain cook, and she will need our assistance with the menu."

35

"We never knows wot's hidden in each other's hearts;
and if we had glass winders there, we'd need keep the
shutters up, some on us, I do assure you!"

—CHARLES DICKENS
Martin Chuzzlewit

M RS. PRATT WAS presiding over the last moments of
the staff breakfast when Miss Ardleigh and the
young miss came into the servants' hall. Seeing them, she
stood up. The rest of the servants hastily followed suit,
pushing back their chairs, their faces carefully bland,
only their eyes registering surprise. Miss Ardleigh had
never appeared in the servants' hall in their time there,
and even Mrs. Pratt had difficulty recalling when she
had last been below stairs. Certainly not since the advent
of Jaggers.

Mudd spoke. "If ye've come about the constable, mum,
Pocket's already bin and back agin."

"I have not, but thank you, Mudd," Miss Ardleigh said.
Mrs. Pratt saw her glance at the plates of toast and egg
and bit of boiled, streaky bacon. Harriet and Nettie were
particularly partial to the bacon, which they did not often

have. It was Mrs. Pratt's effort to make poor amends for Jaggers's ill-treatment. "Have we interrupted your meal?"

"No, mum," Mrs. Pratt lied. She held her face emotionless, but inside she was angrily resentful. Couldn't they even sit down to a meal—plain and parsimonious as it was— without being intruded upon? A lengthy interruption would mean cold food and poor spirits for the rest of the morning. The work was hard enough without that. "D'ye wish to speak to—"

"To all of you, actually," Miss Ardleigh replied evenly. "I have come to apologize, both on my own behalf and that of my sister."

Apologize? Mrs. Pratt stared. Mudd was stunned into speechlessness. Amelia and Pocket were gaping like codfish and Harriet made a small sound, almost a whimper. Nettie wrung her hands. Clearly, it was up to Mrs. Pratt to reply.

"Apology ain't necess'ry, mum," she said, looking back at Miss Ardleigh with narrowed eyes. Apologize? What mistress ever apologized to a servant? It wasn't in the nature of things.

"I fear that it is necessary," Miss Ardleigh said, "even though my words are embarrassing to me and perhaps to you. I find that I must resume management of the household. It is clear to me now, and should have been before this, that my sister is ill-suited to the task of mistress. For yielding up my responsibilities without considering the possible consequences for all of us, I apologize. For her abuse of your rights, I most sincerely apologize."

"Oh, mum!" Harriet burst out passionately, and then bit her lip with a sideways glance at Cook. Mrs. Pratt gave the girl a cold stare, but it was Miss Ardleigh she was angry with. Did she think that by sweeping in here like the Queen herself and dosing them with a spoonful of sweet talk, she could change what had happened—not just last evening, but last spring, when Jenny was turned out? Did she think she could win them over, could erase the memory of those terrible hurts with an easy smile or two? Well, there was more in Mrs. Pratt's heart and mind than Miss Ardleigh knew, if *that's* what she thought!

"From now on," Miss Ardleigh said, "you are to take your direction from me." She looked around at the cheerless room, the cold stone floor, the fireplace absent of fire. "We will begin by restoring the furnishings to this room. Where were they taken?"

"To . . . to the attic, mum," Mrs. Pratt said, blinking.

"Good," Miss Ardleigh replied. "Please have them returned, and the carpet, and see if another chair or two can be found." She shivered. "And unblock the fireplace. It is far too cold in this room to comfortably enjoy your leisure hours here."

Mrs. Pratt allowed herself a small flare of triumph at the thought of the return of the sofa, while Harriet and Nettie seemed nearly overwhelmed at the prospect of a restored fire *and* a carpet. Pocket shifted his feet, grinning.

Miss Ardleigh continued. "Cook, my sister clearly exceeded her authority yesterday when she requested your notice. I do hope you will consent to remain with us."

Mrs. Pratt swallowed. The situation, which had boggled the brain to start with, was becoming curiouser and curiouser.

"That is settled, then," Aunt Sabrina said. She smiled. "You and I will meet this morning to discuss meals, pantry stores, and so forth, and you will acquaint me with any new procedures you have instituted for managing the kitchen. Mudd, you will please inform me about the current state of household accounts, the distribution of responsibilities among the upstairs help, and the state of the grounds."

Mrs. Pratt saw Mudd's eyebrows shoot up and he opened his mouth to speak. But she gave him the slightest shake of her head, and he closed his mouth again.

Miss Ardleigh regarded him curiously for a moment. When he said nothing, she looked around the table, her eyes resting on each one in turn. "In the meantime," she said, "I hope that each of you will accept my thanks for your patience and forbearance. Our household can only run smoothly if we all do our proper parts. I will do mine, I assure you."

That was too much for Amelia. "Bless ye, mum," she said fervently.

Mrs. Pratt cleared her throat sternly, and Amelia had the grace to blush. She always was a forward chit, giving herself airs, putting herself above her station. But even Nettie looked as if she were ready to dance, and Pocket's grin fair split his face. Mrs. Pratt supposed that the younger ones couldn't be blamed for being bamboozled. She herself had heard similar promises before, although not to the extent of returning the fire and the sofa. After the sad business with Jenny, Miss Ardleigh had personally promised that she would rein Jaggers in. But nothing had come of it then, and Mrs. Pratt wasn't going to hold her breath until something came of it now. Anyway, Mrs. Pratt reminded herself murderously, it was *Jaggers* who should be here apologizing, not the mistress.

Miss Ardleigh smiled. "That will be all, then," she said. "We will have guests for luncheon, Cook—an additional four, I believe. Please see me"—she unclipped her watch and consulted it—"in the library an hour from now, with suggestions for the menu." Gathering up her skirts, she swept from the room, her niece behind.

The other servants finished the cold breakfast and left to be about their work, chattering about the prospect of increased daily rations and the exciting prospect— although Miss Ardleigh had not mentioned it—of being released from compulsory prayers. Only Mrs. Pratt and Mudd were left, staring at one another from opposite ends of the table. There was a long silence.

"She'll have t' be told about the accounts," Mudd said. He shook his head with a dark look. "She's not goin't' be 'appy. An' Jaggers is like t' be furious."

"Let her be," Mrs. Pratt said, bleakly smug. "Let her get wot's comin' to her for diddlin'. Little enough, a'ter what she's done." Mrs. Pratt and Mudd had suspected for some months that Jaggers was manipulating the household accounts, but it was only in the last few days that Mudd had confirmed their suspicions through some adroit backward checking. "I figger she knows we know 'bout th' accounts, anyway," she added, draining her coffee. "That's why she come on so sharp yesterday, threat'nin' to sack me. Left to herself, Mudd, ye'd be nex't' go a'ter me."

"What do yer suppose 'as come o'er the mistress, takin' things into 'er own 'ands?" Mudd asked. Reflectively, he ate the last crust of toast. "D'ye think there'll be jam on th' table, an' beer, now that she's runnin' th' manor agin?"

"Dunno," Mrs. Pratt said blackly, "an' don' care. A bit o' jam won't heal what's hurt." She banged her cup on the saucer. She could not help herself. Un-Christian as it was, a poisonous rage, bitter as bile, rose inside her when she thought about Jaggers.

Mudd was thoughtful. "Not t' put too fine a point on't, Mrs. P., but ain't it time t' turn the other cheek?"

"Jam and fire don't go far wi'me," Mrs. Pratt said, from the depths of her wounded spirit. "Who knows wot's hidden in Miss Ardleigh's heart? She didn't raise a hand to help poor Jenny, nor e'en offered to help her find a place, which she culd've done."

Mudd stood up. "Well, I fer one," he announced, "am ready t' let bygones be bygones."

Mrs. Pratt glared at him. "Fine fer ye, Mudd. But fer me, Miss Ardleigh is guilty as Jaggers. Both of 'em deserves wotev'r they git. I only hope it kin be *me* wot dishes it out."

36

"We must leave the family's skeletons to rattle in the dusty dark."

—ANONYMOUS
A Mother's Plot, 1887

KATE NEVER KNEW exactly what went on between Aunt Jaggers and Aunt Sabrina in the library that morning. When Aunt Sabrina dismissed her, she went first to the kitchen to speak to Mrs. Pratt, who was sweeping the floor with an amazing energy.

"Don't know, 'm sure," she said snappishly, when Kate had asked her about the brown felt hat.

"I felt," Kate pressed, "that I had seen the hat before. I recalled the young man who came visiting last evening—Tom Potter. He had such a hat."

Mrs. Pratt stopped sweeping, her face pulled into a scowl. "If yer thinkin' 'twas Tom Potter who came skulkin' roun' the libr'ry, miss, yer wrong."

"But he has reason to dislike—"

"Aye, he has that," Mrs. Pratt said firmly. "But he ain't the sort t' descend t' skulkin'. Me word on't."

And that, for the moment at least, seemed to be that. Although Kate sensed that there was a great deal more to be learned, she was not going to get it out of Mrs. Pratt. She took a basket and scissors and went out into the mild, bright morning to cut flowers for the luncheon table's centerpiece.

After the night's rain, the asters and roses were bedraggled, but Kate had no difficulty finding more than enough. As she filled her basket, she was frankly glad that Aunt Sabrina had not asked her to attend the meeting with Aunt Jaggers. However Jaggers had managed to extort control of the household, it was an authority she valued and she would not easily yield it up. The confrontation between the two aunts was bound to be a painful one, embroidered with old bitterness and—Kate felt sure—laced with ancient secrets. Kate would have liked to know those secrets, but she was glad to be spared the pain of learning them.

And there was the earlier meeting with all the servants to mull over. While her aunt had talked, Kate had observed their faces and had been surprised to observe that not all were equally delighted with Aunt Sabrina's announcement. Amelia, Nettie, Harriet, and Pocket seemed quite pleased, especially at the prospect of gaining a few creature comforts and perhaps a bit more leisure. Mudd, however, had seemed perturbed at Aunt Sabrina's request that he bring her the household accounts. Why?

Kate frowned and clipped a pink rose, still heavy with raindrops. She dropped it into her basket. Was there something about the accounts that Mudd did not want to reveal? Kate's first thought, for Mudd's reaction fitted neatly into a scenario that Beryl Bardwell was considering for "The Conspiracy of the Golden Scarab," was that Mudd himself had been mishandling the household funds and feared to be found out. If true, Kate thought regretfully, it was a pity. In spite of their initial difficulties, she had come to like him.

And she liked Mrs. Pratt, too. But the cook had been even less pleased than the butler by Aunt Sabrina's announcement—which was very odd, Kate thought. She had expected Aunt Jaggers's downfall to bring a smile of triumphant vindication to Mrs. Pratt's face. But in actual fact, her expression had grown blacker and blacker while Aunt Sabrina was talking, until she looked like a summer thunderstorm. It was as if her anger was focused on both the sisters.

No, it was more than anger, Kate thought. It was hatred she had seen in Mrs. Pratt's eyes. It could only be because of Jenny Blyly—which brought up Tom Potter and the brown felt hat.

Kate shook her head, frowning. The below stairs situation was clearly complicated, woven through with as much anger and bitterness as that upstairs. Aunt Sabrina would do what she could, but perhaps the problem could not be solved with the simple removal of Aunt Jaggers. She looked toward the French doors onto the terrace, open to the mild morning, and wondered what her aunts were saying to each other in the library. As she did, someone hurriedly pulled the doors shut. Whatever was being said, her aunts did not wish to be overheard.

37

"If the desire to kill and the opportunity to kill come always together, who would escape hanging?"

—MARK TWAIN

SABRINA TURNED from the doors. "And *that*, sister," she said with a bleak emphasis, "is all there is to it. Now you must make of it what you will."

Bernice felt as if she were choking on the rage that was roaring like an inferno inside. "How can you . . . how can you *dare* to insult me so?" she cried, struggling for words. "How can you—"

"I can, because I have right on my side," Sabrina said simply. "You will no longer direct the servants, and you are to accept the presence of our niece without question." She went to stand beside her desk.

"Right!" Bernice exclaimed. Her voice rose. "After what you did?" She laughed bitterly. "When society knows, you will be completely ostracized. Your name will be destroyed. And *their* names and their future—"

"I am quite prepared to confront my fate," Sabrina said. Her voice was quiet, expressionless. "And I am prepared to allow the others concerned to meet their own. But if society learns of this, it will only be because you have recklessly spread it abroad." She reached down and picked up a letter opener in the shape of a dagger, turning it in her hand. "When you do that, Bernice, you will no longer have a home at Bishop's Keep. For the rest of your days, you will live in a rented flat, subsisting on your widow's pension."

Bernice stared at her sister. "You would not turn me out penniless!" Her throat felt raw, lacerated with the pain of pent-up fury.

"I shall," Sabrina replied, "if you force me to do so." Her face was a mask. Only her gray eyes held life, a suppressed, flashing energy—charged, it seemed to Bernice, with a malicious hatred. "It appears, sister," she added icily, "that we have reached an impasse. If you destroy me and mine, I shall destroy you, quite utterly."

The last words echoed in the silent room, in the empty hollow that had been Bernice's heart. Sabrina had gained the upper hand.

"It is the Irishwoman," Bernice muttered blackly. "She is the one who has turned you against me. Before she came—"

"Bernice!" Sabrina whirled around. "It is absurd to cast recriminations on anyone but yourself." Her voice vibrated, only just in control. "Or on me. If I had not allowed you to—"

"Spare me your self-pity," Bernice cried, the taste of loathing acrid on her tongue. "When you feel the full brunt of society's censure, then you can blame yourself. And pity him, whose career you will have—"

Her face suffused with furious color, Sabrina raised the hand that held the dagger. Bernice flinched. But she was maddened with anger. She could not stop her words.

"—Whose career in the church you will have utterly ruined."

"No more," Sabrina cried, knuckles white around the hilt of the dagger, forearm quivering with murderous violence. "Get out of my sight, Bernice! And stay out, for I cannot promise that I will be able to control this arm!"

Bernice stared at her sister. She felt as if both she and Sabrina had been stripped to the skin and stood mortified in their nakedness—their fear, their anger, their hatred, all exposed to the world. Everything was coming apart. There was nothing to hold on to.

For the first time in her life, Bernice Ardleigh Jaggers was absolutely terrified.

38

"Having taken pains to obtain and compare abundant evidence on this subject I should say that the majority of women (happily for them) are not very much troubled with sexual feelings of any kind. . . As a general rule, a modest woman seldom desires any sexual gratification for herself. She submits to her husband, but only to please him; and but for the desire of maternity would far rather be relieved from his attentions."

—WILLIAM ACTON
The Functions and Disorders of the Reproductive System, 1884

"I AM VERY glad we are able to spend this time together, dear Kate," Eleanor Marsden said, tucking her hand into Kate's arm as they walked along the path to the small lake at the foot of the garden. She turned to look into Kate's face. "I may call you Kate, mayn't I? It is a more *friendly* name than Kathryn." She reached up to smooth an escaped lock of Kate's hair. Her eyes danced. "And you look like a Kate, with that red hair, all flyaway, and the pink in your cheeks, which I warrant is not paint."

"Hardly." Kate laughed. "I will be Kate to you," she said, "if you will be Ellie to me." She was glad, too, for the chance to be with Eleanor. And to get away for a few minutes from the poisonous atmosphere of the house, where above stairs and below, everything seemed terribly out of kilter. Aunt Sabrina and Aunt Jaggers had obviously quarreled very badly; Mudd's face was anxiously somber when he took the account books in to Aunt Sabrina a little while ago; and Mrs. Pratt, preparing the luncheon in the kitchen, was sullen and unspeaking, with an angry, brooding look.

"It is a bargain!" Eleanor exclaimed spiritedly, holding Kate's arm closer. "I already feel, you know, as if I have found another sister." She added with an artless smile, "A dear, older sister, one who has seen something of the world and can give me the very best advice."

Kate smiled a little. She could understand that Eleanor might view her as much older, although the difference in years was probably not much more than five or six. There was a marked difference in their manners. Eleanor was gay, exuberant, even girlish—although Kate was well enough acquainted with her by now to suspect that her constant smiles and vivacious glances covered deeper feelings that could not be shared with her family or her society friends, feelings so deep and perhaps so at odds with those she was expected to have that Eleanor herself was not even aware of them. Kate, on the other hand, knew her own temperament to be far more reserved and thoughtful. It was perhaps that sober reserve that attracted Eleanor to her and made her feel as if her confidences would be honored with respectful consideration.

Eleanor twirled the pale blue ruffled parasol that exactly matched her lavishly trimmed dress, with its wrists and high neck frosted with French lace. "I bring Patsy's regrets," she said, and then added, "but I must confess that I encouraged her to go to London with Mama this morning, so that you and I could have this time alone.

I hope your luncheon plan will not be upset by having three guests instead of four."

"Not at all," Kate said. "Bradford and Sir Charles will arrive in time for luncheon?" Kate was still not accustomed to the late luncheon hour; the meal was never eaten until after one, and when guests were expected, it was even later.

"Yes," Eleanor said. They turned a corner in the path and came out on the grassy shore. She waved her hand carelessly. "They have gone to Colchester, Bradford on some stuffy errand having to do with money, and Charles to do more of his detecting."

"Ah, yes," Kate said thoughtfully, "his murder." She wondered if Sir Charles had taken her suggestion about interviewing Mrs. Farnsworth. She regretted it now; on reflection, she felt it would have been better not to have spoken at all. "What a lovely brooch," she said, changing the subject. She lifted her finger to touch it, a flashing diamond in a circlet of pearls. "A gift?"

Eleanor nodded. "From Mr. Fairley," she said. Was there a heavy note in her voice?

"I'm sure you are excited," Kate said, watching her. "The two months before the wedding must seem to stretch out like an eternity."

"Yes," Eleanor said. Yes, her voice definitely held a lower tone. And her glance, not so gay or flashing just now, was downcast, and colored with something like embarrassment or even shame.

"Ellie," Kate said quietly, "if you would like to speak to me about anything that troubles you—"

Eleanor clasped Kate's hand. "Oh, Kate," she exclaimed in a shaking voice, "I would, oh, I would."

"My dear Ellie," Kate said with genuine sympathy, "what is it?"

Eleanor released Kate's hand and turned her face away. "It is ... I mean to say ... That is, I—" She bit her lip nervously, and then turned to face Kate. "I want to know—if you know, dear Kate—about the . . . about the wedding night!"

Kate stared at her. "The wedding night?"

"I have asked Mama," Eleanor said, the quiver in her voice barely in check. "But all she will tell me is that I must do my duty. She will not tell me what my duty *is*, except to say that I must please Mr. Fairley. How can I please my husband if I have no idea how to do so?"

Kate felt herself very much at sea on this subject, but she took a deep breath and embarked upon the deep, asking her friend the same question she would ask herself in the circumstance. "Can you not allow your natural feelings to be your guide?"

"My feelings?" Eleanor said blankly. "But that is what I am asking you, Kate. What ought my feelings to be?"

Kate tried a different tack. "Well, then, can you not trust Mr. Fairley? He is a widower, is he not, with experience in such matters?" Of course, as Kate understood it, all men had experience. That was an essential part of their freedom, to have as many mistresses as they chose. Her thoughts flashed, unbidden, to Sir Charles. How many mistresses had *he* had?

Eleanor began to pace along the walk, her steps agitated. "That is another of my concerns, Kate. Having been married, Mr. Fairley *has* experience, vast experience. Will he not expect far more of me than I am able to offer?" Her face was suffused with pink and she spoke with an effort. But she continued to speak without waiting for an answer, her passion testifying to the force of her dammed-up feelings. "And while I can scarcely imagine what the act must be like, it seems so *brutal*, so unnatural!" She closed her eyes, the pink paling, her voice falling to a frightened whisper. "So painful."

Kate could feel Eleanor's fear. "I wish," she said quietly, "that I could reassure you out of my own experience."

Eleanor's eyes opened and she stared at Kate. "Oh, my dearest, you cannot think that I believed you to have—"

Her hand went to her horrified mouth. "Just because you are an American and Irish—!"

Kate laughed and took her friend's hand. "Well, if you *did* believe me to be experienced, I must disappoint you, Ellie. The truth is that I have never kissed a man with passion. You are far beyond me in that, and likely to remain so. You will be *my* teacher, and tell me what it is like."

Eleanor's color came again and she shook her head vehemently. "Oh, no, Kate, you are wrong. I have kissed Mr. Fairley, yes, but modestly, and only once, when I gave him my sacred word that I would marry him. But not with passion. My mother says that no good woman ever—"

Kate turned to face her friend. "Eleanor Marsden, you must *forget* your mother!" she exclaimed. "You will shortly vow yourself, body and soul, until death, to Mr. Fairley. You cannot do such a thing without even tasting his kiss!" She seized Ellie's other hand and gave them both a shake. "Promise me, Ellie. The next time you are with Mr. Fairley, you will *kiss* him. And then the next thing, and the next after that, will seem less dreadful."

Eleanor's eyes were wide and very blue. "Do you really believe that a kiss will set my fears at rest?"

"I cannot swear to that," Kate said, wishing she knew more about Mr. Fairley, and what lay in his heart toward Eleanor. She squeezed Ellie's hands as she dropped them, and managed a smile. "But you might find it enjoyable. And when you have kissed him, you can tell me what it is like, so that I will know, too." Again, unbidden, Sir Charles's face came into her mind.

Eleanor turned and they began to walk again. "Thank you, Kate," she said, subdued. "If you think it would help, I will try." There was a silence, and then she picked up her pace and her voice took on a determined cheerfulness. "There are so *many* things to do. I am to have final fittings for my trousseau at Worth's next week. And there are yet shoes to be bought and gifts for the wedding party, and the flowers to be arranged, and—"

"Ellie," Kate said, "do you love him?"

"Love Mr. Fairley?" Eleanor's laugh was quick and nervous. "Why, of course I love him! Don't be silly. At any rate, it is a very good match. Mama and Papa are ecstatic, and all my friends are envious. Why do you ask?"

"Because," Kate said soberly, remembering the long relationship between her aunt and uncle, "marriage at its best is difficult. Unless there is love to leaven it, it is a flat, hard loaf. It is not a loaf to relish, nor will it nourish."

Eleanor stared at her. "Why, Kate! You are a poet at heart, I swear—a philosopher, a *romantic*!"

"I fear that I am a romantic," Kate said with a wry smile, "at least where marriage is concerned. I will never marry for less than love—which means, I suppose," she added, "that I will never . . . marry." She stopped, struck, suddenly, with the realization that she *was*, truly and deeply, a romantic. Eleanor, on the other hand, was profoundly pragmatic. She accepted her social responsibilities and did what was set before her to do without question. Whatever her heart might whisper in the dark of the night, she would go on playing the role she had been trained since birth to play.

"Not marry!" Eleanor exclaimed in amazement. "Be forever a *spinster*!" She tilted her pretty head, frowning. "You must be one of those freethinking women who reject men's control and want the vote."

Kate picked up a small flat rock and threw it as her boy cousins had taught her to do a long time ago, across the open water. It skipped four times, perfectly, then settled with a splash among the lily pads on the other side. A startled swan, coal-black, raised its elegant head as if to question. With a satisfaction far out of proportion to the mere achievement of rock-skipping, Kate watched the circles widen in the still water, interlacing with one another, a series of rippling rings. Finally she spoke.

"You are right," she said. "I am too independent ever to allow a man to dictate my beliefs and my behavior. I could never be less than an equal partner. As for the vote, I plead guilty to trusting my opinions as confidently as those of most men." She turned back to Eleanor with a small smile. "And not only that, but I confess to believing that I could responsibly hold office."

Eleanor's mouth forgot for a moment its practiced smile and a certain wistfulness came into her expression. "Oh, Kate, such self-assurance! If *only* I had your ability to face the future undaunted. Perhaps then I should—"

She stopped, considering the choices she might exercise. Then, to Kate's regret, her face lost its seriousness and her gay smile returned. "But you had best not confide your political ambitions to Bradford, and most especially *not* to Sir Charles. I fear they would both be terribly annoyed."

"Or terribly frightened," Kate said thoughtfully. "I feel sympathy for them. It must be very difficult for one entire sex to contemplate the changes in the world these days. Women campaigning for suffrage, choosing their own marriages, earning their own livings—"

Eleanor took Kate's arm and turned them back toward the house. "I admire the sentiment of independence and those who are bold enough to express it," she said. "But I must also confess to enjoying the comfort of being cared for and the luxury of being loved by someone who can afford it. I daresay Mama is right when she says that a large income is the best recipe for happiness." She trilled a laugh. "Now, we had best go back, do you think? Bradford and Sir Charles will be right along."

"Of course," Kate said dryly. "We must not keep the men waiting."

39

"In the last third of the nineteenth century England's cultivated acreage declined by nearly three million acres. In the same years, British industry lost its ability to be competitive. Hoping to improve the situation, many eagerly latched onto any scheme for industrial development. Among these was the development of the motor car."

—JEROME HUCHSTABLE
The Automobile Industry in Great Britain

AT THE SAME moment, Bradford and Charles were traveling in the Marsden carriage from Colchester to Bishop's Keep. Charles, having spent the first hour of the morning searching fruitlessly for information about the Order of the Golden Dawn, and the second in unproductive conversation with Inspector Wainwright, had determined to give up his investigations altogether.

"It is futile," he said sourly, watching the countryside flash past the carriage window. "If the killer is caught, it will be because the police stumble upon him."

Bradford roused himself from his inward contemplations with some difficulty. "What d'you expect?" he asked gloomily. "Police are a grubby, incompetent lot. You have better things to do with your time than mucking about with them."

"I suppose," Charles said. Of course, there was still the vicar, who might be persuaded to tell what he knew. And Kathryn Ardleigh, who had some reason to associate Mrs. Farnsworth and Monsieur Armand and could perhaps be led to reveal it. Or he could return to Mrs. Farnsworth and see if he could rattle—

"No, by Jove!" he exclaimed out loud, striking one hand with the other fist, "I'm no Holmes, and this is no fiction, where all is made right in the end. This is one of those situations where the whole truth will never be known. I'm bloody well done with it."

"Right," Bradford said. He looked up, his face set, as if he also had come to a conclusion. "Sheridan, I need your advice about a matter of some consequence."

Charles turned away from the window. "If I can," he said.

"I spent yesterday afternoon with Perkins, the estate manager," Bradford replied, dejected. He took off his hat and flung it on the seat. "The estate has fallen into a bit of a hole." He paused. "A pit, actually. Hard to see how things are to be dug out. Rents are off disastrously—not just ours, of course. It's this agricultural depression. Foreign corn pouring in at a fraction of what we can produce it for, farmers bankrupt, farms uncultivated, tenants defaulting on their rents. And bad weather these last two years, harvests rotting in the fields."

"It seems worse here in Essex than elsewhere," Charles said as they passed an empty cottage, the thatch of its roof fallen in, the bare ribs of rafters exposed to the sky. In a neighboring field, two thin cows were making a rough living on nettles. "Some of the land looks quite derelict."

Bradford spoke with heavy gloom. "There are over a dozen tenant cottages empty on the manor, barns falling in, fields uncultivated. Perkins says new farmers can't be gotten because the buildings and the roads are so decayed. We'd have to lay on at least thirty thousand pounds out of capital just to make the damned farms livable."

Charles looked at him. Coming from a family whose commercial investments had removed it from dependence on the land, he knew about the dreadful agricultural situation chiefly from reading and looking about him. The evidences of the depression were certainly everywhere— farm workers flooding the city, families dispossessed, crime on the increase. It was a desperate situation.

But as far as Marsden Manor was concerned, the solution seemed to him quite logical and obvious. "You have access to the railroad," he pointed out. "Could not the fields be converted from crops to pasture, and the enterprise from grain to dairy? The London market, I understand, is clamoring for milk and butter."

"That's what Perkins suggests. But it's doubtful the pater would do something as radical as that, even if it would keep the rotten old ship afloat." Bradford shook himself as if shaking off a burden that wasn't his. "Anyway," he added, "having given the matter a great deal of thought, I have concluded that money can no longer be earned from the land. I have therefore made—out of my own funds, left to me by Grandmama—an investment in quite a promising venture. Through it I expect to refloat the family fortunes."

Bradford spoke with grim determination, as if by very force of will he could buoy up the family's prosperity. Behind the determination, though, Charles glimpsed something else. Anxiety, perhaps? The shuddering apprehension that the investment was not so promising as it seemed?

"If you have already made the investment," Charles remarked, "you do not require my advice." From their earlier conversation and from what he had heard the day of Tommy Milbank's visit, he thought he could guess what this venture was, and who its promoter might be. "Harry Landers, is it?"

Bradford turned. "You know of him?"

"I have heard of his British Motor Car Syndicate," Charles replied evenly. "Landers is said to be successful in selling licenses on the motorcar patents he has acquired. Unfortunately," he added, "manufacture is not likely for some time, given the restrictions on motor vehicles and the present state of their development. And, of course, manufacture is where the investors will make their money."

Charles did not look at Bradford as he spoke. Decorum forbade his asking how much his friend had invested in Landers's scheme, but it was likely to be quite a sizable sum. Charles had heard rumors that a number of wealthy peers had been persuaded to invest heavily, one or two even mortgaging family estates to raise the necessary capital.

And no wonder. Landers—if a huckster—was eloquent in his promotion. Even more, he and others who advocated the new industry were fundamentally right about its glowing future. Staunchly as the Home Office might oppose it, and ridiculous as the idea might seem, someday everyone would have a motorized vehicle. But that day was well into the next century. If Bradford were counting on this venture to supply enough quick cash to keep the family fortunes from foundering, he was riding for a fall.

"Exactly what advice," Charles asked cautiously, "are you seeking from me?"

Bradford leaned forward. "An opportunity has arisen to make another investment," he said with a show of eagerness. "There is to be a motorcar exhibition at Tunbridge Wells early next year, which will certainly attract public attention and increase pressure on the

245

government to relax the ridiculous laws. And I have received news just this morning—this *very* morning, Charles—that Landers has signed an agreement to develop several French patents. The stock will be floated under the name of the Paramount Horseless Carriage Company, for £750,000. It is a solid opportunity. Rock solid. Practically guaranteed."

"Seven hundred fifty thousand pounds!" Charles whistled. "Landers thinks in round numbers."

"Indeed," Bradford said earnestly. "My acquaintances at the *Financial News* say that this is the inauguration of a very great industry, which will not only prove profitable in itself, but will augment the profits of innumerable other industries. It will make the entire nation rich, Charles! What Britain has lost in its fields will be regained on its roads!"

Charles looked at Bradford with some suspicion. His friend had obviously already committed himself to Landers's grand ventures and even grander rhetoric. What then could he—? He paused, suddenly realizing what was wanted.

"Marsden," he said, "I believe it is my purse you are soliciting, rather than my advice."

Bradford had the grace to color. "I believed," he replied somewhat stiffly, "that you might be interested in a financial venture that promises an extraordinary return."

Charles put on a regretful face. "Thank you, but no. I fear that my income is not sufficient for investment in speculative ventures." Especially, he added to himself, those that he believed were fatally flawed. While Bradford's friends at the *Financial Times* might be bullish about Landers's enterprises, the more conservative men he knew at the magazine *Engineering* were already virulent on the subject, seeing Landers as a shameless, vulgar self-promoter, playing to the credulity of the investing public.

He feared that his friend, to coin a phrase, was about to be taken for a ride. He did not intend to go along.

Then another thought, much more chilling, occurred to him. He had heard that Landers and his cohorts were not above using disgraceful tricks to get what they wanted. Had Bradford fallen so deeply into the man's clutches that he was required to redeem himself by soliciting others? He glanced at his friend. The question, delicate and indecorous as it was, hung on the tip of his tongue, but one look told him it would be fruitless to ask. As they turned off the road into the lane leading to Bishop's Keep, Bradford's face darkened, and his smile had vanished. He was clearly not in the mood for further confidences.

40

"When you least expect it, you hear the dreadful click which is driving the world mad . . . Wherever you be, on land and sea, you hear that awful click of the amateur photographer, Click! Click! Click!"

—MUSICAL COMEDY ACT OF THE 1890S

"MY DEAR KATE," Eleanor said, blotting her lips delicately with a damask napkin, "it was a lovely luncheon."

Kate smiled. She was grateful that her guests could not see into the kitchen, where the upsets of the morning had created turmoil and confusion. It was a marvel that the luncheon dishes—asparagus soup, sole in lemon sauce, fricasseed chicken, and the love apples that Mrs. Pratt disdainfully called "tommytoes"—were indeed tasty, and that the serving had gone as smoothly as it had.

"Our compliments," Bradford said, "to your cook." He looked around at the blooming garden, appearing to have recovered somewhat from the dark humor from which he had suffered upon his arrival. "And such a splendid setting, too. I had not realized that the gardens of Bishop's Keep were so fine. Lovely roses, Miss Ardleigh."

"I only regret," Eleanor said with a slightly questioning look, "that your aunts are indisposed. Please let them know that we are sorry they could not be with us."

Kate inclined her head. "I shall," she said, refusing to give in to Eleanor's inquisitiveness and tell her why they were indisposed. "I shall convey your message." She smiled around the table. "I understand that the British often play croquet after luncheon."

"To be sure!" Eleanor cried, clapping her hands. "And isn't it lucky that there are four of us? We are evenly matched—the women against the men."

"But that would hardly be fair," Bradford objected. "You two would be soundly trounced." He smiled at Kate. "Shall we, Miss Ardleigh, test the strength of the Anglo-American alliance?"

"Agreed," Kate said, "if Sir Charles will promise to put away his camera for the duration of the game. I have no intention of allowing him to take my picture while someone is savaging my croquet ball."

"Put away his camera?" Eleanor repeated blankly. "Why, he brought no camera with him."

"Yes, he did," Kate said. "It is in his pocket." Sir Charles's eyes met hers. She was foolishly glad that she was wearing her best white lawn and a wide-brimmed straw hat trimmed with silk flowers. "Show them, Sir Charles," she said lightly, "how you have been toying with us."

Sir Charles bowed his head. "You have caught me out, Miss Ardleigh." He reached into the pocket of his loose tweed Norfolk jacket and brought out a small shiny metal box, a little larger than a double deck of playing cards.

"*That* is a camera?" Eleanor asked disbelievingly. "But it is much too tiny!"

"It is something quite new," Charles replied, putting it on the table. "An American invention, actually."

Bradford leaned forward to examine the camera. "Ingenious, these Yankees."

"It is a Kombi camera," Charles said. "Patented two years ago. The first detective camera to take roll film instead of plates."

Kate looked at the camera curiously, thinking that Beryl Bardwell might use such a device to provide the telling clue in her mystery. "Detective camera?" she asked.

"That is the name often given to miniature cameras," Sir Charles said. He held it up to demonstrate. "It has a very basic shutter, worked by this lever. This model is rather primitive—the lens is marginally acceptable and it has no viewfinder, so that composition and focus are a matter of chance. But I expect the basic concept to influence the design of future cameras. The Americans seem to have taken the lead in this technology, as in many others," he added regretfully.

"But one would require a magnifying glass to look at the photographs," Bradford objected.

"The negatives are an inch-and-a-half wide," Charles replied. "Twenty-five to a roll. They can be developed as positives and viewed through the camera lens, giving them a three to one enlargement. Or, thanks to the new gaslight paper, the negatives can be printed in a larger size."

"You have been taking surreptitious snapshots ever since you arrived?" Eleanor accused. She gave him a mock frown. "What a naughty man!"

Sir Charles made a small gesture of apology. "Only a few. Several of the three of you. One or two of a groom in the back courtyard, currying a horse. And the cook, doing business with an ill-clothed boy selling produce at the kitchen door."

"Gypsies," Eleanor said with a grimace. "One sees so many of them nowadays, lighting fires of sticks beside the road to boil a dirty tea can. And the children, so ragged. Sleeping under ricks and in ditches." Her tone hardened so that it was, Kate thought, remarkably similar to Aunt Jaggers's. "It's disgraceful."

Kate looked at her, thinking that it might not be possible to disagree without offending. But Sir Charles, unexpectedly, showed her that it was.

"Pitiful, rather than disgraceful, I should say." He spoke with a sympathy that Kate found surprising. "I doubt they are gypsies, Eleanor. Mostly decent, hardworking folk who find that the times have turned against them—their cottages taken back by the landlords, employment vanished, workhouse full. Life has been hard of late, for some."

Eleanor, to her credit, looked abashed. "Perhaps I do not see all I should."

Sir Charles smiled, his look lightening, and Kate admired the easy, natural way he turned the subject. "I should have liked to see more of our young vendor," he said. "But the lad took to his heels when I made an unwary move and showed my camera. Some still think it unlucky, you know, to have their pictures taken."

"But not us," Bradford said. Mudd came back to the table just then and Bradford picked up the camera and handed it to him. "Will you oblige us, my good man, by taking our photograph? We should commemorate this happy occasion."

Mudd backed away, looking apprehensive. "Me, sir? Oh, no, sir. I couldn't at all. I don't know how."

"It is very easy," Sir Charles said. "Just aim, hold steady, and push the lever."

Kate had to laugh at the sight of Mudd, holding the camera as if it were the Queen's crown. She laid aside her hat and she and Eleanor leaned close together, while Bradford and Sir Charles stood behind. Mudd operated the lever with a trembling thumb. There was a faintly audible click. With a look of relief mixed with pride at having successfully carried out the complicated task, he handed back the camera.

"And now," Eleanor said, standing up, "no more photographs. Come, Sir Charles, you and I shall show this pair the spirit that has led the British Empire to govern the globe."

"Ah, yes," Sir Charles said dryly. "'And upon this charge cry 'God for Harry! England and Saint George!'" He looked at Kate. "*Henry V*, Act Three."

Kate lifted her chin. "'England shall repent his folly.' *Henry V*, Act Four." She was immensely gratified to see the look of surprise that crossed Sir Charles's face. Did he think that only the English read and remembered Shakespeare?

As it turned out, the Anglo-American team split wins with the British, so that when two rounds of croquet were completed, both sides claimed victory. After the match, they toured the ruins on the other side of the lake. It was the first time Kate had seen them, although they were not much to remark on—just the remnants of old stone enclosures, fallen to rubble and populated by rabbits and robins. After their walk, the guests departed, Eleanor insisting that Kate and her aunts must come to tea as soon as possible.

Reluctantly, Kate went back inside. The afternoon had been unexpectedly pleasant. Eleanor had lighted the gathering with her usual vivacity. Bradford had finally come around to a gay but rather nervous and uncertain amiability. Even Sir Charles had unbent enough to laugh over the mock battles on the croquet field, between mock-serious lectures on the effect of grass height and moisture on the velocity of the croquet ball. He had even promised to give her copies of the photographs he had taken earlier that day. Kate now knew that an ironic playfulness lurked under his serious facade, and she found herself liking him a great deal.

At teatime Kate went to the kitchen. Mrs. Pratt was steaming something savory in preparation for dinner. Kate lifted the lid and sniffed it appreciatively, then busied herself making a tea tray for Aunt Sabrina. She left it with a knock outside the door and had a solitary tea for herself, with the latest copy of *Longman's Magazine* in front of her, open to the third installment of "The Matchmaker," which she was studying for plot development.

The aunts appeared downstairs only after dinner was called, and when they met at the dining table they averted their eyes and did not speak to one another. Aunt Sabrina engaged Kate in bursts of animated conversation punctuated by gloomy silences, while Aunt Jaggers sat opposite, glowering and snappish. Aunt Sabrina, as if to make a show of naturalness, allowed Mudd to serve her a large portion of the savory mushroom pudding that Cook had prepared, talking gaily to Kate all the while. Served next, Aunt Jaggers seized on the remainder, taking it spitefully so that none was left for Kate. Tired as she was and depressed by the disharmony, Kate ate only a little soup and the fricassee remaining from luncheon. Mudd, for his part, was no more silent than usual, but there was an unveiled grimness in his face that reminded Kate that he and Mrs. Pratt held little good feeling toward Aunt Sabrina and none at all to Aunt Jaggers. She felt a real relief when the awful dinner was over and she could escape to her room.

It was a meal that Kate was to mull over for a long time to come.

41

"In quiet she reposes:
Ah! would that I did too."
—MATTHEW ARNOLD
Requiescat

THE NEXT MORNING, Kate woke and dressed as usual. Alone in the breakfast room, she openly ignored Aunt Jaggers's interdiction and read from the newspaper. Having finished both breakfast and the newspaper, she glanced at the clock. Nine o'clock. Aunt Sabrina would certainly summon her if she was wanted, and after yesterday's upsets, it was probably better not to disturb her. What to do?

Feeling at loose ends, Kate put on sturdy boots and a coat and went to climb over the ruined stone walls of the old keep. Tiring, she sat in a quiet corner with her back against a wall of dark flint cobbles, watching the mist rise from the quiet lake and thinking back over the events of the past few days.

The relationship between Aunt Sabrina and Aunt Jaggers had frozen into an icy glacier, and the scarcely disguised animosity of the servants added to the chilly foreboding that seemed to Kate to seep throughout the house like the tendrils of mist over the lake. If she were no longer to work for Aunt Sabrina, should she stay on? Would it not be better if she gave her notice? It was not what she wanted to do, but she did *not* want to stay in a place where the atmosphere was so poisonous that it infected even her own usually buoyant spirits.

At ten, she went indoors and climbed the stairs to her room. If Kate had no work to do, Beryl Bardwell had an abundance. She settled herself at her desk, took out the manuscript of "The Conspiracy of the Golden Scarab," and dipped her pen into the inkwell. She was about to begin drafting the scene in which Mrs. Bartlett plotted the murder of the Egyptian gentleman, when she heard cries in the hall and the noise of hurrying feet.

Kate went to the door and threw it open. "What is it, Amelia?" she asked. The maid had a foul-smelling, lidded chamber pot in her hands.

"Oh, miss!" Amelia cried in a panic. "Mrs. Jaggers is took terr'ble sick!" Averting her face from the stinking pot, she hurried down the hallway to the stairs.

Kate went to her aunt's bedroom. The heavy velvet drapes were tightly drawn against the daylight. In the dimness, she saw Aunt Jaggers in her white cotton nightgown, doubled over in bed, clutching her heavy abdomen. Her face was contorted with a wrenching pain and her skin had a jaundiced cast that frightened Kate. The bed sheets were twisted and rank with sweat and liquid excrement. Mrs. Pratt straightened up, holding the washbasin into which Aunt Jaggers had vomited a greenish gray slime. Vomit slicked the cabbage rose carpet beside the bed. The fat terrier, ears and tail quivering nervously, cowered in the corner.

"Has the doctor been sent for?" Kate put her hand on Aunt Jaggers's forehead. It was wet with perspiration and the skin felt clammy.

"Pocket's gone, miss." Mrs. Pratt turned away to dump the contents of the basin into a half-full bucket. There was, Kate thought, a tone of grim satisfaction in the cook's voice, and her glance at the desperately ill woman huddled on the bed seemed coldly pitiless. Kate thought of Jenny. It would be no wonder if Cook derived a dour compensation from the woman's suffering.

Aunt Jaggers arched her back with a loud cry, and a convulsive shudder shook her whole body. Her eyes rolled in her head, showing yellowy whites, and she shrieked in pain. Then she flung herself over the edge of the bed and began to retch into the basin that Mrs. Pratt once more thrust forward.

Kate ran for her own room and brought back basin, water, and clean cloth, and when Aunt Jaggers was once again lying on the pillow, exhausted, she began to apply the wet cloth to her forehead. Her aunt's eyes were wide open and staring fixedly, the pupils sharply dilated. Her pulse, when Kate at last managed to find it, was slow and irregular, although she was breathing fast, in shallow gasps.

The next hour was a melee of confusion, Mrs. Pratt with the basin, Amelia with the chamber pot, and Kate intent on keeping Aunt Jaggers from flinging herself off the bed in her convulsive thrashings. Dr. Randall arrived at last, a stout, genial-looking gentleman whose heavy jowls were frosted with old-fashioned white mutton chop whiskers.

"Indigestion, is it?" he asked in a booming voice. He opened his bag and took out his stethoscope. "Let's see, let's see."

But when he looked up from a quick examination of Aunt Jaggers, his glance was worried.

"What is it?" Kate asked. "What's wrong with her?"

Aunt Jaggers roused herself with an effort. "Poison." Her voice was a threadlike whisper. "I've been poisoned."

"Don't be foolish," Dr. Randall replied with loud heartiness, as if he were speaking to a deaf person. "Been eating oysters? There's been some trouble with taint hereabouts. Several taken ill."

"No, no oysters," Kate said.

Aunt Jaggers began to flail frenziedly, and a stream of wild words poured out of her.

"Hysterical," Dr. Randall said. He took a bottle out of his bag. "This should set matters right straightaway, I warrant." He measured out a thick liquid into a teaspoon.

But the medicine, whatever it was, brought no quick improvement, and within five minutes Aunt Jaggers had vomited it violently into the basin. The doctor looked on, perplexed, stroking his nose with his thumb. Kate stood with Amelia at the foot of the bed, watching apprehensively. At last Aunt Jaggers quieted, her limbs relaxed, and she seemed to pass into a deep sleep, her mouth slack, her breath hoarse and raspy, a slug's trail of saliva on her flabby chin.

"Ah," the old doctor remarked with some relief, "we're past the crisis, I'd say." He put the bottle of medicine on the bedside table. "Spoonful of this every three hours, and keep her warm and quiet. I expect to find her greatly recovered when I return this afternoon. *Greatly* recovered," he added loudly, with an admonishing look at the sleeping Aunt Jaggers, as if instructing his patient in the course of her improvement.

"What do you think has made her ill?" Kate asked.

"Hard to say," Doctor Randall replied. "You are certain about the oysters?" As Kate nodded, he snapped his bag shut. "What did she eat for breakfast?"

Kate shook her head. "I don't know."

"No one ate, 'cept fer th' young miss, sir," Mrs. Pratt offered. "According t' Mudd, that is."

"Dinner was about eight last night," Kate said.

"Not likely food poisoning, then," the doctor remarked with an air of authority. "Symptoms would have been felt within four or five hours." He looked at Kate. "You seem healthy enough. Any symptoms?"

Kate was about to answer when Nettie rushed into the room, her eyes big, her thin face pale. "It's Miss Ardleigh," she gasped. "I went t' do her bed an' found her on th' floor. She's bad sick!"

Leaving Amelia to watch over the sleeping Aunt Jaggers, Kate and the doctor ran to Aunt Sabrina's room, Mrs. Pratt, and Nettie at their heels. The scene there was much like Aunt Jaggers's room: bed clothing rank and disarranged, the basin overflowing with vomit, the chamber pot brimming. Aunt Sabrina was sprawled on the floor by the door, her nightgown drenched with cold sweat, the bellrope clutched in one hand.

"Pore lady," Nettie whispered. "She musta pulled an' pulled an' pulled it straight off th' wall."

"Weren't nobody t' hear below stairs," Mrs. Pratt said sadly. Her voice hardened. "We all bin tendin' t'other one."

Kate summoned Mudd, who was hovering in the hallway. He and the doctor managed to lift Aunt Sabrina onto the bed. Her breathing was so shallow that Kate thought at first she was dead, but once in the bed her eyelids flickered.

"Mother," she moaned. Her breath was foul with the smell of vomit, and her nightdress reeked with her waste. "Don't be angry, Mother. I did not mean to soil myself."

"Out o' her head," Mrs. Pratt said judiciously.

Dr. Randall dispatched Nettie for the medicine he had left with Aunt Jaggers and began his examination. Kate stepped to the other side of the bed and took Aunt Sabrina's cold, clammy hand.

"It will be all right, Aunt," she said quietly.

Aunt Sabrina's eyes flew open, the whites yellowed and sickly looking. An expression of confusion came over her face. "Who—?"

"It's Kathryn." Kate smoothed her aunt's matted hair away from her face. "Your niece."

Aunt Sabrina stared at her wonderingly for a moment, and then the confusion seemed to clear.

"Kathryn," she whispered. Saliva trickled out of one corner of her mouth and she spoke with what seemed like intense effort. "I . . . must see . . . the vicar."

Dr. Randall straightened up. "Things haven't arrived at that state yet, my dear Miss Ardleigh. You'll be up and around in no time, I promise it." His face belied the assurance of his words.

Aunt Sabrina leaned over the bed to retch into the basin Mrs. Pratt held. When she finished, Kate gently pulled her back and began to wipe her forehead. She reached up to clutch Kate's hand.

"I . . . must see the vicar," she whispered thickly. "Must tell him . . ." Her eyes closed and her voice trailed off in an incoherent string of muttered syllables.

Kate leaned closer. "Tell him what, Aunt?"

"Tell him . . . to tell Jocelyn . . ."

"Jocelyn?"

Aunt Sabrina's eyes opened wide and a spasm of pain twisted her face. "My . . . child," she grated between clenched teeth.

Dr. Randall straightened up, shaking his head. "Delirious."

"She does not have a—?"

"Absolutely not. Known her all her life. Splendid woman, but never had a husband, never had children. Can vouch for that." He frowned, looking around. "Where the devil is that girl with the medicine?"

Nettie rushed back into the room, her eyes open and staring, her face ashen. "She's dead!" she cried hysterically. "Mrs. Jaggers is *dead*!"

"Dead!" Mrs. Pratt gasped, and tripped the basin, spilling vomit on her skirts.

"I swear it," Nettie cried in a wild voice. "Her eyes is open, but Mudd says 'tis true."

"Dead?" the doctor said incredulously. He stood as if frozen. "But—"

"Go," Kate commanded, with all the authority she could muster. "I'll stay here."

"Dead?" Aunt Sabrina struggled frenziedly to raise herself. "Bernice is—?"

"Please, Aunt," Kate begged, gripping her shoulders and pushing her gently down to the pillow as the others hurriedly left the room. "Whatever has happened, we will take care of it. You must rest and get well." Kate didn't want to think about what had happened in that other bedroom, or what would happen if Aunt Sabrina—

Aunt Sabrina's eyes were locked on Kate's and a new urgency seemed to grip her. "The vicar has my . . . will," she said slowly, distinctly. The angles of her face seemed to have altered, and Kate could see the outline of the fragile bones under the nearly transparent skin. "See to the . . . letters and the cipher manuscript, in the safe. Give everything . . . to Barfield."

"Barfield?"

"The vicar."

"Of course," Kate said. "But you are going to be just fine, Aunt Sabrina." She smiled with a confidence she did not feel. "Just rest and—"

"I . . . leave it to you, my dear Kathryn," Aunt Sabrina whispered. "Jocelyn . . . has no need." Her mouth relaxed in a faint ghost of a smile. "You must . . . carry on. You are the last . . . Ardleigh."

Kate smoothed back the loose gray hair. "Please," she said desperately, "just rest. You are going to get well." She tightened her grip on her aunt's hand as if to pull her back from whatever dark precipice lay ahead. "You are going to get well," she repeated fiercely.

A few minutes later, Aunt Sabrina lapsed into unconsciousness. She died a little after one o'clock that afternoon.

42

"Cui bono?—Who benefits?"

—Cicero

D R. Randall turned from the sheet-covered figure, his face somber. "I want to see all the servants in the library. You, too, Miss Ardleigh. There must be a thorough examination."

Kate smoothed the sheet. "An examination? But why?" she asked wearily. Her chest was heavy with sadness, her eyes blurred with tears.

"Why?" The doctor's white whiskers bristled, and Kate realized that he was holding on to his composure with difficulty. "The disease that killed your aunts may be contagious, that's why! We may have to quarantine this place." He waved his arms like an irate bandmaster. "Assemble the servants, please."

A half hour later, having looked into throats, taken pulses and temperatures, examined eyes and tongues, and listened to hearts and lungs with his stethoscope, Dr. Randall dismissed the others and kept Kate behind. He wore a look that Kate, nearly overwhelmed by shock and grief, could not decipher.

"If we are dealing with a disease," he said, going to stand in front of the fire, "there is no evidence of it."

"Thank God for that," Kate replied fervently. She sat down in the Morris chair, shivering. "It would be terrible if others were to suffer as my aunts suffered this morning." Her muscles felt stiff and sore, her throat hurt, and her head was throbbing. But it was grief that afflicted her, not illness. She had not had much love for Aunt Jaggers, but they were relatives and she could not wish her dead. As for Aunt Sabrina—

Kate covered her face with her hands. She loved and admired Aunt Sabrina. It had been dreadful to sit helplessly by her bed, watching her slip farther and farther away, into a place from which there could be no return. And this death had brought memories of another, when Kate's mother died of measles so many years ago. That aching void in her heart, so long covered over, seemed opened again by the death of her aunt.

Doctor Randall cleared his throat and Kate looked up. "I have confidence in my examination," he said gently. "But I suggest that the servants not be allowed to leave the house for any lengthy period of time—in case the symptoms should manifest later." He looked down at the fire. "I fear," he added uncomfortably, "that another question must now be addressed."

"Yes," Kate said, trying to keep her voice steady. "My aunts are dead. If not by illness, how?"

"Exactly." The doctor shifted his weight. "The circumstances, Miss Ardleigh, are definitely suspicious. Mrs. Jaggers mentioned—poison."

Kate stared at him. "But she was hysterical! You said so yourself!"

"And I thought so," the doctor said somberly. "But the alternatives, I fear, are not limitless."

Kate pulled in her breath sharply.

The doctor looked at her as if gauging her ability to hear his next question without going to pieces. "Do you know of anyone who might wish your aunts dead? Any . . . enemies?"

Kate closed her eyes. She could feel the laughter rising hysterically in her throat. "Enemies?" Her shoulders shook, and a wild giggle threatened to escape her. *Everyone* in the house had been an enemy of someone else in the house!

The doctor put a beefy hand on her shoulder. "Steady on, Miss Ardleigh," he said in a fatherly way. He turned to his bag and took out a flask. "Here," he said, unscrewing the cap and pouring an amber liquid into a small cup, "have a swallow of this." Kate gulped the whiskey he offered her and sat still for a moment, letting the heat of it warm and steady her. The doctor helped himself to a sizable swallow and then another, capped the flask, and replaced it in his bag. "I am afraid it will be painful to speak to the constable about this matter. But he must be summoned to interview the servants while events are fresh in their minds." He wiped his mouth with the back of his hand. "There is sure to be a coroner's inquest."

Kate nodded numbly.

"And both your aunts . . ." His look was sympathetic. "Both must be autopsied, I fear. I do not have enough evidence to certify a specific cause of death."

"I understand," Kate said.

"I will see to summoning the constable."

"Thank you." Kate sat still while the doctor opened the door and went in search of Mudd.

The doctor gone, the library seemed appallingly vacant. The chair, the lamp, seemed to wait for Aunt Sabrina, and the things on her desk—her pen, her notes, even the vase of autumn asters—seemed like ghosts, shadows, shades of her. In some indiscernible, indefinable way, Kate felt the impossibility of separating her aunt from the things she loved and lived with, and could not help but believe (though she knew it was not so) that at any moment Aunt Sabrina would open the door and come in.

But the only person to enter was Amelia, who brought an inquiry from Mrs. Farnsworth, by messenger, concerning a certain person who was supposed to be a member of the London temple. Kate looked up the information and gave it to Amelia for the messenger, together with a brief note, unsteadily written, informing Mrs. Farnsworth of her aunt's death.

Mercifully, Kate did not have long to wait for the constable's arrival. At half past three, she heard the crunch of gravel outside and opened the French doors to look out. The constable had arrived on a bicycle. She went back to her chair in front of the fire, and after a few minutes, the doctor brought him into the library.

"This is Constable Edward Laken, Miss Ardleigh," Dr. Randall said. "I have informed him of the circumstances of your aunts' deaths." He spoke slowly and gently, as if he were speaking to a child. Did he think her bereavement somehow made her more fragile? Or did he fear that, confronted by the constable and the need to consider the cause of her aunts' deaths, she would fly into hysterics? He picked up his bag and went to the door. "I must see to other patients," he said in a comforting voice, "but I leave you in capable hands. Do not hesitate to send for me if there is a need."

"Thank you," Kate said. When the doctor had gone, she turned to the constable. "I am sure you have questions," she said, steadying her voice by keeping it low.

"I fear so, Miss Ardleigh." The constable was a slender man with sandy hair, a ruddily thoughtful face, and alert gray eyes. His navy serge uniform was brushed, its buttons polished, his boots shined. "I am sorry to intrude on your grief, but if the questions are answered now, perhaps there will be no need for further intrusion." His voice was well modulated and suggested an education beyond that of the village school.

"Please ask what you must," Kate said, shivering in spite of the fire. Aunt Sabrina's shawl was hanging over the arm of the chair. She fingered it for a moment, then draped it around her shoulders. "Do you wish to speak to the servants?"

"Yes, ma'am," the constable said. "But I have several questions for you first, if I may."

Kate saw that the constable's level gaze held a certain regard, but something of the defensive as well. Remembering that her policeman uncle had often felt himself scorned by the upper class, Kate understood the look. But it would not make the man easier to know that she herself came from a policeman's family and sympathized with his situation. So she only said, "I will answer if I can."

Acting with deference and authority at once, the constable took a notebook and pencil out of his pocket. He wrote down the names of her aunts, the names and approximate ages of the servants and the length of their service, and her own name. She described her relationship to her aunts and her position at Bishop's Keep, and saw as she did so a slight shift in his posture.

He looked up. "You are employed here, as well as related?"

"Yes," Kate said. "My aunt was engaged in a work that required typing and other clerical duties, which I provided." She paused, wondering what she should say of the difficulties of the past few days. She was about to mention the situation when Constable Laken spoke again.

"I understood that Miss Ardleigh had no relatives other than her sister? And yourself, of course."

Kate hesitated. In her delirium, Aunt Sabrina had spoken of a child. But Dr. Randall had vigorously rejected the idea. Aunt Sabrina's words—her last words—echoed in her mind. "You are the last Ardleigh."

"I believe that is the case," she said.

"Who benefits from the deaths?" the constable asked.

Her eyes widened. "Sir?"

"Who inherits the estate?" His tone was studiedly offhand.

"I do not know," Kate said. It was not a question she wanted to think about right now. "I understand that the vicar has a copy of my aunt's will. Perhaps he could provide you with the name of her solicitor."

Constable Laken pocketed his notebook. "I will speak with him. Might I see the servants now, Miss Ardleigh?" His eyes were guarded. "Privately, if you please. That is, without you or the butler present."

Kate was momentarily taken aback. Did he think she might influence their answers? Did he imagine that she or Mudd might wish the servants to conceal some fact that might have a bearing on her aunts' deaths? But no doubt it was better this way. He would learn of the below stairs animosity from the servants themselves. She bit her lip, remembering that more than one of them had good reason to want Aunt Jaggers dead.

"Of course," she said. She rang the bell for Mudd. He opened the door instantly, a silver tray in his hand.

"I was about t' knock, Miss Ardleigh." He extended the tray, with a card. "I have asked th' gentl'man to wait i' the drawin' room."

"Thank you," Kate said, taking a card. "Constable Laken wishes to interview the staff." Feeling diffident about acting the part of mistress even though she knew it was expected of her, she added, "Would you please take him to the servants' hall and assemble them there?" She glanced at the card and saw with surprise that it was Sir Charles's. "And please ask Amelia to show the gentleman in."

"Yes, ma'am," Mudd said. He gave the constable a disdainful glance and proceeded him through the door.

A moment later Sir Charles came into the room. "My dear Miss Ardleigh," he said, with a look of such sympathy that Kate felt nearly undone. "I am so sorry. What an awful thing. Unimaginable." He spoke almost awkwardly, as if the words were not adequate to his feelings. His eyes were on hers, warm with concern. "Are you . . . well?"

"Yes, thank you, Sir Charles." Kate felt the blood coming to her face and an unaccustomed confusion inside her. She looked away quickly, and gestured to the chair on the other side of the fire. "Please sit down. I am sorry I cannot offer you tea, but the servants are otherwise engaged just now. The constable is with them."

He sat down on the edge of the chair, still looking at her. "I didn't know until I came . . . That is, I did not know of your trouble. I merely called to leave the photographs I took yesterday, as I promised." He took an envelope out of his pocket and put it on the table beside the chair. "The constable. Does that suggest—?"

"Dr. Randall does not know the cause of the deaths. There will be autopsies and a coroner's inquest. The doctor suggested that the constable be summoned immediately, and I thought it best to take his advice. I am sure his inquiry is simply . . . routine."

Kate shivered, pulling the shawl closer. She might speak lightly of the inquiry to Sir Charles, but she was perfectly aware of its significance. The constable was a perceptive man. Even if Mrs. Pratt and Mudd were not forthcoming in their answers, he would certainly sense their bitter enmity toward Aunt Jaggers and their resentment toward Aunt Sabrina. Kate did not think, she could not bring herself to believe, that either the cook or the butler could have gone to such awful lengths for revenge. But the constable might think differently. She shivered again. Perhaps she should have insisted on being present when he spoke with them. It was gradually dawning on her that until the matter of the estate was settled, all authority for the household rested upon her shoulders. She was responsible for the servants' welfare.

Sir Charles cleared his throat. "I take it, then, that the doctor has ruled out food poisoning?"

Kate returned her attention to the conversation. "He seemed to doubt it, since neither was taken sick until this morning. Had it been food poisoning, he said, the symptoms would have appeared earlier. In any event, the three of us shared the same table last night—"

Kate stopped abruptly, struck by a thought. They had shared the same table, yes. But they had not eaten the same food. Aunt Jaggers and Aunt Sabrina had consumed the pudding. She had eaten only the soup and fricassee left from luncheon.

Sir Charles leaned forward, watching her face. "What have you thought of, Miss Ardleigh?"

"My two aunts ate something I did not," Kate said slowly. "A pudding."

"What sort of pudding?"

"A mushroom pudding."

Sir Charles' eyes were intent. "What were the symptoms of their illnesses?"

When Kate had told him, he stood up abruptly. "There is a line of inquiry I must pursue."

Kate stared at him. Was there something about the mushroom pudding? Was it possible that—

She rose. "What line of inquiry?"

In answer, Sir Charles half turned toward the door. "I must speak with your cook," he said.

"She is with Constable Laken." Kate frowned. "Please tell me, Sir Charles," she said with greater distinctness, "what line of inquiry you aim to pursue."

But again he did not answer. "Laken?" he inquired with great interest. "Do you refer to *Edward* Laken?"

"I believe that is his name," Kate acknowledged. But she was not to be put off. Was this man so arrogant that he would refuse outright to answer her question? She put her hand on his arm. "This inquiry, Sir Charles," she said for the third time, with urgency. "What is it you think has happened?"

He stared down at her hand, then up at her face, taken aback. He felt himself flush. "I fear it would not be appropriate to discuss my suspicions at this time. I—"

Kate pulled her hand back. "Not appropriate!" she exclaimed. "My aunts have died of an unknown cause, and you talk of hypotheses! Sir Charles, I find your behavior most appallingly—"

"Forgive me for intruding," said a voice, thin and trembling. The vicar stood in the open library door, his hair a wild silver halo, his face ashen. "And for admitting myself. I came as soon as I heard. To . . . to offer comfort."

"Of course," Kate said, feeling a rush of sympathy for the old man. He looked as if he had greater need of comfort than she. "I am very glad you did. Please come in and sit down by the fire." Aunt Sabrina had had a special affection for him, and he must be feeling her death very deeply.

Sir Charles bowed to the vicar, then turned to Kate. "I will not trouble you further, Miss Ardleigh. I can find my way to the servants' hall."

"But I want to know—" Kate began angrily, then stopped. She might compel Sir Charles to tell her what he was thinking, and she could certainly detain him until she could accompany him to the servants' hall. But compassion required her to talk with the vicar at once, and besides, Aunt Sabrina had entrusted her with a private message to the vicar that was not for other ears. She raised her chin with a look of sharp displeasure. "Good day, then, Sir Charles," she said coldly.

The vicar sank down in the chair as Sir Charles hurriedly left the room. He shook his head and dropped his face in his hands. "Death becomes harder and harder to bear," he murmured, more to himself than to her. "But this one is hardest of all. Oh, my poor, dear Sabrina."

43

"Any discriminating diner will attest to the truth of the old adage, The proof of the pudding is in the eating of it."

—MRS. BARNSTABLE
Kitchen Cookery, 1872

CHARLES HAD NO difficulty finding his way below stairs. As he went, he brooded upon the look in Miss Ardleigh's eyes when she had spoken back to him, alternating between fire and chill, and the urgent touch of her fingers on his arm. But she had no cause to challenge him, he told himself, feeling wounded. He had withheld his idea only to keep from causing *her* pain. In fact, no other woman he knew would have attacked him in so headstrong a fashion when he was simply trying to spare her.

Women. They were either fragile and fainting or— viragoes. Being an American and Irish, Miss Ardleigh belonged, doubtless, in the latter category. Although he had thought it possible, before he came this afternoon . . .

He shook his head, perplexed. He did not know what he had thought, exactly. He had certainly not planned to develop yesterday's photographs in such haste, nor to make a special call to bring them to her today. But since the luncheon less than twenty-four hours ago, her image had imposed itself persistently upon his thoughts—her russet flyaway hair, her mouth that could be sternly sober and inviting by turns, her steady hazel-green eyes, her quick wit—

He quickened his pace. Well, if he had been attracted to the woman yesterday, he was saved from fatal error by having met the spitfire today. He straightened his shoulders, recalling himself to the task at hand. Miss Ardleigh was, after all, an altogether unsuitable person for any serious—

He did not complete the thought, being distracted by the sight, in the passageway outside the servants' hall, of five people. The butler, the parlor maid, the groom, and two girls in gray stuff dresses with pinafores were leaning or sitting against the wall, arms folded, faces variously impassive, nervous, and in the case of the two girls, frightened. The cook, Charles concluded, must be with Constable Laken in the servants' hall. Constable Laken. Edward Laken. Ned. It had been years since Charles had seen him, for their lives had taken very different ways. But the name opened an album of memories as bright and clear as any photograph: the warm summer days two carefree boys had spent lazing under fragrant hayricks; swimming in the deep, cool waters of the River Stour; stalking the wild mushroom through gloomy woods below East Bergholt.

The wild mushroom. Fungi were less of an interest to Charles now than they had been when he and Ned Laken were twelve. Ned had wanted to be chief of Scotland Yard when he grew up, and Charles had planned to be the world's greatest mycologist. His juvenile ambitions along that line had been encouraged by his grandfather, a connoisseur of mushrooms who had taught him to recognize the marvelous variety to be found in the woods and fields around East Bergholt. That was a long time ago, and his grandfather was dead. But Charles still remembered what he had learned from the old man. From Kathryn Ardleigh's descriptions of the fatal symptoms, he had a very clear notion of what had caused the deaths of her aunts.

Charles went past the waiting group of servants, feeling their eyes on him, and into the kitchen. It was an ordinary kitchen, high-ceilinged and drafty and no doubt the devil to work in. The only light came from a high window in one wall and a fire in the fireplace. A heavy coal range stood in one corner with a simmering pot of soup at the back; on the table, covered with a cloth, were dishes for luncheon, if anyone had thought to eat it—a roast joint, a cheese, sliced tomatoes, and cucumbers. The sideboard was stacked with pots and bowls and empty of foodstuffs, with the exception of the spices that were used in daily food preparation. Charles looked around. Where the blazes did they store the food?

He went to a door in the wall and opened it. It led through a short passageway to the outside, but off to the right was a pantry with shelves for produce, root vegetables, and the like. It smelled of onions and faintly, of something else, of damp earth and rotted wood. It was dark. Very dark.

Charles returned to the kitchen and found a candle on the mantel. He lighted it at the fire and returned to the storeroom to search the shelves, starting at the top. On the floor at the back, in a willow basket covered with a damp cloth, he found what he was looking for. He sniffed appreciatively. The earthy scene brought back the memory of walks with his grandfather through the autumn forests.

Gently, one at a time, Charles took the mushrooms out of the basket, examining each and placing it in its proper pile. Judging from the great variety, he thought, they had been collected in the woods, rather than in a mushroom house. The most numerous by far were the common field mushrooms, *Agaricus campestris*, whose smooth gray-white tops and pink gills had a clean, crisp look. Beside these Charles placed the horse mushrooms, which had the same rounded shape but were much larger, with grayish gills rather than pink. Next to these he piled several velvety buff-colored specimens of *Lepista saeva*, and a handful of *Lepista nuda*, also known as the Blue Cap—not to be eaten uncooked, but pleasantly aromatic when properly sautéed. He also found a few satiny yellow *Cantharellus cibaria*, which seemed to him to smell of apricots, and one large *Hydnum rufescens*, the wood hedgehog, not frequently collected, owing to the skill required to cook it without bitterness. But it was not until Charles reached the very bottom of the basket that he found, with almost no surprise, what he was looking for: one large and marvelously healthy specimen of *Amanita phalloides*. The Death Cap.

Admiring, he held the lethal toadstool in his hand for a moment, thinking what an extraordinarily beautiful specimen it was, how pearly its soft flesh, how perfect the fan of its radiating gills, how delicate the circumference of the volva that still embraced the lower stem. Such a glorious specimen, and so lethal. He wondered briefly if the other had been this perfect—since it was his hypothesis that there had been at least one *A. phalloides* in the pudding.

Charles gently placed the toadstool on the table. So, then, assume that there had been two, and presume innocence. Someone who did not know his mushrooms had accidentally included two *A. phalloides* among the variegated assemblage of edible fungi in the basket. He frowned. That seemed doubtful, however, because of the presence of *H. rufescens*, which was usually collected only by a mushroom connoisseur with sufficient knowledge to ensure its proper preparation. Which led to the conclusion that the person who collected two *A. phalloides* did so with deadly intent. A defensible conclusion, but difficult of proof.

Or set aside for the moment the motive of the collector, and search instead the intention of the one who had prepared the deadly pudding. Given a basket of edible mushrooms which included (either by accident or design) two or more fatal fungi, the cook should have recognized and quickly discarded the intruders. Unless, of course, the cook were inexperienced or incompetent—or inspired by a deadly intent to slice it up and add it to the pudding.

Charles stood up. He shook out his handkerchief, placed in it the splendid specimen of *A. phalloides*, and tenderly tied the corners into a bundle, which he pocketed.

It was time to look into the preparation of the mushroom pudding.

44

"Mushroom Pudding
¾ lb. of flour, 6 ozs. of chopped white vegetable butter,
1 tsp. baking powder, cold water, 1 qt. button or cup
mushrooms, pepper and salt."

"Make a crust with the flour, baking powder, and
5 ozs. of the butter. Line with it a greased pudding-
basin. Put in the mushrooms with the remaining oz.
of butter, pepper and salt and moisten with a little
water. Finish off like a beefsteak pudding. Boil or
steam for one and one-half hours or longer."

—MRS. BEETON'S BOOK OF
Household Management, 1871

ONE OF THE girls was gone from the line outside the
servants' hall, her place taken by a stout, scowling
woman of middle age whose black brows were drawn
together over small, suspicious eyes. She gave Charles a
dour look as he rapped at the door, then went in without
waiting for a summons.

The constable was sitting at one end of the table, talking
with a seated girl of eleven or twelve, her hair plaited

into a single thick braid down her back, her face so white the freckles stood out, giving her a fragile look. Charles frowned. He was steadfastly against the employment of young children, and his heart went out immediately to the girl sitting on the edge of the chair, nervously answering the constable's questions.

The constable looked up, irritated. "I said no interruptions," he barked, and then pushed back his chair, his face blank with surprise. "Charlie? Charlie Sheridan, is that *you*?"

"It is, Ned," Charles said, and gave his old friend a warm handshake. "How many years has it been?"

"All of twenty, I'd warrant," Laken said. His ruddy face split with a grin. He stood back, shaking his head. "*Sir* Charles, is it?"

"An honor bestowed liberally is scarcely an honor," Charles said with a dismissive wave. "I was only one of dozens the Queen showered with her largesse. So you are of the Scotland Yard sort after all."

"In a manner of speaking, I suppose." Laken glanced at the girl, who was gaping up at them. "I'm just finishing up here. Shall I treat you to a pint at the Head afterward? You can tell me what you have been up to."

"Yes to the pint," Charles said, pulling out a chair, "although we may have to choose a later day. If it's all the same to you, I'd like to join this business." He smiled at the girl. "Which are you, child? Scullery or tweeny?"

"Scullery, sir," the girl said nervously. "Harriet."

"Ah, good, Harriet," Charles said. He took out his bundle, put it on the table in front of Laken. "D'you remember, Ned, our tramps through the woods in those long-gone days, and what we often found there?" He untied the handkerchief.

The constable studied the mushroom carefully, an intent look on his face. "Is this what I think it is?"

"Quite. Do you mind if I ask a question or two of the young lady?"

The constable nodded, and Charles turned to the girl. "I would like you to tell me what you can about the preparation of the evening meal. Did you assist?"

"Oh yes, sir." The girl beamed with obvious pride. "Cook said I were a great help."

The constable leaned forward. "How was that?"

The girl was eager. "Well, I done as usual, cleanin' pots and straight'nin' the table. Then she let me cut up th' mushrooms fer th' puddin'." She spoke with a sense of having learned a new skill, one that was usually reserved to those of higher place in the kitchen.

"Go on," the constable prompted.

"Well, ye see, sir, things were'n a frightful state on account o' we hadn't 'xpected to do luncheon fer comp'ny. And then th' sweets tray were knocked into th' fire, which weren't nobody's fault. We was just too busy, we was, wot wi flyin' round, tryin' to get it all done up proper. An' then Cook had t' make a new sweet 'cause th' other were all over soot an' she asked me t' cut up th' mushrooms fer th' puddin'. I'd never done't before, so she showed me."

"And what did she say?" the constable asked.

"She said as there was diff'rent kinds an' I was t' cut 'em all up together like th' one she done."

Charles slid the open bundle in front of the girl. "Did any of the mushrooms you cut up look like this?"

The girl glanced at the specimen. She answered without hesitation. "Yessir."

"Are you sure? This is important."

"Yessir," the girl replied. " 'Twas th' very last one I cut up. 'Twas so beautiful, I wanted t' put it in. I knew t'wud make th' puddin' taste grand."

Laken looked sharply at Charles. Charles nodded very slightly. The girl caught the glance.

"T'weren't nuthin' wrong with it," she said defensively. "If it'ud bin bad, it wudn't o' bin in th' basket, wud it?"

277

Charles nodded reassuringly. "Can you tell us where the mushrooms came from?"

"Sometimes Cook gets 'em in th' woods. Sometimes Pocket picks 'em. Sometimes they're bought."

"Yesterday's mushrooms," Charles said. "Were they picked, or bought?"

The girl hesitated, obviously wondering why she was being asked so many questions about the mushrooms. "I dunno, sir. Cook just handed me th' basket."

"I see," Charles said. He smiled. "Do you and Cook get along?"

The girl's smile echoed his. "Oh, t' be sure, sir," she said brightly. "She's almost like me mum. She kep' Mrs. Jaggers from—" She caught herself in midsentence, her guilty expression mirroring her realization that she might be saying too much.

"From what, Harriet?" Charles asked gently. When she did not answer, he said, "Come now, child, someone will tell us. If not you, one of the others. What did Mrs. Jaggers threaten to do?"

"She din't threaten, sir." The girl's anger was artless. "She done it! She beat me till Cook made her stop. An' she beat Nettie too, an' locked her in th' cellar in th' dark o' night, blackin' grates, e'en a'ter her candle went out." She began to sniffle. "Not t' speak ill o' th' dead, sir, but Mrs. Jaggers weren't a kind woman."

"And how did Cook make her stop beating you?"

Harriet looked up, torn between her reluctance to betray Cook's rashness but proud of her daring. " 'Twas only water, sir. Nothin' wot'd harm."

"Water?"

"Cook dumped th' slops on her head. Then Jaggers give her th' sack."

"She did?" The constable's eyebrows went up.

"Yes, but th' young miss put a stop t'it." Harriet's sniffles gave way to tears, and the sorrow of long-held and deeply felt offense. "T'weren't just th' way she beat me, sir, or Nettie. Before us'ns 'twere Jenny, who died cause o' her." The tears and the words, intermingled, flowed faster, punctuated by hiccups. "An' Jaggers took th' fire an' th' sofa an' th' jam, an' Miss Ardleigh was goin' to give 'em all back an' now she's dead too an' I'll have t'find a new place." The thin shoulders shook with the awful realization of unknown horrors ahead, and tears streaked unchecked down the pallid cheeks.

"That's enough for now, Harriet," Laken said quietly. "You may go. But you are not to speak of this to anyone else, in any circumstance. Do you understand?"

With a gulping nod, the girl wiped her nose on her apron. Then she stood up and almost ran from the room.

Laken reached for Charles's bundle and poked at the toadstool with his finger. "I take it that you found this on the premises?"

"In the kitchen storeroom," Charles said, "in a basket with various edible mushrooms. The symptoms of the poisonings are consistent with ingestion of *Amanita*— severe abdominal cramps, vomiting, violent diarrhea, jaundice, coma. These may occur up to twelve hours after the fungus is ingested, and death can take place within fifteen."

The constable was thoughtful. "So it appears that the two women died of eating the mushroom pudding prepared by Mrs. Pratt, who—if the girl can be relied on— may have strongly resented her employers. You concur, I take it, with my feeling that the girl's involvement was quite innocent?"

"That is my impression as well," Charles replied. "Mrs. Pratt had both means and opportunity, and the girl has revealed a possible motive. You may find others when you begin to probe. I would especially dig into this business about the dead girl, Jenny. There is also some connection to the parlor maid, who seemed to feel her death quite keenly."

"Jenny Blyly," Laken said. "They're sisters." He stood up. "This part of the job is not my cup of tea. I frankly prefer to go after poachers."

"Are you going to take her in?"

"Yes. People seem more ready to tell the truth when they're not surrounded by the comforts of home." He looked around at the bare, bleak room. "However comfortless it may be."

Charles would have liked to hear Cook's story. But one of the unfortunate responsibilities of staying at Marsden Manor was the requirement of punctual attendance at tea. He stood.

"Then I leave you to it, old man," he said. "Would you mind conveying my farewell to Miss Ardleigh? I will let myself out by the kitchen door." There was no point in once more confronting the woman who had met his well-intentioned efforts with such an ill grace. He would only be embarrassed by her apologies when she learned that she had him to thank for apprehending the killer in her kitchen.

Laken held up his hand. "One more question before you go," he said with a thoughtful look. "Could the young woman have eaten the mushroom pudding and showed no ill effects?"

"Not likely," Charles said. "In fact, she told me that she did not eat any pudding."

Laken's thoughtful look deepened. "I wonder why not," he said.

45

"The tragedy of English cooking is that 'plain' cooking cannot he entrusted to 'plain' cooks."

—COUNTESS MORPHY
English Recipes

DEEPLY ANNOYED, KATE remained after Sir Charles left the room to pursue his inquiry, whatever it was. But it was not fair to burden the poor vicar with her irritation. The vicar had come to share her grief over the death of someone they both cared for, and she owed him nothing less than her full attention.

She rose. "The servants are engaged with the constable, so I cannot offer you tea." She went to the cabinet where Aunt Sabrina kept several bottles of liquor. "Would a glass of brandy do instead?"

"It would indeed," the vicar replied. His smile was a feeble one, and he took the glass she offered him with a shaking hand. His shaggy mane of white hair was disarranged and his collar was crooked. "The constable, you say?"

"Yes." She sat down across from him. "Would you care to hear the details of the morning?"

"If it would not be too painful."

It was painful, indeed. But she had the sense that the old man would find no calm within himself until he learned what had happened from someone who had shared Aunt Sabrina's last moments.

When she finished, he leaned back and closed his eyes. He was silent for a long time, and when he spoke, it was with such a soft voice that she didn't quite hear him.

"Such a rich life."

"I beg pardon?"

He opened his eyes, pale blue and watery. "Your aunt. She was a remarkable woman who insisted on living her life as she thought best, regardless of others' opinions." He shook his head. "I envied her," he said softly. "She was free of the constraints that bind so many of us to our accustomed ways. And yet she was generous to those who had fewer gifts. Sabrina was a woman of many charities."

Kate said nothing. Perhaps it seemed to the vicar that her aunt had been unconstrained. But however self-governing Aunt Sabrina's earlier life may have been, in the past few years Aunt Jaggers had tyrannized her.

"You said that the constable is here," the vicar remarked.

"Dr. Randall could not be sure of the cause of death," Kate said. "It seems there will be an inquest, and probably autopsies. The doctor suggested that the constable be asked to interview the servants while the details were still fresh in their minds. I concurred."

"Quite right," the vicar said. "Quite right. But if Sabrina and her sister did not die of illness, how—?" He looked at Kate, alarm widening his eyes. "Did the doctor suggest . . .? Is there a thought of . . .?"

He answered his own question with an emphatic shake of the head. "No, of course not. I am sure that some obscure disease or condition will be discovered to be the cause."

Kate rose and added another lump of coal to the fire. She knew the word that the vicar could not bring himself to utter. Poison. The same word had occurred to her when Sir Charles had responded so abruptly to her mention of the mushroom pudding. If the pudding had been at fault, the poisonings must have been accidental, arising from ignorance in gathering the mushrooms or carelessness in cooking them. Even though all who handled mushrooms were carefully schooled in the dangers, the newspapers frequently reported such accidents.

But Beryl Bardwell had read too many sensational stories and concocted too many murderous plots to accept that easy answer—especially given the state of high tension at Bishop's Keep. If Aunt Sabrina alone had died, Kate might have suspected Aunt Jaggers to have been responsible. Her treatment of poor Nettie and little Harriet were only two examples of the woman's sudden bursts of ungovernable passion, and there was that business with Jenny as well. Aunt Jaggers hated her sister, and it was very likely that she would inherit the estate. Yes, if Aunt Sabrina alone had died, Kate would immediately have suspected Aunt Jaggers of slipping a poisonous mushroom into the pudding.

But if the pudding were indeed the lethal weapon, Aunt Jaggers could hardly have been the killer. She had eaten two portions of it—hers and Kate's—with a greedy relish.

Kate picked up the poker and stirred the fire. There was another way to interpret the tragedy. Aunt Sabrina had clearly been desperate to escape from whatever threat of exposure her sister was holding over her head. "If I had not already decided to put an end to her intimidations and cruelties, this would be the last straw," she had said when Kate told her that Aunt Jaggers had discharged Cook. Kate had flinched then at the pent-up fury in her aunt's words. What if that fury had inspired Aunt Sabrina at last to take matters into her own hands? What if her desperation to escape from her sister had driven her to kill?

But Aunt Sabrina had also eaten the pudding. If she had decided to kill Aunt Jaggers, she also intended to kill herself as well. Which was not, Kate thought with a deep sadness, beyond the bounds of possibility. She remembered Aunt Sabrina's instructions to turn over to the vicar the letters and cipher manuscript, almost as if she expected to be incapacitated. Unthinkable as it seemed, Aunt Sabrina might have felt that murder and suicide were the only ways to find release from her tormentor and to forever conceal the secret Aunt Jaggers threatened to reveal.

The vicar looked at her. "You are thinking . . ."

"That the constable will soon tell us what he has learned," Kate replied evasively, going back to her chair. She could not share her speculations with the vicar. She had not a shred of proof on which to base them, and they would only trouble his Christian spirit.

"No doubt." The vicar made a tent of his fingers against his thin lips. "Did your aunt speak to you about her . . . concern for the German letters?"

"Yes," Kate said. "Thank you for reminding me. She wanted me to give them to you, and the cipher document." She looked at him. "There is some question in my mind about the letters," she added hesitantly. Was now the time to mention the business? But Aunt Sabrina had seemed quite urgent about them, so perhaps there was something more here than she understood. It might be best to say what she thought.

"I had already gotten a start on translating the letters when Aunt Sabrina asked me to lay them aside. I feel they are not . . . that they are . . ." She took a deep breath. "I am no scholar of the German language, sir, but I have learned something of its grammar and spelling. In my opinion, the letters were not written by a native German speaker. I believe them to be forgeries."

The vicar's eyes narrowed, but Kate suspected he was not surprised. "You are quite sure?"

"No," Kate admitted. "I could be mistaken, or there could be another explanation for what I have observed. Perhaps they should be shown to some other person who might—"

"There is no need," the vicar said. His tone had the finality of a judge pronouncing a sentence of death. "Your observations are corroborated by a letter from Mathers, in Paris."

Kate sat upright. "What did it say?"

"The letter denounced Westcott as a forger and a fraud, and the author of Fräulein Sprengel's putative correspondence. Your aunt brought it to show me. As you might imagine, she was extremely distraught."

Kate nodded, remembering. "She was indeed. She was still highly disturbed when she returned yesterday evening."

The vicar's mouth twisted, as if he were tasting something foul. "It seems that the respected Dr. Westcott bestowed upon himself his own forged authorization to establish the Order of the Golden Dawn."

Kate stared at him. "If the letters are forgeries," she said slowly, "then the Order founded on their authority is—"

"A sham." The vicar spoke with a weary distaste, darkened with anger.

"And the cipher document?" She recalled that some of its pages had a watermarked date of 1809, suggesting that it was over eighty years old, while others were unmarked. But the author of the document might have found a cache of old paper, and while the writing looked brown and faded, a sepia ink might have been used to make it appear so.

"If you and Mathers are right in your accusation, one must suspect that the cipher document is also a piece of fakery." Agitated, the vicar heaved himself out of the chair and began to pace back and forth in front of the fire. "The truth of the matter is that Westcott has made fools of all who trusted him. The Order of the Golden Dawn is a hoax and a fraud."

"But what could Dr. Westcott gain from such an action? Money?"

"Something worth more to him than money," the vicar replied. "Repute. Public acclaim. Power over others." He spoke with increasing passion. "Self-aggrandizement. Self-magnification. These are powerful motives. People kill for far less. A modest deception is nothing to balk at."

"Who knows about Mathers's accusation?"

"Only you, I, and Mrs. Farnsworth," the vicar said. "Both your aunt and I felt the matter should be held strictly confidential, and that some sort of committee should be convened to inquire into it."

"And how does Mrs. Farnsworth view the situation?"

"I do not know, for Sabrina went to see her after she visited me. I would not be surprised if Mrs. Farnsworth discounted Mathers's indictment. She and Westcott are close friends, some even say . . ." He paused in his pacing and cleared his throat uncomfortably. "Excuse me for offending you, my dear. Some say they are lovers. And Mathers has been a pest since the beginning. He has challenged Westcott's authority on several occasions. Worse, he regularly harasses people for money for his work in Paris."

Kate recalled the conversation she had overheard at Mrs. Farnsworth's. Mathers had been "that miscreant Mathers," who had made "unprincipled charges." At the time, she had understood nothing of the exchange, except that the doctor was furious at Mathers and Mrs. Farnsworth anxious to smooth things over. Now, however, the situation was much clearer.

"Do you believe that Mrs. Farnsworth might want to conceal Mathers's accusation?" she asked.

The vicar resumed his pacing. "I would expect her to. She has a great deal at stake in the success of the Order.

She has suffered financial reverses, to the point where she has only the house on Keenan Street and one servant. Members of the temple in Colchester contribute heavily to her support, and are also assisting her in her efforts to re-establish her acting career. If the organization is discredited, the members will be disappointed and angry, some even furious. Their support for her will certainly dissolve."

Kate could easily understand. If members of the Order believed that Mrs. Farnsworth and Dr. Westcott were lovers, they might even believe that she had been a partner to the fraud. That would be the end of the temple, and of the soirees that attracted such well-known people as Oscar Wilde, Willie Yeats, and Conan Doyle. No wonder she rejected Mathers's accusation.

The vicar paused once more in his pacing. "Your discovery of the inconsistencies in the letters is crucial. That proof will no doubt persuade her that it is best to expose the fraud now, whatever the personal consequences, for it is bound to come out eventually. I shall have to speak to her in a day or two." He turned to Kate. "But there are matters of more immediate consequence that must be tended to, Miss Ardleigh—Kathryn, if I may?"

Kate nodded gravely. "I suppose you are speaking of the funeral arrangements."

The vicar's expression was infinitely sad. "Yes, of course. But in the meantime, the estate must be managed, decisions must be made. Since you are your aunt's heir—"

Kate gasped.

"You did not know?"

Wordlessly, Kate shook her head.

"Yesterday, she altered her will, removing her former major beneficiary—"

"Her sister?"

"Yes. Sabrina had come to look upon you almost as a daughter, Kathryn. She wanted you to have Bishop's Keep and sufficient means to support it and yourself, even if you should choose to marry."

Kate bowed her head as the enormity of the realization washed over her, overwhelming her in a torrent of feeling—amazement, incredulity, gratitude. The magnitude of her changed circumstances was utterly beyond belief. Then she remembered something, and raised her head.

"In her last conscious moments, my aunt spoke of a child. She called her Jocelyn. Dr. Randall insisted that she was delirious. You have known Aunt Sabrina for a long time. Do you know anything of a child?"

The vicar stood before her, hands clasped behind his back. His eyes were distressed, but his mouth was gentle. "Kathryn, I cannot discuss this matter with you at the present time. I very much regret that I cannot be more forthcoming."

"I understand," Kate said, although she did not. If Aunt Sabrina had a daughter, why had she left the Ardleigh estate to a niece?

Who was Jocelyn Ardleigh?

46

"Some circumstantial evidence is very strong, as
when you find a trout in the milk."

—HENRY DAVID THOREAU
Journal, November, 1850

STILL THINKING ABOUT his conversation with Charles,
Edward Laken came into the library, one step behind
the stiff-backed butler.

"The constable, miss," the butler said. Laken noticed
that he kept his eyes averted, as if the policeman were
beneath notice. Or perhaps because he held some sort of
guilty knowledge that he did not want the inquisitor to
see.

"Thank you, Mudd," Miss Ardleigh said from her chair
by the fire. "You may go."

When the butler had gone, Laken bowed slightly to Kate
and nodded at the vicar, whom he had known for nearly
twenty-five years. "Good afternoon, sir."

"Good afternoon, Edward," the vicar said somberly. "A
most unhappy business."

"I fear so," Laken said. He turned to Miss Ardleigh,
whose face was shadowed under her heavy mound

of mahogany hair. "But I am pleased to tell you, Miss Ardleigh, that we may have discovered the person responsible for your aunts' deaths."

"Indeed!" she exclaimed. Her surprise was mixed with distress, Laken saw—quite understandably so. She knew that if he had discovered the murderer already, it could only have been one of the servants. Most people did not want to believe—*could* not believe—their servants capable of such a deed.

"Yes," Laken said. "Sir Charles Sheridan, as you may know, is a mycologist." He looked at her. It was perhaps a term that required explanation. "That is," he added, "an expert on mushrooms."

"I know what the word means," Miss Ardleigh said, with some asperity.

Laken immediately regretted his assumption. But there was something else about her look that made him wonder. Was the mention of mushrooms entirely a surprise to her? Had she suspected, or perhaps even known—

"And what exactly did Sir Charles find?" Miss Ardleigh was making an obvious effort to speak calmly.

"He found what is most likely the means of murder," Laken replied. "A Death Cap."

"A deadly mushroom!" the vicar gasped.

"Quite so, sir," Laken said gravely. "The symptoms of *Amanita* poisoning are exactly those exhibited by the victims, and Sir Charles located a remaining toadstool in the kitchen storeroom. The scullery maid has told us that she cut up its match for the mushroom pudding—quite unwittingly," he added. "The circumstantial evidence points to the cook, although—"

"Mrs. Pratt!" Miss Ardleigh exclaimed, her eyes opening wide.

"I understand your consternation, ma'am," Laken said, bowing his head. "Every effort will be made to get at the truth, I assure you."

The fact was that the constable had serious reservations about the cook's guilt. As Charlie Sheridan had observed, the evidence clearly pointed in her direction—the circumstantial evidence, that was. But although Laken rarely had such a serious crime as a murder to investigate, he had over the years met his share of criminals, and he had come to respect his intuitive assessment of guilt or innocence. In this case, while he felt it appropriate to take Mrs. Pratt to the village jail for questioning, he did not think it altogether likely that she was the murderer—or at least, the sole instigator. Of course, some crimes were born of passion, rather than greed. But there remained in his mind that fundamental principle of law, *cui bono*. He would discover as quickly as he could the identity of the heir. At the moment, he reminded himself, it was quite probable—indeed, as far as he knew, a certainty—that Miss Ardleigh herself was the last Ardleigh. *She* was the one most likely to benefit from the deaths of the Ardleigh sisters.

But he did not think it proper to share his thinking with Miss Ardleigh, who was frowning at him. "You are arresting Mrs. Pratt?" she asked.

The vicar went to Miss Ardleigh's chair and put his arm around her shoulders. "I know the idea of the woman's guilt must disturb you, my dear," he murmured. "But you must admit that we cannot see into the soul. It is possible for a person to appear blameless to the outer view, and yet to harbor an inner nature that is quite the contrary."

"There is good reason to believe her guilty," Laken said, watching Miss Ardleigh closely.

"Your evidence is only circumstantial," she said, rising. "I do not believe that Mrs. Pratt committed murder."

Laken's eyes narrowed very slightly. The woman spoke with a surprising confidence—surprising, that is, unless she knew that the cook was not guilty because she knew who was. "May I know the reason for your assurance?" he inquired carefully.

She hesitated for a moment. "We are friends," she said finally.

Laken stared at her. "Friends?" An odd term indeed, coming from—He stopped himself, recalling that Miss Ardleigh had described herself as an employee, her aunt's secretary, which made her a kind of superior servant. In that role, it was quite likely that she had become friendly with the other servants. And she was an American, which perhaps also made her less likely to impose a barrier between herself and them. In his limited experience, Americans were an egalitarian lot.

"I see," he said mildly. "I must suggest, however, that friendship is no warrant of innocence."

"It is in this case," Miss Ardleigh said, her voice sharp edged. She seemed annoyed by his failure to understand and irritated at her annoyance. "If Mrs. Pratt had determined to kill either of my aunts, she would not have used a weapon that might have killed *me*. She could not know that I would not eat the pudding."

"I see," Laken said. He paused, letting the silence linger a second longer than was comfortable. "Why did you not eat the pudding?"

Miss Ardleigh went to stand with her back to the fire. If she was offended by the question, she did not show it. "Because," she said in a factual tone, "Aunt Jaggers helped herself to my portion as well as hers. What was left to me was what remained from luncheon."

Laken made a mental note to confirm her report with the butler, while Miss Ardleigh continued, her voice clear and firm. "What is a more compelling argument for Mrs. Pratt's innocence, though, is the absolute certainty of discovery. Once a foodstuff is implicated, the cook is bound to be suspected. Only a foolish person could hope to get away with poisoning the pudding, and Mrs. Pratt is certainly no fool."

Laken looked at the woman. She spoke with an intelligence and a conviction that he could only respect. But there was at the same time the stirring of doubt in his mind. A few moments before, he had thought that she was not surprised to hear that her aunts had died of mushroom poisoning. Now, she was defending the cook with an intensity that might, to a suspicious mind, suggest that she knew Mrs. Pratt to be innocent. Laken's mind, over the years, had become entirely suspicious, for he had learned that the fairest exterior—and Miss Ardleigh was unquestionably fair—could conceal some very guilty secrets.

But he did not speak of any of this. "I admit your point, Miss Ardleigh," he said quietly, "but I intend to take Mrs. Pratt to the jail for questioning. I expect to detain her overnight. If I discover her to be the culprit, I shall arrest her forthwith. If I find that there is no reason to charge her, I shall release her and continue my search."

"I believe you will find her innocent," Miss Ardleigh said. "I suggest that you look elsewhere for the guilty individual. Do you know, for instance, how the mushrooms came to be in the kitchen?"

"Not for a certainty," Laken said. "The scullery maid says that the cook usually picks them."

She was silent, her head bowed. Then she asked, "How do you intend to transport Mrs. Pratt? Not on your bicycle, I should hope."

Laken frowned. The bicycle was decidedly useful, but it presented certain practical problems when he was required to take someone into custody. "Will you permit me to borrow a horse and cart, Miss Ardleigh? I shall see that it is speedily returned."

She set her mouth. "You may borrow the horse but not the cart," she replied, raising her chin. "I shall ask Pocket to bring the carriage round."

Laken's mouth fell open. "The carriage?"

"Forgive me, Kathryn," the vicar said gently, "but it would hardly be seemly to—"

"Seemly?" Miss Ardleigh cried. "Let us not talk of what is seemly on such a day! If Mrs. Pratt must go to jail, it will not be in a cart, like some poor wretch on her way to the gibbet or the guillotine. She will ride in the carriage, with dignity!"

Laken stared at her, astonished. For a moment she glared back, then gathered her skirts in her hand and swept out of the room. He shook his head, bemused. Miss Kathryn Ardleigh was surely one of the most remarkable women he had ever met.

47

"The cook was a good cook as cooks go; and as cooks go, she went."

—H. H. MUNRO
Reginald

SPENDING THE NIGHT in the cramped, unheated stone jail behind the constable's office was not an experience Sarah Pratt would treasure in her memory.

What she *would* remember, however, to the very end of her days, was riding to jail in the carriage. Pocket, to his everlasting credit, had donned his finest livery for the occasion. Cracking his whip with a fine flourish, he drove like the very blazes down High Street, the constable bringing up the rear on his bicycle, pedaling as fast as his feet could go. The carriage rattled at an amazing rate past the apothecary's on the corner, where Sarah's friends Gert and Gilda stopped their gossiping and stared, mouths open, as she drove by. It careened past St. Mary's on the right, where Rachel Elam was on her way to Ralph Elam's grave with an armful of purple asters which she dropped in a heap on the path when Sarah waved at her. And past The Marlborough Head, where crazy Mick, sweeping the steps, banged his broom handle into his nose when she gave him a politely condescending bow.

By the time Sarah arrived at the jail and was handed out of the carriage with a great show of dignity by Pocket, she was feeling only a slight resentment at having her day's work interrupted for a visit with the constable. Granted, she was still a cook, had always been a cook, and would always be a cook, no matter how many carriages she rode in. But the young Miss Ardleigh (God bless her bones) had treated her like a lady, and that gave Sarah something to think about as she prepared herself for her visit with the constable.

As it turned out, however, that visit did not take place until morning. The constable seemed to hold the theory that a night spent on an iron cot in a cold cell might loosen her tongue—or perhaps he had something else more pressing to do. At any rate, he locked her up and sent Lily round from the pub with a bucket of hot stew, a half loaf of bread, and a pint of ale. After that, the cot did not seem so hard, especially considering that she was not the one who had to cook the stew or wash the dish from which she ate.

And as Sarah went to her knees beside the cot, she said a prayer for the soul of the elder Miss Ardleigh and another for the younger, pausing to reflect before completing her address to the Deity. Was it because she was an American that Miss Ardleigh had so little respect for the established distinctions of rank? Were all Americans similarly blind to tradition and social custom? Was that how it was possible that Rachel Elam's brother Stanton, having sold both his cows and gone to America, now owned his own dairy; and his wife, who made indifferent cheeses with a noticeable tendency to sourness, now was able to command three subordinate cheese-makers? Hearing no conclusive opinion on the matter from Above, Sarah Pratt finished her prayers, climbed into her cot, and went to sleep.

But her sound sleep was sadly disturbed by pangs of conscience, for she deeply regretted Miss Ardleigh's death and the manner of her dying. While the mistress had an unfortunate share in Jenny's death, she had been tolerant and gentle; if she had not eaten the pudding, no doubt she would have been true to her word to restore both fire and sofa to the servants' hall, and jam as well.

Jaggers, however, was another matter. Sarah could not feel remorse when she thought of the woman's death. Indeed, she could not help rejoicing—yes, rejoicing!—in every fiber of her being. She felt her own part in the tragedy, deeply, as well she should; she was contrite and remorseful, although she had to admit of a deep satisfaction when she thought of her kitchen with no Jaggers in it. And even though she was not surprised that suspicion had first fallen on her, she knew it could hardly rest there long, for *she* had not been the one to select and chop the mushrooms. Nor could it fall on little Harriet, for such a young, innocent-looking girl would not likely be called to account for the deaths, and Amelia and Nettie and Mudd had nothing to do with the preparation of the pudding. No, they were all safe from accusation. If anyone were called to account, it would be the one who had introduced the fatal toadstool into the kitchen. And in her heart of hearts Sarah could not but hope that *that* person, who was more to be pitied than blamed, would also escape accusation. She would do her best to see that he was exonerated as well, and that the poisoning was viewed as the tragedy it truly was.

So Sarah Pratt's sleep was laced with dreams in which were mingled regret, rejoicing, and relief, with the latter two sentiments prevailing. When the sun rose, she rose as well and almost as cheerily. She washed her face in the chipped basin, straightened her garments, and smoothed her cot, on which she sat patiently until Lily brought in from the pub a dish of fatty bacon, with biscuits and a pint of gravy. Having eaten well, Sarah found herself refreshed, alert, and only a little creaky as to joints. She was ready to answer whatever questions Constable Laken saw fit to ask her. She knew exactly what she was going to say and how, exactly, she would explain the deaths of the two sisters. There was one slightly sticky part, but on the whole Sarah did not expect any surprises.

The questioning began at eight. It was carried out in the constable's office, a room which was little bigger than Sarah's pantry, crowded with a table, two wooden chairs, shelf, and iron stove, with a photograph of the Queen (God give her a long and healthy life) hanging beside the window. The constable took one chair. Sarah settled herself in the other, smiled at the Queen, and prepared to answer the Queen's representative.

The constable opened his notebook. "It would seem," he said, "that the victims died from eating a deadly mushroom."

Sarah refused to feign sadness for Jaggers, but she could certainly feel a dart of it for the dead Miss Ardleigh. It was that sadness she allowed to creep into her voice. "I knew as much."

The constable's face tightened ever so slightly. "And just how did you know, Mrs. Pratt?"

"From th' way th' pore things died." She added authority to the sadness. "Cudna been anythin' but a bad mushroom."

The constable made a note. "A bad mushroom, meaning a poisonous one?"

Mrs. Pratt nodded.

"And just where did you pick the mushrooms, Mrs. Pratt?"

That *did* surprise, and, for a moment, alarm her. She narrowed her eyes. "Who sez I picked 'em?"

"Did you not? Harriet says you often do."

"So I do," she said, "of'en. There's a spot at th' edge o' th' wood where th' meadow mushrooms are fat as dumplin's. But I di'n't pick 'em that day." She settled herself more firmly in the chair. "That day, there was a deal more t' be done than jauntin' through th' meadow pickin' mushrooms. There were comp'ny for luncheon, a great lot o' it. Four, I made it, an' th' young miss, not t' speak o' the two upstairs, which di'n't come down an' wanted a tray. Wi' respect, sir, if yer don't b'lieve me, come t' th' kitchen someday when there's comp'ny t' luncheon, an' see th' goin's-on. I warrant yer, yer'd find no time t'go a-pickin' mushrooms."

The constable looked at her. "Where *did* the mushrooms come from?"

It was the question she had been waiting for. "I bought 'em," she said firmly, "from a gypsy. At th' kitchen door."

The constable appeared startled. "A gypsy?"

"A lad." She allowed the sympathy to enter her voice. "His folks was camped by th' ditch. His father was a tinker, out lookin' fer scissors an' razors t' grind. His mother were sick with th' fever, pore thing, an' his three lit'le brothers was in th' village, sellin' clothes pegs an' cabbage nets."

As Sarah spoke, the constable rapidly scratched in his notebook. She watched him, envying the speed of his writing. She could read, and read perfectly, having been taught by Miss Ellison, the now-retired governess of Dedham National School. Miss Ellison had set her to read in the *Royal Reader*, where the young Sarah had been enthralled by such stories as "The Skater Chased by Wolves" and "The Siege of Torquilstone," from *Ivanhoe*, as well as descriptions of fairy islands constructed by an amazingly industrious mite called a coral, and reports of the vast frozen wastes of the Northwest Territory. Each year Her Majesty's gimlet-eyed Inspector of Schools came in his fine black frock coat with silk-faced lapels to put the young scholars to their annual examination, and

Sarah would be placed in the front rank of the recitation to show off her reading ability. But when it came to shaping letters on paper, she was in a different sort of water. She was slow, and Miss Ellison's daily exercises in penmanship—"lightly on the upstrokes, heavy on the down"—seemed monotonously tedious. She envied those who could write down words as fast as they spilled out of their brains.

"Can you describe this gypsy boy?" the constable asked.

Sarah shrugged, thinking of the young man who had stood before her. "Brown hat pulled down over his face, brown trousers a size or two b'yond him, boots, dirty hands. About this high." She held a hand up to her nose to demonstrate height. "Face brown as a chestnut."

The constable eyed her. "Are you in the habit of buying foodstuffs from gypsies who call at the door, Mrs. Pratt?" His tone ambiguously implied both a doubt of her veracity and of her prudence.

Sarah summoned dignity to her defense. "I am in th' habit, sir, o' buyin' from vendors when they got somethin' I need. Old Willie Hogglestock comes Mondays with his cart full o' fish an' fruit—grapes, pears, apples. Tommytoes, too"—she wrinkled her nose—"nasty, sour red things wot'll make yer sick. Th' gentry eats 'em with relish—why, I don't know. Then there's Hawkins th' dairyman's helper, wot brings milk, cream, an' butter. Used to be a ship's carpenter, Hawkins did. Come on with th' dairyman after his wife threatened to—"

"I see," the constable said hurriedly. "When the gypsy boy offered the mushrooms, you looked through the basket quite carefully, did you?"

"Ah." This was the sticky part, and Sarah knew it. "T' speak God's truth, sir," she said, averting her eyes from the glance of the Queen, "I did not."

"You did not?"

300

"No, sir," she said remorsefully, "an' I'll ferever wonder in me heart whether 'twas my carelessness wot caused th' trouble."

The constable frowned. "And how was that?"

Sarah heaved a dramatic sigh. "Well, sir, I thought to meself that th' boy might not be a good judge o' mushrooms. But I cud see that he needed th' money, mother sick an' father a tinker an' all. So I paid him, an' paid a bit mor'n he asked, part fer pity o' his perdicament, and part out o' wantin' th' mushrooms. The elder Miss Ardleigh was right partial to 'em, an' I thought t' make her a puddin', seein' as she was plannin' t' give back th' carpet." The constable looked confused but did not interrupt. "But as I was reachin' fer th' basket—t' look through it an' be sure th' mushrooms were wot they should be—there was a commotion."

"What sort of commotion?"

"Th' lad looked round, like, over his shoulder, an' there stood one o' th' guests, lookin' at him. The boy took fright an' bolted."

"And then what?"

"Well, there I stood with th' basket in me hand, thinkin' t' sort through it, like. But Harriet had made up th' fire too hot an' th' soup boiled over. As I was tendin' t' that, I burned me thumb." She held it up to demonstrate the red welt. "I dipped it in Saint-John's-wort oil an' bound it up an' went back t' th' mushrooms, which was sittin' on th' table. But th' spit give way in th' fire an' the joint dropped in th' ash an'—"

"Mrs. Pratt," the constable said, "are you telling me that you did not check the mushrooms?"

"Yes, sir," Sarah said, low. "I aimed t' do't before settin' Harriet to chop. But th' sweets tray got knocked over an'—" She dropped her head, her shoulders slumped under the weight of so many domestic tragedies. "I made th' crust fer th' puddin', an' Harriet chopped th' mushrooms. An' that, sir, is how th' sad deed was done."

The constable spoke with care. "So there could have been a poisonous mushroom in the basket and you would not have seen it?"

"Yessir," Sarah said. "I mean, no, sir." She frowned, trying to make out which way the question went. "I mean, sir," she added, to make her answer clear, "as I di'n't see no poisonous mushroom. If I had've, it wud never o' got near th' puddin', yer can be sure o' that."

"Did anyone else see the gypsy?"

She spoke truly. "None o' the servants, sir, but me. Th' guest, though—he got a glimpse o' him." Not a good glimpse, though, she thought. "He's th' one wot frightened him off."

"Do you know the name of the guest?"

"Well, 'twas th' Marsdens who come fer luncheon, and he was their guest, a Sir Charles somebody-or-other. The same one wot pushed his way in while you was talkin' t' Harriet."

The constable's eyebrows went up. "Sir Charles Sheridan?"

"If that 'twas 'is name," Sarah said cautiously.

Her answer seemed to satisfy the constable. "Only a few more questions," he said. "Harriet cut up the mushrooms and you prepared the pudding—in what sort of container?"

"Why, a puddin'-basin, o'course," Sarah said. "It were steamed."

"Inside a pot with a cover, on the stove?"

Sarah frowned. "How else?"

"For how long?"

"An hour, most like. Till 'twas done."

"Was anyone else in the kitchen during that hour?"

Sarah thought. "Just me an' Harriet." She frowned. "An' th' young miss. She come in to make tea fer her aunt an' herself."

The constable's mouth tightened at the corners. "Did she go near the stove?"

Sarah's frown darkened. "Cudn't say, sir," she said carelessly. "I had too much t' do t' be watchin' others."

But the constable's eyes were still on her as he shut up his notebook and stood. "I will confirm your report of the gypsy with Sir Charles as quickly as I can. You will not object to being detained meanwhile?"

Sarah smiled comfortably. "Oh, no, sir. I'd as soon have the day t' meself, 'specially seein' as it's washday." She stood. "Yer don't suppose, d'yer, that Pocket could bring th' carriage when it's time fer me t' go back t' Bishop's Keep?"

The constable's lips twitched. "I can't say, but I will inquire."

"Thank ye, sir," Sarah said. She looked up at the Queen's photograph and dropped a deep curtsy, pleasantly conscious that she had met her obligation to the crown while still protecting the innocence of one whose motives she pitied, rather than hated.

The Queen gave her a benevolent smile.

48

"When you have excluded the impossible, whatever remains, however impossible, must be the truth."

—SIR ARTHUR CONAN DOYLE,
The Beryl Coronet

A LITTLE BEFORE eleven, Kate was sitting at the Remington, typing—but not on her book. There would be a great deal to do over the next few weeks, and "The Golden Scarab" would have to wait. She was typing a letter to Mr. Bothwell Coxford, her editor, to ask for an extension of her deadline.

She was interrupted by the sound of cart wheels on gravel. She went to the French doors and saw Mudd, bowler-hatted and wearing his greatcoat, drive up with Pocket in the cart. She threw on her shawl and hurried outside.

"How is Mrs. Pratt?" she asked, shivering in the chilly air.

An hour before, Kate had dispatched Mudd to Dedham to find out what he could about Cook's situation, and fetch her home if possible. Although Harriet had been bidden to silence by the constable, the girl had finally told her story to Kate, who now knew that the deadly toadstool had found its way into the pudding by a tragic accident. This new information had much relieved Kate's mind, since she no longer had to wonder if either of her aunts, or Cook, had been somehow responsible.

But if it was known how the toadstool got into the pudding, it was not yet clear how the toadstool had gotten into the kitchen. Harriet did not know whether Mrs. Pratt herself had gathered the mushrooms from the wood, or whether they had arrived by some other means, and no one else was able to offer enlightenment. But Kate, thinking back over the events of the past few days and recalling the brown felt hat dropped by the would-be intruder, suspected that Jenny Blyly's lover—who certainly had a reason to hate not only Aunt Jaggers but Aunt Sabrina as well—might have brought the poisonous mushroom into the house. Indeed, she would have spoken the name of Tom Potter to the constable, had she been sure that to do so might not further incriminate Mrs. Pratt.

Mudd alighted from the cart. "Mrs. P. is quite well," he said, "an' sends 'er thanks fer inquirin'. She 'as explained things t' th' constable an' hopes he'll soon let 'er go."

"Thank God," Kate breathed fervently. "But why did he not let her come back with you?"

"'E's gone off t' check 'er story wi' Sir Charles." He took off his bowler hat and held it in his hands. "She'ud like t' know whether ye plan t' send th' carriage, miss."

Kate could not help smiling. She had overstated the case to Mr. Laken when she claimed Mrs. Pratt as a friend. But as Aunt Sabrina's secretary, she had felt a fraternal sympathy for all the servants and an outright concern for the two youngest. As mistress, she felt the same compassion but with an added sense of obligation, for she was now responsible for the well-being of the staff. Still, she had to admire the irrepressible Pratt, and she hoped that even in the changed circumstance, a mutual friendship was not out of the question.

"By all means," she told Mudd, "send the carriage." She turned to go back into the house, then turned back. "You said that the constable is speaking with Sir Charles. Why is that?"

"Mrs. P. ses 'twas a gypsy 'oo brought th' mushrooms t' th' kitchen door. Sir Charles saw 'em talkin' t'gether, afore th' lad took to 'is heels."

Kate stood still. A gypsy! Yes! At luncheon, Sir Charles had mentioned taking the photograph of a gypsy boy who had turned tail and fled when he saw the camera. Well, Tom Potter was slender enough to be thought a lad. If the picture were clear enough, it might confirm or contradict her suspicion of his guilt. She turned toward the house. Had not Sir Charles called with photographs yesterday? Had not he left them in an envelope on the table beside the chair where he was sitting?

Kate went swiftly back to the library. Yes, there was the envelope. She picked it up. In it were a number of photographic prints—several of her in various casual poses; two of Bradford and Eleanor, unaware of the concealed camera; the one taken by Mudd of the self-conscious quartet at the luncheon table. She laid the photo aside to study later, and turned eagerly to the last one. Yes, this was it! The slender gypsy boy at the kitchen door, face turned full to the camera, hat slipped to the back of his head.

Kate stared at the photograph for a long moment, puzzled. No, the figure was not that of Tom Potter, nor the face. It was too finely featured, too symmetrically drawn. But there was something familiar about that face, something about the eyes, the mouth—

Suddenly her fingers felt cold and her knees began to tremble. She *knew* the face in this photo! It was—

But that was impossible!

She swallowed. No, not impossible, only improbable. But why—?

She stood still, thinking rapidly. Outside in the hallway a cuckoo clock began to announce the hour of eleven. By the fifth cuckoo, her thoughts began to make a kind of muddled sense. By the seventh, Kate could see how it might have happened. By the eleventh and last, she thought she knew who and how, and even why. Her conclusion seemed improbable, very nearly impossible, but it made sense. It had to be the truth.

But she had to admit to an uncomfortable degree of doubt. She looked down at the photograph again, at the face, the clothing, the hat. The picture was not as clear as she would have liked, and her identification could not be absolutely positive. Still, she was almost sure she was right.

But what should she do? The first and most obvious step was to find Edward Laken and show him what she had discovered—what she *thought* she had discovered. But the constable was the one who had insisted so vehemently, despite her protests, on taking Mrs. Pratt in for questioning. What was more, he had infuriated her by staring when she ordered the carriage for the cook. No. It might be petty, but she would not allow him the satisfaction of making the arrest—or, if she was wrong, the satisfaction of laughing at her.

Then what? Should she show the photograph to Sir Charles and beg his assistance? For a moment, she was tempted. It would be quite pleasantly gratifying to show that arrogant man that he did not have a monopoly on hypotheses: she too could formulate a theory of the crime and provide the evidence to validate it. And it would be delightful to correct *his* incorrect conclusion that Mrs. Pratt was the killer.

But here the same nettlesome difficulty arose. If she was wrong, she would have made a fool of herself in

Sir Charles's quite critical eyes. It would be far better to obtain definitive proof—a confession before a witness, if at all possible—and then turn the matter over to the proper authorities.

But it was not Kate's unwillingness to accommodate Constable Laken or risk Sir Charles's critical judgment that proved to be the definitive factor. What decided Kate was her quite natural impulse to face down the wicked person who had killed her aunts, and Beryl Bardwell's interest in hearing a confession from the criminal's own lips.

But this was obviously not a matter that she could take entirely into her own hands. She would need help. She stood quietly for another minute, sorting through various possible strategies. Then she made up her mind. She knew what she would do. But it had to be done quickly. Time was of the essence.

49

"The hiding of a crime, or the detection of a crime, what is it? A trial of skill between the police on one side, and the individual on the other."

—WILKIE COLLINS
The Woman in White

LAKEN WAS FROWNING thoughtfully as he mounted his bicycle. But instead of riding out in the direction of Marsden Manor, he rode toward the vicarage. An important matter wanted clearing up before he spoke to Charlie Sheridan.

The vicar was among his roses. "Ah, Edward," he said, straightening, a basket of late blossoms in his hand. "Perhaps you would care for a cup of morning tea? A biscuit? I am sure Mrs. Mills can find us a little something."

"Thank you, sir," Laken said, "but I fear I am in a bit of a hurry. I came to ask you to enlighten me as to the Ardleigh inheritance."

"Ah, yes." The vicar seemed burdened by the thought. "It is very simple, really. Miss Ardleigh—Sabrina Ardleigh—recently made a new will. Her sister Bernice was her previous beneficiary. Owing to difficulties between them, Miss Ardleigh determined to exclude her from inheritance. In her place, she named her niece. There are some minor bequests, of course, but the bulk of the estate goes to Kathryn. As it should," he added. "She is the last Ardleigh."

"I see," Laken said. He kept his face carefully blank. "Do you know, sir, when Miss Kathryn Ardleigh learned of her good fortune?"

The vicar looked at him, a slight frown puckering his forehead. "As a matter of fact, I told her yesterday, after her aunt's death. It was a great shock to her."

"You are sure?"

The vicar's tufted eyebrows rose. "Why, man, you're not suggesting . . . Of course it was a surprise!" His face filled with consternation. "You can't possibly suspect that young woman of causing the deaths of her aunts!"

"Thank you, sir," Laken said. It spoke well of Miss Ardleigh that the vicar would rise to her defense so readily. But of course it was his business to think the best of any soul. It was Laken's business to think the worst.

50

"To Sir Charles Sheridan Marsden Manor Dedham Essex stop Most urgent stop Ring inscription reads Armand beloved of Thoth grant him eternal life stop Believe ring property Armand Monet noted Parisian cryptographer stop Failed to arrive London last week stop Send murder details forthwith stop"

—SIGNED SMYTHE-HOWELL BRITISH MUSEUM

CHARLES FOLDED THE telegram and replaced it in his coat pocket. It had arrived just after breakfast this morning, in reply to the letter he had posted immediately after copying the inscription. Having read it, he asked for a horse and set out for Colchester, his mind greatly unsettled.

Was Armand Monet the true name of the dead man in the dig? If so, what had brought a noted cryptographer from the continent to Colchester? Was he linked to the Order of the Golden Dawn, as the peacock feather might suggest? If true, what was the nature of that link? How could it be proved? And how would Inspector Wainwright receive this latest revelation?

But Armand Monet was not the only matter that unsettled Charles. The last two days had been decidedly disturbing, beginning with the luncheon party at Bishop's Keep, where he had enjoyed himself rather more than usual. His pleasure, he reluctantly admitted, was largely due to the presence of Miss Ardleigh, whose russet hair and penetrating hazel-green eyes lingered far longer in his memory than he would have preferred. Perhaps it was the photographs that fixed that grave and yet laughing face in his mind. Certainly it was not a beautiful face, not even conventionally attractive, for the times favored a female face that was demure and diffident. But yet it was a remarkable face. It was a face that suggested intellect, awareness, observance.

He frowned. Observance, indeed. So observant that Miss Ardleigh's sharp eye had caught him in the act of taking surreptitious photographs. Oddly, he had not minded being found out, but had been intrigued. Other women of his acquaintance saw little beyond what they expected, or more precisely, were expected to see. But Miss Ardleigh seemed to cultivate the habit of observant inquiry. He recalled the first day they met, when her attention to his photos and fingerprints had been more than that strictly required by social convention. She seemed genuinely fascinated by things that were not normally of interest to women. He had even thought that, with the proper cultivation, her interests might encourage between them a bond of friendship. But that was now quite out of the question, after what had happened yesterday.

He had developed the photographs, as he promised, and had ridden with them to Bishop's Keep. He told himself that he merely planned to drop them off, but in the depths of his being he felt a secret anticipation at the opportunity of seeing this unconventional woman again and perhaps even having private conversation with her. He had even considered the possibility of—

But Charles had forgotten what he might have considered, for his visit to Bishop's Keep had proved the undoing of all possibility. Now, he only recalled how he had been greeted at the door with the news of the death of her two aunts. And how shortly after that he had managed somehow to inspire her anger, and she to awaken his irritation. Her insistence on hearing his theory of fungal poisoning—which he had scarcely formulated to himself and was not at all ready to share with another—had seemed unreasonably abrupt, even rude, exactly what he would have expected from a red-haired American woman of Irish parentage. Well-bred women did not as a rule demand to know the thoughts of casual acquaintances; to do so suggested an equality of intellect and experience to which they would hardly pretend. They were deferential, respectful; they did not contradict. Yes, indeed; her outburst had greatly irritated him. It had even—yes, it had even insulted him.

Still, perhaps he should make allowances. Miss Ardleigh certainly had uncommon reason to display emotion on that day; in fact, now that he thought of it, he was surprised that she had not shown more. Most women, in the tragic circumstance of losing two beloved aunts, would have been totally incapacitated with grief. Indeed, the strain on her must have been extraordinary. At the time of their conversation, she was acting as mistress. She was probably well within her rights to know the actions of visitors with regard to her servants and on her property.

Her property? It suddenly dawned on Charles that he had heard of no other close relatives. Could she be, *was* she the last Ardleigh? He frowned. If this was indeed so, some might construe the mysteries of the deaths in a distinctly unfavorable way. In fact, Miss Ardleigh was perhaps fortunate that the cook had been so ready a suspect. Without that, Miss Ardleigh might well have found herself in that position. And if it proved that Mrs. Pratt was indeed not the killer—

Charles did not wish to follow this line of inquiry. His horse had just passed the old half-timbered house that still bore the scars of the Civil War siege 250–odd years before. He crossed over the River Colne on East Bridge, and rode up East Hill Street, which rose at a sharp angle up to the crest where the ruins of the castle stood. Begun during the time of William the Conqueror, the castle had been a royal fortress and royal prison (a certain Sir Thomas Malory was said to have been rescued therefrom in 1454), and then a baronial residence. It now was in private hands, although he understood that there was a move afoot to purchase it for the borough and make it into some sort of museum.

He paused for a moment and looked at the massive stone walls. When construction of the keep began in 1076, various Roman ruins must still have been visible, especially that of the Temple of Claudius, where the defenders of the town the Romans called Camulodunum had made their final stand against Queen Boadicea and her Icenian army in the first century. Boadicea. Ah! there was a woman. Her passion and zest for life, her warlike power, shone through the darkness of those early centuries with all the fervor and flame of a firebrand. There were no women of that sort now, and it was a pity. Or, if there were, they struck one as abrasive, unmannerly—

He abandoned that sentence and returned to the thought he had originally meant to pursue before he had been sidetracked by Boadicea. It was a thought of which Tennyson would have approved, or Arnold, some vague reflection on the inexorable, inescapable round of life and death, and the unfortunate truth that there was little justice to be had in either. A few minutes later he was entering the Colchester police station.

"Good morning," he said to Sergeant Battle, who was crouching over the desk in the outer office, a pen in his heavy hand, an inkpot at his elbow, and a pile of papers before him.

The sergeant gave him a dark look. "Mornin'," he returned shortly. Charles remembered that his last visit had begun on just such a sour note. Obviously, Inspector Wainwright's pessimism was infectious. Sergeant Battle had caught it.

With a determined cheerfulness, Charles related his reason for coming and asked the sergeant to inform the inspector. While he waited, he sat in a chair by the window and surveyed the room, which held little of interest other than a blurred photograph of the castle, a fanciful etching of Balkerne Gate in the time of the Romans, and a framed citation from the Borough Council for exemplary and heroic police effort. His gaze finally came to rest on a somewhat shabby valise sitting on the floor beside the sergeant's desk. It was a well-traveled leather bag, of the sort that might be owned by a man of the middle class. It appeared to have a monogram engraved on the clasp. Having nothing else to look at, Charles went to the valise and knelt. The initials on the clasp were A.M.

The sergeant re-entered the room and immediately stumbled over Charles. He scowled. "'F I may inquire, sir, is there somethin' about that valise wot int'rests you?"

Charles rose. "How did you come by it?"

"Mrs. Grogan."

"Mrs. Grogan?"

The sergeant sat down and resentfully picked up his pen. "She owns a boardin' house on King Street."

"Why did she bring it here?"

The sergeant dipped his pen in the inkpot. "Owner left it."

"Have you examined the contents?"

"I've more important things t' do than fiddle th' lock on somebody's valise." The sergeant began to write with great industry. "Inspector says fer you t' show yerself in."

Charles stood looking down at the sergeant, wondering how he would react if the inkpot at his elbow were to leap suddenly to the floor. He pushed that unworthy thought out of his mind. "Right, then. I'll just speak with the inspector."

"Good, sir," the sergeant said, signing his name with a flourish and beginning on another paper. "You just do that."

The inspector was not writing; he was reading. Apparently, the stack of reports that began on Sergeant Battle's desk ended on Wainwright's table. It was a moment before he put down the paper and looked up.

"Battle says you know something about the ring."

"I do." Charles took out the telegram, unfolded it, and handed it to the inspector, who scanned the yellow sheet with his lower lip stuck out. After a moment he laid it down.

"Cryptographer?" He scowled. "What the bloody hell was a cryptographer doing in Colchester? Some kind of spy, was he?"

"I doubt that," Charles replied. It was an interesting idea, though; if true, it would add an extra fillip of intrigue to the case. "I have been developing a theory that the man's death was in some way related to a secret society known as the Order of the Golden Dawn. Its insignia is a peacock feather."

"Is it, now?" The inspector's voice held an edge of sarcasm.

"Yes," Charles replied evenly. "But there is another lead which may prove more productive at the moment. If I am not altogether mistaken, you have just come into possession of the dead man's valise."

The inspector's eyes narrowed.

"The proprietor of a boarding house on King Street has delivered to you the unclaimed luggage of a boarder. The initials on the clasp are A.M."

Wainwright's look was that of a man betrayed. "Battle!" he thundered.

The sergeant materialized in the doorway. "Sir!"

"Did someone bring in a valise?"

The sergeant stiffened. "Yessir."

"Why wasn't I told?"

"It just got 'ere. I thought 'twas a reg'lar unclaimed bag."

Wainwright glared. "*Don't think*. Fetch it here, at the double."

Sergeant Battle returned forthwith, valise in hand, and set it on the inspector's table. The inspector examined the monogram and tried the clasp. It was locked. He spoke between his teeth. "Don't stand there like a stork, Battle. Bring something to force this."

A moment later the sergeant was back with a large screwdriver. The inspector inserted it under the clasp, which obligingly popped open. Neatly arranged within the valise were several shirts and sets of undergarments, two fresh collars, a pair of silver-backed brushes, and a thick leather-bound volume with gilt lettering on the spine.

The inspector leafed through the book and handed it to Charles. "Codes," he grunted. "Ciphers. Definitely a spy."

"Actually," Charles said, looking at the title page, "the book is a treatise on cuneiform writing, in French. Monet must have been interested not only in codes and ciphers, but in the pre-Hellenic languages of the Middle East." He paused, his eye caught by a passage in the text. "Fascinating, this. Here is a translation of the tablet of King Nabu-Apalidinna, from Sippar. Seventh century B.C. Neo-Babylonian. I examined it recently in the British Museum, but I didn't have a clue as to what it said."

The inspector was thumbing through a slim black book he had taken from a pocket inside the valise. He tossed it on the desk, vexed. "More codes and gibble-gabber."

With some regret, Charles put down the cuneiform text and picked up the black book. "This is in French also."

Sergeant Battle brightened. "A *French* spy."

"It appears to be the business diary of a Monsieur Armand Monet, 17 Rue du Pont, Paris." Charles leafed quickly through the pages, scanning the tidy, dated notes. The man wrote a clean hand and kept detailed records of his activities.

The inspector glared. "Well?"

"Monsieur Monet was an exceedingly busy man." Charles turned several pages. "He seems to have become involved with the Ahathoor Temple of the Order of the Golden Dawn in the spring of last year. That is the temple in Paris," he added in explanation, and then murmured "ah," as he found a name he recognized. "It appears that Monet was also a friend of Mathers."

"Mathers? Who the devil is that?" The inspector was obviously not pleased to receive such a lot of new information, so thoroughly out of order and disconnected, and not in the form of a written report.

"Chief of the Paris temple. Give me a moment, if you please." Charles leafed through the book until the pages became blank, then leafed backward for several pages and began to ready Monet's notes. "It appears that Monet was in Colchester at Mathers's request," he mused, half to himself.

The inspector looked on with his arms folded. Sergeant Battle stood stiffly at attention.

After a few minutes Charles closed the book and laid it on the inspector's desk. He spoke crisply. "We have work to do."

"What work?" the inspector asked.

"Monsieur Monet's diary tells us a great deal," Charles replied. "Why he came to Colchester, with whom he spoke here, and what he planned to do."

"Does it tell us who killed him?"

"Not in so many words," Charles said. "But it does suggest a possible motive. And it tells us the name of the person of whom we must inquire. That person may be able to direct us to the killer." He started for the door.

The inspector turned to the sergeant. "Well, man?" he bellowed. "Are you going to stand there the whole bloody day? Come along. And fetch your notebook!"

Charles was halfway out the door when he thought of something. He turned back, bumping into Wainwright. "Excuse me, Inspector. I doubt that the cuneiform treatise has any relevance to the case at hand. I'll just borrow it, if you have no objection."

The inspector's mouth pursed. "You're not a spy too, are you?"

51

"I prithee now with most petitionary vehemence, tell me who it is."

"O wonderful, wonderful, and most wonderful wonderful! and yet again wonderful, and after that, out of all whooping!"

—WILLIAM SHAKESPEARE
As You Like It, III, ii

KATE GOT OUT of the pony cart at the corner and, after lingering an appropriate time, walked down the street to Number Seven, carrying Aunt Jaggers's tapestry knitting bag. She marched with spine erect, chin up, and shoulders straight. Outwardly she was a woman of calm and deliberate demeanor, a woman who knew her purpose.

But within, all was chaos. Within, Kate found herself nearly overwhelmed by the sheer folly of her mad scheme. The ride from Bishop's Keep had given her time to consider what she was about and to think better of it. She had played a few juvenile tricks in her day: lurking, for instance, outside the steward's cabin on the ship, on the lookout for Mrs. Snodgrass's diamonds. But she had never done anything as absurd as this. She had never accused

320

anyone of *murder*. And to make matters worse, not even a few glances at the photograph she was carrying with her could restore her confidence, for she found herself uncertain about the identity of the gypsy boy. Guilty or not guilty, she was no longer sure.

But it was too late to change her mind. The die was cast. Arrangements had been made, and if she did not do her part—Well, she had to, that was all. She owed it to Aunt Sabrina, if not to Aunt Jaggers. Two lives wasted, and for what? At the thought, her purpose firmed. She went up the steps and rang the bell.

There was silence within. Kate rang again, mentally scrabbling for something to say. Should she be delicate or direct? Should she open the conversation with a forthright challenge, or allow the discussion to take its own course, following its natural meander into the topics she wished to pursue?

But before Kate could devise a plan of action, the bell was answered—not by a servant but by the very person she had come to see.

Kate made herself smile. "Good morning, Mrs. Farnsworth."

"Why, good morning, Miss Ardleigh," Mrs. Farnsworth replied. "Please, come in. I am afraid you have caught me answering my own bell, since it is my maid's half day." Her golden brown hair was bound back loosely and her green gown flowed without a waist from the shoulders, giving her a look of pastoral innocence, yet with a complexly mysterious knowledge behind the eyes, like one of Rossetti's maidens.

"Thank you," Kate said, masking her relief in formal politeness. She had recalled the vicar saying that Mrs. Farnsworth had only one servant, and had hoped that the woman might be out.

Mrs. Farnsworth's eyes became shadowed. "I was appallingly grieved—and shocked—to hear of your aunt's death. Your note did not elaborate. Please, come into the parlor and tell me what happened. It was a tragic accident, I assume."

Without answering, Kate followed her. The room was dim and chilly, palely lighted by the gas lamp on the wall beside the fireplace and warmed by a fire so small as to be almost symbolic. Kate noticed that the coal hod on the hearth was nearly empty, and wondered if Mrs. Farnsworth had simply allowed herself to run out, or was effecting a necessary economy.

Mrs. Farnsworth put her hands into the embroidered pockets of her dress. "If you like, I can prepare tea. One learns, you know, not to depend upon one's servants for *all* the necessities of life."

"Thank you, no tea," Kate said. She sat on the plum velvet settee facing the fire—on the edge, as decorum demanded—while Mrs. Farnsworth took the chair where she had obviously been sitting, wrapped in a paisley shawl. Between them was a small rosewood table that held a glass dish of shells and several small framed photographs of Mrs. Farnsworth in various costumed poses.

Mrs. Farnsworth pulled the shawl around her shoulders. "Now, please, Miss Ardleigh," she said, "if it is not too trying, perhaps you will tell me how your aunt died."

"It is very trying," Kate said, "but I will tell you." Lacking a strategy by which to plot a more devious course to the subject, she simply spoke what came first to mind, which was the truth. "She was poisoned."

Mrs. Farnsworth's hands flew to her mouth. She gasped. "Poisoned!"

Kate kept her back straight, her eyes fixed intently on Mrs. Farnsworth. Since they had already arrived at their subject, she would take the offensive. She could do no worse than fail. And even if she were mistaken about Mrs. Farnsworth's role in her aunts' deaths—now that she was actually here, the possibility of error seemed dreadfully real—she doubted that the woman would make an issue of the matter. There was, after all, the business of the forged letters. Kate screwed her courage to the sticking point and plunged ahead.

"Mrs. Farnsworth, this is not a stage and you and I are not merely players. You know very well that my aunt was poisoned, for you provided the means of her death. *You* killed her."

Mrs. Farnsworth's brown eyes grew large and she gave a little gasping laugh. "*I*! My dear Miss Ardleigh, what fearful lunacy is this? Have you lost your mind?"

Have I? Kate wondered to herself. But she had nowhere to go but forward, doggedly following the track of what seemed to be the truth. "I am accusing you," she said, "of the murders of Sabrina Ardleigh and Bernice Jaggers."

The open mouth and widened eyes registered incredulity, the simultaneous headshake a sorrowful pity. "I very much fear that you *have* lost your mind, Miss Ardleigh. Perhaps it is the grief of untimely death, for which I hope you will accept my deepest condolences. Sabrina was my friend. But frankly, my dear, I have not an idea in the world who this Jaggers person is whom you say I have . . ." The slightest smile, as if of disbelief, lifted her lips, ". . . poisoned."

"Bernice Jaggers was the sister of Sabrina Ardleigh," Kate said, her eyes on the other's face. That little smile had hardened her resolve. "The evening before last, both ate of the mushroom pudding that was prepared from mushrooms you brought to Bishop's Keep. Among them was a Death Cap. My aunts died yesterday." She felt a deep icy chill, a winter in the bones. "Both were ill for hours. They suffered agonizing deaths."

Mrs. Farnsworth cast her eyes down. "I am most sorry for your sad bereavement, Miss Ardleigh." There was a catch in her impassioned voice and when she looked up, the trace of a tear in her eye. She leaned forward, speaking with urgency. "But I assure you that I have never called at Bishop's Keep. And never having been there, I certainly could not have brought such a thing as . . . mushrooms." She made a little grimace, as if the word summoned up images of dirt and leaves. "Or a . . . Death Cap, did you say? I regret that I do not know what that is."

Kate's heart was in her throat, and she was oblivious to the chill room around her, the pale gloom, the dying fire. Had she made a terrible mistake? Had she accused a woman who was guilty of foolishness but innocent of murder? But she had no other course. She could only pursue. She steeled herself.

"You came," she said, relentless, "twice. The first time, you attempted to break in to the library to steal the forged letters and the cipher document; as you escaped, you left a hat. The second time, you came in the disguise of a gypsy selling mushrooms."

Mrs. Farnsworth sat quite still. Only her eyes moved, with a quick, darting motion, right to left, and there was a slight mottling high on her cheeks. For the first time, Kate began to think that she might be right. With the thought came both relief and a heightened apprehension. If Mrs. Farnsworth was the killer, how could she wring a confession from her? The woman was as cold and icy hard as a glacier.

When Mrs. Farnsworth spoke, her voice was distant. "I see that you insist on persevering in these scandalous and absurd accusations despite my assurance that I have absolutely no idea what you are talking about." She rose, her bearing imperious, contempt and revulsion in her face. "I must, therefore, decline to speak with you any further. Please leave."

She was the perfect picture of offended, outraged sensibility. How could the actress be dislodged from the role? Kate reached into the knitting bag beside her on the settee and took out the envelope. "I fear that it will not be as easy as that, Mrs. Farnsworth. There is proof of your visit."

The other woman's eyes darkened imperceptibly, but her face remained impassive. When she spoke her voice was without inflection. "Proof? What proof could you possibly have?"

"This photograph," Kate said. She opened the envelope and held it up. "It quite clearly shows you in your gypsy costume at the kitchen door, a basket of mushrooms in your hand."

Mrs. Farnsworth stood unmoving.

Kate put the photograph on the table. "Perhaps you would care to examine it."

Quickly, as if she could not help herself, the woman's glance went to the photograph. Then, with the subtlest of facial expressions, perhaps just the smoothing of the skin around the eyes, her self-confidence seemed to return. She lifted her chin. "A cursory examination, I suppose," she said with cool amusement, "might suggest that the figure in this photograph could be a woman. It might even be concluded—although the conclusion would certainly require an extraordinary feat of the imagination—to bear a slight resemblance to me."

"And to Rosalind?" Kate asked. "Is the gypsy's costume not *your* costume from *As You Like It*, in which Rosalind, transformed into Ganymede, dresses as a boy?"

Mrs. Farnsworth's tone was colored by a half-contemptuous disdain. "But the taking of life is not sport for ladies. Why in the world should I wish to kill your aunts, Miss Ardleigh? The idea is outrageous!"

"It was not my *aunts* you intended to kill," Kate said, feeling anger, "but my *aunt*. Sabrina Ardleigh, a good and kind lady and a friend to you. And you probably intended to kill me as well. The idea is not at all outrageous when you consider what is at stake. The reputation of Dr. Westcott, your own reputation and livelihood, the continuation of the Order of the Golden Dawn—all of enormous importance to you, I warrant, and worth a few risks."

Mrs. Farnsworth looked down at Kate. Her eyes betrayed the first slightest hint of fear but her voice was still firm. "Miss Ardleigh, would you be so good as to make your point plain? *If* you have a point, that is. As proof, I fear your photograph falls far short."

"The letters," Kate said. She drew a paper-wrapped bundle from the knitting bag. "The letters purportedly written by Fräulein Sprengel authorizing Dr. Westcott to establish the Order of the Golden Dawn. They are not authentic. They are forgeries, as is the cipher document. Aunt Sabrina guessed as much, and Mr. Mathers's letter to you, which she read, confirmed her suspicion—and perhaps her idea that the dead Frenchman found in the Colchester excavation was connected to you. She confronted you with what she knew and told you that she intended to reveal the secret to the Order at large. You had to ensure her silence."

Mrs. Farnsworth started to speak, then stopped. Her eyes met Kate's. Her look was compounded of acrimony, a kind of pitying scorn, and some sort of deeply interior conflict. For a long moment she seemed to grapple with herself. Then she turned and went slowly to the desk in the corner. A moment later, she turned back again and gestured at the bundle Kate had placed on the table beside the photograph. "Those are the letters?"

"They are the documents you attempted to steal several nights ago from the library at Bishop's Keep," Kate said.

Her voice was disbelieving. "You believe me to have been an intruder?"

"Yes. You left your hat behind—Rosalind's hat. Of course," Kate added, "you had to have the letters, for the forgery is not clever. The fraud would be abundantly clear to any objective reader, who could reveal the hoax and show Dr. Westcott to be a sham and a charlatan. And if that happened, the entire Order would collapse—as you well knew."

"I see," Mrs. Farnsworth said reflectively, "that you have given this matter considerable thought. I wonder—while you were thinking, did you think perhaps of some . . . accommodation we might make?"

"Accommodation?"

Mrs. Farnsworth's smile did not touch her glacial eyes. "My dear Miss Ardleigh, you may think me wicked, but I do not think you naive. You come alone to accuse me of—" She pulled her brows together slightly. "You have come alone, have you not?"

Kate inclined her head.

Mrs. Farnsworth laughed. "There, you see? You come alone to accuse me of murder, bringing your proof. What else am I to conclude but that your evidence—the photograph, the documents—is for sale?"

Kate thought quickly. This was perhaps the opening she needed. When she spoke, her voice held an admiring candor. "You are indeed perceptive, Mrs. Farnsworth; you have found me out. In return, then, I will be frank with you."

"Ah, yes," Mrs. Farnsworth said with a dry irony. "Let us *both* be frank."

Kate allowed herself a small smile. "I am not inclined to seek vengeance for my aunts' murders, for I too have profited. I am to inherit the Ardleigh estate. By the same token, I do not seek to sell the evidence of your guilt for money." She paused. Mrs. Farnsworth was watching her observantly, still standing, her eyes intent, her hands in the pockets of her gown. "What I do seek is participation in the Order. I find that I enjoy the association, and I wish to continue and expand it. I would like to hold the office my aunt held, that of Cancellarius." She raised her voice slightly. "I am willing to give you the photograph and the documents, in return for that appointment and for your verbal confirmation to me that everything I have said here is true."

Mrs. Farnsworth made a condescending gesture. "Confirmation? That part, my dear Kathryn—it is Kathryn, is it not?—is easy. Of course you are quite right. I did darken my face with umber and disguise myself as a gypsy boy, after the manner of Rosalind. I did carry a basket of mushrooms, including two fatal ones, to Bishop's Keep. I knew, you see, that your Aunt Sabrina was exceedingly fond of mushrooms; she said as much the afternoon of the gathering. I did not know that your aunt had a sister, but I was prepared to silence you along with Sabrina, since I could not be sure that she had not spoken of the matter to you."

"But she was your *friend!*" Kate burst out, half rising. "How could you kill her?"

Mrs. Farnsworth's eyes glinted. " 'Most friendship is feigning,' " she said, " 'most loving mere folly.' "

Kate sank back. "I am sorry," she said. "Please go on."

"My motive was as you have deduced. Your aunt was intent on telling the world that Dr. Westcott forged the cipher document and the letters that authorized him to establish the Order. Some might say he was foolish in doing so, although I say in his defense that he did not intend to deceive. He only meant to enjoy for a little— quite to himself, quite in private—the pleasure of creating a fictional world in which he was given the blessing of the most ancient authorities for his magical work. He had no intention of sharing the letters with others."

Thinking of Beryl Bardwell, Kate murmured, "But the relationship between life and art is very complex. A fiction can become quite real."

" 'And thereby hangs a tale.' " A smile ghosted across Mrs. Farnsworth's mouth. "You are quite perceptive, Miss Ardleigh. This transformation of art into life might not have happened, however, had it not been for MacGregor Mathers, to whom Dr. Westcott confided his innocent little diversion. It was Mathers who convinced him that the Order should be introduced to the public at large. It was Mathers who insisted on using the letters to lend authenticity to the effort."

"And in time Dr. Westcott began to believe in the truth of his magical fiction."

"Yes," Mrs. Farnsworth said. Her voice was colored by a regretful contempt, as if she were deriding an actor who had been taken in by his part.

"And Mathers now intends to reveal the fraud in order to discredit the doctor?"

Mrs. Farnsworth's mouth hardened. "Mathers is a man full of his own glory, greedy for power. From the beginning, he aimed to destroy Dr. Westcott and substitute his own project. I could not permit such a thing to happen. Quite apart from my . . . friendly feelings for the doctor, I have my own interests to protect. As you have quite rightly guessed, the Order is a substantial part of my livelihood and will remain so, even when I have successfully returned to the stage. At the present time, I am quite vulnerable. I do not intend to let Mathers destroy me."

"But to keep that from happening," Kate said thoughtfully, "you will have to destroy Mathers, in the same way you destroyed my aunt."

Mrs. Farnsworth raised both brows. "I commend your insight, Miss Ardleigh. I am glad to say that little business is well under way. A poison has already been sent in a certain candy in which Mr. Mathers is known to indulge immoderately: Fairley's chocolates."

Kate almost gave way to an hysterical giggle. It was a small and ironically fateful world indeed. But Mrs. Farnsworth would not be telling her these things unless she were meant to be the next victim. She tried to think ahead to what the woman's next move might be.

Mrs. Farnsworth's eyes were frankly defiant. "There, my dear, you have it. I stand guilty of everything of which you have accused me. 'But call me not a fool, for heaven hath sent me fortune.' And with respect to your wish to hold the office your aunt has so recently vacated . . ." She pulled down her mouth with a somber look. "The position must be earned through a long study of the magical arts. Regrettably, you will not have sufficient time to prepare yourself."

She pulled her hand out of her pocket. Fitted neatly into the palm was a small nickel-plated derringer.

Kate raised her eyes to Mrs. Farnsworth's face. Her brown eyes were intent, her mouth determined, her chin firm. A remarkable woman, with the will to use whatever weapon best ensured the success of her scheme. A person whom Beryl Bardwell could not help but admire. But admiration was quickly chilled by the reality of the situation. This was no time to be doing research!

Mrs. Farnsworth gestured with the gun toward the door. "Come now," she said. "We will go down to the cellar. Our business will be much more conveniently concluded there."

Kate glanced at the door, feeling apprehensive. This interview had not gone exactly as she had anticipated. What would happen when they went into the hall? Would it be best to—

"That is quite a small gun," Kate said conversationally, but loudly. "Is it real?"

Mrs. Farnsworth's voice was grim. "It may look like a stage property, but I assure you that it is quite powerful for its size. It does, however, make rather a lot of noise, which is one of the reasons for our trip to the cellar. Since you seem to be an imaginative person, I leave you to imagine the others." She stepped behind Kate and planted the gun in the small of her back. "Shall we, Miss Ardleigh? Out the door and to your right."

330

Kate bit her lip. Her hands were clammy. Having no choice, she walked ahead of Mrs. Farnsworth. When they reached the hallway door, she stopped once more, her hand on the knob.

"Can we not discuss this?" she asked urgently. "Perhaps we could accommodate . . . ."

"No," Mrs. Farnsworth said again. Her voice was thin and flat, with a brittle edge. "No more discussion. Open the door."

Kate opened the door and stepped into the hallway. What happened next occurred with such a rapidity that afterward she was not sure she could reconstruct the sequence accurately. There was a sudden scuffle behind her, a strangled cry, and the gun discharged, the bullet shattering a mirror on the opposite wall. As Kate turned, she saw that Mrs. Farnsworth, helpless, was gripped in the powerful embrace of a resolute Mudd.

Before Kate could speak, an impatient banging sounded at the entrance door. "What's that shooting?" demanded a loud voice. "In the name of the Crown, open this door!"

Kate stepped to the door and opened it. On the stoop, hand raised, mouth open to shout once more, stood a uniformed policeman. Behind him stood yet another policeman. And behind him stood Sir Charles Sheridan. When he saw her, Sir Charles's mouth dropped open. Kate bowed her head slightly.

"Gentlemen," she said, stepping aside so that they could enter. "How good of you to arrive so speedily."

52

"And thereby hangs a tale."
—WILLIAM SHAKESPEARE
As You Like It, II, vii

"**O**OH, AN' HOW did it feel when th' gun went off, please, Mr. Mudd?" Harriet begged. She was sitting on the sofa, her eyes dancing with excitement.

Sarah Pratt leaned back in her chair, her slippered feet elevated to the warmth of the fire on a stool cushioned with a small pillow. She looked around, replete with satisfaction. All the comforts had been restored to the servants' hall, including tea and jam. Things were as they should be, although it was a sad day. Just this morning, they had buried Miss Ardleigh and her sister. The service had been read by the vicar and attended by almost every resident of the village and surrounding countryside. Sarah felt that everything had been quite in order, although the morning might have been a bit less wet.

It was teatime now, and the autumn rain was driving against the window. Pocket had brought in a bucket of chestnuts to roast in the fire. And as he had every meal since the event, Mudd was retelling with enormous relish the tale of his grand adventure with the young miss.

"We can't have th' gun afore we have th' cart," Nettie objected, playing with the terrier's ears. On Jaggers's death, she had befriended the sad dog. "How did yer get to Colchester, Mr. Mudd?"

Mudd obligingly shifted the focus of his story. "As yer know, I drove th' young miss in th' pony cart," he said with an understanding glance at Pocket, who always got sulky at this point in the narrative. When Pocket first learned what happened, he protested that Mudd had unfairly usurped his prerogative, for it was *his* job to drive. But he objected far less after he discovered that Mudd's assignment had involved not just driving the cart, but (upon instructions from the young miss) forcing open Mrs. Farnsworth's kitchen door, stealing surreptitiously up the back stairs, and waiting outside the parlor with an ear to the door, until finally it opened and the lady with the derringer came out. Sarah noticed that Pocket always turned away when Mudd described the silvery gun with the walnut handle, so small it fitted into a lady's hand, yet so powerful the bullet blasted through a mirror and buried itself in the wall.

"I don't care t' 'ear about th' pony cart." Amelia pouted. She gave Mudd a flirtatious sideways glance. "That's too ordin'ry. I want t' 'ear about th' gun, Mr. Mudd. *That's* th' dang'rous part."

Pocket's ears reddened and he became busy with the chestnuts.

"Well, then," Mudd said, basking in Amelia's glance, "th' young miss comes out o' th' parlor with th' lady, 'oo had th' gun."

Nettie pushed the terrier out of her lap. "How c'n she be a lady," she asked tartly, "'f she had a gun?"

"Let that be, Nettie," Sarah said, pouring herself another cup of tea. "A lady c'n have anythin' she wants."

"She 'ad th' gun," Mudd repeated patiently. "Which I already knew, for I 'eard th' young miss say, quite loud an' pert, 'It is a rather small gun. Is it real?' "

"So brave, th' young miss," Amelia sighed.

Sarah savored the image of her mistress fearlessly holding her ground in the face of a lady with a gun. Any ordinary woman would have fainted dead away, and the villain would have escaped.

"Brave," Sarah confirmed, adding sugar to her tea, "an' gen'rous, too." Miss Ardleigh had planned to allow them tea, but she had said nothing about sugar. It was the young miss who had instructed her to see liberally, but not wastefully, to the comforts of the servants—had instructed *her*, because Sarah was no longer simply Cook but Cook-Housekeeper, and a much enlarged ring of keys jangled at the waist of her apron.

In point of fact, Sarah had more to think about than the comforts of the fire and tea and jam, delightful as those things were, especially on a day like today. The young miss, who was very businesslike and efficient when it came to running the household, had set her to counting everything straightaway: all the kitchen stores, the linen, the silver, china, and crystal, even the furniture. Making an inventory, she called it. It was a demanding task that required all of Sarah's skills of observation, organization, and writing, and as she moved from room to room, noting each item in a book, along with its precise function, condition, and location, she began to think well of herself. Her estimation of her abilities rose farther when she consulted with Miss Ardleigh and Mudd, as now required, on the household accounts. If she could do these things, she could manage three subordinate house servants—yes, even four or five or six—with no difficulty at all.

"So I'm waitin' by th' door," Mudd continued, "primed, yer might say, fer action. An' when they come out I grab th' lady right round th' waist." At this point, he always leaned suggestively toward Amelia and offered to demonstrate, which, of course, Sarah could not allow. She frowned to remind both Mudd and Amelia that such playacting was not necessary to the authenticity of the tale.

"So then th' gun goes off, BANG!" Harriet said happily.

"An' th' bullet breaks th' mirror into th' tiniest pieces," Nettie added, "like lit'le diamonds."

"An' then th' policemen come," Amelia put in.

"Yes, an' Sir Charles too," Mudd said, pretending not to notice that his arm was slipping along the top of the sofa, in the direction of Amelia's shoulder. "Th' one 'oo took th' photograph of this selfsame lady sellin' poisonous mushrooms t' Mrs. P—"

"Dressed up like a gypsy!" Harriet crowed, clapping her hands. "An' that's why Cook went t' jail! Because o' th' gypsy's mushrooms, what got in th' puddin'!"

Nettie looked respectfully at Cook. 'C'n ye tell agin 'bout ridin' t' jail in th' carriage, Mrs. Pratt?"

Sarah smiled, benignly (for the moment) ignoring the fact that Amelia was leaning ever so slightly toward Mudd. Riding in the carriage—to *and* from the jail—was a subject she loved to talk about; indeed, she dwelled on it in her waking hours and dreamed about it in her sleep. And not just the breathtaking speed and smoothness of the ride or the feel of the fine leather seats, but the astonishment on the faces of her friends as she rattled along High Street, going in glory. Since Miss Kate had given her such a generous gift, Sarah had felt quite differently about herself. She had even begun to believe it possible, as Rachel Elam's dairyman brother claimed in his letters home, that a person might actually rise above the station of her birth. Might even aspire to something like (she thought with a catch of her breath) a shop of her own.

She shook the thought out of her head and smiled again at Nettie. "Later, child," she said in a kindly tone. "There's somethin' I need t' hear from Mr. Mudd." She bowed to Mudd with some deference. One had to feel a certain regard for a man who had so bravely stepped in to save the young miss from being taken to the cellar and done away with—although Sarah suggested that, given the necessity, the young miss could have taken perfect care of herself.

"Yer've no doubt told it, Mudd," she said, "but I've never quite got th' straight. How was it th' constable come so prompt-like, just as th' gun went off?"

"I didn't get th' straight o' it meself till this mornin'," Mudd replied, "when I read it in th' newspaper. It 'pears that th' lady had already murdered somebody else."

"No!" Amelia squealed, her hands going to her mouth.

"Yes," Mudd said, lowering his voice and making it dreadful. "A Frenchie with a gold ring. She made 'im tipsy an' drove 'im in 'is 'ired rig out to th' excavation. Then she stuck a dagger in 'is 'eart an' shoved him into a pit."

Harriet's eyes grew large and she gave a faint moan.

"She cud'na bin no lady," Nettie said firmly. She began to count on her fingers. "I make it three she murdered, an' she would've murdered th' young miss, which is four, if she 'adn't been stopped. No lady wud've murdered so many, not even fer sport."

Cook looked at Mudd. "How did th' police know t' come?"

"Accordin' t' the newspaper," Mudd said, "Sir Charles deduced 'oo killed th' Frenchie, or near 'nough. 'E was bringin' th' police t' talk t' th' lady. They were on th' stoop at th' very selfsame instant th' gun went off."

"An' then they arrested th' lady," Harriet said.

"Yer see?" Nettie declared triumphantly. "'f she were a lady, she wud'n've bin arrested!"

"T'were a great piece o' luck that yer was there, Mr. Mudd," Sarah said. "T'wud've bin a awful pity t'have lost th' young miss so soon after losin' Miss Ardleigh, God rest 'er. An' Jaggers, th' devil take 'er," she added factually. "If th' young miss had gone, we'd've all bin out o' a place, instead of warmin' ourselves by th' fire wi' tea an' chestnuts."

Mudd spoke sternly, imbued with a sense of new authority. "Don't speak ill o' th' dead, Mrs. P."

But Sarah did not reply. She was gazing into the fire, warm, contented, and full of chestnuts. And she was wondering, if ever she should have her own shop, what kind of shop it would be.

The comfortable silence was broken by the tinkle of the drawing room bell. "I'm wanted," Amelia said, and rose.

"I'll go with yer," Mudd said with alacrity, and rose as well. "Pocket, p'rhaps yer'd better see t' that lame horse." Pocket grudgingly acquiesced, and the three of them left the room.

Mrs. Pratt glanced up at the clock on the mantel. "Time fer lessons," she said.

Nettie clapped her hands, her face glowing. "Come on, Bandit," she said to the terrier. "Time fer lessons."

Harriet, who thought of herself as older and wiser, twisted rebelliously. "When I got my place, I thought I was through wi' lessons."

"Well, yer was wrong, wasn't yer?" Cook said. "Miss Kate wants you two tippity-twitchits t' get on i' th' world, so yer'd best be at it. Yer don't want t' make fools o' yerselves when yer recite fer her in th' mornin'."

She reached under her chair and pulled out the copy of the London *Times* that Miss Kate had given her, with the explicit but inexplicable instruction that the girls were to practice reading the entire first page aloud until they could read it smoothly and well. Handing the newspaper to an eager Nettie, she warned, "An' don't fritter th' time. Fifteen minutes o' lessons, an' then I'll see yer i' th' kitchen. There's work t' be done."

"Yes, Mrs. Pratt," the girls chorused dutifully.

Mrs. Pratt swung her feet off her stool and stood up. When she thought about the changes at Bishop's Keep, it all seemed rather queer. But still, none of the alterations— with the exception of the sad loss of Miss Ardleigh—were excessively hard to bear. As she went off to the kitchen, Mrs. Pratt was humming a tune under her breath.

53

"The truth is rarely pure, and never simple."
—OSCAR WILDE
The Importance of Being Earnest

"THANK YOU FOR bringing tea, Amelia," Kate said. "You may go now." The maid curtsied and left the room.

"I am glad to have this time alone with you, my dear Kathryn," the vicar said, taking the cup she offered. "The past two weeks have been sad for both of us."

"They have," Kate said, thinking that today was the fortnight anniversary of her aunts' deaths. She sat down, straightening the skirt of her mauve dress. She had worn black to the funeral, as was customary, but she had decided not to keep the heavy mourning that English people seemed to expect. Aunt Sabrina would not have wanted it, and to wear it for Aunt Jaggers would be hypocritical.

The two of them sat in silence for a moment, the only sound the clacking of Aunt Jaggers's parrot, whom Kate had pitied and moved out of the lonely bedroom and into the library. At last the vicar put down his cup and leaned forward.

"Since tomorrow is the reading of your aunt's will, Kathryn, I thought it might be well to discuss it with you."

"The solicitor, I understand, is coming here."

"Yes. The will is very simple. It leaves the bulk of the estate to you, with the exception of certain bequests to the church, to charities she favored, and to the servants. The solicitor will no doubt wish to review the situation in some detail, but I can tell you that the estate included a substantial financial holding that will enable you to live off the rents and the interest without diminishing the principal or liquidating any of the properties. You should be able to live as you wish." He gave her an oblique look. "Perhaps you will also wish to carry on with some of your aunt's charities. Sabrina Ardleigh was a great power for good in this parish."

Kate looked down at her hands. When she had first learned of her inheritance, she had not wanted to think about it. Her great good fortune had been gained through the loss of someone she held very dear. But with the Ardleigh estate came many responsibilities, and she was determined to meet them competently. And more: she was committed to using the Ardleigh fortune, if fortune it proved to be, for good ends. What those might be, she as yet had no clear idea, although she had a few disorganized notions, and was willing to listen to the vicar's suggestions. But she did know one thing: fortune or no fortune, she would continue to write. While Beryl Bardwell might no longer be required to live by her pen, the pen remained Kate's way of encountering the world. Kate needed to write, and no fortune, whatever its size, would change that.

The vicar shifted in his chair. "There is something more I wish to discuss with you, Kathryn. On her deathbed, your aunt spoke of a child."

"Jocelyn." Kate had thought much of this, over the past few days. While the doctor had denied the possibility and the vicar had refused to discuss it, she believed that there must be some truth hidden away. What had become of Aunt Sabrina's daughter?

"Yes, Jocelyn." The vicar paused. "The truth is that he is Sabrina's son. *Our* son."

Kate stared at him. "Your . . . son?" The smaller surprise, that Jocelyn was a male, was lost in the larger astonishment of his patrimony.

"Yes, ours." The vicar's eyes met hers with candor and pain. "He was born nearly forty years ago. I will not go into the circumstances, which as you might guess are quite complicated. I will only say that Jocelyn's birth was kept secret from Sabrina's mother and father and from my wife. He was brought up in love and admonition by a man and a woman who cherished him as if he were their own son. I am pleased to say that he entered the church and has risen into a position of prominence." The light in his eyes brightened his entire face. "He is widely respected, admired, loved. A man of considerable reputation and even greater promise."

"And Aunt Sabrina felt she needed to protect him," Kate said quietly.

"Yes. Unfortunately, Sabrina's sister discovered the secret. She threatened to reveal it to the world unless Sabrina allowed her certain . . . privileges." The vicar's leathery face darkened. "Perhaps her revelation would not have been the end of Jocelyn's career, but it would have made life more difficult for him. That is why Sabrina was willing to live in circumstances she would not have chosen. She bartered her freedom and comfort for Bernice's silence. She did it for . . . our son."

The quiet lengthened as Kate thought about the vast reservoir of pain and sadness out of which the vicar's words must come. How extraordinarily complex were people's lives! What depths there were of anguish, of despair and loss—and of pride, dignity, joy. Yes, even joy.

Within her welled up a deep respect, almost an awe, at the incredible richness of life. What she had heard here today, had witnessed in the last week, had experienced in her own life over the past months—all of it dazzled and dumbfounded her. But it humbled her, as well, for she knew that Beryl Bardwell's stories had not even begun to plumb the depths of the human spirit. How much, as a writer, she had to learn! She had not even yet begun!

The vicar stood and began to pace. "I was not sure I should tell you this, Kathryn, because the secret is not just mine. It is Jocelyn's too."

"He knows, then?"

"Yes. His adopted parents thought it best, when he became a man, to tell him the truth. I am proud to say that he bore it bravely, that he unburdened his heart to me and to his mother, and that he has from time to time been in touch with us. I have written to him of his mother's death, although not of the details." He paused and turned. "I tell you all this, Kathryn, because I believe your aunt wished you to know the whole truth, and because I am convinced that you will safeguard it. And because I think you should know that it is not quite true that you are the last Ardleigh, although you are indeed the last by that name."

Kate weighed her thoughts and spoke carefully. "Did my aunt provide for Jocelyn in her will? Or should I, as her heir, make some special provision?"

"No, she did not, nor should you. Jocelyn's adopted family are of considerable means. They have provided well for him." He pursed his lips. "And of course, we in the Church do not pursue personal wealth."

Kate was enormously moved by the old man's confidence. "Thank you for telling me," she said.

The vicar sat down again. The lines on his old face seemed somehow deeper, and his eyes were dark with pain. "There remains only one thing left to be said. I must tell you how deeply I regret that I involved your aunt in the Order of the Golden Dawn. I know that if I had not encouraged her to become a member, she would be alive today." His voice was gruff. "It is a knowledge, my dear Kathryn, that breaks my heart."

Kate reached for his hand, longing to comfort him in his grief. "Please," she said urgently, "you must not. Aunt Sabrina chose her own path. The knowledge she sought through the Order was important to her. You cannot blame yourself because the situation was other than you knew."

"Thank you, my dear." The vicar's voice revealed a heaviness of heart. "Your comfort is welcome, although I fear that nothing can truly comfort me for the loss of my oldest and dearest friend. If you do not object, I would like to ask you for the documents that belong to the Order. I will see that they are placed in the proper hands."

Kate nodded. "That was my aunt's last instruction. You shall have them. You do know, do you not, that Aunt Jaggers destroyed the original of the tarot cards? They were very valuable, I fear."

"Sabrina told me. At the moment, their loss does not trouble me deeply, but I am sure that others will think it a great tragedy. The deck was much prized for the quality of its occult symbolism." He pushed himself out of his chair with difficulty. "Reluctant as I am to go back out in this weather, I must be on my way. It has been a trying week and I am very tired."

There was a knock at the door and Amelia stepped in. "Lord an' Miss Marsden, miss," she said with a quick curtsy, "an' Sir Charles Sheridan."

Kate smiled. "Show them in, Amelia. And please bring another tray of cakes—some of those Nettie made would be nice—and a fresh pot of tea." To the vicar, she added, "I have asked Mrs. Pratt to assume Aunt Jaggers's housekeeping duties. We will likely hire another cook, but in the meantime, she is training our little kitchen maid. If Nettie likes the work and does well, it can become her trade. If she does not, perhaps we can find something else for her. It is a great pity for people to go through their lives doing work they do not enjoy."

"Your aunt would think well of your concern for the servants," the vicar said. "And I am glad to see that you have made friends with the Marsdens. As the first family in the neighborhood, they will be able to introduce you into society." He smiled. "And if you need a friend, please call on me."

"Thank you," Kate said.

The vicar put his hands on Kate's shoulders and gently kissed her forehead. "It is good that you have come to Bishop's Keep, my dear. Had you not, the truth of Sabrina's death might not have been learned, nor the truth behind the falsehood of the Order. For that, *you* are to be thanked."

Kate would have sat still for a moment with those last words, meditating on the mystery of truths behind falsehoods, and falsehoods behind truths. But she heard Amelia's step outside the door, and voices, and rose to greet her guests.

54

"... and bring you from a wild Kate to a Kate Conformable, as other household Kates"

—WILLIAM SHAKESPEARE
The Taming of the Shrew, II, i

CHARLES TOOK HIS seat by the fire as Kathryn Ardleigh settled herself on the sofa. He glanced at her, noticing that the fireglow brought out the golden lights in her russet hair. Since the episode at Mrs. Farnsworth's, he could not help thinking of her as Kathryn—indeed, as Kate. The name seemed made for her.

"Thank you," Kate said with a smile to the maid who brought in the tea. 'You need not stay. I'll serve." Eleanor raised her eyebrows, and Kate seemed to take notice. "I am sure that you think it heretical of me not to let the servants do everything, Ellie," she said lightly, "but I fear you will have to bear with me. I may be mistress of Bishop's Keep, but in my heart lurk a great many of my former habits— such as serving at tea—that I am willfully determined not to relinquish."

Charles could not help smiling.

Eleanor's cheeks were stained. "Of course," she said, inclining her head. She accepted her cup of tea. "It is your household now, Kate, and you must do as you like." She pulled down her brows prettily. "But my dear, I really must say—"

"It's your cook in the carriage, you see," Bradford interrupted with a grin. "I'm afraid you've become quite the neighborhood scandal. Mama is beside herself, of course, and even Papa has given us the benefit of his views, which tend toward a fear of anarchy."

"Oh, dear heaven," Kate said, laughing. She offered a tray of tea cakes to Charles, bending so close that he caught her scent, light and sweet. "I suppose I should apologize, but the gesture meant a great deal to Mrs. Pratt." She sat down again on the sofa, and began to pour the tea into bone china cups. "I am not in the least sorry I did it, whatever impropriety others might see."

Charles spoke with a teasing gravity. "It is not merely the impropriety that has caused such consternation," he said. "It is rather the example. If the Ardleigh cook can ride in the carriage, why not the Marsden cook? And if the cook, then why not the butler, the parlor maid, the tweeny, the gardener—" He chuckled dryly. "One simply cannot tell where all this frivolous carriage-riding might lead. The commons on wheels, Newgate thrown open, the Crown toppled. It could be the American Revolution all over again!"

Kate handed him a cup. "I do indeed see the difficulty," she agreed. She was straight-faced, but her eyes danced. "I would be chagrined to think that by acting nonconformably, I might have sown the seeds of the Empire's collapse."

Charles took the cup, reflecting that a few cooks in carriages might be a good thing for the Commonwealth. Perhaps a revolution was in order.

"In my opinion, it won't be carriages everyone will be riding in," Bradford declared with great seriousness, "but motorcars. *That* is the coming revolution. The motorcar industry will change the world, and those who are trying to hold it back will lose everything."

Eleanor frowned. "Best not let Papa hear you say that, Bradford. He'll have you horsewhipped." To Kate, she said in a deprecating tone, "Papa refuses to allow poor Bradford to mention motorcars at home, so he takes his revenge by talking about nothing else while we are out."

"Papa can go hang," Bradford said fervently. He scowled at Eleanor's wide-eyed look. "By Jove, I mean it, Ellie! And he will, too—he and all those who insist on marching into the future with their heads screwed on backward! The ones who prosper will be those who boldly drive forward."

"It seems that Bradford has made a great success in a certain speculation in the motorcar industry," Eleanor explained. As she took her teacup from Kate, she held out her arm to show off a new bracelet. "His pleasure has made him quite generous. But we can't tell Papa. He really wouldn't approve, even though Bradford is in the way of becoming filthy rich."

Charles looked at his friend. With Bradford's expected wealth, the burden he had borne for the past several weeks appeared to have lightened considerably. The smile he gave Kate was quite a rakish one, and his gaze was warmly and openly admiring. The thought occurred to Charles that Bradford was flirting with her, and he frowned.

"Ellie is correct," Bradford said. "The company in which I have invested has acquired not one but two French patents, either of which will make its fortune." He turned to Charles. "Too bad, old man, that you did not see fit to join me in the venture."

Charles shrugged. "I am a great admirer of self-propelled transport," he said, "but my admiration does not extend to speculation. I'm no gambler."

Bradford hooted. "You've spoken the truth there, my dear Charles. Too careful by half, you are. You could have made a bundle."

"I have begun to think of acquiring my own self-propelled transport," Kate said, settling back with her tea. "It is a great nuisance to wait for Pocket to harness the horses when I would much rather go on the instant. Moreover, it is impossible to travel with any degree of privacy when I must always be driven. And it is such a dreadful waste to require a driver to sit idly and wait for me to conclude my errands." She paused thoughtfully. "Of course, the purchase will require an investment."

Charles looked at her inquisitively. Really, there was no predicting the woman. What did she have in mind now?

Eleanor's face paled. "Kate, you *wouldn't!*"

Bradford leaned forward. "Self-propelled transport, that's the ticket!" he exclaimed. His ruddy face was suffused with excitement. "My dear Miss Ardleigh, I am delighted. I too am planning to purchase a motorcar."

"Oh, dear," Eleanor said faintly. "What will Papa say? Bradford, he will forbid you to drive it onto the manor! Wherever will you keep it?"

Charles chuckled, thinking of the tantrum Lord Marsden would throw if he saw Bradford driving a motorcar. "You might try hiding it in a haystack," he suggested.

Bradford scowled at Charles and sat forward on the edge of his chair. "Pay no attention to them, Miss Ardleigh. May I advise you on your purchase? I have made a careful study of the available models, and I am quite prepared to—"

"Thank you," Kate said, "but I have already made other arrangements. I have consulted with Constable Laken."

"Edward Laken?" Bradford asked, taken aback. "What on earth does the man know of motorcars?"

"I have no idea," Kate replied, offering him another tea cake. "But he certainly knows about bicycles. He is teaching me to ride, and has offered advice as to which one I should buy."

Charles chuckled again, louder. No predicting, and no taming. This was one Kate who would never be conformable.

Bradford frowned. Eleanor gasped. "A bicycle! Dear, dear Kate! Consider your position in society!"

"Not a motorcar?" Bradford asked, clearly disappointed.

"No," Kate said gently. "At least, not just now. When the invention has been perfected, I may be interested."

"If you insist on going about unaccompanied," Eleanor said primly, "you might ride. I am sure that Papa would be delighted to make a horse available to you."

"Thank you," Kate said. "But I believe a bicycle to be better suited to my temperament. Moreover, a horse requires feed and care, while a bicycle needs only a little oil and doesn't sulk when it is not attended to. It shall render me marvelously mobile. I shall ride to Marsden Manor, Eleanor, to have tea with you, and to Dedham to visit the vicar."

Charles looked at her. "I rather believe you are serious," he said, feeling ridiculously pleased.

"I am most serious," Kate assured him. "I plan to invest not only in the machine, but in a new sort of costume, for I have already found how difficult it is to ride in a heavy skirt. I discovered a picture of a French cycling dress yesterday, a variation on a very sensible fashion introduced in America some years back by Mrs. Amelia Bloomer."

"Bloomers!" Eleanor made a face of mock despair. "Kate, dear Kate, whatever shall I *do* with you? I came to invite you once again to travel to London with me, now that you have more time, and give advice on my trousseau. But perhaps I should think better of it." She shuddered. "Bicycles and bloomers, indeed!"

"What my sister and I actually came to do, Miss Ardleigh," Bradford remarked, "is to compliment you upon your identification of your aunts' killer. To be frank, the whole family was amazed. Papa and I were astonished that a woman should have the perspicacity to discover such a clever murderer, while Eleanor, Patsy, and Mama were amazed that a woman should have the courage to confront her."

"And all of us," Eleanor put in, "were absolutely *scandalized* that a woman could bring herself to commit three murders and attempt a fourth!" She shook her head in wonder and disbelief. "The story has been told to me several times, but I confess that I still find it hard to credit Mrs. Farnsworth—whose newspaper picture shows her to be a slight, delicate woman—with such a voracious thirst for blood! I must congratulate you for apprehending her, Kate."

Bradford frowned. "Allow me to make a slight correction, Ellie. It was not Miss Ardleigh who apprehended Mrs. Farnsworth—that would have been beyond a woman's capacity, I fear." Charles glanced at Kate, who had opened her mouth as if to object. But Bradford was continuing. "It was actually her servant Mudd who captured the woman. And as I understand it, Charles and two policemen arrived at the scene and effected her arrest." He glanced at Charles. "Is that not the case, Charles?"

Charles was glad for the opportunity to talk about his part in the affair. At the moment of his arrival, Kate—Miss Ardleigh—had been too excited to understand clearly how he had come to be at the scene. "I had been on the trail of Monsieur Monet's killer for some days," he said, "assisting Inspector Wainwright with the tedious business of tracing clues." He smiled slightly. "To be truthful, I did not suspect Mrs. Farnsworth, but I must at least take credit for bringing the police to the doorstep and rescuing our fair detective from the clutches of—"

"Rescuing me!" Kate exclaimed heatedly. Her hazel-green eyes flashed. "*I* was in no need of rescue, sir! The situation was perfectly in hand."

Charles frowned. "If you mean that your butler managed to subdue the violent woman after she dangerously fired at you—"

Kate pulled herself up. "She did not fire at *me*," she said in a tone of annoyance. "The gun accidentally discharged when Mudd attempted to pin her arms. I was never in a moment's danger. Your appearance, Sir Charles, saved me only from the trouble of summoning the police."

"Bravo!" Bradford said, applauding. "What spirit! My dear Miss Ardleigh, you have quite got the better of our intrepid Sir Charles."

Charles glared at Bradford.

"You did not know, Sir Charles," Eleanor asked, "that the woman had also killed Kate's aunts?"

"I confess I did not," Charles replied reluctantly. "I failed to recognize Mrs. Farnsworth's features in the face of the gypsy boy." With an excess of politeness, he added, "For that recognition, we must all be grateful to Miss Ardleigh."

"Thank you," Kate said, with a somewhat more charitable smile. "Perhaps I would have been quicker to recognize her had I seen her play Rosalind—as you did, I understand."

Charles felt himself coloring. Blast the woman! Why couldn't she be a little more like other women? He wasn't asking her to be as accommodating as Eleanor or Patsy—just a little less like a hedgehog. In his own defense, he added, rather more loudly than he intended, "My identification of Mrs. Farnsworth as Monsieur Monet's killer has been confirmed. The fingerprint I obtained from the whip handle of the hired chaise matches the print of the index finger of Mrs. Farnsworth's right hand. In addition, an ivory lozenge I discovered at the murder scene was broken from the handle of the dagger she used to kill Monsieur Monet—a dagger that was subsequently found, with a broken point, in her possession. And the print that I thought at first to be that of a walking stick I now believe to be that of the heel of her shoe. Its diameter is exactly the same."

Bradford put down his cup. "And are the newspapers correct in saying that the Frenchman was a spy?"

"Nothing of the sort," Charles replied. "The man was an expert cryptographer. He had been engaged by MacGregor Mathers to examine the cipher document on which the Order of the Golden Dawn was based and openly declare it fraudulent. Mrs. Farnsworth killed him to keep him from revealing the truth. She also planned to kill Mathers—"

"That scheme was aborted, I trust," Kate broke in. "I told Inspector Wainwright about Mrs. Farnsworth's claim to have sent a box of poisoned sweets to Mathers. I hope he conveyed the information to the Paris police."

"I believe that the candy has been intercepted," Charles said. He looked at Kate. While they were at it, he might as well clear up the one unanswered question that remained. "The day you visited Marsden Manor, Miss Ardleigh, you suggested that I interview Mrs. Farnsworth in connection with the dead man at the dig. On what basis did you perceive a relationship between them?"

"It was not Mrs. Farnsworth herself that I believed connected to your corpse," Kate said. "I merely suspected that the murder involved a member of her organization. It was chiefly the scarab which caught my eye. Both my aunt and Mrs. Farnsworth wore scarab pendants. And, of course, there was the peacock feather, which many members wear as an emblem of the Order."

"It is all terribly confusing," Eleanor said to Kate, "but now that the mystery has been resolved, you can turn your mind to other things—to a small ball, which will be held at the manor next Friday evening. Nothing very elaborate, for it will be just the local gentry and some of the village folk, and you are still in mourning. But I think you would enjoy meeting everyone. Will you come, Kate? You need not dance, of course."

"I would be glad to come," Kate said soberly. "I will remember Aunt Sabrina with love and affection for the rest of my life, but I am certain that she would wish me to put the events of the past weeks behind me." Her smile was demure. "She would even wish me to dance."

Almost without thinking, Charles spoke up. "I wonder if—"

At the same moment, Bradford said, "I thought perhaps—"

Charles looked at Bradford, his eyes narrowing slightly. Were the two of them going to be at loggerheads over a woman? But it was beneath his dignity to contend with his friend. "Pardon me," he murmured, and subsided, forgetting his irritation at Kate. It was Bradford who provoked him now.

Bradford took the advantage Charles gave him, clearing his throat and giving Kate a confident smile. "Well, then," he said smartly, "I trust you will do me the honor of reserving the first dance for me."

Kate regarded him for a moment. "Thank you," she said. "I shall be pleased to do so." There was a pause, and then she turned, unexpectedly, to Charles. Her eyes were clear and slightly amused. "If you would not think it too forward of me, Sir Charles, I would like to make a proposal to you, and to ask for your help."

There was a longer pause, as Charles gathered his wits. "Of course," he said at last. "How can I be of service?"

"It is the bats, you see," she said.

"The *bats?*" Eleanor exclaimed.

"Yes," Kate said. "I have recently fallen into the habit of walking among the ruins just at sunset, and I have noticed that there are a great many bats—and, if I am not mistaken in my observations, bats of more than one species. They are very curious creatures, quite interesting. I wonder, Sir Charles, if you would object to walking with me one evening and identifying them for me."

Charles stared at her. There are moments in human relationships when what has been ordinary, conventional, and understood becomes extraordinary, different, and unique. This was a such a moment for Charles. A luminous moment.

"Ah, yes," he said. "Bats. My dear Miss Ardleigh, I shall be glad to."